"Forgive me for intruding, Mr. Kidwell," Stephanie said, "but I'm very eager to charter a boat and I was told yours may be available."

"That so?" He chomped on his cigar, his eyes appearing to drift in and out of focus.

"It's very urgent. I have to leave immediately."

"Where do you want to go?" he asked, slurring his words.

"Anywhere."

"That specific, huh?"

"To the next island. Anywhere with an airport."

His brow furrowed. "Mind if I ask why?"

"My life could be at stake. I don't have time to explain. I need an answer. Please." She opened her purse, dug for her wallet and pulled out a wad of cash. "Here's my money," she said, her voice trembling.

Jack eyed the bills. "Since you put it that way…"

PAYBACK

R.J. KAISER

MIRA

ISBN 1-55166-460-7

PAYBACK

Printed in U.S.A.

For
Linda and Dennis Clear
Mary Jones and Kingsley Macomber
Linda Klein and Dave Thomas
Lori Moreland and John Abbot

A special thanks to Taylor Carey,
sailor, scholar, gentleman and friend.

Friday
September 27th

Miami International Airport

The Mercedes lurched to an abrupt halt in front of the terminal building, its tires screeching, causing heads to turn. Grabbing his carry-on bag, he stepped from the car without a word to the driver and went through the doors, moving briskly, all the while calculating, turning the problem over again in his mind.

He hated doing things half-assed, but the woman had given them little choice. There'd been just enough time to make the necessary phone calls to St. Thomas during the frantic rush to the airport. Maybe his plan would work, maybe it wouldn't. The woman was rich and no fool, but she had her vulnerabilities. Every woman did. Oscar Barbadillo was confident about that. He had a nose for women. Still, this one held the key to a hell of a lot of money.

He could see by the arrival-and-departure board that her flight was late. Good. A bit more time. Oscar went to first-class check-in. His ticket was waiting, everything in order.

"You're all set, sir," the agent said, handing him his ticket with his seating assignment.

"Is the flight full?" he asked.

The agent, a short roundish Latina with bottle-blond hair,

shook her head. "Not completely. There are a few seats left in coach."

"First class?"

She checked her computer screen. "About half."

Oscar leaned over the counter, lowering his voice as he gazed deeply into her eyes. "I would like to sit next to a particular passenger, if possible. A friend, Stephanie Reymond. She's coming in on a flight from San Francisco in a few minutes. I forgot to ask whether she was in coach or first class."

The woman regarded him uneasily, the corners of her eyes twitching ever so slightly. "What was the name again, sir?"

"Stephanie Reymond." He spelled it. "R-E-Y-M-O-N-D."

She scanned the screen, furrowing her brow, unconsciously fiddling with the tiny gold crucifix on the chain at her neck. Oscar inhaled her perfume from across the counter, aware that she was aware.

"I'm sorry, Mr. Barbadillo," she said, "we don't have a passenger listed by that name. Not in coach or first class."

He was surprised. "Are you sure?"

"Yes, sir." She met his eyes, but they flickered away after a few moments.

Stephanie Reymond was probably traveling under a different name, he realized. Of course. She would be careful. After all, the woman had twenty million dollars of their money.

"How many passengers are connecting from the San Francisco flight to this one?" he asked.

She hesitated. "Six."

"How many are woman?"

"I'm sorry, sir, I really can't share that sort of information."

He reached into his pocket, then laid his hand on the counter, parting his fingers enough to expose a hundred-dollar bill. "What harm is there in a number?" he asked softly.

The agent glanced up and down the ticket counter, then slid

the bill out of sight. She worked on her terminal for several moments.

"You can't always be sure by names, but it looks to me like two."

"Either of them traveling alone?"

The agent bit her lip. "I've tried to be helpful, sir, because she's your friend, but I really shouldn't say any more. I don't want to lose my job."

His eyes hardened. "You've already lost it, sweetheart. But for the right name, I can see that you get your job back, and there's always this for your Christmas fund," he said, producing another hundred-dollar bill.

"Please," she said, her expression imploring.

He pushed the hundred over the edge of the counter. "If one of them's a woman traveling alone, I'd like her name."

The agent looked as if she was going to break into tears. She twisted her gold chain around her finger, chewing on her lip.

"Whisper it," he said. "It won't hurt. I promise."

The woman looked again at the computer screen, her eyes shimmering. "Jane Turner," she murmured.

"Thank you," Oscar Barbadillo said without smiling. "And Merry Christmas."

He left the ticket counter, his bag in hand. Walking along, he wondered if his stupid fucking cousin had a picture of Stephanie Reymond that might be faxed and, if so, whether there was time to get it before the flight. Probably not, though he'd call San Francisco and see. Oscar checked his watch and started searching for a phone.

This was all Rico's fault, no two ways about it. Oscar hated the stupid bastard and couldn't understand why his uncle Julius didn't just lock the idiot up in some corner office with a bimbo secretary and let him fuck her brains out. That was all Rico was good for—that and playing big man with his gangster friends.

Stephanie noticed him watching her. Normally she didn't pay much attention to men in public, but this one was hard to ignore. He was good-looking, Latin—she assumed Cuban. He had presence, a blatant sexuality that was apparent in the way he stood, the way he moved. What concerned her was that there was something dangerous about him, too. Menacing, though it was hard to say why.

She knew she had to guard against paranoia. If he was going to arrest her or shoot her, there wasn't much she could do about it. Maybe her luck had finally run out. Or the guy might be an ordinary pervert, preying on a woman alone.

She consulted the wall clock. It was a few minutes past seven in the morning. Her flight to St. Thomas wouldn't leave for a while. Would he be on it? she wondered. That would tell her more about what he was up to.

Stephanie Reymond wasn't the type men pursued in public. Not that she wasn't attractive, but she was over forty, understated and she never flirted. Polite, pleasant and proper—her mother's three marks of a lady, the three P's. That was the philosophy she'd lived by through over twenty years of marriage. Which only served to remind her that she had much bigger problems than a man leering at her.

There was no question they would be looking for her. Had she escaped San Francisco undetected? That was the critical question. The trouble was, she was so exhausted her mind was a muddle. The night before, she'd gotten a few fitful hours of rest in that motel in San Rafael, and she'd had an hour nap yesterday afternoon, killing time before her flight. Five or six hours' sleep in forty-eight. It wasn't nearly enough.

The Cuban, broad-shouldered in a tailored sport coat, his angular face coldly handsome, moved to a seat on the opposite side of the waiting area. When she glanced his way, and their eyes met, the intensity in his gaze unnerved her. She tried staring him down, but she wasn't tough enough. He won.

Stephanie shifted uncomfortably and recrossed her legs. More passengers began arriving and she tried to put him from her mind. God knew, the events of the past few days had given her plenty to think about. She was now a widow, though it hardly seemed possible.

If she felt any guilt at all, it was because she couldn't feel sad. Jean Claud had not only been unfaithful, he'd betrayed her with her sister and put her life in jeopardy. So, maybe she was entitled to hate him. Now that she thought about it, maybe she was glad he was dead, too. One thing was sure, he had certainly disabused her of any illusions.

About a month before, when she'd seen Audrey about filing for divorce, her friend was amazed when she admitted that she hadn't slept with Jean Claud in years.

"No sex at all?" Audrey had said. "*Five* years?"

"Audrey, *I* haven't had sex in five years. Which is not to say that Jean Claud hasn't."

"Honey, you need more than a divorce."

That was, of course, true. But Stephanie was too embarrassed to admit that she and Jean Claud had never had much of a sex life. Or that he was the only man she had ever slept with.

Her problem wasn't a lack opportunity. She'd been propositioned a number of times, once even with Jean Claud's collaboration. That had been the low point of their marriage—until a few days ago. She had been thirty at the time, and Zanny was finally old enough for them to vacation without her. One of Jean Claud's investor clients, Tom Ashby, had invited them to his chalet near Aspen. She'd expected several couples, but there was only Tom. The second afternoon, while she was skiing, Jean Claud returned to San Francisco on a "business emergency." She'd spent the next two days fighting off Tom's unwanted advances before she managed to get on a flight home.

Jean Claud's nonchalant response upon her return told her all she'd ever need to know about the man she'd married. "It's not like you have much of a sex life," he'd intoned in that soft French accent of his, hardly bothering to put down his

Wall Street Journal. "And I always had the impression you liked Tom."

"Dear God!" she'd exclaimed, incredulous. "You told him he could have me?"

"Not in so many words. I simply explained that we led separate lives and that I thought you might be interested. I obviously was mistaken."

She'd stood in the front room of their house, still in her ski clothes, sputtering. "I can't believe this," she'd said, crying, utterly humiliated. "How *could* you?"

"I made a mistake," he'd replied evenly. "You won't accept it, I'm sure, but it was meant as a kindness."

"To *whom?* Tom or me?"

"Stephanie," he'd said, irritated, "you, of course."

"I just want to know one thing," she'd said, trembling, tears flowing. "Was I part of the package on some investment? Did you offer me as an incentive?"

"Absolutely not. It came about over several martinis. Tom told me he was very attracted to you and I told him...about our situation."

"Our *situation,*" she'd said, her teeth clenched, her nails digging into her palms. "You mean that I'm so deprived I'd screw any man my husband shoved in my direction?"

"Stephanie, I've admitted I was wrong. You have my apology. Now, can we let it go?"

She'd stomped from the room and didn't speak to him for three months. If it hadn't been for their daughter, she'd have divorced him right then. But she couldn't saddle Zanny with a broken home, especially considering how close the girl and Jean Claud were. Parenting had been the one bright spot in their marriage. They both adored their child. Still, the incident had taught her one thing—between them, the marriage was unquestionably over.

Stephanie knew she had to take a share of the responsibility. It was her fault she'd been pregnant when they married, and she'd made the decision to put her family first. Had Zanny not been severely asthmatic, Stephanie might have pursued a career as an accountant. But the demands of parenting a sickly child had been great, so she'd limited her activities to charity work and a place on the board of the Stanford Alumni Association. Zanny and Jean Claud had been happy, and she tried hard to make that enough. But it wasn't. For years she'd been kidding herself.

Eventually, Tom Ashby became a footnote in their marriage. Jean Claud had gone on, unfazed. Perhaps it was that, as much as what he'd actually done, that she found so wounding. And that was why, twelve years later, she could still resent him for it.

Of course, marrying Jean Claud had been a dreadful mistake, though it had taken years for her to fully accept that. He'd been her professor at Stanford, so cool, detached, cerebral. A young bachelor in his thirties, with an untarnished reputation, Jean Claud had wooed her ever so subtly, his quiet aloofness quintessentially old world and brimming with rectitude and savoir faire. She'd blamed herself when she'd gotten pregnant and was so grateful when he'd stepped forward to do the right thing that it had never occurred to her that they didn't belong together, that they'd worked out absolutely nothing and, for that matter, that she didn't know the man's heart and never would—not even, it turned out, at the bitter end.

If the lack of love and Jean Claud's insensitivity hadn't killed the marriage, the death of their daughter definitely had. For a year now Stephanie had lived with the terrible image of Zanny's battered body lying on that gurney in the hospital morgue. The girl had only been nineteen, a sophomore at Stanford, when she was taken from them by a tragic, senseless auto accident. Yet, despite her terrible pain, Stephanie had realized, even as they buried their child, that she and Jean Claud no longer had a reason to go on.

And the definitive proof of that had come this week. It was amazing how innocently it had begun. On Wednesday—God, could it only have been two days ago?—she'd told Jean Claud that she was heading to Stanford for an alumni meeting. She'd stay in Palo Alto with a friend and wouldn't be back until the next day. Then, after he'd left for his office, she'd sneaked into his study for a look at his computer files. Audrey had told her it was imperative that she get some idea about Jean Claud's finances before she filed for divorce. Her friend and lawyer had been horrified when Stephanie told her she didn't exactly know what they were worth or where, precisely, he'd invested her money.

"A lot of it's in those start-up companies of his," she'd said. "He's done very well for me. My money's growing in leaps and bounds. At least, that's what Jean Claud's said."

Audrey's expression had been absolutely scathing. Stephanie had felt like the biggest fool alive. Modern women did not blindly put everything in their husband's hands. This was the eve of the twenty-first century, for God's sake!

All true, of course, but Jean Claud had been very old-fashioned. And unyielding. They'd struck a deal early on, and he had scrupulously lived up to his end of the bargain. He'd married her, provided for her, asking nothing in return except that she maintain their home and raise their child. Her charitable endeavors had been exemplary, universally lauded. Stephanie Reymond was known as the matriarch of the Stanford Alumni Association and was directly responsible for millions in donations to the endowment.

But here she was, sneaking around her own house, feeling like a thief. Eventually she'd screwed up her courage and turned on his computer. His files were protected by a password, but she'd managed to figure out his code. After trying "Suzanne," Zanny's real name, and "Yvonne," his mother's name, she'd tried the name of the town in France where he was born and his brother's name. None worked. Then she had tried Jean Claud's pet names for their daughter. "Chou-chou" and "petit amour" failed before Stephanie finally struck gold with "Zanny." As if by magic, the directory of all his files opened up.

Everything was there—bank accounts, personal stock port-folios, even funds he'd squirreled away in France. She felt a curious elation. Never would she have thought all those hours studying accounting at Stanford would bring her to this. Except for the annual reports of charitable organizations, these were the first books of accounts she had seen in years. Wouldn't Jean Claud love the irony.

She realized at once that she'd stumbled on a wealth of information. Knowing Jean Claud's balance sheet would make Audrey's day, she copied the files. She was about to turn off the computer when she noticed a miscellaneous folder in the directory. Out of curiosity, she opened it.

At first it appeared to be another investment portfolio, but the sums were greater, the values of various blocks of stock running well into the millions. Was this the treasure Audrey thought Jean Claud might have hidden away?

Stephanie began to see this was no ordinary portfolio. Rather, it appeared to be a parallel set of books to those of his venture capital firm. Included were careful records of the flow of funds, the sources and amounts. This was a secret record of off-the-books transactions of gargantuan proportions. The source of most of the funds was listed under a company in Long Beach, California, Inter-America Ventures—a name that meant nothing to her. She wasn't sure, but it was starting to look as though Jean Claud was hiding the true source of the funds he was investing in various start-up ventures. Why? she wondered.

Stephanie made copies of Jean Claud's files. Part of her agonized over having snooped, but Audrey was right—there was no point in litigating under a severe disadvantage. Audrey had been elated when she'd called with the news that she'd gotten the financial data. But when Stephanie had dropped the bomb about the secret investment portfolio, she was met with stunned silence.

"Audrey?"

"Steph, we've got a problem."

"What sort of problem?"

"Remember the detective I hired to check into Jean Claud's business affairs, Hal Sedman?"

"Yes."

"Well, he told me he was going to L.A. to follow up a lead he'd uncovered in connection with Jean Claud's business."

"So?"

"He never reported back to me, which is unusual. So I called his office this afternoon."

"And?"

"Hal's body was found last night in San Pedro Bay. The police believe he was tortured and murdered."

"Oh my God."

"There's no way to be sure it has to do with our case, because Hal didn't say Jean Claud was the only reason he was going to L.A. But something else happened this morning that leads me to believe there is a connection."

Stephanie felt her chest tighten. "What, Audrey?"

"Last night our office was broken into. We thought maybe it was a petty crime at first, somebody looking for computer equipment or whatever. But the burglars seemed to be interested in my files. The police thought it was done by professionals. They asked if I was involved in any sensitive litigation. I told them I had several divorce actions and custody cases in progress, and some routine estate-planning work, but nothing that would cause anyone to break into my office. But that was before I heard about Hal Sedman and Jean Claud's portfolio."

"You think there's a connection?"

"It depends. Do you have any idea where this Inter-America Ventures outfit is located?"

"Long Beach."

"That's what I was afraid of. Could be Inter-America was what Hal stumbled onto."

Stephanie felt sick.

"The worst part," Audrey went on, "is that Hal was tortured. Somebody wanted information out of him, and my guess is they got it. Like I said, that doesn't necessarily mean it had to do with our case, but with my office broken into the night his body was found, you've got to wonder.''

"Audrey, you don't think Jean Claud is mixed up in a murder, do you?"

"Honey, I don't know what to think. It could be whoever killed Hal was breaking into my office to find out who has an interest in Jean Claud Reymond's dealings. I hope I'm wrong, but it's all starting to fit."

"So what should I do?" Stephanie asked.

"I think you should go somewhere for a couple of days. Monterrey or someplace like that.''

"What'll I tell Jean Claud?''

"The less the better.''

Stephanie had agonized over whether to run, as Audrey suggested, or simply confront Jean Claud. She wouldn't mention the files or the murder in L.A., but she hungered to tell him the marriage was over.

After packing, she took a good long walk to think things through. It was midafternoon by the time she returned. She'd decided to leave town and was at her desk in her bedroom, composing a note to Jean Claud, when she heard his car in the driveway. Why, of all days, had he chosen today to come home early?

Jean Claud left his Jaguar in the driveway, which meant he wouldn't know that her car was still in the garage and that she hadn't left. If he assumed she wasn't home, she'd be able to avoid a confrontation.

Moments later, she heard the front door open and close.

Opening the bedroom door to see if he was coming upstairs, she was surprised to hear his voice. Then she realized he was on the phone. She went to the extension on the bedside table and carefully lifted the receiver. It was a woman's voice she heard initially, but by the time she got the phone to her ear, Jean Claud was speaking.

"I haven't time to talk now, darling," he said. "I've got an important call to make."

The woman on the other end of the line sighed. "Oh, Jean Claud."

The words were murmured, the sounds brief, but there was something familiar about the voice. Stephanie listened intently, the color in her cheeks rising. But it was Jean Claud's voice she heard again.

"Hey," he said, "don't give me a hard time. Stephanie's down at Stanford for an alumni meeting and she won't be home until tomorrow. We can spend the night together. Meet me at the beach house in a couple of hours. Say, six-thirty. That'll give me time to take care of my business and get over to the coast."

Again the caller sighed.

He chuckled. "I'll be there as quickly as a can. But now I must go. *Ciao*. I love you." And then he hung up.

Stephanie, her hand trembling, set the receiver back in the cradle. Jean Claud had a lover. And he was meeting her at the beach house! Suzanne's favorite place on earth. The bastard wouldn't, he couldn't. They'd practically designated it a shrine after Zanny's death. It was like thumbing his nose at what little they held sacred.

She sat on the bed, trying to pull herself together. Before she did anything, she would wait for him to leave. Even if he came upstairs, it was unlikely he would come to her room. He hadn't so much as stuck his head in the door since Zanny's funeral.

Again she heard his voice, stole to the phone and lifted the receiver. This time it was a man talking with her husband. She assumed Jean Claud was making a business call. She was about to hang up when the mystery voice turned angry.

"Reymond, you don't realize how serious this is. Julius Behring won't accept the fact that the money's gone, that it was a bad investment."

"What choice does he have? He's not the only one who

lost on that deal. Some very good clients of mine also took a bath.''

"You don't get it, do you?" the man said. "If Julius Behring invests money with you, he's your best client by definition. He expects to be first in line."

"Dave, you know how venture capital works. There are risks involved."

"Don't you remember I told you these people expect a decent return, and if they get it, the money will begin to flow and it won't stop? We've got to find a way to make them whole."

"How?" Jean Claud lamented, sounding less confident than usual. "You want me to steal it from other investors?"

"You're the investment guru, not me, Reymond. I'm the guy with the connections, remember? I promised you money, a little dirty on the edges, maybe, but lots of it. Well, I delivered. Now you've got to step up and make sure things work out."

"Dear God."

"And another thing. They want to know who in the hell you've been blabbing to about their deal."

"What do you mean?"

"Some P.I. has been snooping around, asking questions about Inter-America Ventures, embarrassing questions."

"I don't know what you're talking about," Jean Claud said.

"They seem to think you do. For your information, Professor, the sonovabitch was found floating in San Pedro Bay. The same thing could happen to us."

Stephanie's mouth dropped open.

"I'm warning you," the man continued, "these guys play for keeps and they've got very nasty friends. I thought I made it clear—the only risk with these guys is pissing them off."

"But I haven't spoken to anyone about this," Jean Claud moaned. "Honestly, I have no idea why anyone would involve a private investigator."

"Well, Julius has got to figure it's either you or me or somebody we talk to."

"Like who?"

"Like your wife, for example."

Stephanie's blood went cold.

"Why would Stephanie hire a detective to check up on my business dealings? She couldn't care less."

"Maybe she's divorcing you, Reymond," the man said. "Or has that never occurred to you?"

There was a silence. "It's possible, I suppose."

Stephanie flushed. She began trembling, her hand shaking so violently she could barely hang on to the receiver.

"Okay," her husband said, sounding surprisingly cool-headed. "Give me the bottom line. How much time do I have?"

"With luck, I can buy a day or two."

"There's no way I can raise that kind of money that fast."

"That's not an answer the Behrings want to hear. When I talked to the son, Rico, he was so livid he told me you'd better deliver or you'd find a stick of dynamite crammed up your ass. That's a direct quote, by the way."

"Look, Dave, I've got somewhere around thirty million dollars coming out of a company that's going public next month. Halcyon Technologies. Tell the Behrings they can have half their money out of that."

"Half in a month? Promising all of it in two weeks probably won't earn a return call," Dave said. "Eight days ago they said a week, remember? You're lucky you're alive."

"What kind of people are these? You told me they were businessmen."

"They are. But the son, Rico, is a nutcase. He loves having men around him with guns. Killers fascinate him. He said that once, right to my face."

"Dear God." Jean Claud said again. "Surely this Rico can see that killing me won't get their money back. Just talk to him, Dave. Halcyon is going to be a winner, guaranteed."

"I'll try. But I can't make any promises. I'll tell you this, Reymond, you'd be smart to pack your bags, just in case."

The conversation ended. Stephanie replaced the receiver. She wasn't sure what Jean Claud was involved in, but in the course of fifteen minutes, one thing had become patently clear—the man downstairs was an absolute, complete stranger.

The passenger agent announced the flight on the public-address system. Searching out the Cuban, Stephanie saw that he was getting up. It looked as though they'd be going to St. Thomas together. Picking up her alligator case with the computer disks and the money inside, she began moving with the crowd to the entrance to the jetway. The Cuban seemed to be hanging back. He wasn't nearby as she went through the door-way leading to the plane. Could it be he wasn't going on the flight?

She had a window seat toward the rear. The seats next to her were empty. She had imagined him coming down the aisle and sitting next to her. The thought made her nauseated. Then, when she saw him appear at the entrance to the coach cabin, her heart nearly stopped. But he didn't come down the aisle as she feared. He simply stared at her. What was he trying to do? Scare her? Intimidate her? Well, he was succeeding.

After a while he went back into the first-class cabin, and she sagged in her seat, relieved. He was torturing her, that's what he was doing. The worst part was she didn't know why. He wasn't a cop or the FBI, that much she'd pretty well decided. The only thing left was that he was somehow connected with the people who'd killed Jean Claud and Jane and that private investigator.

A few more passengers trickled in, including a shiny-faced couple who took the seats next to her. The young man immediately introduced himself and his wife. Their names were Brian and Tiffany Harvey, they were newlyweds from New Jersey, on their honeymoon. Stephanie congratulated them,

thankful for their presence. They were a welcome relief from
the anxiety of the past half hour or so.

She gave them their privacy, but watched them from the
corner of her eye, listening to them cooing at each other.
Stephanie envied the joy of the young couple, wishing she
was in some happy place. And not just to escape her present
predicament. She wanted a different life, or at least to erase
the last few years of the one she had.

As the plane pulled away from the gate, Stephanie decided
she was safe, at least for the moment. Fatigue weighing
heavily on her, she wished she could sleep. Outside, the tropical Miami landscape—the palm trees in the distance, the Ber-
muda grass, the air that almost *looked* humid—were all so
alien. How different it was from the foggy Northern California
coast where, only last Wednesday, her life had been changed
forever.

As she'd driven to the coast, tracing the golden shoulder of
Mount Tamalpais, the tops of the towering eucalyptus touched
by the misty fog of late summer, she'd forgotten about the
danger Jean Claud was facing. Instead, she'd focused on her
husband's infidelity, wondering who his mistress was.

Stephanie had made the trip countless times. Often she and
Suzanne had gone to the coast for the afternoon to sit on the
deck of the beach house overlooking Bolinas Bay. Even as a
child of eight, Zanny loved to stare at the sea, watching the
gulls. So they had sat together, bundled against the brisk Pacific wind, pungent with salty mist—Stephanie with her nov-
els, Zanny with her dreamy eyes and long sighs.

As she drove past the Muir Beach Overlook, Stephanie realized she had no idea what she hoped to accomplish at the
beach house. Her initial intent had been to get away, as Audrey
suggested. She'd packed a suitcase and put the computer disks
with the copies of Jean Claud's files in her purse. But then
she decided she couldn't live without knowing the truth.

Whether she actually confronted him, skewered him with guilt, remained to be seen.

And so she drove, wiping tears from her eyes as she followed the road that snaked past weathered barns and abandoned farmhouses until at last she reached Stinson Beach. Her pulse quickened. Not so much from fear of what she would find, as fear of how she'd react. This was uncharted territory—contending with a betrayal that touched not only their marriage, but the memory of their child.

The fog had thickened, making it impossible to see much more than a hundred feet ahead. The lights of approaching vehicles emerged from the gloom only moments before gliding past. But Stephanie knew every swell in the road. She exited Shoreline Highway at Calle del Arroyo, following it to the point where it divided into Seadrift and Dipsea Roads. She took the left fork, Seadrift, which ran down the ocean side of the spit of land separating Bolinas Bay from the lagoon.

Out on the spit the mists were thicker, the houses along the road ghostly shadows. She could barely see the pavement, forcing her to drive at a crawl. The beach house was at the far end of the spit, beyond the point where Dipsea Road looped back into Seadrift. Coming to the intersection, Stephanie rolled to a stop. She lowered her window to sniff the air. It was wet, cold and smelled strongly of the sea. She heard the wail of a distant foghorn and the faint rumble of the surf.

She raised her window and proceeded through the intersection. Nearing their house, she was able to make out the blurry shape of first one car parked at the edge of the road, then another. The first was Jean Claud's Jaguar, the second car was a Mercedes, one she didn't recognize. She assumed it belonged to her husband's lover.

Stephanie drove on a way, turned around and came back to the house, parking opposite the woman's car. There was no sign of life at the beach house, no lights. Perhaps they were in bed.

Her key ring in hand, she climbed out of the Acura and

gently closed the door. Then she walked across the road to look inside the Mercedes. On the passenger seat was an alligator case. It drew her attention because her sister, Jane, a real estate agent, had one that she used to carry her multiple-listing book, cellular phone and notebook computer. How ironic that...

"Oh my God," Stephanie muttered, backing from the car. She glared in the direction of the house, then at the Mercedes again. It couldn't be. No. Not her own sister. It had to be a coincidence.

She checked out the car. It was new. Jane *did* get a new Mercedes every couple years. How long since she'd seen Jane's car? Six months? She hadn't seen it when they'd had lunch recently. Then she thought of her sister, calmly eating lobster bisque and counseling her to divorce. What gall!

A knot formed in her stomach. For a moment she thought she might be sick. How could they? She didn't know who to hate more, Jane for her betrayal, or Jean Claud for his cold-hearted depravity.

She looked back at the house. It couldn't be innocent. She'd heard him speaking to her with affection, and yes, the voice she'd heard had been vaguely familiar. Now she knew why. Stephanie never would have imagined this, yet, in retrospect, it seemed patently obvious. Jean Claud and Jane had always been friendly. Allies against her.

It wasn't as though she and Jane hadn't had differences, they had. They shared a mother, but Stephanie's father had been considerably more successful than Jane's. And although he'd died young, he'd provided generously for his child. Jane had been bitter about Stephanie's inheritance. Still, Stephanie never would have thought childhood jealousies would lead to this. How could she have been so oblivious to what was going on?

She went to the front door, careful that her heels didn't clunk on the wooden walk. Then she quietly let herself in. The slider to the deck off the great room was open and the breeze was billowing the drapes. She saw a bottle of champagne and two glasses on a table by the sofa. Clothes were strewn everywhere. She looked around, realizing they were in the loft. Zanny's loft!

Stephanie held her breath, listening carefully. She could barely make out Jean Claud's voice. Then she heard a giggle. Jane's giggle.

"Can we stay all night?"

"I don't know why not, my darling. Stephanie won't know whether I'm home or not."

"She wouldn't care, anyway. All she can think about are her damn causes. How could she be so stupid? If I'd married you, Jean Claud, I'd never have let you get away."

"Ah, but then her loss is your gain, *n'est-ce pas?*"

Stephanie's blood boiled. The rage and hurt were so strong they choked her, and she had to cover her mouth.

"Oh, Jean Claud," Jane said. "I could do this for a million years. Promise we'll be together soon."

"Nothing will keep us apart. Nothing."

Stephanie hated them, but she also felt disgust. It suddenly seemed pointless to climb upstairs. Maybe all she'd really wanted was to be sure. As she turned for the door, her eye fell on a photo of Zanny at ten, sitting in the sand, hugging her knees, auburn hair like Stephanie's blowing across her pretty face.

She walked over to the fireplace and took the picture from the mantel. Then she went to the slider, pushed aside the billowing drape and went onto the deck. The photo clutched in her arms, she started across the sand, taking Zanny away from that place.

Tears flowing down her cheeks, her sense of urgency grew stronger. She began to run, going no place in particular. Just away. Reaching the water's edge, she was weeping so hard she could barely breathe. She staggered to a halt and collapsed.

She lay there, clutching the framed picture of her daughter as she sobbed, her body heaving, the sand caking against her face, her mouth, her eyes. It was like the day Zanny had died in that horrible car accident all over again.

Then it happened. The world seemed to explode, the roar so deafening that her brain went numb. For a few moments she couldn't feel anything, but she knew she was alive because of the shrill ringing in her ears. Lifting her head, she saw that their beach house was a tangle of ruins, enveloped in flames.

As reality began to sink in, she realized that her husband and sister had just been blown to bits. The horror of it was too much. Shaking, she lay in the sand, unable to move. She didn't know how long she was there, but finally, she got to her feet and staggered toward the fire, the photo in her arms. Nearing the burning remains, she became aware of the acrid smell of the fire and the heat. No one could have survived in that inferno.

She made her way to the street, certain that help would soon be on the way. Both her car and Jean Claud's were littered with debris. Peering up the road, she couldn't see anything through the fog. No lights were visible in the nearest house, though she saw some broken windows. The heat generated by the fire was tremendous.

She went to her car and, pushing aside some boards, managed to get the door open. Her key ring was no longer in her hand. She must have lost it on the beach. She grabbed her purse from the front seat. Jane's Mercedes had been partially shielded from the blast by the other cars and was relatively untouched. She went to it and tried the door, but it was locked. Staring at the flames, the heat drying her skin, she realized there was nothing to do but wait.

In the distance a siren sounded and she was glad. The police were already on their way. But how would she explain what had happened?

She glanced around warily. Surely whoever had done this was long gone. Or were they? She tried to think. Maybe she should call Audrey. Maybe the attorney would still be at the office.

Digging her cell phone out of her purse, she dialed. Audrey answered on the second ring.

"Audrey," she said, her voice shaking. "It's Stephanie. Something terrible has happened. Jean Claud's dead. A bomb."

"What?"

Fighting back sobs, she told Audrey what happened.

"Steph," Audrey said, "get out of there immediately. Go to a motel, anywhere but home."

"But what about the police?"

"I'll deal with them. In fact, a couple of detectives are coming to talk to me about Hal Sedman and the break-in. I told them I'd stay late at the office. But we can discuss all that later. Get out of there, Steph. When you're someplace safe, call me."

Though it didn't seem possible, Stephanie's heart was pounding even harder than before. "Okay," she said. "I will."

Audrey hung up. Stephanie looked around at the glowing fog, trembling at the thought that whoever had done this might still be nearby. The siren off in the distance meant help was coming. Her instinct was to wait for the police to arrive, but Audrey had insisted she leave. Perhaps Audrey felt *she* was in a better position to explain things—like their connection with the dead detective in L.A., why they were investigating Jean Claud, and why Stephanie's life was in danger. Stephanie was reluctant to second-guess an attorney, and she knew the longer she waited, the harder it would be to go. If she was going to leave, the time was now.

The trouble was, she'd lost her keys. And besides, her car was littered with debris. Then she remembered that Jane kept an extra car key under the front fender on the driver's side in one of those little magnetic boxes. She checked and, sure enough, it was there. Without wasting any more time, Stephanie removed the ignition key to the Mercedes, opened the door and climbed in, putting Zanny's picture and her purse on the seat with the alligator case. Then she remembered her suitcase was still in the back seat of her car. She would need her things.

Stephanie got out, crossed the road, dragged her suitcase from the car and put it in the trunk of the Mercedes. Then she got back in, turned the car around and headed up the road. Nearing the intersection, she could see the blurry lights of an emergency vehicle flashing as it came toward her on Seadrift. She turned onto Dipsea Road and made her way back to the Shoreline Highway. For several moments she sat at the intersection, almost catatonic, trying to clear her head. Glancing at Jane's alligator case, she realized for the first time that any evidence that her sister had died with Jean Claud was with her. The vehicles left at the house were the Jag and her Acura. Perhaps Jane's remains could be identified, but maybe not. For a while, anyway, the assumption would be that Stephanie was the one who'd died with Jean Claud. But did the killers know who they'd murdered? Had they been lurking in the shadows, watching? Had they seen her leave the beach house? There was no way to be sure.

The big jet roared up the runway. As the plane rose, Stephanie found comfort in the low throb of the engines and felt herself sinking rapidly toward a drugged-like sleep. Her heart still pounded from having relived that terrible afternoon at Stinson Beach, but the need for rest overwhelmed her. Even the Cuban didn't matter. Nothing did but the strangling fatigue. Within moments of her last conscious thought, she was asleep.

The Atlantic Ocean

They were somewhere over the eastern end of the Bahamas when Stephanie awoke with a start, the explosion ringing in her ears. It was a dream, of course, the desperate heave of her chest a result of fear—the trauma of having seen her husband and sister blown to pieces. She was far away from that horror now, but it was only a temporary respite. She still had the Cuban to contend with and God knows what waiting for her in St. Thomas.

Brian and Tiffany Harvey were playing cards, oblivious to her anxiety. For the first time in years, she was facing her problems alone. Jean Claud had been nothing if not conservative, and he'd insisted on sheltering her way more than was necessary. Of course, that was her fault as much as his. Even Audrey had said as much. Stephanie was much too smart, much too strong to allow herself to be a victim the way she had. But fate had given her an opportunity to redeem herself. She was facing the challenge of her life.

Stephanie's thoughts returned to that terrible afternoon of the bombing. It had been twilight by the time she checked into a modest motel in San Rafael, just off the freeway, near Third Street. Since she was in Jane's car, she'd decided to check in under her sister's name.

After registering, she'd gone directly to her room, double-locking the door and using the security chain. The place was dingy and smelled of stale tobacco, but for the moment she was glad to be alive. After dumping her purse, the photo of Zanny and Jane's case on the bed, she went to the phone and dialed Audrey's number. The office answering machine picked it up.

"Audrey, it's me. If you're there, please pick up the phone. I've got to talk to you."

She waited. Nothing. She was about to hang up when she heard the receiver being lifted on the other end of the line.

"Who is this?" It was a man's voice and it sounded gruff.

Stephanie was shocked. To the best of her knowledge, Audrey didn't have any men friends, at least none that would be in her office, answering her phone. "Who are you?" she demanded.

"Detective Wells of the San Francisco Police Department," the man replied.

"What's happened?"

"Will you tell me your name, please?"

Stephanie started to reply honestly, then thought better of it. How did she know he was really a cop? "Leslie Hartell," she said, using the name of her best friend, the first name to pop into her mind.

"What's your connection to Miss Saulter?" the avowed officer asked.

"A personal friend," Stephanie replied. "What's happened to Audrey? Why are you in her office?"

"There's been an accident," he said, hesitating. "Well, *accident* may not be the proper term. I'm afraid Miss Saulter has been shot."

"Oh, dear God. Is she all right?"

"I'm sorry to say she's dead."

Stephanie was stunned. "Oh no, not Audrey."

"We're trying to locate next of kin," the officer said. "Is there any chance you could help us in that regard?"

Stephanie barely heard the words. Her mind was reeling. Jean Claud and Jane dead. Now Audrey.

"Miss Hartell?"

"Huh? Oh, no, I'm afraid not," she said. "I don't know her family. I'm sorry, I have to go."

She hung up and burst into tears. Her world was collapsing around her. Wringing her hands, she got up and paced, trying to think clearly. Audrey's last words to her were to get out of town and now Audrey, too, was dead. Stephanie's instinct was to run as fast and as far as she could.

Outside she could hear the monotonous hum of freeway traffic. Pulling back the curtains, she took a deep, fortifying breath and watched the lights of passing cars. Where would she go? What would she do? Then she thought of the conversation only a week earlier when she'd called her friend

Leslie in Washington to say that she'd finally decided to leave Jean Claud.

"Oh, Steph, you poor thing," her friend had said. "God, you need me, don't you? Damn. I'd have you come here in a flash, but Warren and I are on our way out the door for two weeks in Europe. Why not go to our place in St. Thomas? A little time alone in the sun will be good for you. I'll call from London to see how you're doing. Then, when we're back in Washington, I want you to come here and stay as long as you like."

Stephanie had declined the offer, deciding to wait until Leslie got back. But that was before everything had literally blown up in her face. Suddenly, the Virgin Islands seemed a godsend. Remote. Safe. A few days at Leslie's place would be an opportunity to calm down and figure out what to do. Most importantly, she'd be out of danger. Or so she'd thought.

In retrospect, she realized the smart thing would have been to go to the police right then. But Audrey's death had really rattled her. Stephanie had felt so alone, so confused, so uncertain about what to do. The two people she'd have turned to—Leslie and Warren Hartell—were away in Europe. Waiting in the Caribbean for them to return seemed an easy, uncomplicated solution to her problem. Even so, she'd hardly slept that night in the motel, planning her escape. Her one salvation was that everyone would think she was dead, since it was *her* car buried in the rubble at the beach house.

But Stephanie knew she had to be careful. She knew not to use her credit cards and she wanted to avoid using Jane's. Fortunately, she had cash. Jane, who'd always carried a lot with her, had over five hundred dollars in her wallet. Stephanie had three hundred and fifty-five in hers because she'd used her credit card for a recent lunch with a group of friends and they'd repaid her in cash. That was a lot, but even so, she would need more money if she was going to buy plane tickets and meals. In the morning she'd go to the bank.

She'd always had money of her own. Between her personal

savings and checking accounts, she had seventeen or eighteen
thousand she could put her hands on immediately. Yes, she'd
withdraw several thousand to tide her over, but not at her
branch. If she wanted to drop out of sight quietly, she would
have to go someplace where the clerks wouldn't recognize her.

That night in the motel room, as she lay awake in her bed,
Stephanie had tried to look beyond the immediate crisis and
imagine what would become of her life. Considering her inheritance, work wasn't a necessity. Whatever happened, she
wouldn't be under financial pressure.

At dawn she'd called the airline and made reservations. After breakfast at Denny's she'd gone to the bank and withdrawn
her money. Not once had she seen anyone watching her. But
in spite of her caution, it was obvious now that someone had
spotted her at the airport. That was the only way she could
explain why the Cuban was tormenting her. He had to be one
of *them.*

To this point she'd been in public and he couldn't easily
accost her. He was obviously confident she wouldn't go to the
police, given that she was on the run. Maybe that was a mistake. Perhaps she *should* go to the authorities now. St. Thomas
wasn't shaping up to be the safe haven she'd thought. Besides,
if she'd been compromised, there was no longer any reason to
keep silent. The last thing she wanted was for people to think
she was guilty.

She tried to figure out what it was, exactly, that these killers
wanted from her. Surely they didn't think she had control of
Jean Claud's investment funds, that she could repay them
when he couldn't.

How ironic that Jean Claud's skill as an investor had been
the key to her financial security, but might also prove to be
the key to her downfall. Whatever his failings, her husband
had certainly done well by her financially. He'd invested her
inheritance for her, and Stephanie had given him a great deal
of latitude. She'd seen no need for high-risk investment and
had told him twenty percent of her portfolio was the most

she'd wanted in venture capital. As far as she knew, he'd honored that request.

Over the years he'd periodically reported how well her portfolio was doing. Sometime before Suzanne had died, he'd given Stephanie a report that showed he'd tripled her net worth, which meant she was worth over four million dollars. One day it would have gone to Zanny, but now…

A thought suddenly came to her. If Jean Claud had been mixed up in some crooked scheme with unscrupulous people, what might he have done with *her* money? Her blood ran cold. She recalled the desperation in her husband's voice during that phone call from the man named Dave. Suddenly she felt an urgent need to know the status of her own portfolio.

The answer was probably on the computer disks, which she'd put in the alligator case. Jean Claud had kept records of everything in his computer. All the books of her personal portfolio had been there, as well. Thank God she'd copied the files and had the computer disks with her.

A sobering thought struck her. Could that be what the Cuban was after—Jean Claud's files? Audrey knew she'd made copies. If the Cuban was involved in her friend's death, Audrey could have told him about the disks before he shot her.

The insight sent a fresh wave of fear through her. Those people Jean Claud had been dealing with… What was their name…? Behring, that was it. The Behrings, Inter-America Ventures, Dave—everybody involved in Jean Claud's shady deal—would be very interested in Jean Claud's files. And because of Audrey, they probably knew she had them.

What should she do? She'd intended to examine the disks in detail once she got to St. Thomas, but maybe she should have a look now. With a new sense of urgency, Stephanie lowered the tray table, slipped her sister's laptop computer from the alligator case under the seat and booted it up. She couldn't be sure Jane had the right software, but she was happy to discover the system was set up identically to Jean

Claud's. That was a pleasant surprise, and it also made her
wonder.

Perusing the hard drive, she discovered that most of the data
files concerned Jane's personal finances and her real estate
business. Stephanie didn't want to waste time on them, and
she slipped one of Jean Claud's floppies into the disk drive.

For several minutes she looked through his accounts, mem-
orizing the various places he'd stashed their money, aware that
when the time came to settle Jean Claud's estate, it would be
helpful to know where everything was. Then she began to look
for the data on her own portfolio. She found the file. There
was a record of investments made over the years, mostly in
equities, the bulk of those in Fortune 500 companies. But then
she noted that about ten months earlier Jean Claud had liqui-
dated almost the entire portfolio and dumped ninety percent
of her assets into a company called Halcyon Technologies—
an investment of nearly five million dollars.

Stephanie was shocked. Jean Claud had never mentioned
that he was considering such a bold move. It was a risky
decision, regardless of how great the company's upside potential might be. What could have been his motive?

Stephanie checked their joint portfolio and found that the
bulk of those monies—roughly two million dollars—had also
been invested in Halcyon. That meant virtually everything she
had, except for the house, was riding on one obscure company.
Halcyon Technologies. Why did that name seem familiar?

Then she remembered.

Halcyon was the name that had come up in the phone conversation between Jean Claud and Dave. Jean Claud had said
he was going to be making a ton of money when Halcyon
shares were sold to the public next month. And he'd told Dave
that the money they owed the Behrings could be repaid out of
those funds—with *her* money, in other words.

Feeling sick, she glanced around. Next to her, Tiffany Harvey was asleep, her head on Brian's shoulder. The young cou-

ple's innocence again struck her, painfully emphasizing the difference between their carefree existence and hers.

Just then the curtain separating the first-class cabin from coach opened and the Cuban appeared. Stephanie blanched. As she watched him coming down the aisle, her heart began to race.

She quickly stuffed the computer back into the alligator case and kicked it under the seat. As he approached, the man looked directly at her. He was no less frightening than before, but now she had a better understanding of what was going on. With Jean Claud dead, they'd probably decided to wring the Halcyon money out of her. They were after her, all right, because of the information on the computer disks.

The Cuban reached her row and, to her dismay, stopped and said, "Mrs. Reymond, we haven't had the pleasure of meeting. I am Oscar Barbadillo, a business associate of your late husband. Seeing we both seem to be headed to St. Thomas, I thought perhaps we could have lunch."

Stephanie was speechless. She glanced at Brian Harvey, who looked up at the man. Tiffany was awake now, also watching. Barbadillo waited, his eyes moving over her, making her more uncomfortable.

"I...I'm not going to St. Thomas...for business," she stammered.

He shrugged. "We can have a friendly conversation."

Stephanie was unsure whether to reject the invitation outright or play him along to buy time. Finally, she opted for the latter. "Why don't you tell me where you're staying and I'll give you a call, Mr. Barbadillo."

"I don't have a hotel yet. Why don't we go directly from the airport?"

"I'd rather not, thank you. I'm very tired."

"Then give me your number."

His voice had grown more commanding. And the way he looked at her made her increasingly uneasy.

She swallowed hard. "I'm staying with friends."

"Don't they have a phone?"

"Yes, but the number's in my suitcase."

He glanced down the aisle. "Maybe we can talk more when we get to St. Thomas," he said as the flight attendants approached with a serving cart. "We have some very important things to discuss."

Stephanie nodded and watched him retreat toward the first-class cabin. Her hands were shaking. Barbadillo had addressed her as Mrs. Reymond, and he'd referred to her *late* husband. For him to know who she was and that Jean Claud was dead, he had to be involved in some way. Maybe she had more reason to go to the police now than ever.

Charlotte Amalie

St. Thomas, U.S. Virgin Islands

Jack Kidwell lay on the examining table staring at the ceiling, looking for Africa or a butterfly or the shape of a woman's bare tit. He'd engaged in this pursuit before, of course—at the clinic in Immokalee when he'd broken his arm at age ten. They'd given him a shot of something and he'd felt no pain. He'd just lain there, searching for images on the ceiling. Bill Toussaint's exam room had a few watermarks overhead, but Jack couldn't, for the life of him, envision a damn thing but rusty brown smudges that looked like...well, rusty brown smudges. His imagination had obviously expired right along with his innocence.

The notion of bare tits still interested him, but that was hardly news. Not even the alcohol had stifled his sex drive, though for two or three years now Bill had been warning it would.

The door opened and Dr. William Toussaint entered, his lab coat as stiff as week-old white bread. Bill came to the table and looked down at him. "Jack," he said, "I can't give you a clean bill of health. I wish I could, but I can't."

"What do you mean? There's not a thing wrong with me."

"By outward appearances, no. But your liver's enlarged. Considerably more than last year. It's obvious you've been drinking like a fish."

Jack sat up on the edge of the table. "Sure, I hit the bottle, sometimes pretty hard, but I'm sober now, aren't I? And I'm sober whenever I've got passengers aboard and I'm under sail. That's all that matters."

"That's between you and the maritime authorities," Toussaint replied evenly. "My job is to report the status of your health and the fact is, it's not good. I'm sorry."

Jack shook his head, trying to control his anger. "Nothing would satisfy you, Bill—nothing short of me becoming a teetotaler."

"That's not a half-bad idea."

"Come on, now," Jack protested, getting to his feet. "This is no laughing matter. I'm on probation as it is. You send in a report that I'm drinking and they'll jerk my license."

"That's between you and them."

"No, goddamn it, it's between you and me. You're the one who's saying I'm unfit. And it's your word that counts."

Bill Toussaint, an Englishman who was one-sixteenth black, his skin as smooth as milk faintly tinged with chocolate, drew up his slender frame. His blue eyes flashed. "I'm saying you've got an enlarged liver due to alcoholism. That's a medical fact, not an accusation. What they do with it is their business."

Jack began pacing, the seriousness of the situation becoming obvious. "You know exactly what they're going to do with it."

"You want to know what my major regret is in this thing is?" Bill asked. "That we're talking about your license, not your life."

"Fuck my life," Jack retorted. "What's it worth if I can't

earn a living? Your only legitimate concern is the well-being of my passengers. Booze has not caused one bit of harm to a single living soul.''

"Present company excluded," Bill Toussaint said.

"Yeah, well, that's *my* choice, Doc."

They looked into each other's eyes for several long moments, friends, yet on this issue, enemies. "Jack," the doctor said finally, "sit down for a second." He gestured toward the examining table.

Jack felt a lecture coming, but he had little choice. He climbed back up on the table. "Okay, Mom, what have you got to say?"

"I'm a medical doctor, not a shrink," Bill began. "I know I'm out of my element here, but I'm going to tell you what I think, anyway. You're the shell of the man I once knew. Look at you. How long has it been since you've shaved?"

"So I ran out of blades a few days ago. Is that a crime? I'm clean. I showered."

"That's not what I'm getting at. When you first came down here, you were a hell of a guy. Sure, you could party even then, but you had fire in your soul, purpose. You cared about life. You cared about people. I liked you."

Jack heard a tremor in Bill's voice. He could tell he was speaking from the heart and it kind of got him. A lump started forming in his throat. He hated emotion. Always had. "But then demon rum turned me into an asshole—is that it?" As usual, Jack found a smart remark to make it easier to get past his feelings.

The doctor leaned against the counter. "No, Jack."

"What then?"

"To put it bluntly, after Alicia died, you gave up. I know losing her was a blow, maybe the worse thing you'll ever experience, but she was the one they buried that day, not you."

"That's the first thing you've said that's wrong, Bill. My corpse is playing out the string, and I do whatever I can so I don't notice the pain." He pointed at Bill. "But I don't mess with anybody else's life. I don't drink and drive. I never screw a woman if it'd hurt her. And I don't blubber on other people's shoulders. That may not make me a model citizen, but there's a whole lot worse out there. I just want to be left alone, and for some goddamn reason, I can't get anybody to understand that."

Bill unfolded his arms. "Well, this is a debate nobody's going to win. I've got only one option I can live with and that's to tell the truth. I can't give you a clean bill of health when you're dripping with eighty-proof scotch whiskey."

Jack's shoulders slumped. "Let's get to the bottom line, Dr. Toussaint. What do I have to do to get out of purgatory?"

"Come back in a month without having had a drink. Simple as that. You won't have to tell me whether you've succeeded or not, your liver will."

"Jesus Christ, I'll be out of business."

The doctor absently wiped the counter with a tissue he plucked from a neatly aligned box. He was as fastidious as he was honest. "Remember the first time we met, Jack? You were selling those condominiums."

"Jesus, don't remind me."

"You were the slickest damn salesman I'd ever seen," Bill said. "And I mean that as a compliment. You were passionate, convincing, high-energy. You were a man who was going to set the world on fire."

"Well, it was my last hurrah. I'm in retirement now."

"You've given up on life."

Jack gave him his best woebegone look. "Doc, enough already."

Bill contemplated him. "Okay, here's what I'll do. I'll send a report in with a recommendation that there be a follow-up exam in a month, saying this exam isn't conclusive."

"That's the crumb?"

"Yes."

Jack considered the implications. The real question was,

could he stay off the sauce for a month? The probability that he couldn't scared him. Not so long ago he still claimed to be in control. In recent months he'd stopped kidding himself. The result had been predictable. He was drinking even more.

He rubbed his hand over his jaw, thinking. Maybe Bill was right. God knew, the sirens' call was as strong as ever. He could see himself going down the companionway, walking to the locker, unscrewing the cap of a virgin bottle and taking a long, gluttonous swig. He could feel the delicious burn of the scotch just thinking about it. Lord, how he worshiped that feeling.

"So that's it?" Jack asked. "Sober for a month or I go to hell."

"Sober for a month and, if you pass the test, reexamination in six months."

"Oh, Jesus Christ, Bill."

"This is one challenge you won't be able to sluff off, my man. You've got to look this tiger in the eye."

Jack could see he wasn't going to wiggle out of this one. Bureaucrats and the medical profession would be ruling his life until he found a way to beat them. He took his shirt off the hook on the back of the door. "All right, you win."

Bill Toussaint smiled. Jack smiled back. He liked the son-ovabitch, but he'd have relished nothing more than to pop him one just then. He shook Bill's hand and went out of the room.

"Thanks, Doc," he said over his shoulder.

"See you in a month," the doctor called after him.

"Fuck you, Bill," Jack said under his breath. But at the moment he happened to be passing the little nurse with the sweet round ass and she gave him a disapproving look. "Sorry," he said. Then he went through the door to the waiting room. The half-dozen or so patients glanced up as he strode out the door.

The heavy tropical air, fragrant with bougainvillea and cooking smells, filled his lungs. He took a couple of deep breaths and realized that, despite the early hour, he could use a drink. That was bad. If he succumbed, it would be the beginning of the end. Jack knew that. The sad part was, he almost didn't care. Looking up at the blue sky, he shook his head. If he was a betting man, he'd bet against himself. Thank God he wasn't that foolish with his money.

Harry S Truman Airport,

St. Thomas

Stephanie continued to agonize over her situation as the plane touched down on the green Caribbean island. She'd been brooding ever since the Cuban, Oscar Barbadillo, had come to speak with her, doing her best to keep a cool head despite the terror she felt. She hadn't eaten the meal the flight attendant had brought and maybe that was a mistake. Between her sleep deprivation and lack of food, she felt woozy and shaky. But she'd made a decision about Barbadillo. The very last thing she'd do was go off with him. She didn't want to wind up dead like Jean Claud, Jane and Audrey.

She had to be very careful. Her sister's alligator case contained not only the prize Barbadillo and his friends were after, but also the key to her own financial security. The first order of business was to secrete it someplace safe while she worked things out. In hindsight, she realized fleeing San Francisco had been the biggest mistake of all.

As the plane taxied toward the terminal building, Brian Harvey pulled a carry-on bag from under the seat in front of Tiffany. It gave Stephanie an idea. She hadn't talked to the kids a lot, but the girl had told her about their wedding and Stephanie had made all the appropriate sounds. If she was going to do anything about the alligator case, this was the time.

"Excuse me, Tiffany," she said, "but I was wondering if I could ask a favor."

The girl's bright eyes were full of innocence. "Sure."

"I don't want that man who came to speak to me to see my case and I was wondering if you would mind carrying it off the plane for me."

"I'd be glad to," the girl said.

"Perhaps you can put it in a locker for me."

"Okay."

"But if we could take it to the ladies' room first, I'd like to go through it," Stephanie said.

Tiffany nodded.

"Is everything all right?" Brian asked. "That guy seemed kind of strange."

"He *is* strange."

Stephanie didn't want to explain, and the Harveys seemed content to leave it at that. Within minutes they were at the gate and the passengers prepared to deplane. Seeing Jane's case in Tiffany's hands, Stephanie felt better about facing Oscar Barbadillo.

With nothing but her purse in hand, Stephanie followed the newlyweds. The first-class cabin was empty, but Barbadillo was waiting for her at the bottom of the boarding stairs. The air was warm, but the sight of his coldly handsome face, his menacing eyes, made her shiver.

"Mrs. Reymond," he said, falling in beside her, "it's important that we speak."

"Why is that?" she asked, moving briskly, not looking at him.

"For your own good."

"I think I'm the best judge of what's for my own good," she said. "I'm sorry, but I have no desire to talk to you, much less have lunch with you. So, please, leave me alone."

Barbadillo brusquely took her arm and pulled her aside. His eyes were intense, if not angry. "You don't seem to understand the trouble you're in. If you cooperate, things will go much more smoothly. If you don't, I can't be responsible for what happens."

"Are you threatening me?"

The tiniest smile broke at the corners of his mouth. "If you want to consider it that."

"What is it you want?"

"To talk to you about your husband's business."

"I know nothing about Jean Claud's business," she said.

His smile was broader, his fingers tightening on her arm. "You expect me to believe that?"

"Frankly, I don't care what you believe. But if you don't leave me alone, I'm going to the police. In fact, I think that might be a good idea, anyway."

Stephanie jerked her arm free and started walking across the hot tarmac toward the terminal building. Brian and Tiffany had gone on ahead, but they turned to look back at her. Seeing her coming now, they proceeded. Barbadillo had not come with her and she didn't look to see where he was. In being firm, maybe she had dampened his ardor. She could only hope so.

Catching up to Tiffany and Brian, she followed them into the building, a rather ancient edifice with a corrugated steel roof and open sides. Inside the barnlike structure was a covey of tour guides. A porter pointed the milling passengers toward the baggage-claim area. Stephanie glanced back. Oscar Barbadillo was strolling at a leisurely pace and didn't look particularly angry or upset. That concerned her.

The passengers had spread out some. Stephanie tried not to stick to close to the Harveys so as not to draw attention to either them or Jane's case. Reaching the baggage-claim area, she kept to the middle of the throng. There was no sign of Barbadillo. Could he have given up? Or was he lying somewhere in wait?

She felt perspiration forming on her lip. She glanced at the alligator case in Tiffany's hand. The girl said something to Brian and, giving Stephanie a knowing look, walked toward the rest rooms. Stephanie waited several moments, then followed her, her heels clicking on the concrete floor. If Barbadillo was watching, she didn't see him.

She noted the luggage lockers just outside the rest rooms, deciding that was where Jane's case should be stashed. Inside the ladies' room, she found Tiffany waiting. The girl handed her the alligator case.

"Are you sure you're all right?" Tiffany asked.

"I'm fine," she replied though her heart was pounding and she was dewy with perspiration.

"Is there anything else I can do?" the girl asked.

"There is one thing, if you'll give me just a minute."

Tiffany nodded. Stephanie went into one of the stalls and locked herself inside. She sat down and, though she felt like crying, she pulled herself together. Opening her purse, she removed the envelope with the cash she'd gotten at the bank. After counting out ten one-hundred-dollar bills, she stuffed them in her wallet. Then she put the envelope with the remaining four thousand in the alligator case. She had another twelve thousand in travelers' checks. Two thousand of that went into her purse, the rest into the case.

She removed the framed photograph of Suzanne, wondering if she dared leave it. In the end, she wedged it into her purse. That left only the computer disks. She considered dividing them but knew they'd probably be useless unless she had them all. She put them inside the case with Jane's laptop. Everything was together, to be lost or preserved in one fell swoop. The next step was to hide the case.

Leaving the stall, she went to where Tiffany was leaning over a basin, examining her face in the mirror. Seeing Stephanie, she turned, tucking a hank of dark blond hair behind her ear. It was a gesture not unlike Suzanne's.

"If you'd be good enough to put the case in one of the lockers outside the door," she told the girl, "I won't keep you any longer."

"No problem."

"Here are some quarters," Stephanie said, taking a dollar's worth from her coin purse. She put them in Tiffany's hand, along with a couple of twenty-dollar bills. "This is for you and Brian to buy yourselves a bottle of champagne."

"Oh, that isn't necessary."

"I'd like you to have it. Please."

The girl acquiesced. Taking the case, she left the rest room. Stephanie told herself everything was under control now. She'd taken precautions. Short of them killing her, she'd be fine.

After a couple of minutes Tiffany returned, handing Stephanie a locker key. "You sure you're all right?" she asked. "I mean, can I call someone for you?"

"No, I'll be fine, thank you."

"Well, I'd better go then. Brian's waiting. Have a nice vacation."

"And you have a nice life."

Tiffany grinned, a bit embarrassed. Stephanie watched her as she left, thinking of the last time she'd seen her daughter alive. It was over a year ago. Suzanne had been home from college for the summer.

Fighting off the emotion threatening to erupt, Stephanie told herself that trading sorrow for fear was not much of an improvement. She transferred her attention to the key, wondering what to do with it as two women came into the rest room. Turning from them, she stuffed the key in her bra, then casually examined herself in the mirror. Once the women had gone into the stalls, Stephanie wet her hands and ran her fingers through her short, wavy auburn hair. The face looking back at her had seen better days. So had her taupe linen suit. She smoothed the collar of her blouse and turned up the sleeves of the jacket another notch. There was not much to be done about the haggard look, but she took consolation in the fact that she'd earned it.

Drying her hands, she tried to prepare herself mentally. She had faced adversity before. The year since Zanny's accident had been hell, albeit of a different type. But she'd gotten through that and she'd get through this, too.

Taking a deep breath, she headed to the baggage-claim area, which was teeming with passengers and porters. She saw a couple of policemen standing off to the side, but Oscar Barbadillo was nowhere in sight. The policemen seemed to be watching her, which struck her as odd. She had half a mind to go speak with them immediately, but decided the first order of business was to get her suitcase.

The bags were arriving as she walked up. Edging forward, she searched for her suitcase. It was on the second train of baggage cars. She grabbed it and backed out of the crowd. A porter took it from her, plopping it onto his handcart.

"Taxi, missus?" he asked in a musical accent.

Stephanie glanced at the policemen, who continued to watch her. She wondered if she might be better off taking a taxi to police headquarters. It might be easier to speak with someone in authority there. "Yes, please," she said to the porter.

"Right this way."

The man was not young, but he swung his body rhythmically as he walked.

Outside, the taxis were loading passengers. The porter went to an empty spot at the curb, signaled the next one in line, then put her suitcase on the sidewalk. Stephanie opened her purse to get some bills for a tip.

Just then she felt a hand on her elbow. She flinched, expecting it to be Barbadillo, but it was one of the policemen she'd seen inside, a slender young mulatto with a sparse mustache.

"Stephanie Reymond?" he said.

The other officer, also young, but more heavyset and darker, stepped to her other side. She looked back and forth between them.

"Yes, I'm Stephanie Reymond," she said.

The first man nodded. "Please come with us."

The second man picked up her suitcase. The first started to lead her away.

"Hey, man," the porter called after them plaintively. "What 'bout me?"

Stephanie and the officers stopped. "Give him some money," the thinner officer said.

She gave the man the two one-dollar bills in her hand, which he took with a grunt of thanks before shuffling off. The cops led her toward a police cruiser parked farther up the loading zone.

"It's just as well you found me," she said to them. "I was going to take a taxi to the police station."

They ignored her comment. While the heavyset man put her suitcase in the trunk, the other one opened the rear door of the patrol car. Stephanie slid in. The door slammed closed behind her. The two cops got in the front, separated from her by a wire-mesh screen. The engine started and they pulled away. As they passed the entrance to the terminal, Stephanie caught a glimpse of Tiffany and Brian climbing into a van. Again, she envied them their innocence.

The police car entered the main road, which led over a low hill to Charlotte Amalie. No one said anything. Stephanie was relieved to think she would no longer be facing danger alone. She could see now she'd done the wrong thing in fleeing. It would have been better to have gone straight to the authorities. If the police wanted to make a big deal of it, they probably could, but it was certainly understandable that she'd been terrified, considering everybody around her, including her lawyer, had been killed. As a practical matter, the worst she was guilty of was poor judgment.

Reflecting, she was surprised that the police had been able to track her down so quickly. She'd been sure it would take weeks to figure out that she wasn't the one who'd died with Jean Claud. Oscar Barbadillo had found her easily enough, but presumably he and his friends were responsible for the trouble and knew to look for her.

The cruiser moved along the road at a rapid clip, the driver ignoring the potholes and giving bicyclists minimal latitude.

The two young officers obviously had nothing to say to her.
Presumably their orders had been to pick her up and nothing
more.

Stephanie leaned forward in her seat. "Are we going to
police headquarters?" she asked, deciding to initiate the conversation.

The men ignored her.

"Excuse me," she said more loudly. "Could you please
tell me where you're taking me?"

"You'll see," one said.

That struck her as a curious response. And it gave her pause.

"I'm not under arrest, am I?"

"You're being taken in for questioning."

"About what?"

"You'll find out soon enough."

Stephanie did not like their attitude. The U.S. Virgin Islands
might be a territory, but it wasn't a foreign country. The Con-
stitution applied. She was at a loss whether to protest their
offhand manner or wait and see what happened. Maybe it was
a mistake, but in the end she decided not to risk antagonizing
them. As they'd said, she'd find out what was going to happen
soon enough.

Charlotte Amalie

Jack Kidwell was having a bad day. Ever since leaving Bill
Toussaint's office, he'd wandered around the quarter like a
lost child. The irony was that he *was* lost—a lost soul, whose
only purpose had been pretty much reduced to getting through
the day. Did he fight this thing, or did he give up?

When a guy wasn't sure if he had it in him to help himself,
he was a goner. So why didn't he just go find himself a bottle
and be done with it? The pain would be gone—at least the
short-term pain. Yet he hesitated. Why? Pride? He had nothing
left to be proud of. Could it be fear? Of what? Death was all

that was left. Maybe what bothered him was that he was taking the coward's way. It was too quiet and lonely. Maybe what he secretly longed for was to die with his boots on, to go down firing away at the demons bedeviling him. The trouble was, he couldn't figure out how.

Jack realized after a while that his wanderings weren't as aimless as they seemed. He'd come to the little park on the hillside across the street from Sonia Velasco's place and, finding a bench nestled under a banana tree, he plopped down to consider why he was there. Sonia was not only a friend, she was a former lover. Jack wasn't sure which relationship had brought him to her neighborhood. Perhaps it didn't matter. Each had its allure, its advantages and its problems. But for the moment it seemed enough just to contemplate the possibilities.

It had been a while since he'd seen her. That, probably, was due to pride. It was one thing for a man to admit his frailties to himself, a very different thing to admit them to a woman. And usually it wasn't necessary. Women, by and large, were quick to do that for you. Sonia was rather special, if only because she was the best lay on the island, bar none, though he didn't much like it that she always smoked a cigar after sex. If she had any other faults or flaws of character, she did a good job of hiding them.

Sonia Velasco was Swedish or Danish—he could never remember which—and she attributed her prowess in bed to the skills of her late husband, Enrique, an expatriate Cuban mulatto artist with charm, wit, charisma, though only a modicum of talent. Enrique had sold his art to the New Yorkers from the cruise ships, but spent enough time in other women's beds that Sonia eventually lost what qualms she had about dalliances of her own. That was when she'd taken Jack as a lover, some four or five years ago. Since Enrique's untimely death at the hands of an irate cuckold—an irony Jack had trouble digesting—he and Sonia had been friends more than lovers, though they still had sex every couple of months out of mutual regard. That is, they did until his drinking had gotten out of control and his pride wouldn't allow her to see him in his deteriorated condition.

The question at the moment was, did he swallow his pride and take refuge in her arms, or did he let his rudderless boat quietly drift away? There were sound arguments either way. Perhaps what held him back was that, if he allowed her to save him, he would owe her. There was also the question of whether it would work. Sex, he'd long since discovered, was a palliative, not a cure. Like booze. But the advantage to booze was you didn't need anybody else.

Not that there wouldn't be something in it for Sonia. She had her needs. That was the part that concerned him most. He had enormous respect for her ability to accept life's vicissitudes—a talent he unfortunately did not share—but women had a lesser aptitude for stoicism.

No, the real problem—and Sonia knew it as well as he— was that they had little more in common than a mutual understanding of their bodies. At forty-five, she retained much of her beauty even if she was, as she insisted, on the downhill slide.

Staring up in the bright morning sun at her second-story flat with its balcony and rusted iron railing, he thought of the last time he'd been with her. After they'd made love, he'd watched her stare at the ceiling fan in her boudoir, the pale skin of her neck and chest blotchy from their lovemaking. She'd savored her cigar and the last of her orgasm, pooching her well-shaped mouth to emit sensuous rings of smoke that drifted into the gentle currents of the creaky old fan until they were broken and disbursed like days passing into memory. Jack liked it that she could be with him yet forget him at the same time.

Though he was never sure, he surmised it was Enrique she thought of at those moments. There was no disputing that her husband had been the love of her life. And while Jack never felt used by her, he'd always been able to give of himself without feeling the onus of loving or being loved. But would that hold if he were to put his soul in her hands?

He remembered the day they'd met over a bin of oranges at an outdoor market. She'd let him carry home her purchases, then had made him some fresh-squeezed juice as a reward. The first words out of her mouth were that she loved her husband, but that he treated her badly. She'd endured his dalliances as long as she was able, but had decided to take a lover. The rest, as they say, was history.

The last time he'd visited her, she'd greeted him in a soft flowing caftan, kissing him on the mouth before leading him to the bedroom. "I haven't been screwing anyone else," she'd said in her soft Scandinavian accent as she'd undressed, letting her bra drop away from her large, well-shaped breasts.

"Meaning?"

"I'm a little hungrier than usual."

"I'll be careful," he'd said.

He had noticed a certain eagerness in her lovemaking, though it fell well short of desperation. For the most part, Sonia was her usual self—equally in control and out of control, luxuriating in her own sexuality as much as his. Her greatest strength as a lover was her understanding of a man's sexual desires. She knew not to be obsessive and to measure her own pleasure with as much care as she measured his. A woman who could take her pleasure gracefully was the equal of one who could give it unselfishly. Sonia was adept at both.

Jack felt a need to screw that was almost the equal of his need for a drink. He could picture himself walking across the street, climbing her stairs and rapping on her door. Then, when she looked into his eyes, the moment of truth would come. He would either manage a quip or break into tears. Pride kept him from finding out which. No, he would not burden Sonia with his frailties, he would deal with them on his own. And let the goddamn chips fall where they may.

The accident on the road from the airport held them up for

a while, the cops leaving her in the car while they tended to their duties. But they didn't stay long, turning the work over to a couple of other officers who'd arrived on the scene. The cops still weren't very communicative, leaving Stephanie uncertain whether to be angry or compliant. She'd never been in police custody before, even for her own protection. No one had spoken for several minutes, and she was getting progressively more ill at ease.

They passed a baseball field on their left, then a high-rise hotel. To the right was the bay. The highway traced the waterfront. After a quarter of a mile they were in an older section of town and turned onto a side street. Stephanie was eager to reach the police station and speak with someone in authority.

The buildings on either side of the narrow street were two and three stories high, stucco and concrete, all old. A few blocks from the waterfront, they pulled over and the officers got out. Stephanie peered out the window at the nondescript building opposite the car. The mulatto opened the door on the passenger side. "This is where you get out."

"This isn't the police station."

"Temporary headquarters, lady. Our regular offices were damaged in the hurricane."

Stephanie was skeptical, but she was hardly in any position to argue. She climbed out of the patrol car and the officer took her arm, leading her to the door. The other cop had gotten her suitcase from the trunk and joined them in the small entry leading to a flight of stairs.

The three of them went up, Stephanie growing more and more wary with each step. What if these men were abducting her with the intention of assaulting her? More than one cop had abused his authority, taking advantage of a woman. But they'd known her name when they approached her, leading her to believe it couldn't be a random abduction. Nothing was making much sense, but that was hardly a surprise. She was exhausted and her brain was muddled.

At the top of the stairs, the officer holding her arm told her to go up the next flight. On the third floor there were two doors. The cop knocked on one and a man in shirtsleeves with a gun and holster strapped to his side opened the door. He was Hispanic, sturdily built, in his mid to late forties. Stephanie assumed he was a detective.

He looked at her, then at the cop. "So, it's Señora Reymond, is it?"

"That's what she says."

The man motioned for her to enter. She hesitated, fear now gnawing at her gut. The cop gave her a gentle push, and she passed reluctantly through the door into what looked like the front room of an apartment, though it was empty except for a desk and a few chairs.

"That her suitcase?" the Latino asked.

"Yeah," the other cop said, handing it to him.

He put it down, said, "Thanks and *adiós*," closed the door and locked it with a key, which he dropped into his pocket.

Stephanie, who'd watched him anxiously, was completely flummoxed. "Who are you?" she demanded. "Are you in charge here?"

"No," came a voice from behind her. "That would be me."

She spun around. Standing in the door leading to the back rooms was Oscar Barbadillo. "Oh my God," she murmured.

Barbadillo, who was in shirtsleeves now, didn't quite smile, but she could tell he was pleased by her surprise. He strode casually to the desk, and sat on the corner of it, resting his folded hands on his crotch. "So, Stephanie, we meet again," he said, favoring her with an amused grin. "You don't mind if I call you Stephanie, do you?"

"What do you want?" she demanded, doing her best to mask the terror she felt.

"For starters, you can come over here and talk to me like a proper lady. Nobody can carry on a conversation from across the room. Besides, I want to smell your perfume. The way a woman smells tells a lot about her, you know."

His words, not to mention his tone, terrified her. Stephanie didn't move.

"Didn't you hear me, Stephanie?" he said, his tone sharper. "I said come here!"

She could hear the breathing of the other man, who was behind her, knowing that at any moment he might hit her over the head. Still, she refused to budge.

"Ay, carumba!" Barbadillo said. "She won't listen. Carlos, encourage the woman to come to me, will you please?"

Stephanie felt a large, warm hand on her back, which promptly gave her a shove. She staggered forward, righting herself before she fell. Deciding there was nothing to be gained by further resisting, she took the last few steps separating her from her tormentor. Though her heart was raging, she tried to be brave, meeting his gaze, projecting as much contempt as she could.

Barbadillo looked at her body, just as he had on the airplane. Then he reached out and took her hand, smiling into her eyes with his evil smile. "You are a beautiful woman, you know that?"

Stephanie jerked her hand free. Trembling, she said nothing.

He tossed his head inquisitively. "How old are you?"

Her eyes narrowed. "Look, what is it you want, Mr. Barbadillo?"

His expression grew cruelly sober. "I want to get to know you, Stephanie. It's so much more pleasant if we are people with each other—I, a man, you, a woman. So let's make an effort, okay? Now, I asked you a question. It may not be the most polite one, but I would like to know the answer."

She drew a fortifying breath. "I'm forty-two."

His eyebrows rose. "So, it's true! To look at you, I would never have believed it." His smile was the warmest yet. "I'm younger, Stephanie, but I don't feel it. To me you are still a flower. Very lovely." His eyes moved down her body once more. "A very attractive woman."

"Why are you doing this?" she asked. "Your flattery

means nothing to me.'' She glanced over her shoulder at Carlos, who was still at the door, his arms folded defiantly. ''I'm a prisoner. Why?''

''Because for the moment, this is what I wish. Now please, *querida,* let's try to be friends, shall we?''

''I have no desire to be friends with you.''

He shook his head disapprovingly. ''You are not in a good mood, Stephanie. Why is this? Is it because you're tired? Are you still sad at the loss of your daughter? Or are you bitter because your sister was your husband's lover?''

''How do you know all this?'' she demanded, shaken.

''I know many things about you,'' he replied. ''Your husband was an associate, as I told you. But as we talk, I learn so much more. I have a gift for understanding women. You, for example, have never known a real man. I can tell by your manner, the way you look at me. Oh, you may have had sex, but you are practically a virgin. Reymond never had you, truly. It is obvious. You are like a colt who's never been ridden. And you are crying out to experience a real man. You may not know this in your conscious mind, but it is true. Me, for example. Deep in your heart, you would have me take you.''

Stephanie's eyes filled with hatred. ''You are disgusting,'' she said, seething. ''A pervert. And I refuse to stay here another minute.''

She spun on her heel. Barbadillo reached out and grabbed her arm. Stephanie swung at him, slapping his face hard. He shook off her blow and slapped her back, knocking her off balance, making her cheek sting. Then he grabbed her jaw, his fingers digging into her flesh.

''If you ever strike me again,'' he shouted into her face, his eyes wide with anger, ''I will drag you into the bedroom and make a woman of you, whether you are ready for me or not.'' His tobacco-tinged breath washed over her. ''Do you understand?''

Stephanie nodded, terrified. Barbadillo released her, but continued to scowl.

"Carlos, bring her a chair," he commanded. "Then take the suitcase into the other room and take it apart. Tear out the lining, open every box of Tampax, check everything."

The chair was brought and she sat in it, and Barbadillo returned to his perch on the desk, above her. "So," he said, his tone softer again, "here we are, two people, potential friends or potential enemies. The choice, Stephanie, is yours."

"How did you get the police to bring me here?" she asked.

"The officials are very understanding in St. Thomas. And I can be very persuasive."

"What do you want from me?"

"Cooperation," he said, again resting his hands on his genitals. "Honest answers to my questions."

"If you want to know about my husband's business, Mr. Barbadillo, I can't help you. I know nothing. Jean Claud was very closemouthed about his work and only told me the most general things."

"Hand me your purse, Stephanie."

She complied.

Barbadillo unzipped it and peered inside. "Women and their purses," he muttered, shaking his head. Turning it over, he dumped the contents onto the desk.

She watched him, feeling violated as he poked through her things. He picked up the framed photograph of Zanny, studying it.

"Suzanne was a lovely girl," he said. "She looked like you and that is very fortunate. Jean Claud was not the most handsome of men."

Stephanie, swallowing her contempt, said nothing.

Barbadillo picked up her appointment book and paged through it, then he went through her wallet, leafing through her bills. "Were you expecting to stay long in St. Thomas?"

"A week or two."

He nodded, then examined her purse more closely, bending and poking the leather to see if something might have been sewn inside, she assumed. Satisfied there was nothing hidden there, he set it back down.

Then he got up, went behind the desk and took a cigar from the inside pocket of the coat hanging on the chair. Fishing a lighter from the side pocket, he lit the cigar, blowing smoke toward the ceiling. Savoring his cigar, he regarded her through the ribbon of smoke curling before his face. "That is the worst thing about that bastard Castro. A good cigar is hard to come by."

Stephanie watched him draw on the cigar, his manner pointedly, obscenely sensual. Lifting his chin, he again blew smoke toward the ceiling again. He gave her a wry smile and set the cigar down in an ashtray on the corner of the desk.

The top couple of buttons of Barbadillo's white shirt were open, the dark hairs of his chest showing. His shoulders were very broad and, with his shirtsleeves rolled up, he evoked a masculine, virile image. Not wanting him to sense her awareness of those things, she lowered her eyes, shifting in the chair uncomfortably. But, reminding herself how evil the man was, she looked at him again, regaining her defiant frame of mind.

"How long are you going to keep me here?" she demanded.

Barbadillo slowly came around the desk and moved behind her chair. He put his hands on her shoulders and began massaging her tense muscles, which grew more tense because of his touch. If he noticed, he paid no attention, continuing to knead her flesh with his strong fingers.

"I will keep you here until I get what I want."

"I have nothing to give you," she said bravely.

"Oh, I think you do. More, maybe, than I first thought. Women, you see, are strange creatures. They resist because they must. The harder they fight, the more satisfying the victory for the man. But submit eventually, they must. If it is the right man."

Stephanie twisted free of him and got to her feet, facing

him. "If you think I have any interest in you as a man, you're sorely mistaken. I want to leave. Now!"

He frowned. "I'm afraid that won't be possible. You see, the decision is mine, not yours. And I do have a very strong interest in you, Stephanie, an interest that is growing by the minute."

"You *are* sick," she said.

"No, determined. I like having my way."

Barbadillo was playing mind games with her, she could see that. What she didn't know was how far he would push things, whether his sexual-predator act was for effect, or if he was actually sick enough to carry out his threats.

"What must I do before you'll let me go?" she asked, rubbing her throbbing cheek.

"Okay, let's take care of business first," he said, his tone surprisingly reasonable. "Here, you sit in this chair and I'll get another."

Turning her chair, he went and got one that was against the wall, placing it so that the two chairs were facing each other. He motioned for her to sit and she did. He went and got his cigar and the ashtray. Puffing on the cigar, he put the ashtray on the floor beside the other chair, then sat. They were close enough that their knees nearly touched.

"Here's the problem, *querida*," he said. "My associates and I invested twenty million with your husband in what was supposedly a surefire investment, which was to provide a very nice return. According to your husband, it didn't. The stock is practically worthless. But we're very suspicious and we have our own...investors who are counting on us. We find out your husband's other investments are doing fine. It could be he is taking the profits elsewhere and saddling us with the losses."

"That would surprise me," she said, "because I know for a fact Jean Claud has an excellent reputation in the venture capital business." She figured he was alluding to Halcyon Technologies, but she wasn't about to tip her hand about that.

If there was to be any salvation, it was in convincing him that she was nothing but a dumb housewife.

"Well, we aren't about to drop twenty million and congratulate him for his excellent reputation," Barbadillo said dryly.

"So you killed him."

"No, of course not. Murder is not only a crime, it is, in this case, counterproductive. Your husband has plenty of money. It's just a matter of recovering what is ours. We have this little problem, though, that he is no longer with us."

Stephanie hated him for his cavalier, pseudo-innocent manner. He knew damn well that lives had been snuffed out needlessly—if not by him, then by his friends.

"You look skeptical, Stephanie," he said. "Is it that you don't believe me?"

The man was very perceptive and she knew she had to be careful. Oscar Barbadillo was chipping away at her defenses.

"I believe you," she said, "I just don't understand your point."

"My point is, you are our best hope of recovering our money."

"I don't know how I can help you, because I don't know a thing about how Jean Claud handled his investments."

"He handled your personal portfolio, did he not?"

Stephanie blinked. How could he know that? Then she understood—Audrey. They'd forced her to tell them everything before they'd killed her. But Stephanie knew she still had to play dumb. "Did Jean Claud tell you that?"

"Stephanie," he said, putting his hand on her knee, "there is so much I know about you. Unfortunately, there are a few things I do not. That's why it's so important that you and I become friends." He gave her knee a squeeze. "Let me describe my problem," he went on. "After Jean Claud met with his unfortunate accident, friends of ours dropped by your house. They...let's say, searched the place, discovering, among other things, that the hard drive on Jean Claud's computer had been wiped clean. My friends did discover that you had previously made copies of his financial records, which means you are in possession of the only copy of the information we need to recover our money. You see how simple the problem is?'' he said, giving her knee another pat. ''All I need to know is what you've done with the copy.''

''I don't have the disks,'' she said.

''Well, it's true they aren't in your purse. Are they in your suitcase?''

''No.''

''You're sure?''

''Yes.''

Barbadillo reached down for his cigar and took a drag, reflecting as he did. Then he pursed his lips and expelled the smoke into the air. Stephanie had never liked cigars or cigar smokers, but Oscar Barbadillo did it with more flair than any man she'd ever known. At a certain level he was fascinating. If he weren't so creepy, she could almost have admired him.

''Carlos!'' he said, calling to the man in the other room.

''What?''

''Have you found anything?''

''Plenty of underwear and shit, *amigo*. No computer stuff. No files. Nothing like that.''

''Are you finished? Have you taken the suitcase apart?''

''I'm doing that now. There's nothing here.''

Barbadillo gave her a woebegone look. ''Stephanie, what have you done with the disk? Is it under your clothing?''

''No.''

''But it is no place else. It must be there.''

She had an image of him making her strip in front of him and it was enough to make her sick. She forced her tired brain to think, her desperation growing. Did she tell him the disks were in the locker at the airport and hand over the key? Would that satisfy him? Or would he kill her, anyway? She knew an awful lot and he'd been pretty open with her. Too open.

And what about her inheritance, her portfolio? If the information Barbadillo was after included the key to getting the funds coming out of the Halcyon sale, then he and his friends would take everything and she'd have nothing.

"Stephanie," he said in a singsong voice, "you aren't talking, *querida*. The disks are in you panties, aren't they?"

"No, I told you they weren't."

His eyes narrowed. "Then where are they, goddamn it!" he shouted.

She flinched, his sudden burst of anger shocking her.

"Where!" he yelled. "What did you do with them?"

"I put them in my safe-deposit box in my bank in Mill Valley."

"What?"

"They're in my bank."

"Bullshit," he scoffed. "When could you have done that?"

"Yesterday morning before I went to the airport. Where do you think I got all that money and the traveler's checks?"

He contemplated her, taking another drag on his cigar. She returned his gaze, doing her best to stare him down. She knew her life could very well depend on her resolve.

"I'm sorry," he said in a surprisingly soft tone, "but I don't believe you. I'm going to have to search you. There is no other way."

Stephanie tensed, the suggestion making her nauseated.

"Stand up," he commanded.

She got to her feet, backing away, making the chair screech on the wooden floor. "You have no honor," she said, her fear of him soaring. "You're using this as an excuse."

Barbadillo rose as well. "I must have the disks," he said, though by the look in his eye he might just as well have said, "I must have you."

Stephanie took off her suit jacket and, holding it up, turned it back to front. "See, no disk."

He inched toward her, ever so slowly, not stopping when she threw the jacket at him. Ignoring the symbolic rebuff, he continued his pursuit, the slight smile on his lips not exactly sadistic, but close.

"You could see the disk if I had it on me," she lamented, almost in tears.

"I can't be sure unless you take off your clothes."

A feeling of panic rose in her and she ran to the door. Carlos must have locked it. She began pounding on it with her fists, screaming for help. But who would come to her aid? The police? She knew the chances of that were nil.

Stephanie spun around. Barbadillo still pursued her, relentlessly and with terrifying deliberateness, seemingly amused. Her back to the door, she saw Carlos across the room at the entrance to the back hall, having come to see what all the commotion was about.

"Let me beat it out of her, Oscar," he said. "Why fart around?"

"Go back and play with her underwear," Barbadillo said. "I'll take care of her my way."

He was right in front of her now. Her back pressed against the door, tears of desperation welling in her eyes. She felt hopeless. Did she tell him where the disks were, or would that be the same as signing her own death warrant? If she could convince him they were in the bank, then he'd realize he needed to keep her alive.

Oscar was in her face now. The smell of his cigar was on his breath. Reaching up, he brushed her cheek with the backs of his fingers. She trembled and that appeared to amuse him.

"Please don't," she mumbled.

Unmoved, he ran his hand down across her shoulder, then slipped it under her arm, dragging his palm up her side, all the while his eyes boring into hers. Moving still closer, he thrust his hand behind her back, using both hands now, probing her skin with his fingers.

"Any disks under your blouse?" he asked in a tone so matter-of-fact it disgusted her. "Maybe taped to your skin?"

"I told you, they aren't with me!"

"Maybe, *querida*, but I've got to make sure."

Barbadillo felt her back and waist, then brought his hands around front, moving them over the plane of her stomach and up under her breasts, peering into her eyes as he searched her. He gave her breasts a playful caress and she was sure he'd feel the locker key in her bra, but he didn't linger.

"This isn't all that bad, is it?" he said, his lip curling.

"I've never been so humiliated in my life," she said, glaring with contempt.

"Oh, Stephanie, if you'd just relax, you might enjoy this."

"I hate it," she said. "And I hate you."

Oscar shook his head. "Well, I'm afraid we're not quite through. You're going to have to take off your skirt."

She fought back a new rush of panic.

"You don't like the idea, do you?" he said gently, using the tone one used with a child. "Maybe that's because that's where you hid it, under you skirt."

"I told you, I don't have it with me!" she said, sobbing now. "Why can't you believe me?"

"Because I'm a suspicious man," he snapped. "And we're talking about millions of dollars. Your money *and* mine! What would you endure to save your inheritance, huh, Stephanie?" His tone had grown harsh again.

"Leave me alone," she cried, her body shaking violently.

"Yeah, okay, I'll leave you alone...after I find the goddamn disk!"

Reaching down, he grabbed the hem of her skirt and yanked it up. Then he violently spun her around, holding up her skirt and pressing her against the door with one hand as he patted down her hips, her butt and thighs with the other. She wept as he ran his hand up between her legs.

Angry, he jerked her around again so that she faced him, grabbing her by the throat and pressing his face practically into hers. "Where are the goddamn disks?" he shouted.

All she could do was sob.

Barbadillo reached down and pressed his hand against her

pubis, shocking her. Applying more pressure, he lifted her on her toes. "You see, *querida,* there are two ways of doing everything. Do you want to deal with me or that gorilla in the other room? I'm a cream puff compared to Carlos. He'll cut you into little pieces. Is that what you want?"

"The disks are in the bank!"

Barbadillo let go of her and turned sharply away. Stephanie smoothed her skirt, tears running down her cheeks. Oscar paced back and forth in the middle of the room. She realized then that she'd outlasted him. At least for now.

"I still don't believe you," he said, pointing at her with an accusing finger. "You stashed them somewhere. Was it on the plane? Did you give them to another passenger? What did you do with them, Stephanie? They're not in the bank in California. I don't believe that. You brought them because you need them to get the money, don't you?"

"They're in my safe-deposit box," she repeated.

He stopped pacing, his dark glower full of hatred. "Carlos!" he shouted. "Maybe I need your help after all!"

"No," she said.

"Tell you what," he said. "I'll give you five minutes to think about this before Carlos goes to work. Five minutes to come up with a better answer."

Carlos appeared at the door. "Is it my turn?" he asked, sounding positively gleeful.

Stephanie wiped her eyes and looked at her tormentors. "I need to go to the bathroom," she said.

"Fine," Barbadillo said. "That'll give Carlos time to plan his conversation with you."

"I don't need to plan no conversation," Carlos said. "You want some information, I'll make her tell you. It's that simple."

"The lady might think better of her stubbornness," Oscar said. "Women can be very reasonable when they want to be, you know." He looked at her. "The can's in back, down the hall."

Stephanie glanced at the desk where the contents of her purse were spread out. "Do you mind if I take my purse?" she asked.

Barbadillo tossed his head as if to say, "Go ahead."

She picked up her jacket from the floor, slipped it on, then scooped the contents into her bag. The picture of Suzanne was intact, and the money was still in her wallet. When she turned, Oscar was looking at her legs.

"Too bad things didn't go a little better between us," he said. "You're a good-looking woman and I like you. You've got guts, *querida*. You're smart, grown-up. That is good considering the way most broads are these days. It's a shame you didn't trust me. It would save us both a lot of trouble. And damn it, I really hate the sight of blood."

Swallowing hard, Stephanie put her purse under her arm and headed toward the back of the apartment. Finding the bathroom, she stepped inside, locking the door behind her. The image in the mirror was not pretty. The haggard, red-faced woman could have been someone else. It didn't seem like her. Perspiration ran down her back, she felt sullied and wretched, and she didn't know what to do.

After taking a few deep breaths, she looked around. The fixtures were antiquated. The porcelain surfaces of the basin, tub and toilet were stained. She did have to go to the bathroom, so she relieved herself, noticing as she sat on the stool that the louvered grate over the small window above the tub was hanging by one small hinge and appeared ready to fall off. Could it be a route of escape? she wondered.

Before flushing the toilet, she climbed up on the tub and lifted the grate enough to peer outside. There was no fire escape, but there was a flatbed trailer truck parked in the alley below. It was stacked high with bales of rags. The distance was probably fifteen or twenty feet to the top bale.

Her heart raced at the prospect of escape. She'd probably break her neck in the fall, but she didn't like her chances with Oscar and Carlos. Flushing the toilet, she grabbed her purse, then raised the grate. It creaked. With her head out the opening, she tossed her purse onto the truck. Judging by how it bounced, the bales were reasonably soft. That was encouraging. The trick would be to shimmy through the narrow opening.

There was a knock on the door. "Time's up," Barbadillo said. "Come on out."

"I just have to wash up," she replied. "I'll only be a minute."

"Make it quick."

Knowing she had to hurry, she struggled to get herself out the window. She could get as far as her chest easily enough, but she didn't have the strength for the last push she needed. There was nothing to hold on to. Lifting her leg, she managed to hook her toe on the showerhead. The pressure broke the hinge on the grate and it crashed into the tub.

She heard voices outside the door. "Damn it, open up!" Barbadillo shouted. "We'll break the goddamn door down. Come out of there!" His shoulder slammed against the wood. Then again.

She'd gotten her waist to the window ledge when the bathroom door crashed open.

"*Jesucristo!*" she heard Barbadillo holler when he saw what she was doing.

She was teetering when he grabbed her ankle. Kicking out with her free foot, she caught him in the chest, knocking him away. It was enough to thrust her out the window. She did a somersault in the air, landing flat on her back on the bales of rags.

The impact knocked the wind out of her. She lay staring at the sky, gasping for air, when she saw Oscar Barbadillo stick his head out the window.

"*Puta!*" he screamed. "You'll pay for this!"

He pulled his head back in the window. Stephanie knew they'd be coming for her. Snatching her purse, she crawled to the edge and slid off the trailer, dropping the last five feet to the ground.

Her heart racing, she looked both ways, then dashed toward the shorter end of the alley, afraid one of the men would get there before she did. But she made it to the street without seeing them. Thank God they'd been on the third floor. Deciding they'd come from the left, she ran to the right. It was a short half block to the next street. As she dashed across the intersection, she practically ran into a cruising taxi. The driver had to slam on his brakes to avoid hitting her. Even so, she fell over the hood.

The man started to get out, but Stephanie signaled him to get back inside. She jumped in on the passenger side as a shout came from up the street. It was Barbadillo and Carlos, the latter with his gun drawn, running toward them.

"What goin' on, missus?" the corpulent driver asked, his eyes round as pie plates.

"Go, damn it!" she screamed. "Just drive!"

The cab lurched forward as Oscar Barbadillo came running up. Stephanie heard the whap of his fist on the trunk as they careened off. The driver looked in the mirror and started to brake. Stephanie whacked his fat arm.

"Keep going," she shouted breathlessly. "Those men are trying to kill me!"

The taxi surged ahead, tires squealing. They'd gone half a block before she glanced back. Oscar had run after them for twenty yards, but stopped, knowing it was useless. When the taxi reached the Waterfront Highway, the driver looked at her, his face glistening with perspiration, fear in his eyes.

"Missus...I..."

"Take me to the airport," she said, her chest still heaving. "I'll pay you a hundred dollars! I've got to get off this island. Now!"

They'd gone several blocks before the cabby found the courage to speak. "Shouldn't I be takin' you to the police, missus?"

The police were the last people she wanted to talk to. She had no way of knowing if Barbadillo had bribed just the two at the airport or half the force. And at this point, she wasn't willing to trust anyone. "I'll go to the police somewhere else," she said. "I just want to get out of here."

"You got a plane ticket?" he asked, hunching over the wheel as he drove. "You know there's a flight you can take?"

Stephanie realized that the airport might not be the place to go. Barbadillo might figure she'd head that way. Those policemen could have returned.

"Maybe I don't want to go to the airport," she said upon reflection. "Is there any other way to leave?"

"There be ferryboats and sea planes, missus. There's ferries to St. John leavin' all the time."

"Take me there then, please."

Stephanie laid her head back, trying to calm herself. Her heart pounded, her cheek throbbed where Barbadillo had slapped her. She'd scraped herself getting through the window, but she wouldn't think about that now. She had to focus on not getting caught again. But at least she knew now she had a damn good reason to feel paranoid. It was small consolation, but it was something.

Frenchtown

Jack Kidwell glanced around the littered deck, as disgusted with his boat as he was with himself. He'd walked all the way back from town, passing half a dozen bars. He'd resisted the temptation to go in for a drink, but now that he was home, he had trouble finding purpose. If he had an ounce of gumption he'd clean the old tub. But it was hard to give a damn, knowing Bill Toussaint had effectively put him out of business. He could clean the boat up three weeks from now and only have to do it once.

Procrastination was as much a vice as drink. Alicia used to

chide him about it, but her words were always gentle. She hadn't been Miss Organized herself, but she'd had a keen sense of responsibility, a commodity he'd been short of—at least since he'd lost everything in Florida and came to the Caribbean. Just thinking about her put a weary ache in his heart. A world that had rejected her was not a world he wanted any part of. The trouble was, escape was not easy, except with booze.

Jack thought of the nice sweet bottle of scotch in a locker below, waiting for him to pop it open. Oh, it would be so easy. And so nice. Would one drink do all that much harm? He knew it would because there was no stopping once he got started. But he also knew his resistance was wearing down.

Jack rubbed his jaw and stared across the sleepy marina, bathed in afternoon sun. Alcoholism was a bummer. If you were going to beat it, you had to do it by inches. One day at a time. God, he was sick of the phrase.

Jack heard her heels on the wooden dock before he noticed her. For a brief instant, he thought it was Alicia. But his soaring heart crashed when he remembered the dead didn't walk around in the afternoon sun. The girl in the short little dress, that showed more of her cocoa thighs than it covered, was Tanya Brown. She waved. He waved back, the sour taste of disappointment fading into a cold, hard reality that was as painful as sobriety.

"Captain Jack!"

He concentrated on the firm flesh and long legs. "Hi ya, sugar," he returned.

Tanya made her way up the boarding ladder to the deck of the *Lucky Lady,* her smile as wide as her strides were long. She had a beach bag slung over her shoulder.

"Jesus," he said, "they're letting high school out earlier every year."

"High school?" she said with a scowl. "This girl was finished with high school, man, long before you started fucking her." She grabbed his ear and pulled his face down to kiss his mouth as if it was something she'd been doing for twenty years. "Otherwise you might be in jail."

Jack inhaled her pungently erotic scent, smiling his concurrence. "Thank goodness for small favors." He gave her cheek a pinch. "What brings a pretty young thing like you out to see a crusty old sea dog like me?"

"Baby, you shouldn't gotta ask."

She smiled Alicia's smile and it almost broke his heart.

"I did bring you a few little things," she said, putting down her bag. She opened it, extracting a 1.75-liter bottle of Chivas Regal and laid it in his hands as though it were frankincense or myrrh. "That's from my daddy."

Jack gazed at the label and weighed the bottle carefully. To him it was more like the Christ child himself than any offering or tribute. Bill would have said the Antichrist, but that was beside the point. "Just what I need," he mumbled.

"*And,*" Tanya said, "Mama sent a big container of chicken and dumplings."

She took a cylindrical ice cream-like container from her bag and handed it to him. Jack sniffed it dutifully, giving a nod of approval before setting it down.

"Your mama's a sweetheart."

"They both think you're the cat's meow," Tanya said. "Whatever that means."

"It means Bobby still owes me a bomb. Half the money in that plane of his is mine."

Tanya's look of impatience made it clear to him she didn't want to hear about it. "Which reminds me—Daddy said he was going to be a few weeks late on his payment this month. He's eleven thousand behind on his fuel bill and if he don't fly, nobody gets paid."

It was not what Jack wanted to hear. This was the third time this year Bobby had missed a payment. And with his license having been jerked, Jack wouldn't be producing any income for at least a month. He'd been counting on Bobby's check to tide him over.

"Tanya, that money is important. I—"

"I don't know nothin' about that, Captain," she said, cutting him off. "The money thing's between you and my daddy. Don't got nothin' to do with me, no way."

He wondered about that. He'd been curious for a long time just how her family dealt with their relationship, finding it easier to pretend it wasn't a problem. But this was proving to be a day for courage. "I don't mean to bring up a sore subject," he said, "but what, exactly, do your parents think's going on between us?"

"Baby," she said, "I don't think we want to talk about that, either."

Her tone said it all. "Oh, Jesus."

She gave him one of her seductive looks. "It's not so bad, Captain. They think I'm twenty-one and if I want your white babies, fine. If I want to tell you to go to hell, that's fine, too."

He knew right up front that most anything Tanya said was fifty percent bullshit. She'd had a crush on him forever. And she did like to have a good time. He'd rationalized that, as long as she was cool with it, he was, too. But it was rationalization, pure and simple. She might be twenty-one, but she was still a girl. And her goddamn father was a bastard for not beating the shit out of him for screwing her. But, of course, Bobby had to think of the money, too. Damn, it was really a disgusting situation, for which he was as much to blame as anyone.

The problem was, he could close his eyes and Tanya became Alicia, fleetingly perhaps, but still Alicia. That was hard to ignore. With a few good, stiff belts in him, Tanya's allure was as strong and irresistible as silky-smooth Scotch. And in combination—Tanya and booze—they could be deadly. Jack saw the chances of him surviving the evening without succumbing to be very slim, indeed.

"You know, sugar," he said, "the biggest favor you could

do for me now would be to take that sweet little ass of yours and go on home to your mama.''

She acted disappointed. "That what you want, Captain Jack?"

How did he say yes? But then, how did he say no? "I've got a little problem," he said. "It's got nothing to do with you, Tanya, but I'm in a difficult position."

"You got VD?"

He shook his head, laughing. "No, nothing like that."

"A woman?"

"No, not that either."

She moved toward him until her round hard breast touched his chest. Then she reached down and gently grasped his genitals. Within seconds he was hard. "Don't see any problem here," she cooed.

Jack wondered how a girl so young could have such confidence in her sexuality. And why she was interested in him, for chrissakes. Her father's debt could explain the timing, but not her passion. Tanya liked to fuck and she especially liked to fuck him. She'd once told him she started having sexual fantasies about him when she was eleven, back in the days when Jack was still living in Florida and had the world by the balls. Bobby Brown was his pilot, Tanya a prepubescent nymph. To think he was screwing her made him feel like a pedophile. To his credit, he had waited until she was nineteen and no longer a virgin.

Jack took her wrist and removed her hand from his groin. Tanya frowned with disappointment.

"You really don't want to?"

"Of course I *want* to," he said.

"So then, how about we get all comfortable and have some of my mama's dumplins first?"

"Shit," he said, "you're going to be the death of me."

The beat-up pickup truck pulled to a stop in front of the

marina. Stephanie handed the wizened old man a twenty-dollar bill and said, "Please don't tell anyone you brought me here."

He shook his head. "No, ma'am."

Stephanie had no idea whether he would honor her request, but she was reduced to putting her faith in people she didn't know. She'd spent the past few hours at the ferry port, waiting to leave the island, afraid Barbadillo would find her before she got away. He never showed up, but the police had. A vanful of them. And though she wasn't absolutely sure they were looking for her, she couldn't take any chances. Slipping away, she'd found the little old man loading his truck with crates of vegetables and asked if he'd give her a ride. He'd looked at her suspiciously, wary until she'd produced some bills.

"Where does you want to go?" he'd asked.

"Is there a marina where I can charter a boat?"

"There be one at Frenchtown and I do got a delivery out that way."

"Please take me there."

Now Stephanie watched the truck pull away, then headed for the gate to the marina. The man in the guard booth was talking to a heavyset woman with a full plastic shopping bag at her feet. They were laughing and having a good time.

"Excuse me," she said, interrupting. "I'd like to charter a boat. Who do I talk to?"

"There's a whole mess of boats inside," the man replied. "Go ask. That's all I can say."

That wasn't very helpful, but she thanked him, anyway. Spread out before her was a forest of naked masts. A maze of docks ran through the marina. The majority of them had to be private boats, which left her wondering how she'd find those available for charter.

She saw a teenage boy mopping the deck of a large sailboat and asked where the charter boats were located. He directed her to the other side of the marina. As she went out on the last dock, there seemed to be a bit more activity. On the first boat she came to, a man was at the boom, flaking the mainsail.

"Excuse me," she said, calling to him.

He turned, his skin glistening in the late-afternoon sun.

"I want to charter a boat. Who do I talk to?"

"Captain's in town and he ain't going to be back for maybe an hour or two," he replied. "You have to talk to him."

Stephanie thanked him and moved on. There was no one aboard the next couple of vessels that she could see. On the fourth, two men, both older, were on deck. One of the men, who wore a captain's hat tilted back on his head, puffed on a pipe as he watched her approach.

"Aye, ma'am. What can I do for you?" he said, seeing she had a question. His accent was noticeably British.

"I'd like to charter a boat to take me…off St. Thomas," she said.

"You've come to the right place, then. Where would you be wantin' to go and when?"

"It doesn't matter where. Someplace with an airport."

"An airport? Don't you know they've got one right here in St. Thomas?"

"Yes, but I can't fly from here. It's very important that I leave immediately."

He took off his hat and scratched his thatch of stringy white hair. "That would be a problem then, lass. Weather permitting, we're takin' a Canadian group out in the morning. In three days time the boat will be available for hire, if you can wait that long."

"I'm afraid I can't." She groaned. "Is there anyone else here who could take me immediately?"

The man shrugged. "Most charters are booked in advance, as you might imagine. You'd do better to book through an agency, if you don't mind me sayin' so."

"I don't have time," Stephanie said, her frustration level rising. She looked back up the dock as though she half expected to see Oscar Barbadillo and Carlos making their way toward her.

"You can ask around," he said, stroking his chin. "A bit

earlier I saw Winslow, skipper of that Cambria 44 you see along the way there, but he's got a party coming in this evening, I know.''

"There must be somebody." She was on the verge of tears.

"Cap'n," the man's companion said, extending a bony hand toward the end of the dock. "What about Jack Daniels?"

The first man chortled, nudging the other with his elbow. "Charlie's right, miss. You might try Jackie. His boat's likely available since he's in port more than he's at sea. Can't vouch for the condition of the boat…or him, for that matter."

"Which one is it?" she asked, looking.

"Last on the right."

"His name is Daniels?"

The man chuckled. "A bit of a joke, lass. His proper name is Kidwell. Jack Kidwell. Not a bad bloke, truth be known. Friendly with the ladies, if you see that to be a virtue. Haven't noticed him around this afternoon, but most likely he's aboard. Could be he's sleepin' one off."

It was not the most reassuring description, but Stephanie didn't see that she had much choice. "Thank you, I'll speak with Mr. Kidwell."

The man saluted her and Stephanie moved down the dock to the last boat. The craft was much like the others, though the deck was cluttered. The name on the bow, *Lucky Lady*, struck her as ironic—she wasn't sure whether as an omen it was good or bad.

Stephanie glanced back, again afraid of seeing Barbadillo or the police, but the only sign of life was seabirds and the man she'd seen working on the first boat. The sun had dropped behind the hill between Charlotte Amalie and the airport. Dusk was approaching. She couldn't dawdle.

Taking hold of the rickety handrail of the boarding ladder, she climbed onto the deck. As she stepped over a coil of line, she heard the faint sound of music coming from below. That came as a relief.

"Hello!" she called tentatively. "Hello!" There was no

reply. Moving a few steps farther along, she called out again.
"Mr. Kidwell? Hello?"

She went around an overturned bucket and mop, stepped
over a snatch block, halyard tails and various odd bits as she
moved in the direction of the companionway and the steps
leading belowdecks. The music grew louder. It had a Caribbean beat. Jack Kidwell either couldn't hear her because of it,
or was sleeping off a drunk. She took a long, deep breath.
With Jean Claud's killers after her, she had no alternative but
to awaken Kidwell if necessary.

As she descended the steps, she kicked aside a dirty beach
towel, wondering how on earth the man avoided breaking his
neck. "Mr. Kidwell," she called out over the ever louder beat
of the music.

There was no response.

It was dark belowdecks, the only light coming from the
ports on either side of the main salon. The cabin was like a
fraternity house the morning after a drunken party. The close,
dank air smelled vaguely of booze, food and cigar smoke.

The music seemed to be coming from the aft cabin. As she
carefully made her way toward it, she heard the sound of a
woman's voice, low and sensual. Stephanie froze. That other
captain's comment about Jack Kidwell being friendly with the
ladies suddenly took on graphic meaning.

The door to the aft cabin was slightly ajar and, as Stephanie
crept closer, she was able to look inside. A lovely young mulatto, completely naked, was astride a man with deeply tanned
skin, her torso gyrating, her head thrown back as she moaned.
Stephanie could not see the man's face, but she saw him cup
the girl's breasts and rub the nipples with his thumbs. The
sight was so unexpected, so erotic, that Stephanie was mes-
merized.

"Oh, Jesus. Oh, Jesus," the girl kept saying. "Don't stop."

Stephanie was stunned but also fascinated. Her cheeks
burned with embarrassment, not only because of her modesty,
but because she'd allowed herself to get caught up in someone

else's private moment. She started to turn away, only to look back when she heard either the girl or the man make a sound.

"Time to come, you little bitch," the man said. "Captain's ready." The words were not kind, but there was a tenderness in the tone.

"Oh, Jesus. Oh, Jesus! A little more. Oh…eee!"

"Come on, sugar," he growled.

"Now! Oh, Jesus, now! I'm coming!" she cried. "I'm coming."

The girl's head rolled and pitched like someone in the throes of a seizure, her shrieks punctuated finally by an, "Oh, God!"

Stephanie could see the man's torso arch, lifting the girl off the bunk, and she saw the sensuous body collapse onto his chest, spent.

The girl was gasping and it sounded as if she was crying, as well. "Dear God, dear God," she murmured.

The lovers were soaked in sweat. The man ran his hand over the young woman's back and haunch with a tenderness that was at once gentle and impersonal. For the first time in a few minutes, Stephanie took stock of herself. She felt an empathetic glow of sexual arousal.

Shocked, she forced herself to back away, nearly tripping over a carton as she headed for the stairs. But as she started up the companionway, she remembered that Oscar Barbadillo was tracking her down at that very moment. Whether Jack Kidwell was a drunk or a womanizer didn't matter. She needed him. Badly. Turning, she faced the aft cabin.

"Mr. Kidwell!" she called out more resolutely than before. "Could I speak with you, please? Hello? Mr. Kidwell?"

There were no embarrassed squeals from the cabin, no scurrying about, just the music. She was about to call out again when the radio or cassette player abruptly went dead.

"Who's there?" came the man's voice. There was irritation in it.

"I'd like to speak to you about a charter," she replied, her voice tremulous. "I'm sorry to disturb you, but it's urgent. I'll wait...upstairs." With that she scurried up the companionway, unable to move half as quickly as she'd have liked.

Topside, Stephanie took a couple of deep breaths of sea air, her face flushed, her clothes and hair soaked with nervous perspiration. Her dignity was in shambles. She was embarrassed. But overriding it all was the danger stalking her.

Pulling herself together, she paced back and forth across the littered deck, casting an occasional glance along the dock, certain that at any moment her enemies would appear. She peered impatiently down the companionway. There was no sign of anyone. No music, no voices. Nothing. Didn't the bastard realize this was an emergency? She was just about to head down again when Jack Kidwell appeared at the base of the stairs, a cigar between his teeth, a glass of whiskey in his hand.

The man was quite large, well over six feet and bearlike, though that impression came more from his unsteady gait than the dense mat of hair on his chest and the tangle of his shaggy blond hair. He had on a pair of faded cotton shorts. His feet were bare, his face unshaven. It was difficult to tell his age, but Stephanie placed it at just over forty—the same as her own.

"You rang?" he said, not bothering to remove the cigar from between his teeth. He kept a hand on the grab rail to steady himself. It was obvious he was intoxicated.

Stephanie repressed the mild revulsion, trying hard to affect a dignified demeanor. The cigar made her think of Oscar Barbadillo. That, and the way Kidwell looked her over, made it hard not to recoil.

"You're not a hallucination," he mumbled, "because I distinctly heard you speak." He rewarded his own cleverness with a grin.

"Yes, Mr. Kidwell. Forgive me for intruding, but I'm very eager to charter a boat and I was told yours may be available."

"That so?" He chomped on the cigar, his eyes appearing to drift in and out of focus.

"It's very, very urgent," she said. "I have to leave immediately."

"Immediately's pretty soon, you know," he said, slurring his words slightly.

"Yes, I know. But I have to depart right now, without delay."

"Where do you want to go?"

"Anywhere."

"That specific, huh?"

"To the next island. Anyplace with an airport."

His brow furrowed. "Mind if I ask why?"

"I'll pay cash in advance," she said, ignoring the question. "Five hundred dollars."

"That's a pretty good reason," he said, more amused than was justified.

"I'll give you an extra hundred if we can be under way in fifteen minutes."

Kidwell puffed on the cigar. "That's pretty damn immediate. Too immediate, probably. There's a lot more to putting to sea than you'd think." He looked up at the sky. "And it could be we're in for some weather."

"Please," she said, "my life could be at stake. I need to know if you'll do it or not."

He rolled the cigar between his teeth, squinting at her through the curl of smoke. "At stake how?"

"I don't have time to explain. I need an answer. Please."

"There's a slight problem," he said waving his hand dismissively. "I'm indisposed."

"I know I'm coming at an awkward time but—"

"Sugar, if you'd have come a minute earlier…you'd have…ruined my evening. As it is, I'm not enjoying this a whole lot."

"Please, Mr. Kidwell, yes or no?"

He scratched his head with his cigar hand. "How about at sunrise? The boat needs to be cleaned up and I have to take on provisions, not to mention a couple cups of coffee.'' Another grin.

"I don't care what it looks like and I don't need to eat," she returned. "Just get me off this damn island *now*. I'll make it a thousand dollars."

"Jesus Christ. What did you do, rob a bank?"

Deciding on one last attempt, she opened her purse, dug for her wallet and pulled out the nine remaining hundreds. "Here's my money," she said, her hand trembling.

He eyed the bills. "Since you put it that way…"

"Jack, what's happening?" It was a lilting feminine voice behind him.

Kidwell turned around. The mulatto girl, her slender figure sheathed in a little cotton jersey dress, emerged from the companionway. She was in strappy sandals and carried a beach bag. She slipped her arm around Jack Kidwell's waist and cast an unfriendly glare in Stephanie's direction.

"Hello, sugar," he said, grinning first at the girl, then at Stephanie. "This lady needs to go sailing, so I'm afraid we'll have to finish our conversation another time."

The girl glanced at the bills in Stephanie's hand. "Yeah, man, I heard. So, you're going?"

"I'm afraid duty calls."

She laid her head on his shoulder and eyed Stephanie, obviously not pleased with developments. "You're no better than a hooker, Captain Jack," the girl said. "You know that, don't you?"

He chuckled. "Flattering assessment, but I can hardly argue with your logic." He patted her fanny. "I'll be back in a few days. I'll give you a call. And tell Mom and Dad thanks for the food and drink."

"Sure." She did a little shimmy with her body against him and kissed his chin. "So long then, baby."

The girl left, moving past Stephanie with a slinky walk. Kidwell took another puff on his cigar and watched her go down the dock. He shook his head regretfully. "Hell of a conversationalist, that one."

"Look, I'm terribly sorry to have spoiled your evening," Stephanie said, "but I really had no choice."

Kidwell turned his attention to her. "My sense of propriety, not to mention my curiosity, demands that I ask why the urgency."

"Isn't it enough that my life's in danger? Can't the particulars wait?"

He shrugged. "If that's as specific as you're going to get, I guess it'll have to do. I never argue with cold, hard cash."

Stephanie again peered up the dock. The girl was about to disappear from sight. There was no one else around. "How long before we can be under way?"

"How particular are you about your accommodations?"

"Not particular at all."

He nodded. "Luggage?"

She lifted her purse.

"I see." Kidwell drained his glass, stamping out his cigar in the bottom of it. "Disgusting habit, smoking. Don't do it, normally. But you succumb to one vice and all the others tend to sneak right in," he said, sounding sad. He set the glass on the deck, almost losing his balance. "This may be an impertinent question, but do you have a name?" he asked, drawing himself up.

"Jane," she said, scarcely hesitating. "Jane Turner."

"Well, Jane Turner," he replied. "Welcome aboard the *Lucky Lady*."

"Thank you, Mr. Kidwell."

He gave her a long, appraising look, as though to be sure who and what he was dealing with. "Incredible as it may seem, we have rules on the *Lucky Lady*. First and most important is that all charter passengers pay in advance."

"How about when we clear the harbor?" she returned.

"Rules are made to be broken. But not this one."

"Half now," she said. "Half when we clear the harbor."

"This particular rule may, however, be bent on occasion." She smiled. He smiled.

"We seem to have a knack for compromise," he said. "A man and a woman can't always do that effectively."

Stephanie thought again of the "conversation" Jack Kidwell had been having when she arrived. The thought that he might wish to converse similarly with her sent a shudder through her. Redirecting her thoughts, she counted out five hundred dollars and handed the bills to him. "I'm all for making compromises," she told him, "but be warned, I'm not much of a conversationalist."

His smile told her he got the point. Again, she glanced warily down the dock.

"Your money's the right color," he said. "But am I correct in assuming that you might be more comfortable out of sight?"

"Yes, I think so."

"Follow me, then."

He started down the stairs. Stephanie followed.

"Watch your step," he said. "The clutter is the price you pay for not waiting until morning."

"No problem."

"I keep the fore shipshape for unexpected customers," he explained. "I'm sort of like the boy in that story, the one who never bathed but always washed his ears because that's all his mother ever asked about."

"I get the point."

Once they were below, he turned on the lights and apologized again for the condition of the boat. When he looked at her, he stared at her face, his expression inquiring.

"What happened to your face, sugar?"

Stephanie touched her cheek. She'd forgotten about being hit. "I walked into a door."

"Yeah, well, the door must have been pretty pissed."

He led the way to the fore cabin. The berth, a double-size bed, was made up and inviting. Seeing it, she realized she hadn't slept in a bed since California. She went over and sat down on the corner of the berth.

"Nice," she said. "It'll do quite well."

Jack Kidwell seemed pleased, though it was hard to tell how much of his satisfaction was due to contentment and how much it was due to her legs, which he scrutinized unabashedly—probably out of habit. "When you're paying premium prices you want clean sheets," he remarked.

"What I'd like more than anything, Mr. Kidwell, would be to know we're under way."

"Get to work, in other words."

"Yes, if you would."

"Well," he said, starting to turn away, "make yourself at home, Miss Turner." He paused. "It *is* Miss, isn't it?"

"Yes."

"That wedding ring you're wearing is for purposes of general deception. You're in disguise, in other words."

Stephanie smiled, embarrassed. She'd been aware of her ring a couple of times during her flight, but hadn't given it a thought since. "Yes, exactly," she said, knowing she wasn't very good at this.

"I thought so." Then he left the cabin.

The smell of booze and cigar lingered after he'd gone. The air was already close, so she took off her jacket and opened both ports. The cross ventilation afforded some relief. She badly needed a shower and a change of clothes, but her things were back with Oscar Barbadillo so she would have to make do. Thank God, she'd at least had the presence of mind to take her purse to the bathroom.

Reaching into her bra, she removed the locker key and put it in the zipper pocket of her handbag. If she hadn't stashed Jane's case in a locker, everything would now be in Oscar Barbadillo's hands. Compared to her life, that wasn't the end of the world, but she didn't relish the thought of losing everything she had to these people.

Stephanie pondered the situation, uncertain why Inter-

America Ventures was so sure the computer disks were critical to recovering their money. It made her wonder if they knew something she didn't.

Up on deck, she heard Kidwell preparing the boat for departure. Stephanie knew virtually nothing about sailing. From her hilltop home in Mill Valley she'd watched sailboats plying the water of the bay. The poetry and grace of a flotilla moving like a flock of birds in the setting sun had always appealed to her, but she'd been a remote and silent witness. This would be her first time at sea in a small boat.

Through the open port she could hear Jack Kidwell cursing as he struggled with something—probably the sails. Operating a boat was work. It took skill. She'd learned enough from her friends who did take part in the sport to know that. This yacht of Kidwell's was a good deal larger than many boats sailed for sport, as well. She assumed he was a competent sailor, but there was no way to be sure. He was a drunk and a womanizer, albeit one with a hint of charm—that much she could safely say. What he was like sober remained to be seen. She could only hope it would be an improvement. It hardly mattered, though. Jack Kidwell was all she had.

She didn't even want to speculate on what his story was. It would probably only make her more nervous. She began pacing impatiently, wondering if there was anything she could do to speed up their departure. If she offered to help Kidwell, she'd probably only get in the way. And if she was on deck, she might be seen. How Kidwell might react if Barbadillo or the police showed up was not something she wanted to consider, let alone face. She couldn't count on him not to betray her, and God knew he had no reason to protect her unless it would be to get the balance of the money she'd promised. He certainly wouldn't risk his neck to save hers.

Stephanie wiped her moist forehead, wishing she wasn't so grungy. Then it occurred to her she might have some moist towelettes in her purse. Digging through it, she found one, crumpled but usable. Opening the packet, she sat on the berth and washed her face and neck. It felt heavenly, especially on her sore cheek.

She unbuttoned her blouse and ran the towelette under her collar and over the top of her chest. Hearing someone clear his throat, she glanced up to see Jack Kidwell in the doorway. She flinched.

"Sorry to interrupt," he said, his expression betraying no regret whatsoever, "but while I was getting the boat ready, my brain finally caught up with events."

Stephanie's heart sank. "You've changed your mind."

"No, no," he said, "not that."

"You want more money."

"No, not that, either."

"What then?"

"I really could use some fuel for the engine," he told her. "And we're low on fresh water."

"What does that mean?"

"No water, no bathing, among other things."

"Oh, God," she said, closing her eyes. "The one thing I'd die for."

"Die for? You mean you'd be willing to give me an hour to refuel and resupply?"

Stephanie was torn. How did she balance the benefit of a delay against the danger? "Is it absolutely necessary?"

"Not absolutely, no."

She agonized. "Then we'd better not do it."

Kidwell leaned against the door, his bare feet crossed at the ankles, his hand on his hip. He rubbed his grizzled jaw. "You're really afraid, aren't you?"

"Yes."

"That color in your cheek. A present from a friend?"

"That would be one way to put it."

He stroked his chin. "I'd offer you a beefsteak, but all I've got aboard are canned goods, some dried stuff and bulk items. And not a great deal of it, either."

"That's okay. I'm fine. Don't worry about me."

She could see the questions streaming through his mind. He was obviously not happy with her reticence.

"We're going to have to agree on a destination, Miss Turner."

"What are the options?"

"You want to get to an airport."

"Yes."

"Well, we've got San Juan, Puerto Rico, about a hundred nautical miles to the west. St. Croix is about fifty to the south. But I'm not eager to make either passage at night, especially not with the threat of weather I'm seeing."

"What do you propose?"

"My preference would be to lay off the coast until daylight. Maybe head east, in the direction of St. John."

"If that's what you think is best, then let's do it. But as quickly as possible. Please."

"I understand you aren't eager to talk about your problem, but if I understood the nature of the threat, I might have a better idea what to do. In other words, I'm wondering if I should plan on evading the Coast Guard, the police, search planes and so forth. I think you get my point."

She realized then that she had to take him into her confidence, if only partially. At least now he seemed reasonably in command of his thinking. He even sounded sober, which was encouraging. But she did need to tell him something. "I'm not a criminal, if that's what you're concerned about. As a matter of fact, I was kidnapped by some…pretty shady characters…this afternoon."

"What do you mean by shady?"

"They're corrupt businesspeople who cavort with hoodlums and criminals. And they're under the mistaken impression I have information they need. By a twist of luck, I managed to escape."

"But not until they'd popped you one," he said, pointing to his cheek.

"Right."

"Why didn't you go to the police?"

"Because I believe the police—or some of them, anyway—are in complicity with the kidnappers."

He considered her comment. "That's quite a tale, Miss Turner."

"It's true, though."

He contemplated her, looking skeptical.

"You don't believe me, do you?"

"I don't know that it matters. As long as your money's green, I don't have any grounds for complaint. Unless I'd be getting myself into the soup along with you, of course."

"I can't promise you won't be in danger," she said, hoping to appeal to whatever chivalric impulses he might possess.

"That's not much of a selling point," he said. "But I'm not exactly a virgin when it comes to encounters with the dregs of society. All the same, I do have this thing about not getting involved in drug deals."

"This has nothing to do with drugs, I assure you."

Jack Kidwell took a deep breath, his broad chest expanding. It was an attractive chest, muscular, deeply matted with hair. But Stephanie did not want to see him in that way. She wanted to stay as distant and aloof from him as possible.

"Let me ask you this," he said. "Do you really need to get to an airport or do you just need to lay low?"

"What difference does it make?"

He shrugged. "It may be easier to hide than flee. And it gives me more options."

"I guess more than anything I need time to regroup," she said, checking her watch, aware that every passing minute could be bringing Oscar Barbadillo closer. "Assuming you're able to get me out of here in one piece."

"While I'm getting under way, I'll see if I can come up with a plan," he said. "If your friends are determined, and have sufficient resources, we might be better off to head somewhere they wouldn't expect. There's no point in taking you someplace only to have them standing on the dock waiting."

Stephanie shivered at the thought. "Lord…"

He contemplated her again, stroking his chin. "You look uncomfortable, like you'd really like to get out of those clothes."

"If you only knew. I've had this outfit on since San Francisco."

"San Francisco, eh?"

She was afraid that was revealing too much, but it was too late. "Yes."

"Let me have a look around. I imagine I can come up with a few things left on board by former passengers."

"Thank you, but don't get me any of your girlfriend's things. I don't think she'd appreciate it."

"Tanya's not really a girlfriend, though I don't imagine that matters to you one way or the other."

"No, Mr. Kidwell, it doesn't."

He looked as though he wanted to explain, but finally decided against it. "Fine," he said. "That's fine." Then he left the cabin.

The Caribbean Sea

It was not promising to be a very good night for sailing. Jack glanced at the sagging mainsail, barely filling with the light breeze. Since he had cut the auxiliary at the mouth of the harbor, they'd only attained a couple of knots. Worse, perhaps, he didn't like the looks of the sky. A storm was in the offing; the barometer was confirming it. Unfortunately he couldn't verify it with the weather service. A few days ago he'd spilled some scotch on his radio and had forgotten all about it until he'd tried to listen to the weather report, only to discover he had no radio. It was not only dangerous, it was illegal to sail without properly functioning emergency equipment. But the voyage was turning out to be unorthodox in so many respects that a breach of safety regulations hardly seemed that big a deal, not when he had no business putting to sea to begin with.

Bad as all that was, it was probably the least of his worries. His passenger was clearly in more desperate straits than he, and he'd plunged into the adventure with no idea what he'd gotten himself into. If there was a redeeming feature in this, it was that he'd found a little excitement and had something to care about, if only looking out for his own butt. Jack did like being at sea, though. He'd never considered it work and always felt a bit guilty taking money for it.

At the moment the southern tip of Water Island lay off to the starboard, and dead astern was Hassel Island. Beyond it, he could see the lights of Charlotte Amalie twinkling in the dark. Jack decided this was just what he needed—to be under sail. Bill Toussaint thought he was helping matters by keeping him ashore, but he was wrong. If Jack was going to escape the allure of booze, it would be this way, by going to sea.

He spun the wheel, bringing the vessel on to the port tack so he could take advantage of the little wind they had. It would be slow going and dangerous if it turned dead calm. For the moment, though, they were moving.

After setting the boat on the new tack, he trimmed the sails, engaged the wheel brake and let her steer herself through the night. He leaned back against the cockpit coaming and watched the moon come up. The large silvery disk illuminated the dark water, enabling him to see miles in every direction. Even without running lights, the smallest boat would have been easily visible. That was a plus from the standpoint of safe navigation. But it also meant he couldn't hide easily.

The air was mild. He hadn't had time to change because their departure had been so hasty, but he had grabbed a tattered sleeveless T-shirt and his well-worn topsiders. If Jane Turner was going to come aboard at the spur of the moment, she'd have to expect that the skipper might be unshaven, unwashed and without underwear.

The truth was, she was lucky to have caught him before

he'd drunk himself into a stupor. Once Tanya had stripped and offered to pour him a drink, Bill Toussaint's speeches—the threat to his health and livelihood—had gone down the drain as easily as that first scotch had gone down his throat. He'd given up on life, choosing short-term pleasure, instead, because he knew it was inevitable. And Tanya, bless her little heart, had given him the excuse he needed. To the extent that pride mattered, he could blame her for being too seductive a temptress.

But then Jane Turner had come along, her predicament, her desperation giving him an excuse to pull out of his hole. How long it would last, he had no idea, but he was engaged, and for the moment that was enough. Sonia had once asked him what he lived for and, after reflection, he'd been shocked to discover he no longer knew. When he'd admitted that, she'd taken it upon herself to explain his problem to him. "It's because you've got nobody, Jack," she'd said. "And you really ought to do something about that." It was a nice idea, but he knew that would never happen.

He took in a long, slow breath of sea air. From experience, he knew he was eighty percent sober, back in that zone where pain was reality. This was not a good place to be. Thank God he was at sea and responsible for someone.

But he wondered about Jane Turner. She was not your usual sort of woman—certainly not the type he'd expect to come walking onboard his boat with a purseful of cash and no luggage. It wasn't as though he didn't meet all kinds. He'd skippered around everything from society ladies to tramps, spinsters to party girls. Single women, married women and some who couldn't quite decide what they were. Some wanted to get boffed, some just wanted to tease, others were strictly voyeurs. And it often didn't make much difference whether their guy was around.

He had laid more than one matron while her husband was fishing or golfing. One had even climbed into his bunk, naked as a jaybird, while her old man was snoring in the fore cabin.

But it was apparent Jane Turner had priorities other than sex, though he'd already sensed more than a little chemistry between them. That didn't mean a lot, though. The queen of England could give off vibrations without sex so much as crossing her mind. He'd been on the planet long enough to know some things were just part of the human condition. Still, something about this woman interested him. Maybe it was the novelty of her situation. She did have him thinking, wondering about her, wondering if she was sleeping.

When he'd left her below she'd seemed both emotionally and physically drained—too tired to do more than thank him when he'd taken her some dried fruit and the few articles of clothing he'd managed to scrounge. Though the offering wasn't very enticing, she'd seemed grateful.

Still, she'd made it clear she wanted a formal relationship, which was okay by him. He liked the thought of adventure, he needed to work and he needed money. Fun and games were not high on his list at the moment. If he had misgivings, it was that he didn't have a better handle on what was going on with her. Maybe she was a little too mysterious. He was dubious about the corrupt businessmen, though he did believe something criminal might be involved. What was most troubling was that she didn't fit the profile. The woman belonged in a drawing room, not on a sailboat. Yet he wouldn't describe her as a snob. She was real, human. He'd even seen flashes of a lighter side.

When he'd brought her the cotton T-shirt dress that little Italian Lolita who'd been aboard with her mother had left behind, Jane had held the dress in front of her and said, "The last person to wear this was probably a pubescent French girl. I don't think it's me, Mr. Kidwell." Jack hadn't told her how close she'd come to guessing the truth.

She'd thanked him for the clothes, saying the shorts would do fine, even though they were a couple sizes too big. At her request he'd brought her a pan of water so she could take a sponge bath, warning her they'd have to conserve water since she wouldn't let him replenish the supply.

"I wasn't sure at first," she'd told him in a moment of candor, "but my impression is you're a gentleman."

He'd grinned. Judging by the way she said it, it was wishful thinking as much as anything. "I'm not sure whether I should thank you or assure you that you're right," he'd rejoined.

"Either will do."

"Thank you, then." He'd left the cabin after that, probably to her chagrin, though he hadn't bothered to look back to see how she'd reacted.

Earlier, when she'd first come aboard, she must have heard him and Tanya going at it, so her initial impression of him couldn't have been reassuring. He'd seen no point in trying to disabuse her of it. Some things were best left unsaid.

Seeing it was time to tack, Jack swung the *Lucky Lady* to starboard, ducking under the boom as it swung over the cockpit. Then he sat down again, pondering the moonlit sea. Of all the possible lives he might have chosen, this one made the most sense, he told himself. Yet, given the depths to which he'd fallen, it obviously wasn't enough. Not after Alicia, anyway.

Glancing up, he was surprised to see Jane Turner making her way toward him, steadying herself on the lifelines and stanchions. She'd changed into one of the T-shirts he'd given her. Her shorts were cinched with cord. Her legs, he noticed, weren't bad—not bad at all. She had nice skin that was pale as bone china in the moonlight. And her hair had been wetted and smoothed back, accentuating her bone structure. She was actually quite striking.

Jane Turner wasn't the kind of a woman whose looks jumped right out at a guy. When he'd first seen her, she'd struck him as conservative, conventional, even mundane. But he realized he might have been a bit hasty.

"Good evening, Miss Turner," he said. "You look a little

more comfortable. How do you feel?'' He motioned for her to sit.

''I'm exhausted, but I do feel like a new person,'' she conceded, dropping onto the cockpit seat.

''How's the cheek?''

He took her chin and turned her head so he could see it. She appeared not to like being touched in such a familiar manner, so he let go of her. ''It looks like you'll live.''

''It could have been much worse,'' she said. ''But the reason I've come up is to pay you.'' She held out four bills and a traveler's check. ''Our agreement was that once we cleared the harbor you'd get the second half.''

Jack regarded her outstretched hand, hesitating before he took the money. After glancing briefly at the check, he stuffed it in the pocket of his shorts. ''A woman of her word.''

''You've kept your end of the bargain,'' she said. ''The least I can do is keep mine.''

''So far so good.''

''Yes, so far so good.''

Jack looked at her mouth and the way her hair waved around her ears. He noticed her hands were slender, patrician. She'd removed her wedding ring.

''Not much wind,'' he said, pointing up at the mast. ''The breeze hardly fills the sail.''

She glanced up. The top was lightly luffing, the sheet nearly slack. ''Which means we won't be going very fast.''

''We won't be outrunning any Coast Guard cutters, which may or may not be a problem. You'd know the answer to that better than I.''

She peered toward the dark silhouette of St. Thomas. ''It's a beautiful night, isn't it?'' she said, ignoring the implication of his comment.

Jack found her evasiveness curious, and it made him wonder if things weren't worse than she'd let on. But he decided not to press her. ''Most nights are beautiful down here,'' he said. ''Unless there's a storm.''

"You ever been caught in a hurricane?"

"I've had to ride out a couple. Never at sea, thank God."

She turned her attention back to him. "So, have you been in the Caribbean long?"

"I don't know. Seven, eight years, something like that."

"You evidently had a previous life."

"And you, evidently, are a lot more willing to ask questions than answer them."

She nodded. "Point taken. I apologize."

"Don't. If people are curious enough I'll talk about myself, but seems to me a thing like that ought to be mutual. I, too, get curious."

"I'm sure you do," she said.

"But you'd rather keep your secrets."

"Yes."

He watched her run her fingers back through her damp hair. It wasn't exactly a provocative gesture—at least he was fairly sure she hadn't intended it that way—but he took it as the woman in her saying something to the man in him. Sonia did things like that often, but with her it was conscious. This woman, he could see, was allowing herself to enjoy the caress of the wind—something he suspected she seldom did. And there was something about the implicit daring in that idea that appealed to him.

It was time to tack again, so he warned her about the boom as he brought the boat around. They both ducked under it. The *Lucky Lady* glided off at an angle of ninety degrees to their previous course.

"You're more suspicious of me than ever, aren't you, Mr. Kidwell?" she said after a while.

"Most of my passengers aren't so secretive."

"I'm curious what your imagination tells you about me," she said, studying him.

"You're as innocent as you pretend to be," he replied. "That I'm pretty sure of."

"I don't know whether to be glad or offended."

"Be glad. You're always better off being underestimated than overestimated."

"You're a regular philosopher, aren't you, Mr. Kidwell?"

"A student of the human condition."

"Do you read cards?"

"I'll tell you this, Miss Turner, you're a lot more worried about me than you are about what I know and don't know."

"My, you *are* good," she said.

He could see she was doing her best to sound self-assured, mainly because she *wanted* to be confident. He was succeeding in putting her mind at ease, which was good for both of them. He'd seen it countless times. Women needed to be sure it was safe to play dangerously, though most of the time they didn't even know that's what they were doing.

"What else can you say about me?" she asked.

He studied her until she seemed to become uncomfortable under his scrutiny. "For starters, you aren't *Miss* Turner. It's *Mrs.*"

"Well, you're half-right," she said. "I'm a widow." Her eyes shimmered. "A very recent widow."

"That's connected somehow with why you're running."

"Yes."

"But you don't want to explain."

"No."

They listened to the waves lapping against the hull as the boat cut effortlessly through the water. Jack considered pressing her, but decided against it. There was plenty of time for them to get acquainted.

"You said earlier you'd give some thought to a plan," she said. "What have you come up with? Where are you taking me?"

"Toward St. John," he said, "though I'm beginning to think we shouldn't put in there, at least not at Cruz Bay. For the moment, I'm trying to be unpredictable," he explained. "You see, I'm assuming the danger is real, that the adversary is formidable and has resources. Every commander wants as much intelligence on the enemy as he can get, but I recognize I have to make do with what I've got...which isn't much.''

"You're chastising me."

"No, I'm simply explaining what I'm up against."

"And so?"

"Well, your first request was that I take you someplace with a commercial airport. I figure the bad guys will make the same assumptions."

"I told the taxi driver who helped me escape that I wanted to get to another island with an airport," she said.

"That's good. Your friends will hear about it eventually. A little disinformation can't hurt. If we can get 'em looking for us where we ain't, so much the better."

"But if we don't go to St. John, where do we go?"

"Someplace where we can lay low for a few days. I'm thinking maybe I'll take you to this place I know in the British Virgins. It's a small, private island owned by a former client, a man named Nigel Lovejoy. Nigel's a Brit, a businessman who enjoys the good life. When he was between wives, the two of us spent some time bumming around the Antilles on the *Lucky Lady*. I helped him...shall we say...forget his troubles.''

"I imagine you'd be very good at that, Mr. Kidwell."

"We've been doing the Mr. Kidwell thing long enough," he said. "It's Jack."

"All right. So, what about your friend's island?"

"I figure the thing to do is hide out there for a couple of days. Once we get a reading on the situation, I can take you to Guadeloupe or someplace else down the chain where you can hop a flight to...wherever you want to go."

"Fine, but there's one problem. I don't have a passport."

"Hmm. Well-prepared, aren't you?" he said.

"I didn't plan on going anywhere but St. Thomas. The idea was to get away from the world for a few weeks. Instead, I...well, let's just say it turned out to be not so welcoming.''

Jack casually got to his feet to observe a brightly lit motor yacht passing by a couple hundred yards to starboard. Seeing nothing to be concerned about, he once again took his seat. "Going to Nigel's still makes sense," he told her. "You can take a day or two to figure out what you want to do next. And, in the meantime, you'll be safe."

"Fine. I can use the time to clear my head."

"All that remains," Jack said, "is to get from here to there."

She considered that.

The wind had picked up some and Jack sniffed it. He decided the weather he'd been anticipating might be arriving a little sooner than expected. "I'm sorry to say we're forced to operate with another small disadvantage," he said.

"What's that?"

"I don't have a functioning radio, which puts us at the mercy of what comes along, weatherwise."

"Is there reason for concern?"

"Not a lot," he replied. "But the weather is changeable this time of year. It would be nice to get a report now and then."

"I take responsibility for that," she said. "I forced you to leave when you weren't ready."

"I'm the skipper. Ultimately everything that happens aboard the *Lucky Lady* is my responsibility."

She didn't argue with him. Jack felt better for having made his little speech. It was odd for a drunk to care about something like honor, but he did.

"I'm glad you feel that way, Jack," she said. "It's reassuring. To be honest, when I first came aboard I was wary."

"But desperate."

"Yes, I guess that was fairly obvious."

He surveyed the sea ahead, sensing she wanted to talk, but wasn't sure how much to trust him. She wanted reassurance, and maybe a friend. It was funny how the sea made people open up—the old saw about being in the same boat.

"My problem has to do with money," she announced as

though privy to his thoughts. "My late husband may have lost or squirreled away all our money, including my inheritance from my parents, and I honestly don't know where I stand financially. A guy named Oscar Barbadillo with a company called Inter-America Ventures thinks I either have, or know how to get to, a considerable sum they believe they're owed. That's what this is all about."

"I see." He reflected on what she'd told him. "Are they right or wrong?"

"About me having their money?"

"Yes."

"Wrong."

Jack believed her. "You strike me as a person who's used to living well," he said. "This predicament must be rather trying."

"I've never gone wanting," she said. "Even as a child. I'm thankful for that, of course. How about you?"

"I was dirt-poor as a kid," Jack told her. "I think we were who they had in mind when they invented food stamps."

"Where was that?"

"The Florida Everglades. My dad found work in gas stations occasionally before he drank himself to death. My mother slept with the landlord for the rent money and a box of groceries every month. I was twelve before I figured out why she always came home from her big trip to the supermarket with her eyes red and her skin whisker-burned."

She shook her head. "I'm sorry."

He revisited an ancient emotion, one that had been dormant for a long while. "It's hard to believe people actually live that way," he said, trying to sound stoic, "but they do."

She was silent for a while. Then she said, "You obviously had a difficult childhood."

Jack laughed. "Adulthood has only been marginally better." He regarded her and, seeing her contemplative, wondered if maybe she was thinking about the little exhibition he and Tanya had put on that afternoon. At the time, he couldn't have cared less, but now he was embarrassed. Another drawback to being sober.

He noticed the wind had picked up considerably. Again he tacked, standing before turning the wheel in order to get a better look at the sea. Then he plopped down heavily.

"Believe it or not, you're not seeing me at the top of my game," he said. "Actually, I'm going through a rough stretch."

"I'm not judging you," she said.

"Pride is the issue. Even my old man suffered when he was sober enough to see my mother unpacking the groceries. Which tells you about all you need to know about him."

She was silent again.

"But to answer your original question, I'm no stranger to money. Once I got out of Immokalee and got me some book learning, I went to work, determined to prove I was worthy. Made my first million by the time I was thirty-two, three years ahead of schedule."

"What did you do?"

"I was a real estate developer. You've heard about fellas selling swampland out of their Cadillac convertibles, well I was a latter-day version. We developed commercial properties. Nothing glamorous. But I bought myself sleek boats, fancy cars, big houses and a blond wife with an aptitude for spending money. The whole thing was to prove to the world I'd made it, and to prove it to myself, too, for that matter. You see, it takes effort to get the mentality of a bottom feeder in the Immokalee social structure out of your consciousness."

"So, what happened?"

"The abbreviated version is that my partner swindled me and a whole bevy of investors, then parted for greener pastures with my wife. I was left holding the bag and the consequences. I did eighteen months in the state penitentiary."

She seemed taken aback at his candor. "That hardly seems fair."

"Oh, I'd strayed across the line, too. The only thing I did right was stay and face the music."

"You paid your debt to society."

"I've been telling myself for ten years that, in the long run, ol' Larry may have gotten the worst end of the deal. He got Ellen."

"You didn't love her?"

"How could I? I was still trying to figure out who the hell I was."

"You seem to be awfully self-aware..."

"For a drunk?"

"You have a serious drinking problem?"

"Thank you," he said, meaning it. After a moment he added, "But not while I'm working."

She stared out at the sea and he watched the moonlight play on her skin.

"In case you're wondering, I've never told my story to a client before. In fact, there aren't three living people here in the Caribbean who know it."

"So why did you tell me?"

"I don't know. I guess I felt a sudden compulsion for honesty. And maybe I wanted to put you at ease." He wondered if that sounded a little too pious and maybe too self-serving. "Now that I think about it, it's a crazy notion, trying to reassure somebody by telling them they're in the company of an ex-con."

She laughed. "I'm a lot more concerned about the way you are now, to be honest."

"A changed man. This boat is the product of several years of hard work selling condominiums. And I own a security interest in an airplane, though that's rapidly turning into a bad debt. Bottom line is this, what you see is pretty much everything I've got."

"I don't imagine boats like this are cheap."

"When you consider it's also my house and car, I don't live ostentatiously."

"It's character that counts, Jack, not money."

He smiled, wondering if she was trying to reassure him, or make excuses for him. Mainly he felt good because they'd bridged the trust issue to some degree. They'd communicated and that wasn't always easy. Not for strangers, let alone intimates.

The moonlight softened the contours of her lovely face. In this light her beauty was classical, aristocratic. He liked what he saw. He liked her.

She seemed to grow uncomfortable, perhaps aware of his admiration. "Well," she said, "I'm just beat. If you'll excuse me, I think I'll go to bed."

"Sure."

She scooted to the edge of her seat, but hesitated. "Before I go, there is something I want to tell you. I lied about who I am."

"Yeah, I know. Your name is Stephanie Reymond."

She seemed shocked. "How did you know?"

"Traveler's check."

She blushed, lowering her eyes. "Well, I guess I've proved I'm not a very good criminal," she said, clearly embarrassed. "Jane Turner was my sister."

"But you're standing by your kidnap story."

"Yes. Absolutely."

"And your husband's involvement?"

"Yes, all true."

"He's dead?"

She nodded.

"The guys who kidnapped you?"

"Or people they hired."

Jack wondered why she was taking her husband's death with such equanimity. He didn't detect tremendous sadness or a sense of loss. Perhaps she was bitter or resentful. Or, perhaps it hadn't been much of a marriage. "You've been through a lot."

"Yes, but I don't see any point in going into detail," she

said, pushing a wind-tossed curl off her face. "The more you know, the worse it is for you." She got to her feet, making it clear she wanted to go to bed. "I'll say good-night now. Thank you for all you've done, Jack. You very well may have saved my life today and I want you to know I'm truly grateful."

"Hey, you're paying me well, *n'est-ce pas?*"

She extended her hand in friendship—at least that's the way he interpreted it. "I hope you'll forgive me for being cautious," she said.

"In your shoes I'd be careful, too."

"Good night," she said.

"Sleep well."

He watched her walk away, liking what he saw, the way she moved, the curious blend of sophistication and innocence in her manner. He allowed himself to speculate on his prospects with her and decided they weren't good—not in the time available. He was intrigued, though. It had been a while since he'd rescued a woman, an emotionally needy one, that is. Mostly he avoided those kinds of situations because they could easily turn to quicksand. But in this case, it was already a bit too late. Much as he hated to admit it, he was already hooked.

Stephanie's Grandmother Chandler had once told her that the snake you worry about is the one that's close enough to bite. Having been raised in the wilds of Montana, her grandmother knew something about snakes...and about life. As a girl, Stephanie hadn't understood the figurative meaning of the phrase, though she'd come to understand it as she got older. But until this week, even figurative snakes hadn't posed much of a danger. That had changed. Fate, it seemed, had handed her a lifetime supply in one fell swoop.

As she slipped under the sheets, her body aching with fatigue, Stephanie thought about Jack Kidwell. He was dangerous, she decided, though hardly the way Oscar Barbadillo was dangerous. Barbadillo was sadistic. Jack, on the other hand was...well, simply sexual. And that made him dangerous in her eyes.

Stephanie was beginning to realize she had a problem with sex. Audrey had been shocked to hear that she hadn't had intercourse in years. Of course, Audrey was shocked—it wasn't normal for a woman in good health, married to a man in good health, to live like a nun. But her sexual relationship with Jean Claud had never been good, not even at first, and so for years she'd repressed her libido, even when they did have relations. But recent events had conspired to jar her from her complacency.

First, there'd been Audrey's comment about her celibacy. Then she'd discovered that Jean Claud was having an affair. The betrayal had been painful but the feelings of inadequacy Stephanie felt because of it were almost worse. How had Jane succeeded where she'd failed? Was it her fault? Or Jean Claud's?

She had never played the blame game with Jean Claud, nor had she been bitter about his indifference toward her. She'd simply dealt with her circumstances as best she could, finding enough outside the realm of sex to occupy her energy and passions. After the last several days, though—Oscar Barbadillo's perversity being the crowning touch—she'd seen enough of how the other half lived to know sex had its downside. And yet, the image of that mulatto girl in Jack Kidwell's bed, writhing in ecstasy, had stuck in her mind.

It still embarrassed her to think that she'd watched them, unable to tear herself away. Yes, there was a certain novelty value in it—she'd never seen a real live couple making love before—but it had also made her wonder if she, too, could lose herself that way, give herself up to the physical experience of being with a man. Her conclusion was that she couldn't. It simply wasn't her.

So, why did that image of the two lovers plague her? Was it that the girl had been so lost in her passion? Was it *her* nature that caused her to behave that way, or was it Jack?

Could a man make so much difference? Maybe that's what ate at Stephanie most. She couldn't help wondering how obvious her lack of experience was. Oscar Barbadillo had zeroed in on it immediately. How could he have known her husband hadn't been much of a lover, that he hadn't satisfied her? Had it been simply talk, an attempt to be salacious and lewd?

Barbadillo she could dismiss, even if he had seen something in her that escaped the average person. But Jack Kidwell was another matter altogether. He aroused certain feelings in her, despite the fact she knew the kind of man he was. Was it the profane and the forbidden that allured her? And why now?

As a man, Jack was not terribly mysterious. He was utterly without pretense, which she found refreshing. And that he was almost militant in his candor added to his allure. Still, neither quality explained why she was drawn to him. Could it have been that he was so fiercely independent? She'd never known a man who lived on the edge, and Jack Kidwell certainly seemed to do that.

Fatigued as she was, and desperately craving sleep, Stephanie couldn't make her mind let go. Nor could she block the image of that cocoa-colored girl writhing atop Jack Kidwell. She could almost feel the rhythmic undulations of the girl's body and hear her cries of pleasure. But even so, Stephanie couldn't see herself making love that way with Jack or anyone else; she simply couldn't.

Bel Air,

Los Angeles, California

Julius Behring was vaguely aware of Jay Leno babbling away across the room when he felt a hand on his shoulder. He jerked awake, staring up into the face of his Filipino houseboy, George Molina.

"Mr. Behring," George said apologetically, "sorry to wake you, but your son has arrived. He's downstairs."

Behring blinked at the clock on top of the TV. It was a few minutes after eleven-thirty. Rico wouldn't be coming at this hour unless there was a problem. God, what else could he have done to screw things up? Groaning, he waved George off. "All right. Tell him I'll be down in a few minutes."

The houseboy went off and Behring straightened the recliner and got to his feet. He was stiff, the arthritis in his back and legs biting him. He cursed under his breath, knowing his body was falling apart and there wasn't a damn thing he could do about it.

At least he still had his mind. Christ. Where would he be if he wasn't smarter than all the other schmucks out hustling a buck? And where would Rico be? Rico was a worry. The boy lacked maturity. Too often he went off half-cocked. Worse, he had a dangerous infatuation with violence. In business a man had to be hard, it was true, but foremost he had to know how to use his mind. Rico was still trying to fuck everything in sight -women, enemies, his own goddamn associates, it didn't matter what.

That stupid stunt he'd pulled with the venture capitalist, Reymond, could end up costing them millions. An expensive lesson. He'd learn, though, whether from Julius himself or from his own mistakes. Out in the real world, there were only two ways to end up—the victor or the vanquished.

Julius Behring got his robe from the bed, slipped it on, then checked himself in the mirror. He smoothed his silver hair and left the room, sensing he was in for more bad news. He never should have given Rico a free hand with all that South American investment capital. Now he had to worry about salvaging his son, as well as the money.

Julius knew that these modern investment schemes were much too risky. He knew real estate, he knew automobiles, he knew restaurants, saloons and the import business. The Colombians understood the same things. ''Why get into shit we know nothing about?'' he'd said to Rico.

''But Pop,'' the kid had said, ''this guy Dave Martin, he really knows his stuff. He knows these high-tech people and he knows us. Dave's a straight shooter. Trust me on this.''

Julius knew in his gut it was wrong. Too glitzy, too much *ah* and not enough *humph*—like a hooker in a goddamn gold dress. But Rico had actually put a lot of time into studying the venture capital business. He was trying real hard to be a businessman, and Julius didn't have it in his heart to tell him no. He loses a mil or two, he learns. That was the way Julius had figured it. But *twenty* million?

Naturally he was pissed, but he couldn't blame the kid entirely. Julius had given Rico the reins when he wasn't ready, so he himself had to take some responsibility for what had happened. But he had his limits. If Rico didn't get the mess straightened out soon, Julius knew he'd have to take the operation over, maybe put his nephew, Oscar, in charge. Though his son was president of Inter-America Ventures, Julius had retained the title of chairman of the board and made Oscar executive vice president, in charge of overseas operations. Mostly Julius kept his own counsel, but he did listen to Oscar, who had good sense, even if he had a tendency to be flamboyant.

Rico and Oscar hated each other, which was unfortunate. If they could just learn to work together, they'd all be so much better off. But there was no reasoning with a couple of young bulls. They'd beat each other to death if Julius let them. It was a delicate problem—he had to find a way to salvage the twenty million without humiliating his son.

When he got downstairs, Julius Behring went directly to the library. He found Rico pacing back and forth in front of the fireplace. The boy stopped and looked at him.

Rico was Latin in appearance, like his mother's people, but lacked their handsome good looks. He bore little resemblance to his cousin. Rico had Julius's eyes, which was not a blessing.

Otherwise, he was mediocre in appearance—neither short nor tall, heavy nor thin, good-looking nor bad.

The amused expression on Rico's face was unexpected. What now? Behring asked himself. Jesus, *had* it gotten worse or not?

"Hi, Pop," Rico said. His tone was surprisingly cheerful.

Julius stuck his hands in the pockets of his robe. "So, what's up?"

"Guess what? My brilliant cousin, Oscar, has fucked up. Royally."

"What do you mean?"

"Oscar *had* her, Pop, the Reymond woman. But he let her get away."

Behring leveled his gaze on his son. "Explain."

"I sent Oscar all the information, like you suggested. He met her flight in Miami. He followed her to St. Thomas. Had it set up with the cops to arrest her. They put her in his hands and before he could find out about the computer files, she crawled out a bathroom window and escaped."

Julius dropped into his favorite chair under the oil painting by the realist Renaissance artist Girolamo Savoldo. He regarded his son over steepled fingers, thinking he should be getting this story from Oscar. Rico would put whatever happened in the worst possible light—anything to make his cousin look bad. "There must be more to it than that," he said.

"No, Pop, Oscar fucked up. It's that simple."

"You almost sound pleased, Rico."

"Well, I'm hoping now I won't be hearing that it's me who's always screwing up. I made a mistake with Reymond, but Oscar fucked up our best chance to get back the dough. The question is, are you going to let me go down there and straighten this thing out?"

"That's what you want?"

"Yeah. I *am* the president of the goddamn company, after all."

"So tell me your plan," Julius said.

Rico Behring sat down on the sofa nearest his father. "I think this isn't a job for accountants and lawyers. I think it's a job for serious people."

"Gangsters, in other words."

"Pop, we don't make ice cream for a living. The money we invest is dirty as often as not. Our investors aren't exactly Mary Poppins and they expect results. I say we do what we've gotta do. I say I line up ten, twelve guys who understand these things and I go down to the Caribbean and get our money."

"You want to hire an army of thugs to find a housewife on an island?"

"This broad's not stupid, Pop. She made a fool of Oscar and we all know how brilliant he is."

"There's no need to slam your cousin, Rico. It's because of his connections and hard work that we've got all that investment money flowing in from South America and other places. He's done a lot of good for this company in a very short time."

"What are you saying, Pop? That you plan to give him a medal for letting Stephanie Reymond get away?"

"Are we sure she's gotten away? Do you know this for certain?"

"Oscar found out she left St. Thomas on a sailboat called the *Lucky Lady*. He's got the local cops watching all the ports and airports in the Virgins, and he claims that the islands are locked up tight as a drum."

"So, what are you saying? That you don't believe it? That the woman's already on the French Riviera?"

"No, but we can't fuck around. Oscar might be good at getting money out of people that have more bread than they know what to do with, but this thing is over his head. I was the one who told him to hire every plane he can to start searching first thing in the morning. And I also told him to spread the word there's big money for anybody who fingers her. You see, Pop, this is *my* area of expertise. I understand these things."

Julius could see his son did not realize he was missing the point. Managing an army of thugs was not exactly laudable, not for a businessman with aspirations. True, they did a lot of business with people who lived on the wrong side of the law, but Inter-America Ventures did not itself deal in drugs, numbers, prostitution or the rest of it. Julius Behring had built his empire providing investment services to people who had no other place to go. Yes, it was a risky line of work, but life was risky. And he'd always been very careful who he dealt with and how he transacted his business. At the moment his greatest fear was that the loss of this money would lead to more serious problems. Deals went bad when somebody didn't do what they were supposed to. That's why he'd always kept his word and produced what he promised.

"Is Oscar sure we can trust the police?" he asked.

"The right guys have been paid."

"That can't be cheap."

"No, Pop, it's costing us a bundle. But you know better than me how important getting Reymond's files is. As long as the broad's got the stuff, we got no choice but to track her down and nail her butt to the wall. And I'm going to do it, too. Our biggest problem is maybe the weather."

"The weather? What are you talking about?"

"Oscar says some goddamn storm is coming in from the Atlantic. A hurricane. It's not supposed to hit there. He said down in South America or some fucking place, I don't know. But it's supposed to get windy and rain a lot all over the Caribbean. It could slow up the search. But I'm going to find the bitch. I swear I will."

"Yes, but can you do it without drawing too much attention to us and our investors?"

"Pop, nobody but us knows what's going on. The cops in Frisco and the FBI think Reymond's wife was blown to pieces with him. And if one of my guys wasn't watching the house, we wouldn't know it, either. It's her and us, but we can't be farting around. This has got to be taken care of, and like now.

The best thing is for me to go down there and take charge. Swear to God, Pop.''

Julius gave his son a look, but didn't say what he was thinking. Oscar might have let Stephanie Reymond crawl out a window, but Rico was the one who'd had her husband murdered, a guy who was going to have thirty million in his pocket in a month. Behring's own broker had confirmed that Halcyon Technologies was being sold to the public in two or three weeks, which meant Reymond could have paid them back. But now the bastard was dead.

"Excuse me, Mr. Behring," the houseboy said from the door, "but would you like something to drink?"

Julius normally didn't have anything to drink after his usual martini before dinner, but tonight he needed something. "Yeah, George, bring me a glass of sherry. You want anything, Rico?"

"No, Pop."

"Just the sherry," Julius said to the houseboy, waving him away.

The man left the room. Julius turned his attention back to his son.

"Have you had any luck locating Dave Martin?" he asked. "Shouldn't he be able to tell us how Reymond distributed the money out of these public offerings?"

Rico drew himself up, beaming. "Pop, that's the good news."

"Oh, you mean maybe I'm not going to have another ulcer, after all?"

"I'm not a complete fuckup," Rico said. "I had some guys looking for Martin and they found him down in Mexico. I got the word a little while ago."

"And?"

"They're bringing him back to L.A. as we speak. I should be able to talk to him tomorrow. But he's already told us where Reymond's money is going to be."

"*Going* to be?"

"You know the company Reymond is selling in a few weeks?"

"Yeah, Halcyon Technologies."

Rico scooted to the edge of the cushion, rubbing his hands. Julius watched him, seeing some of the same boyish innocence as seven years ago when he was twenty-two and graduating from USC. Rico might have gotten a fancy title in the interim, not to mention a wife, a child and a home, but the truth was, he'd hardly changed. He was still a boy.

"You see," Rico began, "Reymond set things up so that when the company goes public, his broker has instructions to transfer the funds from the sale of the stock into his offshore account, a bank in the Cayman Islands."

"You're telling me that's where my money will be."

"According to Martin."

"Then what?"

"From there the money's supposed to get distributed to the various secret investors, like us."

"But if Reymond's dead..."

"The money goes in just the same. But with Reymond out of the picture, getting the dough out is going to be complicated. That's the part we've got to figure out."

George brought him his sherry, carrying it on a silver platter. Julius took the glass.

"You've had a long day, George," he said. "Go to bed."

"Yes, Mr. Behring."

"Get me up at six. And have the masseur here early, too. I can't screw around tomorrow."

"Yes, Mr. Behring."

Julius sipped his sherry, focusing again on his son. "Rico, I don't want to disillusion you, but did it occur to you that with Reymond dead there may be no way to get that money out of the Cayman Islands, unless maybe it's his estate or the federal government?"

"That's not a problem, Pop. Dave Martin told the boys in Mexico that Reymond set it up so the money could be withdrawn by anyone who knows how. It didn't have to be him. Dave says he doesn't know the specifics, but when he gets here, I'm going to find out if that is true."

"It's true," Julius said.

"How do you know?"

"Use your head, son. If Martin knew how to access the account, then he would have been able to get the money himself. Reymond wouldn't have risked that. It's got to be somebody else who's authorized to make a withdrawal."

"Like who?"

Julius took another sip of sherry. "It seems to me there were only two logical choices. Either the mistress or the wife."

"It would have to be the mistress," Rico said, "because his fucking wife was divorcing him. But the mistress is dead."

"True, but the method Reymond set up for getting the funds—probably a code—isn't dead. The question is if the dead broad carried it in her head or it's written down somewhere."

Rico got to his feet and began pacing. "You're saying we tear the mistress's place apart to see if we can find it."

"That would be a good start, Rico." Julius cleared his throat, staring at the amber liquid in his glass. "Tell me, Rico, what was the first thing Reymond did when he realized you were coming down hard on him?"

Rico was silent.

"He panicked, didn't he?" Julius said. "Destroyed all the files on his computer. He figured the jig was up, so he wiped everything and went into hiding, right?"

"So?"

"What do you think the chances are that all the information on that Cayman Island bank account—perhaps including codes and procedures for making withdrawals—was in that computer?"

Rico just stared at him. "I don't know."

"I don't know, either. But I have a hunch Reymond erased

everything because he didn't want the account information to fall into the wrong hands. Ours, for example.''

"Oh, I get it, Pop," Rico said, a wide smile filling his face. "That's why you told me to have Oscar get the computer files from the wife."

"Well, I wasn't sure until you told me about the Cayman Island account and what Martin said about access. I hoped there'd be something important in Reymond's books of account, but I had no way of knowing just what. Now I think I do."

"So, catching up with the Reymond broad is even more important than before," Rico said.

"That's the way I read it, son."

"Hey," Rico said, sitting on the sofa again, "what if she already knows how to get the money out of the Cayman Island bank?"

"That's a possibility we have to consider. The good thing is, the money's not there yet and it won't be until they have that sale of Halcyon stock."

"So we have time."

"Maybe. There's always a possibility the FBI or somebody else will step in. Until we've got that computer data in our hands, we can only guess."

"Oh, shit," Rico said, putting his head in his hands, rubbing his temples.

Julius watched him. "What's the matter?"

"I just thought of something. I hope Oscar's more fucked up than I think he is."

"What do you mean?"

"Well, my brilliant cousin told me he searched Reymond's wife before she escaped. She didn't have the computer disks on her."

"Are you sure?"

"That's what Oscar told me."

"Jesus," Julius said, shaking his head. "Well, all the more

reason to find her. Even if she doesn't have the data on her, she knows where it is.''

"According to Oscar, she claims it's in her bank safe-deposit box.''

"What safe-deposit box?''

"Up in Frisco.''

Julius drained the last of his sherry and considered that.

"Are we fucked, Pop?''

"Not necessarily.''

"You don't believe her?''

"She went to the Caribbean, didn't she? That's where the money will be. I don't think that's a coincidence, do you, Rico?''

"No, I guess not.''

"But if the computer data *is* in her safe-deposit box, that means the critical information is in her head. At least that's true if she wants the money, and I suspect she does.''

"Which means we got to find her either way.''

"Bingo. I'd say Mrs. Reymond is the key to getting our money back, the key to everything.''

Rico popped to his feet again. He had that wild look in his eye like a kid playing cops and robbers. "So, am I in charge, Pop?'' he asked. "Oscar hasn't done so good. Actually he screwed up real bad. This is a job for muscle. It's a job for me.''

Julius rubbed his gray-stubbled jaw. For once Rico was probably right. Accountants and lawyers weren't going to solve this. Heavy-handed measures were required.

"Okay, go down to the Caribbean,'' Julius said. "Hire who-ever you have to. Number-one priority is finding that woman. But I don't want you throwing your weight around with Oscar. Remember what I tell you, huh? Two heads are better than one.''

"Sure, Pop,'' Rico said. "Two heads are better than one.''

"All right,'' Julius said. "It's late. Go home to your wife.''

A flicker of disgust passed over Rico's face, but he didn't

say anything. He clasped Julius's shoulder and headed for the door.

After the boy had gone, Julius stretched his arthritic back and slumped in the chair. He thought of his dear, departed Anita, and he thought of the tart, Rhonda, his son had married. She was trouble. Julius had known it from the moment he first saw her. He shook his head and, unhinging his body, got to his feet. It was a sad, sad world that even in his old age a man couldn't find a little peace.

Saturday,
September 28th

Leinster Bay
St. John, U.S. Virgin Islands

Stephanie awoke with a start, sitting bolt upright in bed, a scream poised on her lips. Her heart pounded, the terror only gradually beginning to dissipate as she realized it was only a dream. She *wasn't* tied up and Oscar Barbadillo *wasn't* burning her with his cigar, though the way her heart was pounding, she'd been certain that was what was happening. Whether she'd actually cried out in her sleep, she wasn't sure.

Calming herself, she listened to the sounds in the night and concentrated on the motion of the boat. A wind had come up. They were rolling more, but she could not hear the hiss of the hull cutting through the water. Had they stopped, she wondered?

She listened again and thought she heard a rattle. Was someone at the door, or was it the creaking of the boat? After her dream, she felt paranoid. True, she'd regarded Jack Kidwell favorably the night before, but now he seemed an anathema, a danger. She hated to think he was in his bunk drinking and that he might get so drunk, he'd pay her a visit.

Stephanie had gotten herself worked up, which wasn't good. Climbing from the berth, she went to the port on the starboard side. It was pitch-dark. The silhouette of land was nearby. They seemed to be anchored in some sort of bay. There was no sign of a town, so maybe Jack had decided to put in at some remote spot to get some sleep. She could only hope it was as innocent as that.

Stephanie returned to her bed and tried to make sense of her predicament. She hardly knew the woman she'd been yesterday, yet here she was, stuck with her legacy. But she'd survived—which was remarkable considering she'd never faced the likes of Oscar Barbadillo or Jack Kidwell before. With luck, her troubles with Barbadillo were behind her. And Jack, well, he was simply someone she'd hired to help her escape, no more important in the greater scheme of things than a taxi driver.

And yet he was all that stood between her and disaster. That gave him power, power that he had to be aware of. The man was no fool, she'd already seen that. His character was the problem. He was a drunk, a womanizer and, by his own admission, a criminal. He'd cheated, stolen and was willing to flaunt the law for money. His saving grace was that he'd made no attempt to hide that, which showed a certain amount of honesty. Or indifference. She couldn't be sure which.

But in an odd way, the man had managed to inspire confidence. He was likable. He had the ability to make his frailties a source of charm. He didn't seem like a con man, though reason told her he was. The real question was if she could count on him to work in her interest.

The pitch and roll of the boat was more pronounced, and the wind had risen. Could it be a storm? Was that why they'd dropped anchor? Her uncertainty made her nervous and she wondered what Jack was doing. Sleeping? Drinking?

She decided to investigate, knowing she'd feel better if she knew what he was up to. She put on the shorts he'd found for her, uncomfortable at the thought of being caught sneaking around in nothing but a T-shirt.

The boat was tossing so much now that she began to feel

nauseated. God, all she needed was to get seasick. As she opened the door of her cabin, the boat rolled and she was thrown against the bulkhead, bruising her shoulder. The main salon was even darker than her cabin. Only the gray disks of the ports were visible against the pitch-black. But then, on closer examination, she saw a faint glow of light coming from Jack's cabin. It brightened and dimmed as the door swung to and fro, faintly creaking as the boat rolled. He hadn't secured the door that afternoon, either, making her wonder if perhaps the latch was broken. Or did he like to keep an ear open to the goings-on in the boat?

Whether he was drunk or sober, asleep or awake in his bunk, she couldn't be sure. Another wave of nausea hit her and her gorge rose.

Stephanie wondered if Jack had some Dramamine. That was an excuse to be up, true, but she did need something for her nausea. And if she found him in a compromising state, she wouldn't disturb him. On the off chance he was awake and sober, she'd ask for help.

Making her way across the dark cabin, bumping into something only once, she found Jack's door. Cautiously peeking in, she saw his berth in disarray, but no sign of the man himself. The light coming from a wall-mounted reading light was dimmed by a cloth that was hanging over it. Could he be in the head? Checking, she discovered it, too, was empty.

The *Lucky Lady* rolled sharply and Stephanie had to grab the doorway to keep from falling. At the same moment she heard a sound behind her. Turning abruptly, she discovered it was a box sliding across the deck. Her gorge rose again and she knew she had to get some fresh air. Jack was probably topside, anyway.

At the head of the stairs she was met with a gust of warm, moist air. It carried rain, large wet drops of tropical moisture spattering randomly—first hitting her shirt, then her forehead, then her arm. The waves surrounding the boat were white-tipped and angry—not the monsters of a stormy Pacific Ocean, but neither were they the tranquil moon-kissed wavelets of the early evening. The wind was hot, tossing her hair, warning of greater fury to come.

Stephanie fought the lurching in her gut. Overhead, the halyards clanked against the mast and the taut lines hummed soprano in the gale.

"Jack!" she cried over the cacophony of the squall. "Jack, are you up here?"

Her hand on the lifelines, she made her way to the cockpit. There was no one there. Had he fallen overboard? Or gone ashore? She gazed through the diaphanous veil of rain at the dark shoreline. Unless Jack had passed out in some dark corner below, she was alone.

Stephanie tried to keep her rising panic under control. She forced her brain to calculate the implications. The fact that they were at anchor probably meant he hadn't fallen overboard. Most likely he was ashore. But for what purpose? And where? She couldn't make out so much as a single light anywhere along the coast. Why would he go ashore here?

Then a terrible thought struck her. What if he'd sold her out? He had to wonder if maybe information on her whereabouts would bring a reward. Was he capable of that sort of treachery? She had no reason to think he wasn't. He owed her nothing. What loyalty she had, she'd bought. It was entirely possible she'd be outbid.

A sudden, pronounced roll threw her off balance and she fell against the coaming. A terrible sickness overcame her and she thrust her head over the side just as she upchucked into the sea.

She'd hardly eaten, which probably made it worse. She lay her head back, her stomach lurching as the rain pounded her body. Her shirt and shorts were soaked and her hair was plastered to her skull. Again her gorge rose and she hung her head over the side just as a wave splashed seawater into her face. She spit and vomited again.

Stephanie wasn't sure how long she lay curled up, her face

pressed to the wet vinyl seat cushion, the wind howling
through the rigging so loud at times that she wanted to cover
her ears and scream. Once she'd tried to get up, but she was
so weak, and her footing so unsteady, that the wind blew her
back down. She began shivering, then crying, her fear as much
a source of torment as her illness.

Stephanie knew she had to get below, out of the rain. She
willed herself to her hands and knees, deciding she was better
off to crawl to the companionway rather than risking a fall
and possibly being tossed overboard.

She proceeded at a snail's pace, weeping, spitting, fighting
the dry heaves, shaking off the constant spray of seawater
showering the deck. She hated it that her life had come to this.
She'd done nothing to deserve it. Nothing.

When she was near the entrance to the companionway, she
heard the throb of a motor. Looking toward shore, she could
barely make out the dark silhouette of some kind of craft moving toward her. Was it Jack? Would he be alone? Or were
they coming for her?

At this point Stephanie almost didn't care. Even the torment
of Oscar Barbadillo would be a form of respite—so long as
they took her ashore.

Seeing no point in pressing on, she leaned against the cabin
house, her bare legs under her. She pushed a wet hank of hair
from her eyes. The craft was closer now, one of those rubberized things. She could only see one figure aboard.

By the time the craft was alongside, she was able to make
out Jack's face. He wore foul-weather gear and was half standing, one hand stretched back to the handle of the outboard
motor. He stared at her, incredulous. Because of the swell and
sloshing of the waves it took him a minute to maneuver so
that he could tie the craft alongside. It was a few seconds more
before he clambered aboard.

"Stephanie," he cried as he reached her side. "What happened?"

She gazed into his eyes more with relief than uncertainty. "I'm sick as a dog," she moaned.

Jack took off his jacket and wrapped it around her. "You've got to get below."

She shook her head. "If I go down there, I might die."

The bastard actually smiled. "Seasickness is rarely fatal."

"Go to hell," she said, letting her head fall against the side of the cabin house more heavily than she intended.

"Sounds like you've got a little life left in you."

"Where have you been?" she demanded. "I thought you'd abandoned me."

"I went ashore to see what I could find out about the path of the storm."

"You went for a weather report? Dear God. I could have told you what to expect. Heavy wind and rain, Jack. Better than ninety percent chance. Lord."

"You still have your sense of humor," he said. "A sign you'll probably survive. Come on, we've got to get you below and into dry clothes."

They went down the companionway, the steps slick with saltwater. Jack turned on a light in the salon, but it was faint because of low batteries. When they finally got to her cabin, he switched on the light and helped her off with the rain slicker. Stephanie sat on the berth, hugging herself, partly because she was chilled, partly because the wet T-shirt was translucent. It was not cold in the cabin, but her teeth chattered, anyway.

"Looks like you got a little too much weather," he said. He took a towel from a cabinet and began drying her hair and face, giving her a good tousling. Then he dried her arms and bare legs.

Stephanie looked up at him, feeling dependent, childlike. It was not a familiar sensation. She couldn't remember if a man had ever dried her off this way, since her father had when she was tiny.

Seeing the extra T-shirt on the chair, he tossed it on the bed beside her. "All right, off with your clothes."

"I'm not letting you undress me!" she said with indignation.

"Think of me as a nurse."

Stephanie rubbed her arms as a wave of nausea rose. "I'll think of you as just what you are!" She swallowed hard, trying her best not to be sick again. "If you want to help, turn around."

Jack complied. "False modesty is a waste of energy when you're battling the elements," he said over his shoulder.

"You can spend your energy as you wish and I'll spend mine as I…"

The boat rolled and pitched simultaneously and Stephanie was sure she was going to toss her cookies, as Zanny used to say. With great difficulty she'd gotten the clinging shirt about halfway off, but her stomach rose and she couldn't fight it off. She doubled over, her head between her knees, and began belching dry heaves.

"May I help?" Jack asked as she continued to retch.

After several moments, Stephanie came up for air. "Oh, God, I want to die."

Jack turned around then and, taking charge, pulled her shirt off. Stephanie made a halfhearted effort to cover her breasts. Ignoring her, he grabbed a towel and wrapped it around her shoulders, vigorously rubbing her back. "Lie back," he commanded. "We've got to get your shorts off."

Stephanie complied, pulling the corners of the towel over her chest. Jack moved forward like a surgeon, grim-faced— probably because it looked more politic—and untied the cord in her shorts.

"I don't have on any underwear," she managed to say in a small voice, her chin quivering.

"Don't worry, I've seen it before."

Lifting her hips, he stripped off her shorts. Stephanie crossed one leg over the other and covered herself with her

hand. Jack did not even look at her. Turning, he shook out
her shorts for no apparent reason other than to occupy himself.

"Can you crawl up to the head of the berth?" he asked.

"Yes."

While his eyes were averted, she struggled to the top of the
bed, dropping heavily onto the pillow. It was hard just to pull
the sheet over her, but she managed. Jack came to the side of
the berth, his legs spread apart to brace himself against the
motion of the boat. He gazed down at her, his hands on his
hips, his expression both paternal and amused.

"Had I known, I'd have offered you some Transderm, but
it's too late now."

"If you have any cyanide, that'll do."

He grinned broadly. "I'll get a little water for you to sip."

Jack left the cabin. Stephanie was surprised to discover she
was having a cold sweat. The nausea was unrelenting. If there
was a way and a place to surrender, she would. Anything to
end this.

Jack returned with a small plastic dishpan and a washrag,
as well as a half glass of water. Stephanie, the sheet clutched
under her chin, watched as he sat beside her. The disorienta-
tion was bizarre. Jack Kidwell's face seemed the only point
of reference.

"I think you'll feel better if I wash some of that saltwater
off your skin," he said. Then, moistening the cloth in the small
puddle in the bottom of the pan, he began to wipe her face,
pushing her hair off her forehead. Next he washed her eyes
and her neck. All the while Stephanie watched him, surprised
at his gentleness.

"You make a good nurse," she said.

"I'm a specialist in seasickness."

"Is undressing your passengers routine?"

"No, actually, you're the first ever. Due to seasickness."

"I'm glad you qualified that."

Jack gave a small smile and put the pan aside. Then he
handed her the glass of water. "Just small sips for a while."

She took a couple, then handed back the glass. He put it on the bedside table.

"How do you feel?" he asked.

"Like hell. The only thing I've had that's worse is a kidney stone. Even having a baby wasn't this bad. It was more painful, but not so unpleasant."

"You have children?"

Stephanie had forgotten he didn't know. "I did."

She started to explain, but emotion rose out of nowhere and she choked up. Jack let it go.

"How about you?" she croaked as tears rolled out of the corners of her eyes.

Jack shook his head somberly. "None." He reached for the towel and, taking a corner of it, dabbed her eyes.

"So, what's the weather report?" she asked, trying to sound more cheerful.

"Not good. There's a category-two hurricane bearing down on the Leeward Islands."

"Where are the Leeward Islands?"

"They're the northernmost of the Lesser Antilles. Roughly from the Virgins down to Guadeloupe. They're projecting it to hit about seventy-five to a hundred miles south of here. But we're feeling the effects."

"So I noticed."

"I knew from the sky we were in for a blow, and the barometer over the last couple hours confirmed it. I just wasn't sure how directly it was going to hit. According to the weather service, it was just a tropical storm and on a more southernly course until about six or eight hours ago. But it's swung north and intensified. We should be in port battening down the hatches."

"Category two is bad?"

"It could be worse. But hundred-mile-an-hour winds are nothing to sneeze at."

"It won't be that bad here, though. Right?"

"Not if the storm holds course."

Stephanie noticed a particularly acute roll and her stomach gave a lurch. "Where are we?"

"Leinster Bay, on the north coast of St. John. When the wind started kicking up, I put in. Figured I'd better know what we were up against. With my radio out and being totally unprepared, looking for a telephone was all I could do."

She could tell he was embarrassed. She knew nothing about seamanship, but it was obvious they'd been sailing by the seat of their pants. He wasn't to blame, though. She'd been the one to force a hasty departure.

"Where did you go?" she asked. "I looked out and didn't see so much as a light."

"Believe it or not, to a pay phone. Much of St. John is a national park and there are telephones along the road."

"So you called in for a weather report from a pay phone?"

"I called a friend."

She noticed his uneasiness. He wouldn't look into her eyes.

"What else happened, Jack?"

He took a moment to formulate his answer, then plunged ahead. "There's apparently a massive search being mounted for us. By your friends."

A heaviness came over her. "I'm not surprised."

"You're worth twenty-five thousand to them," he said. "That's the word on the streets. And they know you're on the *Lucky Lady*."

"That's bad, right?"

"It makes for a difficult game of hide-and-seek."

"So, what's your point? They're going to find us anyway, so you might as well turn me in and pick up the reward? Are you trying to let me down gently, Jack?"

"No, I'm not turning you in. What's twenty-five grand? I used to spend that over a weekend. For nothing. Of course, that was years ago."

"When you were a tycoon."

"Right."

Stephanie didn't know whether to believe him. He might

already have told them where she was and was baby-sitting her until they came to pick her up. Should she confront him directly or try to inveigle the truth out of him? She decided on the subtler approach.

"What happens now?" she asked.

"That's what I'm trying to decide. We're going to have this weather for a while, which means we're tied down, but so are they. There'll be a respite from search planes, but once the weather clears we'll be sitting ducks."

"What you're saying is the game's over. We've lost."

"We're in a corner," he said. "The question is if we risk venturing out in the storm and making our escape under cover of the elements, so to speak."

"You mean you'd actually be willing?"

"Well," he said, "I guess that depends."

She stared at him in the dim light of the cabin, uncertain of his meaning. The conversation had been very offhand, but she sensed they were getting to the bottom line. "Are we talking about money, Captain?"

His hesitation was the answer. But then he surprised her by saying, "Yes and no."

For a second she didn't understand. Was he being coy? Then she understood. It *was* about money, but it was also about something else. Lord, he wasn't going to exact sexual favors on top of getting paid, was he? Surely not.

Jack met her gaze. Stephanie sensed she was now dealing with the person who'd ended up in prison, the con man who'd operated out of the back of a Cadillac convertible, as he put it.

"Why don't you just tell me what you want?" she said, her insides heaving as much from disgust as motion sickness.

"First, I'm risking my neck," he said. "Granted, it's not worth much in the greater scheme of things, but I've got my pride."

"Give me a figure, Jack."

"Let's say five grand for the personal risk."

"And?"

"There's the boat. It could be damaged or lost."

"What's a new one cost?"

"More than the traveler's checks you've got in your purse."

Her eyebrows rose.

"I snooped earlier when you were in the head."

"Sneaky but honest, aren't you?"

"I don't like flying in the dark."

"But if the price is right, you'll consider *sailing* in the dark."

He smiled. "I guess you've got to be quick to get into Stanford."

"How did you know?"

"Alumni-association card in your wallet."

"Where did *you* go to college?"

"State school on a baseball scholarship. I majored in girls."

"More candor."

"People do business best—and, for that matter, make love best—when they know where the other person is coming from," he said easily.

"So you want me to indemnify your boat."

"I'll take your promise that you won't leave me high and dry if the *Lucky Lady* gets trashed."

"That's awfully vague," she said, "not to mention trusting."

"Having decent people feeling a moral obligation is a little like insurance."

"Okay, I'll promise to do what I can within my means. But we're still only partway down your list. What else?"

Jack rubbed his grizzled jaw, looking a little embarrassed.

He did want sex! She felt her stomach clench and knew she was going to be sick again. When she sat up, pressing her trembling fingers to her mouth, Jack handed her the dishpan. Stephanie hung her head over it, retching. When she came up, she was gasping.

She fell back onto the pillow, once more in the depths of

misery. Jack put the damp cloth on her forehead. She was grateful, yet wary.

"Just say it, Jack," she murmured. "What else do you want for my life?"

He absently ran his finger across her cheek, much the way the Cuban had. It made her quail.

"What I'd like," he said, "is more detail about what's going on. The fact that some shady characters are after you because they think your husband ripped them off is a little vague."

"You want to know you're risking your life for a good cause. Is that what you're saying?"

"More or less."

He said it so easily and with such innocence that Stephanie almost felt like congratulating him. But she didn't believe him. Oscar Barbadillo and his friends at Inter-America Ventures wanted her, yes, but they wanted the disks even more. Jack must have found out. If it was Barbadillo he'd talked to on the phone, Oscar would have told him to find out where the disks were.

"You seem unsure," he said.

"Do I? I tend to without makeup."

He gave her a smile and more innocence. "It's not unreasonable that I ask," he said. "The risk *is* considerable."

"How specific do you want me to be?"

"Let's start with what business you and your husband have with these crooks."

Clever, she thought. Start with the innocent stuff, then move in for the kill. "As best I can tell, my husband was accepting investment money for his venture capital firm from illicit sources. It may have been some sort of laundering scheme, I don't know. I guess there were losses and they feel Jean Claud owes them twenty million dollars."

"Twenty million?"

Stephanie nodded. "That's more than I carry around in my purse, too."

"So, why did they kill him?"

"I don't know. They were either vengeful or stupid, I guess."

"They obviously think you have the key to getting their money back."

She immediately thought of the locker key in her purse and wondered if Jack had spotted it while snooping. But his blue eyes were so open and innocent, it was hard to believe he'd gotten that far. They were, however, getting around to the disks, which was where he'd been headed ever since he'd gotten back on board. "I guess twenty-five thousand says they think I do," she said.

"Are they right?"

Clever, Jack, she thought. "No, I don't know how to get their money. So far as I'm aware, it's been lost for good."

He appeared to accept that with equanimity. "You're saying they're barking up the wrong tree."

"Yes."

Now it was Jack probing for truthfulness. He read her eyes, clearly trying to divine the depth of her veracity. "Why didn't you just straighten them out? Seems it would save us all a lot of trouble."

She shook her head. "I tried."

"They didn't believe you."

"Right."

He pondered that. Then an expression of confusion replaced thoughtfulness. "This is probably a stupid question, but why didn't you go to the police when your husband was killed?"

She'd been sparing with her explanations to this point, but decided this was her opportunity to appear to open up. So she told him about Audrey, the divorce, the phone call Jean Claud had received from that man, Dave, and the explosion at the beach house. The only thing she left out was that she'd made copies of Jean Claud's files. "You see, it all started out innocently," she said. "I figured the world thought I was dead and that a week or so in St. Thomas would give me time to clear my head. I also wanted to talk to my friend, Leslie, and her husband before I decided who to trust.''

"But the bad guys were a step ahead of you, apparently.''

"So it seems.''

Jack took that in with equanimity. She watched him closely, figuring the way he reacted would probably indicate how much he knew and what his intentions were. She'd sidestepped the issue of the disks and he wouldn't bring them up unless he knew of their existence.

"Well,'' he said, "they can't get blood from a turnip, but I guess you've got to worry about them killing you while they try.''

"That's kind of the way I look at it.''

He nodded thoughtfully. He was either as clever as she, or totally ignorant of the disks. She hoped for the latter, but knew it behooved her to assume the former. Jack reached for the glass and handed it to her. Stephanie lifted her head and took a couple of sips. Then she listened. The wind had died down and the boat was rocking less than before. Or was she just getting accustomed to the motion?

"Is it my imagination, or is there a lull in the storm?''

"It's a lull,'' he said. "And time to make a decision. Your life is at stake as much as mine. Do you want to make a dash for Nigel's place, or wait and take your chances after the storm's blown over?''

"If you're willing, I assume that means the odds against us aren't too stiff.''

"I'm not suicidal, if that's what you're asking.''

Stephanie smiled and Jack did, too. He hadn't slipped up yet, which either meant he was sincere or very, very good. The smart thing, she decided, was to signal friendship and trust. If she came across as naive, he might let his guard down. But whether Jack Kidwell was guileful or not, their destinies had been hitched together by the storm. The uncertainty was if their true objectives were compatible.

Surprising her, Jack reached out and took her chin. "So, what'll it be, princess?"

His touch sent a flutter through her. "I guess I'm willing if you are," she said.

"Willing to make the crossing, you mean."

She blinked until she realized he was being cute. "What else, Jack?"

His grin was completely devoid of apology. He got to his feet. "Now's the time to put some distance between us and your friend, Barbadillo. It'll be light in a couple of hours."

"Jack..."

He stopped at the door.

"How did you know his name was Barbadillo?"

"You told me last night, Stephanie. You said Oscar Barbadillo, with an outfit called Inter-America Ventures, thinks you have their money."

"Oh," she said. "I forgot."

He studied her. "If I'd talked to Barbadillo on the phone, like you suspect, I wouldn't be taking you to the British Virgins, now, would I?"

"You would if you were trying to lull me into a sense of complacency."

He shook his head. "Why take the risk? I'd simply have said we're safe here." Then, giving her a wink, he left the cabin.

Sir Francis Drake Channel,

British Virgin Islands

By dawn, they'd been at sea nearly three hours. Jack had given her a Transderm patch and it had helped. At first she'd stayed below, sipping water and broth. For the first hour the seas weren't bad. The worse part, according to Jack, was that their course took them almost directly into the wind, making for slow progress. When the gale picked up to thirty-five to forty knots with waves of fifteen feet or more, Jack really had to struggle. Stephanie, battling seasickness again, put on a rain slicker and went topside. The air, and being able to see the horizon, helped, but the fury of the storm scared her.

Jack made her put on a life jacket and she clung to the lifelines, sometimes for dear life when the boat rolled and water rushed across the deck. They were hit several times by waves that came at them like a locomotive, exploding as they crashed against the hull, jolting them. Stephanie looked at Jack, terrified, certain he hadn't anticipated this. After a particularly ferocious jolt she looked around in near panic, wondering if there was a place where they could take refuge.

Astern, St. John was little more than a hazy gray smear on the horizon. Another island—Jack told her it was Tortola—lay five or six miles to port, and on the starboard side there was a string of smaller islands, closer but less sheltering. Stephanie wondered if maybe they shouldn't make for the nearest one. When she found the courage to suggest it, Jack told her there was no safe harbor and the best that could happen was that they'd wash up on a beach. "Conditions aren't that desperate!" he shouted over the roar of the storm. She wondered how much worse they needed to be.

At the end of a long tack toward Tortola, a huge wave rose up like a sea monster. Jack pointed at it and shouted for her to hang on. Stephanie grabbed a stanchion with one hand and a winch with the other. The wave exploded over the starboard bow and rushed along the deck, hitting them like a huge fist, knocking them against the back of the coaming and very nearly over the side. Jack grabbed her by the life jacket and pulled her back as the water subsided around them. Stephanie sat sputtering on the deck while Jack steered.

"That was a doozy," he shouted with false heartiness.

"That's what you call it?"

He tried a smile, but the blowing rain and salt spray made him squint. Spinning the wheel, he brought the sailboat sharply to starboard, crossing the eye of the wind. Even with deeply reefed sails, the pressure was tremendous. Jack had been watching the sails and rigging warily. Stephanie knew they were sailing on the edge; she didn't have to be an expert to see that. As she watched Jack, hoping and praying he was as competent as he seemed, she heard a loud ping coming from the bow. Simultaneously, the jib loosened on the head stay and began shaking furiously, making a terrible clatter.

"Oh, shit," Jack said, "there went the shackle. I've got to fix that or we're going to lose the sail. Here, take the wheel. Hold a steady course and if we heel too far, ease into the wind a bit, but don't let go."

She had no idea what he meant, but he was gone before she could get clarification. Stephanie gripped the wheel, watching him as he moved forward, pulling himself along the stanchion lines when the bow pitched upward and holding himself back when the bow dipped into a trough. Moving along the deck looked treacherous and she was afraid that at any moment he'd be swept away by a wave.

When the boat heeled sharply to starboard, Jack motioned to her to bring the bow more into the wind by making a big circle with his arm in the direction he wanted her to turn the wheel. Stephanie did as he indicated, overcorrecting so that Jack had to signal her to swing back the other way, giving her a thumbs-up when she had it right. Then he went to work replacing the shackle.

She felt unsure of herself at first, much as when she'd learned to drive a stick shift and didn't fully understand the function of the clutch. In time, though, she began to get the feel for the boat and began correlating steering corrections to the response of the yacht. Best, perhaps, was that she was no longer seasick. Fighting the wind and waves enabled her to stay in harmony with the motion of the boat. In that sense it was a little like horseback riding.

As Jack labored, she saw another gargantuan wave coming toward them with the relentlessness of an enormous shark.

Jack, his back to the wind, didn't see it. She began to scream, but he couldn't hear her over the roar of the wind.

Her breath wedged in her throat, she watched in horror as the bow of the *Lucky Lady* rose suddenly on the clifflike face of the monstrous wave. Jack's head spun, but it was too late. The wave broke over the bow with tremendous force, swatting him like a Ping-Pong ball and hurling him over the cabin trunk and along the deck, his body disappearing over the bulwark starboard side, enveloped in a frothy envelope of spray and splash. For several horrifying seconds the boat seemed submerged, the spent wave washing sedately over the stern, coming as high as Stephanie's waist before draining back into the sea.

Panicked, she searched the sea off the starboard side, afraid Jack was lost. But then she saw his head and arms. He was clinging to the lifeline, trying to pull himself aboard. Stephanie wanted to rush forward to help, but she was afraid to let go of the wheel—fearing that if they were swept by another wave they might capsize. On the other hand, without Jack, both she and the boat both would be lost anyway. Torn, paralyzed with uncertainty, she clung to the wheel and watched him struggle, praying he'd get aboard.

For a while it looked as if he'd make it. He managed to get one leg over the side when another large wave hit the *Lucky Lady,* jolting her so hard she shuddered and bouncing Jack violently against the hull an instant before the rush of water scraped him cleanly off the boat.

Stephanie reacted instantly, rushing to the starboard side, thrusting her torso between the bulwark and the lifelines just as Jack came floating by. She reached out as his hand rose from the water, clasping her wrist at the very last instant. The drag of his body nearly pulled her in, but she managed to loop her other arm around a stanchion. He clung to her arm as if it were a rope, the force so great it felt as though her arm would be pulled from the socket.

Their eyes met. She saw terror on his face, the desperation

of life about to slip away. For an instant he seemed to hesitate, as though the thought of letting go had entered his mind. He could save her by abandoning himself.

"Pull, Jack!" she cried, the strain on her body making it difficult to get out the words.

Climbing hand over hand, he pulled himself up, the pain in her arm excruciating. Their faces were only a couple of feet apart. Again, they looked into each other's eyes. Again, she saw doubt.

"Come on!" she pleaded.

Jack made an effort, but she could see he was exhausted. He made a desperate grab at the stanchion, but missed. His other hand slid along her arm and she thought he'd slip away. But then the *Lucky Lady* slewed down another wave, raising her stern from the water. Jack's body slammed against the hull and when the stern dropped, the water rose, popping him up like a cork. For an instant, his head was above hers.

The respite was just long enough for him to grab the stanchion, first with his free hand, then with the other. She took hold of his life jacket. At the same time, the water rushing along the deck reached them, but its force was spent and, with her help, Jack managed to hang on.

He got his leg up and, with her pulling on him, he rolled over the bulwark and into the cockpit. For several moments Jack lay on his back, staring at her, his mouth agape as he breathed. She remained hunkered against the coaming, dazed, breathing hard. He didn't have to say, "Thank you." It was in his eyes.

Jack struggled to his knees when the boat began to heel. Seeing they'd nearly jibed, he frantically spun the wheel. Seconds later they were back on a southeasterly course, headed for one of the smaller islands on the windward side of the channel.

Stephanie crawled back to where he'd planted himself, once more battling the storm from the helmsman's seat. Without a word, Jack put his arm around her shoulders and pressed her hard against him. He kissed her forehead and her cheek with clumsy exuberance. It was the most poignant and heartfelt gesture of thanks she could have gotten. They were bound now, in a new and special way.

Cooper Island

The *Lucky Lady* lay anchored in the shallows on the lee side of the island, bobbing in the relatively tranquil waters, waiting for the last of the storm to blow itself out. Jack had said they wouldn't be going anywhere unless they pumped out some of the water they'd taken on and got the sails and rigging in serviceable condition.

From inside the cocoon of her rain gear Stephanie watched Jack working on the shackle that had nearly cost him his life. It was raining lightly with occasional gusts that served as a reminder of what was possible. "You've looked death in the eye before, haven't you, Jack?" she asked.

He gave her a grin she found totally incongruous. "A few times, I guess."

"Is it a male thing to bounce right up as though nothing happened or is it just you?"

"I'm working to avoid another disaster," he said. "This fight isn't over."

"But aren't you just a little dazed to think you came within inches of buying the farm?"

"Fortunately, Stephanie, I had you."

"Anything I did was purely accidental," she said.

"Say what you will, I owe you one. A big one."

She was grateful for the acknowledgment, but she liked his earlier wordless thanks better. Still, she couldn't help wondering how their misadventure would affect his attitude. What was really going on in his mind? Thoughts of twenty million dollars?

"Jack," she said, "if we were back in St. John and you

knew what you know now about the storm, would you still have come?''

"Probably not."

"So was it a mistake?"

"I knew it was risky."

"Life is precious," she said.

"Thanks to you, we're still fighting," he replied. "And we're way ahead of the game. I'd say we're a good twenty-five miles farther afield than they suspect. Once I get this baby patched, we can make it forty by nightfall, maybe even all the way to Nigel's."

Stephanie shook her head. The man was definitely back up on his horse. Jack glanced down at her from his work and explained what he was doing. The shackle that had broken provided the anchor point for the sail on the *Lucky Lady's* stem head. It had exploded under the torrent's force of the wind on the sail, leaving twisted bits of shiny metal in its place. Fortunately, Jack had a spare shackle in his tool kit and was quickly able to make the deceptively simple yet crucial repair.

"So, how are you bearing up?" he asked.

"Physically or emotionally?"

"Both."

"Physically I'm at about six," she said. "Emotionally it's more like four. I need a rest."

"That was the whole point of making this dash—to get you someplace where you can feel safe."

"I bet I sleep for twelve hours," she said.

Jack put down his tools. "I hate to ask anything of you, considering you're a paying customer, but if you wouldn't mind working the bilge pump while I fix the rigging, we'll be able to get under way sooner."

"Sure. I want to do my part."

Jack led her below to the engine room and showed her how to operate the pump by hand. They'd taken on a lot of water. The air was close below and Stephanie took off her slicker.

She caught Jack glancing at her breasts under the T-shirt. She was embarrassed but things were not exactly normal when in survival mode. And they'd had the bonding experience of saving one another's lives.

"Think you'll be all right down here?" he asked.

"Sure. Believe it or not, I've cleaned a few toilets in my life."

"If it gets claustrophobic and we start rolling again, feel free to come up for air."

"I will," she said.

They were standing close in the cramped space. Jack had another half day's growth of beard on his jaw and, if anything, looked more bedraggled than when she'd first seen him. But there were compensations. She felt an intimacy that transcended superficial considerations.

Stephanie sensed Jack was feeling it, too. His grin was warm. He put his hand on her shoulder. "You're as fine a mate as I've ever sailed with," he said, his voice edgy with emotion. "Thanks again for what you did out there. I'd be fish food now if it wasn't for you."

She shrugged, her cheeks coloring. "Enlightened self-interest."

"I won't forget it," he said.

Stephanie did what seemed like the most natural thing to do—she hugged him, laying her head against his shoulder. Jack held her and for several long moments they clung together. He pressed his face against the top of her head in an endearing way. Then he let go of her, saying there was work to do. He went topside, leaving her ankle deep in seawater.

She started to work, finding the rhythm of the task agreeable, even comforting. It was an odd thing that life had brought her here, to this place where good and bad were in such sharp contrast. When she thought of the existence she'd been leading as recently as a week ago, she was amazed—amazed that she'd fallen so far, but also amazed that her former life had felt satisfactory. She'd found meaning in it, the comfort of familiarity, but in retrospect it seemed so empty, so staid.

Whatever else Jack Kidwell was, he was real and he was a man. Jean Claud, by contrast, had been a phony and a coward. But she also knew it would be a mistake to idealize either Jack or this experience. He had his qualities, but she knew what he was, and it was best she keep that in mind.

Bel Air,

Los Angeles, California

Julius Behring sniffed the honeysuckle in the air, liking it even though his sense of smell was no longer keen. There was lots of honeysuckle in his garden. He'd told the landscaper to put it in when he'd bought the house. Lots of honeysuckle and other plants that smelled good.

The yard had matured considerably in the ten years since he'd purchased the house from Lola Leyton, the film star. She had entertained a great deal and the house had been set up for it. Behring had changed all that. A home to him was a sanctuary. He closed the place in with hedges and walls and filled the grounds with vegetation. The backyard, which he was especially fond of, had a rose garden, a small maze, beds with flowers year-round, a putting green, which he no longer used, the pool area where he occasionally sunned himself, and his favorite spot, the arbor with its flowering vines. Having put in several hours already at his desk, Julius had been in the garden for half an hour now, listening to the bees, enjoying the fragrant air and thinking.

Recently he'd thought a lot about Anita, who'd been dying of cancer when he bought the place. She loved flowers and floral scents even more than he did. Julius had wanted it nice for her in her last days. It had been important to him because he hadn't been much of a husband. Business, his responsibilities came first.

Anita, his little Cuban *chiquita* as he called her, knew all that when she'd married him. "Love me the best way you know how, provide for me and my children, Julio, and I will be happy," she'd told him.

Julius had done what she'd asked, but only that. It was a deal he was willing to make and he kept his end of the bargain, discovering in time it probably wasn't enough. Maybe her Catholic guilt had gotten to him in the end, maybe it had been a mistake to take her as his wife in the first place. In the fifties it wasn't so common for a Jew and a Latina to marry, but Julius Behring had always done everything his own way. Maybe they'd both paid a price. He'd never said so to a living soul, but for some time now he'd been convinced his penance was Rico.

Behring loved his son, but he'd admitted to himself long ago—though never to Anita—that their child was cursed with the worst of each of them. Rico had his mother's fiery temper and passion, but not her heart. The boy had Julius's single-minded determination, but not his judgment. The poor bastard was a loose cannon at times, and dangerous to himself and everybody around him. Oscar, on the other hand, was smart. Julius could forgive him for allowing the Reymond woman to escape. It was a freak thing, that truck parked under the window, but from what Oscar had said when he'd called Julius to tell him what had happened, it had humiliated him to fail and that wasn't necessarily bad. It could help Oscar down the road to be a little more forgiving of Rico's weaknesses. Yet Julius had his doubts that either of them would learn from the other's mistakes. There was too much bad blood between them.

It had been risky bringing his nephew into the inner circle, but Julius had always admired his wife's brother's son. Oscar had the best of Anita's family in him. And his Latin background had enabled him to work effectively with the South

Americans. He was intelligent, loyal, serious-minded and mature, many of the things Rico was not. It was no wonder his son was jealous.

Drawing in the sweet scent of the honeysuckle as if it was sustenance, Behring tried to sweep his mind clear. His mother had preached often about the evil of worry, but it was a lesson he'd never quite learned—women didn't fully appreciate the importance of work, that was the trouble. A guy who didn't understand that was a guy who lived out his days on social-security checks.

Julius Behring consulted his watch. It was time for his mid-morning refreshment. He looked down over the rose garden toward the house. Almost on cue George Molina, in his starched white jacket, came out the sunroom door. He was carrying a silver tray with a tall glass of fresh-squeezed orange juice.

George made his way up the slope. Julius monitored his progress. There was nothing hurried about George. Everything the houseboy did, he did with due deliberation. Julius liked that. Make haste slowly. It was a good philosophy in business and a good philosophy in life.

George climbed the last of the steps leading to the arbor. Julius closed the file, which had lain open on his lap but little consulted, placing it on the table beside him. Upon reaching the shade of the arbor, the houseboy, now in his fifties, looked at Julius, who looked at him. They had been together long enough that they could greet each other without so much as a nod. George's greatest virtue, as far as Julius was concerned, was his ability to anticipate Behring's desires and needs without being prompted. Nor did he question a thing. It was very difficult to find people like that anymore.

George put the glass of orange juice on the table at Julius's right hand. Then he stepped back, the silver tray now under his arm, waiting to see if there would be instructions. Behring stroked his chin. George Molina was silent.

"The tax attorney is due at two?" Julius asked, though he knew the answer.

"Yes, Mr. Behring."

"And that's my only appointment?"

"Yes, Mr. Behring."

"Hmm." Julius picked up the glass. "There hasn't been any word from Rico, has there?" he asked.

"No, Mr. Behring."

"Nor Oscar, either, I suppose."

"No, sir." Again George waited.

"The orchids," Julius said, waving his arm toward the display at the rear of the arbor, "I think it's time to rotate some new plants in from the greenhouse. These are looking tired. Mention it to the gardeners, will you, George?"

"Yes, Mr. Behring."

Julius took a sip from the glass of orange juice. "I'll have lunch in the sunroom today."

George Molina nodded. He knew it was the end of the conversation. He began retracing his steps toward the house, the silver tray under his arm.

Julius tried to relax, get his mind into that nice easy rhythm that came with being in control. It had been difficult of late because of that god-awful mess in the Caribbean. When they'd torn apart the home and office of Reymond's mistress and found nothing relating to his business, Julius figured it was the wife who knew the procedure for getting the money out of the Cayman Islands bank. Whether it was by design or accident, he didn't know. A lot remained murky, but a few things were clear—the woman's money was on the line the same as his. There would be thirty million in a Cayman bank soon, and she was on the run in the Caribbean.

George had nearly reached the house when the telephone at Julius Behring's elbow rang. George stopped and looked back but, realizing Julius would get it, the houseboy continued down the steps. Julius took the receiver.

"Yes?"

"Pop."

"Rico," he said, smiling. "Good to hear your voice."

"Yeah, me, too."

"So, how's the vacation?"

"Good and not so good, Pop."

"Explain."

"Well, we almost didn't get into the fucking island. Some goddamn hurricane was in the area. But we made it."

"Any news from our partner?"

"Haven't made contact with her," Rico replied with surprising subtlety. Julius had schooled him on the importance of obliqueness when communicating by phone. "But we expect to soon."

"Oh?"

"With the hurricane, she couldn't have gotten far. There'll be eyes out looking at daybreak tomorrow. Oscar hired two planes. I hired three more."

"Good."

"Yeah, and we had a turn of luck. Oscar got an anonymous call from this broad saying she's a friend of the sea captain who is with our little pigeon. She says the guy wants to know the score, wants to know if we're dealing and if so how much."

Julius Behring was pleasantly surprised. "What did Oscar offer, Rico?"

"Twenty-five for the woman. A hundred if she comes complete with computer stuff."

"And?"

"We haven't heard back, but our thinkin' is the guy's workin' on the computer part of the deal. Oscar also thinks he knows what happened to the computer disks. When our friend got off the plane in St. Thomas all she had with her was her purse and her suitcase. It didn't hit him until later, but when Oscar first saw her in Miami he thinks she also had a carry-on bag."

"The disks are in the missing bag."

"Yeah, Pop. That's what we figure. They're either in Miami, which we doubt, or they're here someplace. Oscar thinks she could have given the bag to another passenger. We're checking that out. Our friends, the cops, are in the process of running down all the passengers for us. Some of them could be gone already, but who knows, we might get lucky. But if we catch up with our little pigeon first, it might not matter."

"Sounds like you're off to a good start, Rico."

"Yeah, everything's under control. I figure in two or three days I'll have had all the sun I need. And since comfort's the key, I've hired lots of extra help. Folks are so friendly down here, everybody wants to join the team."

"How's Oscar?"

"Pissed, Pop. Pissed that he got outsmarted. He especially hates it that it was a broad. You know how he is about women. Thinks they should all worship his cock."

Julius didn't say anything to that. His nephew was a ladies' man, all right, but Rico was the one with the problem with women, and he didn't even know it. He used them the way he used everything else. Julius had warned him that his abusive attitude was going to be his undoing, but the boy wouldn't listen. And it hadn't gotten any better since his marriage. His relationship with Rhonda, it seemed, had only made his problem worse.

"So, all in all, things are looking up," Rico crowed.

"You may be on to something with the sea captain," Julius said. "What do you know about him?"

"Word is he's a charmer and needs the bread. He also has a past. Did time in Florida for some real-estate scam."

"Sounds like a man we can deal with. Maybe you can afford to be a little more generous, Rico. Let's up our offer to a quarter of a million."

"For the package?"

"For the package."

"That's a hell of a reward."

"There's a lot at stake."

"Christ, why not?" Rico said with a laugh. "Quarter of a million it is, Pop!"

Isola Lovejoy,

British Virgin Islands

Nigel Lovejoy's island was only a few miles off the northwest coast of Virgin Gorda, toward the eastern end of the chain. It was dusk when the *Lucky Lady* floated serenely toward the cove where visiting sailboats took haven. The storm had challenged them all but the last few miles of the voyage, though with far less intensity than the early leg of the crossing. In the course of just an hour, the winds dropped from thirty knots to a caressing breeze. The last clouds moved off to the west, swept along in the skirts of the receding storm.

Stephanie had spent most of the final hours of the trip in the cockpit with Jack, watching the sails, the irregular profiles of the islands drifting by. They hadn't talked a lot once they'd gotten under way again, except about the boat.

"What do you suppose the repairs will cost me?" she'd asked earlier, after he'd unreefed the mainsail to take advantage of the lighter winds.

"Most of it's cleaning up," he replied. "Labor. I may need to have a little electrical work done and some tinkering with the auxiliary engine, but I don't think there's anything major. Structurally, she seems perfectly sound."

"I wish I could say the same," Stephanie said, her mouth bending into a smile.

Jack had given her a sly look. "For a lady who's been through a hurricane, you look just fine."

"Having an excuse doesn't make me feel any better," she said.

"At Nigel's you can have a nice warm shower, wash your hair, and come out as beautiful as you've ever been."

"Oh, heaven."

He gave her knee a friendly pat. She hadn't wanted to make anything of his comment, but there was something about the way he'd looked at her when he said it, and the pat on her knee, that made her quiver inside.

Jack had done nothing overt since they'd hugged down in the hold, but she'd sensed that he was no longer fearful of offending. His subtlety in that regard made his new attitude especially provocative, though she held fast to her cautious ways.

In the fading light of dusk, Isola Lovejoy, its profile flat to the water and prickly with palms, seemed as much an oasis as an island. It was only seven acres in size and was owned in its entirety by Nigel Lovejoy. The major improvement on the island was the manor house, which Nigel had built according to his own design, incorporating both modern and colonial elements.

The water they'd taken on had knocked out the auxiliary engine, limiting Jack's ability to maneuver, and they approached the island with a deliberateness that was agonizing. Once the mouth of the cove was fully visible, the manor house came into view, its white, columned facade golden from the sun-kissed clouds behind them. The structure sat on the slope of the hillock that rose beyond the cove.

Stephanie thought of Mount Vernon as seen from the Potomac, though both the perspective and the grandeur of the manor house were much less assuming. It did look civilized and inviting, however. And the thought of a shower had her drooling. She was a bit in awe at the lush tranquillity of the place.

"Nice, huh?" Jack said.

"It's beautiful."

"Worth braving the storm?"

"All's well that ends well, I guess."

Jack's only response was a nod.

Stephanie moved forward for a better look, walking along

the port side, her eyes on the trees and lawns. Only a few hours ago the *Lucky Lady* had been awash with seas, fighting for her life. Now they were in paradise.

Jack dropped anchor in the middle of the cove. He said he'd take her ashore, introduce her to Malva, Nigel's housekeeper, and come back later to tend to the boat.

"What's our story?" she asked.

"Malva's been alerted that we were on our way and that it's a discreet visit, but that's all. There'll be no need to explain more."

"You make it sound like this is a regular occurrence."

"Do I?"

"Or is it just that you have trusting friends?"

He gave her a quirky smile. "I have trusting friends."

With Stephanie's help he lowered the inflatable dinghy into the water. She had stuffed her clothes into a paper sack earlier, and she went below to get it and her purse. When she returned, he helped her into the small craft. After yanking on the starter cord of the outboard a couple of times, he managed to get the engine going. They putted toward the small sandy beach at the base of the cove as dusk closed in around them.

It wasn't until they were practically ashore before Stephanie saw the huge man in the shadows at the foot of the lawn. He wore a dark brown sleeveless shirt and baggy pants that came to the middle of his calves, and his feet were bare. He was obviously native to the islands. When the bow of the boat plowed into the sand, he moved forward.

"Captain Jack, how you doin', sir?" he said, splashing into the water, his big white-toothed grin coming as a relief to Stephanie.

"Howdy, Joseph," Jack said, stepping out of the boat and into the water.

The two men shook hands, Joseph so large that he dwarfed Jack, himself no waif. Close up, Stephanie could see that the man was not young, his hair white, his big body slightly stooped. But there was nothing frail about him. He had the look of a man who spent his days lifting heavy things, yet was at peace with the world.

"You surely didn't sail that little boat of yours through that storm, did you, Captain?" he said, tossing his head toward the cove.

"I surely did. With the able assistance of Ms. Reymond."

Joseph glanced down at her, bowing deferentially even before Jack introduced them. Stephanie stood.

"Welcome to Mr. Nigel's island," Joseph said, taking the hand she offered in his paddle-like paw. "You two must be mighty fine sailors, comin' through that hurricane, even if it only was the edge. Wasn't so bad here, but we heard on the radio the wind was sure strong down by St. Croix and St. John."

"We came through a pretty good blow," Jack said.

Stephanie moved to the edge of the boat to climb out, but Joseph motioned for her to sit. "I'll pull you up onto the beach, missus, so you don't have to get your feet wet."

Once she was seated, the huge man took hold of the line and dragged the craft a good ten feet onto the beach, seemingly without effort. Then he helped her out of the boat as Jack joined them.

"That all you got?" Joseph said to Stephanie, nodding toward the paper bag in her arm.

"Yes, I'm traveling light."

He accepted that without comment. To Jack he said, "Malva says you should come up to the house. Tess'll have some supper for you soon."

"That sounds good."

"You know the way, Captain. Go on up."

Jack took Stephanie's arm and they started up the sweeping lawn. The light on the house had a moonlike glow, though it was still dusk. She was surprised at how unsteady she felt.

"It'll take a while to get your land legs back," he said.

"Solid ground does feel funny."

"Joseph's wife, Tess, is a hell of a cook, assuming you have a taste for Creole cuisine."

"I could eat anything," she said, only now realizing how hungry she was. "It could come right out of a can and I'd be happy."

As they neared the house, a figure appeared on the veranda. It was a woman in a plain white sundress, an attractive mulatto with her hair pulled back sleek and exotic, a mature woman, perhaps in her late forties.

"Jackie!" she said with unmistakable delight.

"Hi, Malva."

They embraced and for a moment she held his face in her hands, smiling at him with the assurance and familiarity of an old friend. "We didn't think you'd make it."

"I had my doubts for a while, too," he said with a sly grin at Stephanie. "Malva, I'd like you to meet my friend, Stephanie Reymond. Stephanie, this is Malva, queen and reigning monarch of Isola Lovejoy."

"Queen, my ass," she said, giving him a playful slap on the arm. "The day I'm queen of anything is the day I'm dreamin' or dead." She turned to Stephanie, a smile on her lips. "Welcome." Malva offered her hand and Stephanie took it. The woman's grip was firm and more welcoming than her eyes.

"Thank you," Stephanie said.

There was warmth on Malva's face, but also judgment. Stephanie glanced at Jack and saw something unspoken passing between them.

In light of Malva's earthy elegance, Stephanie was even more self-consciously aware of her own tattered condition. She ran her fingers through her brittle hair, feeling gritty and unworthy.

"I bet you'd like me to show you to your room," Malva said.

"Yes, please. And the bath even more."

Malva glanced back into the falling darkness. "Is Joseph bringing your luggage up to the house?"

"I'm afraid this *is* my luggage," Stephanie said, giving the sack a squeeze. "I lost my suitcase in St. Thomas."

"In other words, you'll be needin' somethin' to wear. Follow me," Malva said, leading her inside. "You can look after yourself, Jackie," she called over her shoulder. "You'll be sleepin' in your usual room. Supper's in half an hour or so."

The entry was large and dimly lit by a huge wrought-iron chandelier. The floor was a terra-cotta tile and the furniture Mediterranean—Italian and Spanish antiques, it appeared—but the walls were covered with Caribbean art, sunny and colorful. The main salon, which Stephanie peeked into as they went by, was much more contemporary and relaxed. It was lighter in color, the sofas and chairs cushiony, pillowed and pastel, the art modern and geometric.

The aromas and sounds coming from the back of the house suggested the kitchen. Malva led Stephanie in the other direction, out a wing of the house with what were likely guest rooms lined up on either side. Stephanie's room was at the end. "The guest-of-honor room," Malva said, opening the door.

The four-poster, queen-size bed seemed so sumptuous and pristine after what she'd lived with the past twenty-four hours that Stephanie felt unworthy. And, to make matters worse, when she caught a glimpse of herself in the dressing-table mirror, she was horrified.

Apparently, Malva saw her glancing longingly toward the white-tiled bath, because she said, "That's what you're lookin' for, I guess." "Everything's in there you'll need. Towels, shampoo, body lotion, hair drier."

"I can't tell you how delicious that sounds."

"I'll have clothes for you to choose from laid out on the bed when you get out."

Stephanie sensed a reticence, but it was difficult to tell if it was just Malva's way, or there was something going on because of Jack. He hadn't indicated they had a special relationship, apart from the fact that the woman worked for his friend, but there had been a familiarity between them. The possibilities were obvious. "I appreciate your kindness," Stephanie told her.

"It's my job."

"Have you been here long?"

"Going on five years. But I don't stay on the island all the time. I'd go nuts."

"You aren't from the Virgin Islands originally?"

"No. I was born in Georgia. But my mama was Jamaican and I came down here to the Caribbean with her when I was twenty. Then I followed a man to St. Thomas. That ended, but I stayed. Few years after that was when I met Jackie. Him and me go way back."

The comment didn't confirm Stephanie's suspicions, but it went a long way. She could see Malva was as curious about her relationship with Jack as the other way around. "He's done me a very great favor, so I'm in his debt," Stephanie explained. "I imagine he told you I was forced to leave St. Thomas under emergency conditions."

"No, he didn't explain. In fact, it was Sonia who called. But she did say you weren't the usual charter passenger. There's some things I know not to ask about."

Stephanie saw that explanations weren't necessary and that there was a great deal of trust involved. She did wonder who Sonia was, but decided asking about her was not the politic thing to do.

"Well," Malva said, "I expect you're dyin' to get in that shower, so I'll let you be." She bowed her head graciously and drifted away.

Jack slapped the lime-scented cologne on his face and put the bottle back in the cabinet where he'd found it. The sting persisted for several moments at the corner of his mouth where he'd nicked himself shaving. A spot of blood oozed from the invisible cut, and he pressed the skin to stop the bleeding, taking the opportunity to appraise the way he looked in the mirror. The faded green polo shirt and chinos had long been favorites so he'd brought them from the boat after he and Joseph had secured the *Lucky Lady*. He probably could have found something nicer around the house to wear, but the shirt and pants were clean, if not perfectly pressed, and he'd much preferred wearing his own clothes.

When he'd seen Malva on his way to his room, she'd told him to hurry as there'd be hors d'oeuvres and drinks on the veranda. Tess was already grumbling that dinner was ruined. Jack had shaved and showered quickly, but an hour had passed since their arrival, which meant he was probably holding things up.

Leaving his room, he made his way through the house, encountering Tess, who'd come out as far as the hallway to get a sense for how the party was progressing. She was standing akimbo, her huge round hips like shelves on which her fists rested defiantly.

"You just now goin' out, Captain Jack?" she asked irritably, not bothering with niceties.

"Hi, Tess," Jack said, pinching her jowl. "You're pretty as ever."

She brushed his hand away, the furrows deepening on her gleaming forehead. "This dinner's as good as ruined. Already is ruined!"

"One of your ruined dinners is better than any three unruined dinners from the best restaurants in the Virgins."

"You may know that, Captain Jack, and I may know that, but that don' make my ruined dinner taste any better. Now get on out there and tell Malva dinner's about to be served. One drink and no more!"

Jack went off dutifully.

Arriving on the veranda, where the air had grown soft and still, Jack found Stephanie staring out at sea and Malva at a table, pouring wine into a glass. They both turned at the sound of his footsteps.

Stephanie had been transformed from the sea urchin in the baggy, oversize shorts and T-shirt to a woman of considerable elegance. She was wearing a white cotton halter-neck dress with a slim skirt. Her auburn hair was slicked back, exposing her neck. He wasn't sure what to make of her.

"Soap and water seems to agree with you," he said.

She reacted with embarrassment. "You, too."

"That dress looks like it was made for you, Stephanie."

"Hardly," she said, coloring.

"Really. You look great."

"Thank you." As she said it, she turned back toward the sea.

Jack was amused. It was the reaction of a much younger woman. Their harrowing experience and the intimacy that resulted seemed to have affected her a little more deeply than he'd first thought. The wariness and suspicion had been replaced by self-consciousness, and he decided that was good. At least things were moving in the right direction.

Malva drifted over. She had a sherry in one hand, which she gave to Stephanie. In the other was a tumbler half filled with a tea-colored liquid and a couple of ice cubes, which she extended to him. "Your scotch, Captain."

Jack took it, staring down at the roiling liquid, a mini panic gathering in his gut. He could picture himself muttering, "Cheers," and downing a hearty gulp without so much as another thought. Aware they were both watching, he sloshed the scotch around in the glass, his arm aching with indecision. Then he impulsively thrust the tumbler back into Malva's hand. "I don't think I want a drink tonight," he said.

"Lordy," Malva said, blinking, "what's the world coming to? Never known you to turn down a scotch, Jackie."

"Life is full of surprises," he said, his eyes sliding over to Stephanie.

There was an awkward silence, then Malva said, "Why is

it that a man who hardly shaves always cuts himself?'' Wetting her finger, she rubbed a spot of blood from the corner of his mouth. After a tense moment with Stephanie watching, Malva went back over to the table.

Stephanie fingered the stem of her sherry glass.

"So," he said, "I take it you're all settled in."

"Yes. Malva's been very gracious."

He subtly checked out her body, still struck by how she'd transformed herself and how that had apparently helped her regain her confidence. She seemed aware of his regard, reacting more with equanimity than embarrassment. Malva returned with a small tray of canapés.

Stephanie took an hors d'oeuvres, popping it into her mouth. Jack did the same. Then she snatched another.

"I'm famished," she said. "I must have had five of these before you got here."

"You haven't exactly been treated to gourmet meals," he said. "Actually you didn't each much at all."

"I'm making up for it now."

"Guess I'll go inside and talk to the volcano in the kitchen," Malva said. "Finish your sherry then come on in."

"We'll be right there," Jack said, his eyes on Stephanie.

Malva withdrew. Stephanie sipped her drink, looking at him over the rim of the glass.

"Well, here we are," she said. "You told me you'd bring me to safety and you have. I'm in your debt, Jack."

"You paid me well and saved my life along the way. I'd say we're even, or maybe I still owe you."

"I don't think we need to talk in those terms. As I said, all's well that ends well."

"You're safe for the moment, but you're not completely out of the woods," he said.

"Yes, I know. I guess I need to take a few breaths before I start worrying about that."

He nodded, sensing a noticeable shift in attitude toward him. She probably felt safer now and didn't feel the need to be defensive. But it was too soon to tell just how friendly things were going to be. There was no need to rush things, though, and anyway he judged her to be a woman who wasn't easily rushed.

"You were afraid of me when you first came aboard the *Lucky Lady,* weren't you?" he asked, probing.

"Jack, I hardly had time to be afraid of you. In a way, you were the least of my worries."

"Well, I hope you feel better about me now."

"Of course I do. You've proven yourself under fire, if that's the right phrase." She again sipped her sherry.

"Relationships are strengthened through adversity," he said.

"Friendships are."

He smiled. "Am I pushing a little hard?"

"*Are* you pushing, Jack?"

"I guess I'm curious what you're like in a state of normalcy."

"Even this isn't me, I assure you."

"What is you, then?"

She took a moment to think about that, crossing her arms, her glass in one hand. She seemed aware of his scrutiny, even as she pondered the question. "You know, for the first time in my life, I have no automatic answer. I'm not the person I was three or four days ago, that much is certain." Her brow furrowed. "What an odd problem to have, not knowing who and what I am. I mean, I know who I was, but I can't exactly be that person again."

"Are you saying you can't go home?"

Again she thought. "I suppose I am…at least at some level. Because even though I'd like to say, 'Of course I could go home,' I seem to have trouble with the words."

"Maybe because you don't want to."

She nodded. "I don't want to be the person, the twit, I was before, that's for sure."

He studied her. "I'd say you've had a transforming experience, Stephanie."

She laughed. "Is that what you'd call it?" Her mood darkened. "Well, my husband and sister were killed before my eyes. My lawyer was murdered. I was kidnapped and I've been through a hurricane on a sailboat with…"

"A drunk with a questionable background."

"I wasn't going to say that."

"You didn't have to. I did."

"You aren't a drunk, Jack." There was more hopefulness than conviction in her voice.

"I'm trying not to be."

She processed that, seeming a bit troubled. He was sorry now he'd brought it up. But then, why hide from the truth? If Jack had learned anything in this life, it was not to fear the truth.

Stephanie continued to struggle. But after a few moments, she let go and went on. "Anyway, I've been through all that in a matter of just a few days," she said. "So, yes, I guess I have had a transforming experience."

"How have you changed?"

"My, you do want to make a point of this, don't you?"

"Don't answer if you don't want to."

She looked off, twisting her body back and forth as though the question made her uncomfortable. "It's probably terrible of me to say this, Jack, but you know how I feel? I feel free."

"Free?"

"Yes, and it's not just because Jean Claud's dead. At the purely human level, I'm still traumatized by his death, but you know what? This experience has opened my eyes to the fact that I have been living my life in a cage—one of my own making to a certain degree, but still a cage."

"Interesting."

"I must sound like I'm nuts," she said. "Or at least totally insensitive."

"Not at all, Stephanie, I empathise with you."

"Jack, how can you? My life is…was so alien from yours. Do you have any idea, for example, how bizarre it is that I'm here, in this place, standing here talking to you? If Jean Claud hadn't…well, let's just say I could be at Stanford right now, this very minute, attending an association executive-committee meeting or something of the kind. I've never even fantasized about having an adventure like this. If my mind wandered at all at a meeting, it would be to wonder what I needed to pick up at the supermarket on my way home."

"But now you're free."

"And feeling a little guilty about it. I don't want to seem completely heartless."

"Speaking purely for myself, I'm glad you're here and sorry you feel guilty."

She contemplated him a bit warily. He had pushed, a bit too hard, he realized, and he told himself to slow down.

Jack gave her his most innocent smile. Stephanie smiled back, seemingly uncomfortable with the energy flowing between them. She finished the last of her sherry.

"So," she said, "Malva seems quite fond of you. You must be good friends."

"In a way she's like a sister."

"Sister, Jack?"

Her meaning was obvious from the way she said it. She'd obviously made up her mind about him, and even if there was some attraction there, nothing he could do would convince her she was mistaken.

Glancing over at the scotch on the table, he yearned to gulp it down. Funny how that worked. The least bit of stress and the first thing he thought about was having a drink.

He turned his attention back to Stephanie, watching her push a wisp of hair off her cheek. The gesture moved him. He thought of the way they'd embraced on the boat and he wanted to touch her again, even knowing she wouldn't be receptive. There was something about this woman.…

"Hey, you two, dinner." It was Malva at the door, sleek and cool.

"Oh, good," Stephanie said, "I could eat a horse."

She put her empty sherry glass on the table and, with only the briefest glance at him, went off. He followed along behind, watching her body move beneath her dress. Malva pointed her toward the dining room, then slipped a note in Jack's hand, arching an eyebrow as she did.

He stopped to look at it, having difficulty reading in the dim light. Malva had written:

Sonia wants you to call. It's urgent.

When Stephanie saw that she and Jack were going to be dining alone, she urged Malva to join them.

"I've got an early morning," Malva said. "Mr. Lovejoy calls on Sundays from his home in Cornwall before he heads back to London. It's usually around seven here when he does. Besides, three's a crowd. I'm sure Jackie will keep you entertained."

Her sly look at Jack made Stephanie wonder.

Malva went to the sideboard, took the open bottle of wine and poured some for Stephanie. Then she went to the other end of the table where Jack put his hand over his glass. "So," she said, "found yourself a reason to quit, have you?"

"Why, Malva, you know I'm a responsible man."

She laughed. "You're full of shit, Jackie, that's what you are." Putting a hand on his shoulder, she said, "You two enjoy your supper." She tousled Jack's hair, then withdrew.

Stephanie observed the interplay, knowing there was history there, probably more than Jack had admitted to. He regarded her and she regarded him.

Stephanie picked up her wineglass and took a sip. Then she glanced around. The room had an English feel, with an antique sideboard and a series of staid-looking oils, mostly on the theme of hunting. It was so traditional compared to the rest of the house that she had a feeling it was Nigel Lovejoy's joke, a tongue-in-cheek shot of humor. When she turned her attention back to Jack, she found him stroking his chin.

"I think I need to explain something about Malva," he said.

"No, you don't."

"Yes, I do." He peered at her from the other end of the table which was large enough to seat twenty. "I met her in a bar in Frenchtown not long after I arrived in St. Thomas. I was drunk and got cheeky with a couple of big bruisers who didn't much like my mouth. Malva dragged me from harm's way before I got sliced up and fed to the fish."

Stephanie sipped her wine again. "I see. So, she saved your life and you've been dear friends ever since," she said. "Kind of a recurring theme in your life, isn't it, Jack?"

He grinned as if to say he'd caught her. "Are you suggesting that we, too, can become dear friends?"

"Well, friends perhaps, but not *dear* friends."

"Malva and I were never lovers," he said. "The main reason Malva and I are close," he said, "is because I was once engaged to her cousin. She and Alicia were like sisters. Alicia worshiped her…" His voice dissolved on the last words and trailed off.

His sudden emotion took Stephanie by surprise. Questions immediately came to mind, but before she could ask them Tess entered with the soup tureen, grumbling under her breath, her wooden smile half hidden beneath her puffy cheeks.

"I hopes you enjoys it, missus," she said to Stephanie. "It'll be about the only thing that ain't burned to leather or dried up like a prune."

Stephanie was sorry for the interruption. "I'm sure it will be delightful."

Tess grunted and, after serving her, waddled to the other end of the table where she ladled soup into Jack's bowl, saying only, "Enjoy, Captain," before leaving the room.

Alone again, they were silent. Stephanie couldn't tell if he was thinking of her or the fiancée he'd mentioned. She took a spoonful of soup.

"So, what happened to Alicia? I assume you never married her."

"No, she was killed in a diving accident a few weeks before the wedding. Alicia worked with me as a hand on the *Lucky Lady*. We were a team. She cooked and helped with the sailing. And she was a marvelous diver. Gave lessons. Died trying to save some bastard who'd ignored her instructions and went way too deep. It was so unnecessary."

He'd spoken in a quiet, matter-of-fact manner, but she could see it was painful for him to talk about. And having heard his story, she realized his attitude toward women was probably more complicated than she'd thought. Pain had to figure into it as prominently as selfishness.

"I loved Alicia very much," he went on, his voice thick with emotion. "She was my salvation in more ways than one. When I lost her, I felt as though I'd lost my life." He gathered himself, then said, "I'm ashamed to say I've used that as an excuse for some of the mistakes I've made since. It's not a pretty picture, I know, but it's true."

She fingered her wineglass. "It takes courage to admit it, Jack. Courage most people lack."

"Thank you for saying so, but I can live with the reality of who I am and what I've done."

She ate some more soup. "Out of curiosity, why did you tell me about Alicia?"

"Compulsive honesty, I guess. That and the fact that I don't like surprises—getting or giving them."

"That, too, is commendable."

He smiled. "You're just bubbling over with compliments this evening, aren't you?"

"Compulsive flattery," she quipped.

They fell into silence. Stephanie realized she wanted to do a little soul-baring of her own. After gathering her courage, she said, "My main tragedy is my daughter. We lost her in an automobile accident just over a year ago. She was home from college for the summer, and went out riding with a friend. Their car went off the road and rolled down an embankment…'' Her voice trailed off as the image came into her mind. ''Zanny was my life in many ways.''

Emotion that had been pent-up for a long time flooded her. Tears came to her eyes and she wanted to cry. It was only then that she realized she hadn't had a good cry since that night in the motel in San Rafael. She'd been like a student during finals week, running on caffeine and Benzedrine. But, through everything, her daughter was always with her. No matter what happened in her life, Suzanne would always be there in her heart. Stephanie wiped her eyes with her napkin, chastising herself for having gotten so emotional.

''The picture of the little girl in your purse. Is that your daughter?'' he asked.

''Yes, Zanny at ten. She wasn't quite twenty when she died,'' Stephanie said.

Jack looked up the table at her, his face filled with compassion. Perhaps he was thinking of his own loss as well as hers. Tragedy was one thing they seemed to have in common.

She recalled that moment of affection that they'd shared aboard the *Lucky Lady*. He'd held her. The embrace hadn't been threatening because it was borne of pain and fear and need—some of the same emotions she was feeling now.

After a few minutes Tess mercifully arrived to clear their soup bowls. She served a whitefish in wine sauce, then withdrew.

Stephanie searched for a topic of conversation, realizing a change of mood was called for. ''I suppose since I'm eating at Mr. Lovejoy's table and drinking his wine, I should know something about him,'' she said. ''I believe you said he chartered your boat.''

''Nigel financed the purchase of the *Lucky Lady*, actually. When we met I owned a smaller boat, which I sailed when I was still in real estate. Nigel sort of set me up in the charter business, you might say. That's how it started. Obviously, we've been good friends ever since.''

"What exactly does he do, anyway?''

"Nigel owns an advertising firm in London. Plus he's got offices in New York, Paris and Rome. He's a pretty big player in the multinational arena, but Nigel's smart enough to delegate responsibility. Makes sure he gets in plenty of leisure time. I don't think he'd be offended if I described him as a sixty-year-old English playboy who likes his wine, his girls and his good times. This island is his playpen, the site of many a wild bacchanalia, as he calls them.''

"You paint a colorful picture.''

"Believe me, Nigel is determined to go through this life wringing out every bit of pleasure possible. He's a self-proclaimed hedonist and leaves no stone unturned 'when,' as he says, 'in pursuit of a good time.'''

"That could almost describe you, Jack.''

"If you believe that, you don't know me.''

She realized he wasn't being glib—he meant it. And from his perspective, that was probably true. She was beginning to see that, to Jack, partying was a refuge, not a goal. His real battle was with life itself. In fact, there'd been a moment during the storm, when he'd been washed overboard and she was hanging on to him, trying to pull him back onto the boat, when she'd seen a look in his eyes that said he wasn't certain if he wanted to live or die. At first, it seemed he'd elected to die, but then she'd screamed at him to fight. And he did.

"Why aren't you drinking tonight?'' she asked.

He took a careful bite of fish. "Doctor's orders.''

"Then you weren't being flip earlier.''

"It's only been recently that I've thought of myself as having a drinking problem. But then, I guess that's the pattern. Let's just say, I'm trying life without it for a while.''

"I hesitate to compliment you,'' she said.

"Oh, go ahead,'' he said, giving her a crooked smile.

"There's a lot about you to like.''

''Thank you, but why the warm fuzzies?''

Stephanie considered the question. ''I don't know.''

''I guess I'm feeling the same things,'' he said. ''Maybe we want what happened between us during the storm to mean something.''

''Now that's a frightening thought,'' she said, drinking some wine.

''Maybe I stated it a little too strongly.''

''Why can't we just say we're friends and leave it at that?'' She cut her fish and took a bite.

''That old demon, fear.''

''I like you, Jack. You're attractive and you know it. That's a dangerous combination. Worse, I'm sort of stuck with you. That gives you an unfair advantage.''

He put down his fork and pushed his plate away. ''You haven't been hurt by it yet. Or are you saying you're afraid I might seduce you?''

She colored, astounded that he'd actually said it. ''You have a lot of gall, you know that?''

He laughed. ''You get the bad with the good, sweetheart. That's the way life works.''

Stephanie wasn't sure whether to be flattered or offended. Was this a seduction? she wondered. Of course, she could simply tell him to go to hell, but she didn't want to do that because, for the moment, she needed him. Maybe the thing to do was treat it like a game. She sensed that was what he was doing.

Before she could conjure up a retort, Tess entered the room with a conch soufflé, which she served without speaking. Stephanie lavished compliments on her for the fish. Tess accepted them with equanimity. After the woman left the room, Stephanie picked up her spoon. For a minute or two she and Jack ate, their interrupted conversation hanging over them.

''Tell me,'' she said, opening the discussion again, ''does it go like this with most of your women? This coy, titillating banter, I mean.''

He repressed a smile. "No, every relationship is unique. But surely you know that from your own experience."

"You want honesty? I'll give you honesty, Jack. I was married for over twenty years and I was never with any man besides my husband."

"You're kidding."

"No."

"But there must have been men before him."

He was hinting at a question that her own sister never dared to ask. Apart from Leslie, no one had ever gotten the story of her sexual history from her. Maybe because she felt defensive about it. Her sex life wasn't exactly something worthy of glorification—not considering it was more a source of embarrassment than anything else. And yet, Jack's off-hand comment almost compelled a response.

"Just one," she said after a brief hesitation. "My freshman year of college. I figured I needed to have sex and get it over with, as a sort of last step into adulthood. It was in a motel after a fraternity party. We'd both had a lot to drink. The part I remember best was the discomfort and getting sick."

"My condolences."

"Thank you."

Jack fell silent. They ate for a while, the incomplete conversation still dangling, the pressure in her building.

"So, are you surprised by my sexual history?" she blurted, hardly giving her words a thought. "Or did you have me pegged the moment you saw me?"

Jack rubbed his jaw as though the question were a difficult one. "Naturally, one can never be sure without a little…hands-on experience, shall we say…but you definitely didn't strike me as a libertine."

"That's safe enough," she said, coloring.

"I could tell you were uncomfortable with me," he said. "And with your own feelings."

Her heart began to beat harder as she stared up the table at him. The topic was not only an intimate one, but the conversation itself had turned highly personal. Incredibly, though, she felt drawn right into it. "I saw you making love with the girl," she ventured.

Jack was only moderately surprised. "How did you feel about that?"

Stephanie was surprised he would ask such a question, much less believe she would answer honestly. But she decided to do just that. "I was jealous," she said bravely.

Jack smiled. "That's nice. Refreshing to hear."

"Don't gloat."

"I'm not. I like candor in a person."

"Don't make too much of it," she said. "It wasn't you personally. It's more a commentary on my life."

"Now there's a subject."

"One I'd rather not get into, thank you." She took a sip of wine. Despite her brave words, she was seized by the urge to jump right back into the conversation. Thinking this might be an opportunity to ask him a question that had been niggling at her, she plunged ahead. "But if you don't mind, I would like your opinion about something. That man who kidnapped me, Oscar Barbadillo, said something that shocked me. He said he could tell my husband didn't understand my needs. He said I'd never been with a real man. And he...well, volunteered his services. It was as though he didn't need to do any more than look at me to know. Is that possible?"

"Some guys have a special sense about things like that. Male intuition, I guess."

"I hate to think I'm that transparent."

"There's not a lot of pretense in you, Stephanie. You're as innocent as you appear. Even I can see that."

"Oh, God," she said, lowering her face into her hands. Could she actually be having this conversation—telling Jack about her sexual frustrations and insecurities? It took courage for her to look up at him, but she finally did. "I think maybe I've had too much to drink."

Tess came to clear the dishes. And not a minute too soon.

"Y'all want some coffee?" she asked.

Stephanie said she did. Tess made her way to the other end of the table. "Captain?"

"None for me, thank you, Tess." He got up. "But there is something I have to do. If you'll excuse me for a minute, Stephanie, I need to make a call."

He went off without further explanation, leaving her to wonder who he was phoning. Could it have anything to do with her? Was he selling her out? But if that were the case, why hadn't he simply turned her over to them back at St. John? Unless he was haggling about the price.

Waiting anxiously, she'd just about finished her coffee when Jack returned. His face contained no clue as to what had transpired. She wanted to ask him, but she'd already been outspoken enough that evening.

Ironically, Jack looked especially appealing as he took his seat. Innocent as could be. If he had sold her down the river, he'd disguised it well. But was the bastard secretly gloating? She hoped not—for her own sake, sure, but also because of what it said about him.

He looked at her, smiling as he draped his napkin across his lap. "Coffee good?"

"Better for me than the wine."

"Don't try to undo our conversation," he said. "It was a good, honest one."

Jack, she could see, knew exactly what she was thinking. She hoped to God he wasn't like Oscar Barbadillo, reading her every thought. No, they were nothing alike. She was just insecure.

"Then let's talk about you," she said. "Everything all right at the office?"

He gave her a thoughtful, appraising look. "Maybe we *should* talk a little business."

His tone gave her a sinking feeling. It reminded her of Jean Claud when he had something serious to discuss. That steely directness always sent an icy stab right through her. She braced herself. "Okay, fine. What do you have in mind?"

"Why don't you tell me what you want to happen," he said. "Best-case scenario."

She saw no harm in being dead honest. "I want to go home," she said. "Which probably means going to somebody like the FBI—assuming Inter-America Ventures hasn't bribed them, too."

"Inter-America Ventures…"

"The bad guys."

Jack nodded. "Well, if you want to return to the States, that means getting you to an airport. The trouble is, it has to be one far enough away that it isn't under surveillance by your friends. The international airport in the British Virgins is on Beef Island, which is only hours from here, but I have reason to believe it's being watched. There are other possibilities farther afield that may be safer, but there are obstacles to them, as well. The major requirements would be time, money and a passport."

"That's another problem," she said, suddenly weary. "Unless you take American Express, I don't have any cash left, at least with me. I've got nineteen hundred in traveler's checks in my purse, and I owe you seven thousand."

He considered that. "I'm sure you're good for it, Stephanie. You can send me a check when you get home."

"That's very trusting."

He smiled. "I'm the one with the criminal record, not you."

She thought how different he was from the man who'd staggered up onto the deck of the *Lucky Lady* the previous day, wearing little more than a pair of shorts and a cigar.

"The irony is, I can't be sure what I'll be facing when I get home," she said. "The police will want to know what I've been doing and why. Which is only reasonable since I've been wondering the same thing myself."

"Well, if you decide to run off to South America instead, you're going to need more than nineteen hundred dollars."

"I have more, actually," she said. "It's just not with me. I've got fourteen thousand dollars in cash and traveler's checks back in St. Thomas. If I could put my hands on it, I could pay you to get me out of here and still have a dime left to call a lawyer if I end up needing one."

He seemed to like her attempt at humor. "What are you saying? That you want to go back to St. Thomas and get the money?"

"Hardly. Not considering what we went through to escape. Besides, in the greater scheme of things, fourteen thousand isn't much. I can always send somebody for it later."

"Then what do you propose?"

Stephanie contemplated him, deciding in the end to say what was on her mind. "Mind if I first ask who you called?"

"No, I spoke with my friend, Sonia, in St. Thomas to get an update."

"And?"

"I was told they're still looking for you and plan to intensify the search. There's been no change that would affect a return to the States."

His tone sounded honest, but she had no way of knowing whether what he said was the truth. They were at a crossroads. She anguished over telling him about the disks. She wanted to trust him, but reason urged caution. Ultimately she had to rely on herself. The days of being taken care of by a man were over.

"So, what do you want to do?" he asked again.

She chewed her lip, her insides in a knot. Did she tell him about the disks or didn't she? "Promise you won't betray me, Jack," she finally blurted.

"I won't betray you," he replied without hesitation. "I promise."

She glanced toward each door. "Could we go outside? Maybe take a little walk?"

"Sure."

They got up from the table. At almost the same moment, Tess entered the room with a couple of tarts and the coffeepot.

"Don' y'all want dessert? More coffee, missus?"

"We're going to take a little walk first," Jack told her. "Why don't you leave it on the table and we'll have it when we come back?"

"If that's what you wants, Captain."

They left, Jack touching her waist with his warm hand as they passed through the door. They walked through the dimly lit entry hall, Stephanie's heart beating uncertainly. Jack had her totally confused, her body and her mind going in different directions.

They went onto the veranda. The air had cooled. She stepped to the edge where she faced the ocean breeze to gather herself. Taking a deep breath, Stephanie still wasn't sure whether to tell him about the disks. Jack put his hand on her shoulder in a reassuring way, but now she found his touch unsettling.

She decided to plunge ahead. "There's something else I've stashed away in St. Thomas besides my money," she said, giving him a sideward glance.

"You mean your husband's computer disks?"

Stephanie was incredulous. "You know about them?"

He nodded.

"Barbadillo announced that publicly?"

"No, they've informed me about them through my friend."

"What do you mean, 'informed' you?"

"I hate to be the bearer of bad tidings, Stephanie," he said, "but the price on your head has gone up to a quarter of a million dollars."

Her mouth sagged open. "A *quarter of a million*?"

"Right. But that's for the package—you *and* the disks."

"My God." She searched his eyes in the moonlight, trying to comprehend what he was really saying. Was it that the bounty was too tempting or that their friendship had no price?

Then she understood. Jack had *her*, but he didn't have the disks. "So, what are you going to do?"

He shrugged indifferently. "Me? Nothing."

It occurred to her then that there was nothing he could do, unless it was to beat information about the disks out of her. She was seized with uncertainty. What was Jack's angle? Was he trying to lull her into a sense of complacency? What a stupid question. They were talking about a quarter of a million dollars. Of course he was!

"You seem troubled," he said.

"Jack, how long have you known about the disks?"

"Since I made that call from St. John."

"Why didn't you tell me before?"

"We were about to make that crossing in the storm. I didn't think you needed another reason to worry."

"Or to doubt you?"

"Maybe that, too," he said.

"Why tell me now?"

"Because we're talking about what you're going to do. And you were about to bring it up yourself, anyway."

"You could have played dumb."

"Not a guy who's compulsively honest."

She couldn't help smiling. He either *was* honest, or the smoothest con man she'd ever met—which wasn't much of a contest, of course. He was the *only* con man she'd ever known.

Jack surprised her then by reaching out and caressing her cheek. "You're thinking about that guy selling swampland from out of the back of a Cadillac, aren't you?"

She blinked. "You do read minds, Jack."

"In your shoes, I'd think about that. Anybody would."

Stephanie took a deep breath. They'd come to the moment of truth, this one turning on the question of trust. The best course, she decided, was to proceed cautiously, but to appear open and forthcoming. Jack would eventually tip his hand. All she had to do was watch and listen carefully.

"So, did Inter-America tell you why they want the disks?" she asked.

He shook his head. "I think you'd know the answer to that better than I."

"Obviously they want the twenty million they invested with Jean Claud. They're probably counting on getting it out of a company that's being sold to the public in a few weeks, an outfit called Halcyon Technologies."

"Does that explain why they'd want your husband's computer files?"

She shrugged. "If so, I don't know why."

"Maybe they don't know about the sale and are trying to find out where their money is."

Stephanie considered that. "That's possible, but I have a feeling they're after something more specific. Barbadillo hadn't questioned me long before I managed to escape, but the feeling I had was that he thought I could tell them how to get their money."

"Could they expect you to make good on your husband's obligations? Won't you be in control of his business once his affairs are settled?"

"I'm not sure. Jean Claud never discussed things like that. But I do know he'd set up a secret fund with Inter-America's money. I think he must have been laundering it for them, which means it would have been under the table. I doubt their money would show up in an audit of Jean Claud's assets."

She glanced at Jack, who seemed to be pondering what she'd said. She could smell his cologne mixed with the sweet scent of flowering vines and felt a sudden vulnerability.

"It could be that they know that," he said after a while. "Your husband must have put their money in an account he controlled, probably disbursing the proceeds through an off-shore bank. My partner and I ran a scheme like that in Florida. Only we weren't laundering. We were saving our investors tax money—and saving ourselves a little, as well."

"Is that one of the reasons you went to jail?"

Jack smiled. "No, if they'd caught us at that, I might still be behind bars."

"That certainly inspires confidence," she said with a touch of irony.

"Need I remind you, Mrs. Reymond, that you married a man who did business with people desperate enough to kill him? I, on the other hand, am retired from a life of crime. At present, I'm a simple boat driver."

He put his arm around her shoulders and gently pulled her against him. It was a brazen move in light of their conversation, but she didn't object.

"Let's walk a little," he said.

She was wary, but found herself saying, "Sure," just the same.

Jack took her hand and helped her down the steps, keeping hold of her fingers as they walked. The path of crushed white rock shone distinctly in the moonlight. How long had it been, she wondered, since she'd walked hand in hand with someone other than her child?

"As for your friends at Inter-America," Jack said, his tone reasonable, patient, "my theory is they're convinced the key to getting the funds is on those disks."

"I looked at them briefly," she said, "and I didn't see anything to indicate how the money would be distributed from the Halcyon sale. Of course, I wasn't as interested in that as much as what Jean Claud had done with my own money."

"What do you mean?"

"My inheritance is in that company right along with Inter-America's."

"Which means you two are fighting for the same bone."

"It's more like I'm running and they're chasing me, thinking I have it."

"But in fact you buried it."

"In a manner of speaking."

Jack folded her hand over his arm as they followed the path, which had taken them around the house and down toward the sea on the back side of the island. The vegetation was dense and it was darker, the moon scarcely visible through the trees.

"I guess what this is boiling down to is whether the disks contain the secret to accessing the funds," he said. "Your friends obviously think so. They're betting a quarter of a million on it."

"None of which tells me what to do."

"You have several options," he told her.

"Such as…"

"Well, I could go back to St. Thomas and get the disks for you, but you'd be reluctant to agree to that because I could take them to Barbadillo, tell him where you are and collect a cool quarter of a million."

"But, of course, you wouldn't do that because you're an honorable man and you're my friend."

"True, but you'd be a fool to count on that. I certainly wouldn't in your shoes."

"Why? Because you know yourself better than I do?"

"Because it wouldn't be a smart move, Stephanie. I'm trying to look at this practically, not cajole you into doing something stupid."

She could sense this was leading somewhere. "There must be another option you'd recommend, then."

"I may still be your best bet," he said. "But I think the key is for you to find a way to ensure my loyalty."

"And the best way to do that is…"

"To appeal to my entrepreneurial instincts," he replied. "In other words, if I were you, I'd make me an offer I couldn't refuse."

"Like what?"

"Like a significant piece of the action. Right now, I'm a five-thousand-dollar partner in what could be a thirty- million-dollar deal. I have options, however. I might be able to pick up a quarter of a million by getting in bed with Barbadillo, or I could make a better deal with you."

Stephanie's hand dropped from his arm and she stopped

walking. Jack turned to face her. It was so dark that she could barely make out his features, but she searched them just the same. "Jack, you're blackmailing me."

"No, that's not it at all. An honorable man does not blackmail his friends."

"Oh, that makes me feel a lot better," she said sarcastically. "So, what *do* you call it?"

"Look, Stephanie, I'll be blunt. Right now you've got a hundred percent of nothing. Wouldn't eighty percent of several million be better? If you can take on a partner who'll help you get the result you're after, why cling to a losing strategy?"

"You're saying you want twenty percent of my inheritance."

"Twenty percent of what you're able to get out of Halcyon, assuming I'm instrumental in making it happen. That's a reasonable condition and I'll honor it."

"Why should I pay you, if I can wait until Jean Claud's estate is settled and get a *hundred* percent of what I'm legally entitled to?"

"Didn't you say he'd probably hidden most of the money and it wouldn't turn up in an audit?"

"Who knows what he did?" she said, realizing that was probably true.

Jack reached out and took her by the shoulders, signaling his determination. "If you can get your money through legal channels, fine, but based on what you said, your husband would have that money going into an account that's beyond the reach of the courts, creditors, tax authorities, friends, enemies, wives...you name it. What I'm saying is, you may well have to resort to extralegal means to recover your money."

"And who better to turn to than an experienced criminal?"

"I'll overlook that and consider it a negotiating ploy," he said, dropping his hands from her shoulders.

Stephanie sighed. "It was bitchy. I'm sorry."

"Don't sweat it, Stephanie. We're talking big bucks. I understand you're uptight about this. Hell, so am I."

She fell into a reflective silence. Jack was certainly willing to lay things on the line. He didn't lack for courage. Or was it gall?

The honest truth was she didn't know what to make of him anymore. He'd known about the disks since St. John, and he'd been wooing her ever since. Sure, he was her protector, but Jack Kidwell was a knight in shining armor who knew an angle when he saw one.

Stephanie shivered, rubbing her arms as the night sounds seemed to grow louder. A high-pitched chirping came at them from all directions. She glanced around at the darkness. "Are those crickets?"

"Frogs."

She shivered again. "At least you didn't say snakes."

Jack laughed. Then he stepped over, put his arm around her waist. "Come on," he said, drawing her along the path. "It's only a few more yards to the nicest beach on the island."

Another minute of walking and the sound of surf grew more pronounced. They came out of the trees and onto an open beach, brightly lit by the moon. Jack's arm fell away and Stephanie walked onto the sand, letting the ocean breeze caress her. Jack had gone to a small lean-to nearby where several lounge chairs were stacked. He carried a couple over to where she waited.

"Here, might as well be comfortable," he said, arranging the chairs side by side.

They sat and watched the gentle waves rolling onto the beach. Jack seemed content. Stephanie thought over their conversation and wondered if she wasn't being set up. This whole thing might be an elaborate scheme to get her to tell him where the disks were. Even his comment that she'd be foolish to tell him could have been calculated to get her to do that very thing. Even his offer of partnership might have been a sham—anything to throw her off balance. Now she was more confused than ever.

Jack spoke. "Do you have any idea what the usual arrangements were when your husband disbursed the proceeds from a public sale of stock?''

More probing. But was it for himself or for them? she wondered.

''Only a general idea,'' she replied after a moment. ''Jean Claud's investment bankers would deposit money coming out of an initial public offering into a trust account in the name of his venture capital firm. From there it was distributed to the investors. But I don't know anything about the accounts, who had signature power or anything like that.''

''Do you know the name of the investment banking firm?''

''Yes, it was Meriwether & Handley in San Francisco.''

''Do you know the principals?''

She thought for a moment, then decided there was no harm in telling him. ''I know Tom Handley. We saw him and his wife socially. Tom and Jean Claud were close.''

''I wonder if you could get any information about the procedure from him,'' Jack said.

She rolled her head along the back of the chair to look at him. ''There's a problem with that. I'm sure Tom, like the rest of the world, thinks I'm dead. A call from me would be a bit of a surprise, don't you think?''

''Hmm,'' Jack said, stroking his chin. ''Well, what if I called him, posing as your executor or lawyer or something, and pretended I was organizing your estate and needed information on your assets?''

''I suppose that would be possible. But I don't see what good it would do.''

''You never can tell what might turn up in conversation. People like to show off their insider status, and you sometimes can learn from what they refuse to say.''

''You really *do* have a criminal mind.''

He chuckled. ''Yes, I guess I do. But there *is* honor among thieves, you know.''

She could see how he might have become a millionaire at a young age. All Jack Kidwell seemed to need was a cause that got him excited. A thirty-million-dollar public offering had apparently done the trick.

"So, what do you think?" he said. "Shall we see what we can learn?"

Playing along with him seemed the safest course. "Fine," she said. "If you want to, do it."

"It'll have to wait until Monday to call Handley."

"You think we'll still be alive and well by Monday?"

He reached over and put his hand on hers. "I hope so, sweetheart. Because if we aren't, we went through a hell of a lot for nothing."

Stephanie didn't want to think it was true, but she realized then that Jack might have endured that storm for thirty million dollars, not her. And the funny thing was, she couldn't be sure of his true intentions until it was too late. But she had a decision to make. Jack had an offer on the table from her enemies. Did she try to buy his loyalty, or tell him to take a hike? Either course could lead to disaster. But she couldn't see any middle ground.

The wind rose a little. It felt so delicious Stephanie had trouble believing she was in danger. Why couldn't this be innocent? Why couldn't Jack Kidwell be attracted to *her* and not her money? How nice it would be if she'd simply come to the Caribbean to rest and renew herself as planned, and in the process met a man who was willing to help her out of her shell.

Sighing, she thought of a time a few months ago, one of those rare summer evenings in the Bay Area when the cooling ocean fog didn't come rushing in the Golden Gate as usual, and the temperature stayed in the eighties well past midnight. Jean Claud had been away on a business trip, and she'd gone out back around ten o'clock and gotten into their spa with nothing but a glass of Chardonnay for company. The water had been so sensuous she'd taken off her suit and let the streaming jets of water caress her. She remembered thinking how nice it would have been to have someone with her who she loved, someone who loved her. The saddest part had been that she hadn't been able to come up with a single candidate, not even one from her imagination. That's how alone she was.

"How about a swim?" Jack asked suddenly.

"Now?"

"Sure. The water's as warm as a bathtub. You'll never find a more isolated spot for a moonlight swim."

"I appreciate the invitation, but I don't think so," she said.

"What are you afraid of? Me or the ocean?"

"I'm not afraid, I'm just not interested."

"There is nothing, absolutely nothing, as wonderful as swimming naked in a tropical sea."

"I'll take your word for it."

"If it's modesty, I won't look at you. On my honor as a gentleman."

She gave him a level look. "Jack, why are you being so insistent?"

He shrugged. "I don't see how you're going to trust me with thirty million bucks if you can't trust me with your body."

"Ah," she said, seeing there was a point to this, after all. "I don't recall having entrusted you with my money just yet. Besides, what does one have to do with the other?"

"The point is building trust."

"I'm not going swimming with you, Jack, for the sake of trust or anything else."

"To each his own."

Jack got up and removed his shirt. Then he unbuckled his pants. Stephanie realized he was going to strip right in front of her. She thought about leaving, but that would be priggish. Why should she let him scandalize her? The hell with him. If he wanted to take off his clothes, let him.

She shut her eyes and lay back, doing her best to ignore him, focusing on the air wafting over her body. After a few moments she heard his clothes being plunked down on his lounge chair and, when she opened her eyes, she saw him sauntering toward the water, naked. His buns showed much whiter in the moonlight than the rest of his well-tanned body. He had a good physique, no longer the young Adonis he must have once been, but muscular and in fine shape.

Reaching the water, Jack waded out until the waves reached his upper thighs. Then he dived in and began swimming. Stephanie kept track of him until he was perhaps eighty or a hundred yards out. When he stopped swimming and there was no more splashing, it was more difficult to see him. She lost sight of him for a time, but then picked him up again, only to have him disappear in the obscurity.

Stephanie wondered what he was thinking. Regardless of what his intentions had been, he must think her a prude. Damn it, she thought, why didn't she have the gumption to prove she wasn't as repressed as he thought? Was she afraid of him? Or afraid of the effect he might have on her?

When she searched the dark sea again and couldn't find him, she figured this might be an opportunity for her to take a quick swim. It was one way to prove she wasn't afraid, and she could be back and dressed before he came ashore.

Getting to her feet, Stephanie started taking off her clothes. Her conservative side, her cautious, repressed side, screamed at her to stop. But she kept going and, when she was naked, she dashed toward the surf, scouring the sea as she went. Jack was nowhere to be seen.

Unlike him, she waded into the warm water. He was right, it was heaven. Stephanie luxuriated in the sensation, walking slowly until the water rose nearly to her chin. Then she did the breaststroke, keeping her eyes trained on the sea, vigilant for any sign of him. If she did spot Jack swimming back, she'd simply return to shore and dress before he got there, not in a panic, but casually and with confidence.

After ten minutes and no sign of Jack, Stephanie began to worry. What if he'd gotten a cramp? He might be in trouble. Walking backward toward shore and out of the water where she'd have a better view of the entire cove, she searched as far as she could see. There was still no sign of him. Turning, she plodded to the beach, only to look up and see Jack in his lounge chair, waiting for her. Wearing a big grin, he waved.

Stephanie was knee-deep in water and tried covering herself, knowing she hadn't enough hands. Turning to take refuge in deeper water, she tripped and fell as a wave rolled in. She came up sputtering.

"Would you at least be gentleman enough to turn around?" she yelled at him.

Jack dutifully got up from his chair. He had on his trousers but no shirt. After turning the lounge chair around so that his back was to her, he plopped down again. Stephanie walked up the beach to her chair, snatching her clothes. She stood behind him.

"What a mean trick," she said through her teeth as she hastily slipped on her panties and pulled her dress over her wet body.

"It wasn't a trick. I didn't know you'd gone into the water until I got back."

"How did you get here?"

"I swam to the point over there and walked around the beach. I thought you saw me."

"I didn't."

"Well, no harm done."

"Easy for you to say. I didn't undress for *your* benefit. It was to swim."

"I knew you weren't trying to seduce me," he said, "if that's what you're worried about."

Steaming, she stood in front of him and glared, her hands on her hips. "You are a bastard, Jack Kidwell, an arrogant bastard!"

"Hey, aren't you blowing this thing out of proportion? If you were thirteen, I'd understand it. Honest, Stephanie, I'm not that eager to see you naked. Besides, I already have."

That humiliated her even more, but it was the truth in what he was saying that hurt most.

"Here, use my shirt to dry your face," he said, tossing it to her.

She wiped the saltwater from her eyes and dried her neck. Then she handed back his shirt. "Thank you."

"Listen, I can understand how you'd be upset, thinking I'd played a trick on you. But I honestly didn't. Embarrassing you is the last thing I'd want to do."

His contrition made her feel guilty. She could see she'd overreacted. "You're right, Jack, no harm was done," she said, running her fingers through her wet hair.

He sat upright, dropping his legs to either side of his chair. Then, reaching into his back pocket, he took out his comb. "Here, sit down and let me comb the tangles out of your hair."

She was about to decline but, having said no to every overture he'd made, she decided maybe it was time to show a little courage. Without a word, she sat on the end of the lounge chair, between his legs.

Jack began combing her hair, being careful with the tangles. It was a surprisingly intimate gesture, and yet she didn't feel threatened. Jean Claud had never done anything remotely like this. The closest he'd come was putting suntan lotion on her back.

Jack was making quite a production out of the ritual. She couldn't exactly feel his body heat, but knowing he was so close sent shivers through her. She thought about his comment of building trust and wondered if that was what was going on.

He'd finished combing her hair and leaned close to her ear. "I think we'd make a great team, sweetheart," he said. "And I'd like the opportunity to prove it."

"You asking me to take you as a partner."

"Yes."

Jack, she realized, was making his move. His breath on her neck told her it was a two-pronged assault—he was making a play for both her *and* her money. In her mind there was resistance, but not in her body—at least not when he put his arms around her and cuddled her against his chest. She wasn't sure what to do, though she couldn't help tensing. It was reflex.

"You cold?" he asked, his voice disbelieving of another possibility.

"Maybe a little. I was wet when I got dressed."

He moved his face closer until his warm cheek grazed her ear. He was hovering, threatening to kiss her. Wary, she knew the thing to do was stop him. What he was trying to do was so transparent, and she knew exactly what he was after. The only thing she wasn't sure of was how far he'd go. Yet, oddly, she was equally torn between wanting him to continue and wanting him to stop. It was like waiting for a collision, not willing it, but not preventing it, either. Then, when his lips grazed her neck, she drew a breath. She didn't move, sitting very still as he kissed her skin. His mouth was warm and moist, making her flesh tingle. She tried to resist, but the sensation was too inviting, too compelling. Finally she turned to him, making her mouth available. He kissed her and they sank back against the chair.

"Jack," she said, her protest getting no further than his name.

They kissed some more. This was something she often imagined, but never experienced—being in the arms of a stranger. She watched as he moved his hand over the plane of her stomach. Things kept occurring without her consent, like a game of Mother-May-I gone awry. Jack was in control and she made no attempt to assert herself. It was a self-destructive impulse, yet instead of being horrified, she was glad, happy it was beyond her control.

Stephanie laid her head back on his shoulder, savoring the feel of his body. Above, the moon floated in the star-strewn sky, a silent witness, the last vestiges of the storm forgotten. Would it stop at this? she wondered. Would it be enough to hold her and kiss her?

She didn't resist when he cupped her breast. She felt as

though she were fifteen again, being touched for the first time. And after a couple of minutes she grew very excited. Her breathing became erratic and her heart started hammering. Jack laid his hand on her mound and she arched against it, turning her face to kiss him, allowing his tongue to slide in the corner of her mouth.

This was so unlike her, she could hardly believe that she would be doing this with the man she'd watched making love to that girl. Realizing that he was touching *her* now, that it was *her* body that was aroused, heightened her excitement. Her nipples hardened and she writhed against his hand.

She pulled up her skirt. Jack slipped his finger under her panties and drew it up to her moist center, making her cry out. She gyrated against his hand, drawing the sea air into her lungs in gasps, along with the salty heat of his body. She was amazed by how easily and automatically it was happening. It was as though her five years of abstinence meant nothing.

"Oh, God," she moaned as she felt a climax building. "Oh…"

"Stephanie," he murmured, kissing her more fervently.

She'd surrendered completely now, giving herself to this man of the sea, of tropical nights, of storms and sun and writhing naked bodies. Jack was sex and fantasy, lust and sin.

This was, she began to realize, something that had to be done, like when she gotten drunk and given away her virginity. She could not be with this man and remain innocent. The realization flew in the face of everything she believed, the way she'd lived her life, but it was also irrefutable. From the moment she'd seen that girl writhing on Jack Kidwell's body, Stephanie had known that she would have to experience that same pleasure, know him in the same way.

She undulated against his hand, opening her legs wide. Within moments she came, shuddering, pressing his hand hard against her, unable to breathe, her body rigid, waiting for the storm to pass.

In time it did, though her insides continued to throb. Slowly her muscles relaxed and she drifted back to reality. Shame clamored in the background. And embarrassment. This had been no fantasy, she realized. It was raw, unbridled sex.

Uncrossing her legs, she removed his hand. Jack kissed her ear. "You're beautiful," he whispered. "I can't tell you how much I want you."

She'd been oblivious to his desires until now. He'd given her pleasure and now he wanted his. An odd, guilty panic started bubbling in her. "What do you want, Jack?" she asked, though she knew the answer.

"To make love with you."

She stopped his hands from roaming over her and held them against her stomach. "I know you've given me pleasure and now you want yours," she murmured, "but I don't want to make love."

"Why not?"

How did she explain? There wasn't an explanation that didn't sound selfish, insensitive. "I should have stopped you."

"Why?"

"Because it isn't fair that you aren't...satisfied."

"Stephanie, I thought we were making love, not scratching each other's libidos. I don't have a score sheet and you shouldn't, either."

Pushing his hands away, she scooted to the end of the chair, then got to her feet, pulling her skirt down before turning to face him. She was red-faced, utterly humiliated, grateful for the partial darkness. Jack looked up at her, partly perplexed, partly annoyed. She could see it on his face.

"Did that offend you?" he asked.

"Jack, I don't know what got into me. I'm thoroughly embarrassed and ashamed."

"Are you saying that for my benefit or for yours?"

"Please don't make this any harder than it is."

"I'm having trouble understanding the problem."

"Dear God," she said, bringing her hands to her face. She wanted to turn and run, but she was determined to salvage what dignity she could. "Do you know how long I've known you?"

"Something over twenty-four hours."

"Yes, and I've been a widow for only a few days. You know my sexual history. I'm…traumatized by what I did— not what *you* did, what *I* did."

"You think I think you're a slut? Is that what you're saying?"

Stephanie abruptly turned away from him, crossing her arms over her chest. Tears came from nowhere and started rolling down her cheeks. She bit her lip hard, trying not to sob.

"I'm sorry," he said, "that wasn't fair."

She shook her head. "It wasn't your fault. That's what I'm trying to tell you. I'm *apologizing,* Jack. To you!"

She heard him climbing from the chair and she cringed, knowing he was going to touch her. He put his arms around her, and he felt so warm and strong, she wanted all the more to cry. Unable to help herself, she sobbed a couple of times.

His lips were by her ear. "I'm sorry," he whispered. "I badly misread you."

She wept more deeply, and he turned her around and held her tight against his body. She pressed her face into his neck, crying. Jack stroked her back. She felt like a silly child. "I just want to go home," she said. "I'm so tired."

"What you need is sleep. We'll deal with your situation in the morning."

She looked up at him, sniffling. "Why are you being so understanding? Men are supposed to hate this. What I did was unfair. Why aren't you mad at me?"

He gave her a sad grin and wiped the tears off her cheeks with his fingertip. "I don't know, kiddo, maybe I'm just a nice guy."

Sunday
September 29th

Rico Behring had had a little too much Jamaican rum and woke up with a hangover. But with that hurricane blowing outside—even if it was only the ass end—there hadn't been much to do except drink and fuck. When the morning sun came in the window, warming his face, he lifted his head from the pillow and saw that the blonde was gone. Then he heard the sound of the shower.

Dragging himself from the bed, he went into the bathroom. The place was steamed up. The hooker, whose name he couldn't remember to save his soul, was singing softly as she soaped herself behind the frosted glass door. After relieving himself, Rico wrapped on the door with his knuckles.

"Make it snappy, babe. I've got work to do. Time to go home."

"Yeah, sure," she said.

Rico returned to the bedroom and put on his robe. Then he went into the sitting room. Oscar was lounging in an armchair, in a powder blue sport coat, black shirt and trousers. His legs were crossed and he had a cigar in one hand. He had that goddamn superior look on his face. Oscar always looked superior.

"Morning, cousin," Oscar said. "Sleep well?"

"Fuck you, Oscar."

He just smiled.

Rico couldn't look at him without remembering the way Oscar, who was five years older, used to torment him when they were kids. Once, when his family had visited the Barbadillos in Florida, Oscar and his friends took him out to the garage and made him take off his clothes so the neighborhood girls could see his pecker. It still rankled him, after all these years.

"What's the matter," Oscar asked, "didn't the hooker give you a good time?"

"She was a piece of ass," Rico replied dryly. "What do you want for finding her, a medal?"

"It wasn't easy coming up with a blonde with big tits on two hours' notice, Rico. Not in this place. The locals have a corner on the market, and they ain't blond."

"So you're a hero," he said, going to the table by the window where a breakfast of juice, coffee and pastries was waiting. Standing, he took a slug of the orange juice, wincing when it hit his stomach. He put down the glass. "So, have we got a line on the Reymond broad?"

"No, but we're looking," Oscar said, drawing on his cigar. Jutting his chin, he exhaled. To Rico, he seemed to be saying, "Fuck you."

"You damn well better find her," Rico said, dropping into one of the chairs and pulling the robe over his bare leg. He stared out the window at the bay, filled, it seemed, with a million boats. "I still can't believe you fucking had her in your hands and let her get away."

"Believe me, I'm as pissed about that as you are about blowing her husband to pieces when he was the one with our money."

"Don't get on my case!" Rico said, pointing his finger threateningly. "I told them to scare the shit out of the sonovabitch. I didn't tell them to kill him!"

Barbadillo exhaled more smoke, a little smirk at the corner of his mouth, as if to say he didn't believe it.

Rico was steamed. If Oscar wasn't his goddamn cousin, he'd beat the goddamn arrogance right out of him. "Point is, none of that shit matters if we can put our hands on the broad and the computer disks," Rico said. "Where do things stand, anyway? Update me."

"The planes are out looking for her. So far there's nothing, but they tell me Kidwell can't hide a boat like that forever. It's just a matter of time."

"I hope so," Rico said. "The old man is anxiously waiting to hear we got this under control."

"Personally, I think our best shot is the boat jockey."

Rico perked up. "Any word from him, yet?"

"His lady friend hasn't gotten back to me, but she said she would after she talked to him. It's still early."

"Any luck getting a line on her? If Kidwell doesn't play ball with us, it'd be nice to track him down and beat what we want out of him. His friend should be able to tell us where he's hiding , if we can find *her,* that is."

"Already working on that, Rico. She's white, I figure, and speaks with some kind of European accent. How many women can there be in the Virgin Islands who know Kidwell and fit that description?"

"If you locate her, I want to know about it," Rico said, pouring himself some coffee. "I'm not going to let another broad slip through your fingers."

"Tell you what," Oscar said. "I won't let her get away, if you don't blow her to pieces. Fair enough?"

"Fuck you, Oscar."

"Let's keep things in perspective, that's all I'm saying."

Rico tore off a chunk of pastry. "You want to do something useful," Rico said, stuffing the pastry into his mouth, "find me a real woman. A nice, classy Cuban broad. You gotta know a hundred, Oscar. Fly one in from Miami, if you have to."

"I thought you were happily married, cousin. Or has Rhonda stopped giving you blow jobs?"

Rico flipped him off, smirking. "You know what your trouble is, Oscar? You spend so much time trying to get in their heads, you never get any ass."

Oscar puffed on his cigar, grinning. "The real pleasure of sex is in the mind, Rico. You do that and the body takes care of itself."

The door to the bedroom opened and the blonde stepped out. Seeing them, she froze momentarily. Rico and Oscar both looked at her. She'd combed her hair and put on makeup, but her face was puffy. The sizzle was gone. Rico realized what she reminded him of—a Christmas tree in the middle of January.

"Oh, sorry," she said. "Didn't mean to interrupt. I'm going, okay?"

"Hold on, sugar," Rico said. "I want to ask you something."

She had a wary look. "What?"

"How was I last night? Was I a stud or was I a *schmuck*, a *putz?*"

She frowned. "Huh?"

"Scale of one to ten," Rico said. "Was I good, or was I bad?"

"No, wait," Oscar interjected. "That's not the right question. Mind if I rephrase it?"

Rico rolled his eyes. "Sure, why not? You're the expert."

"What's your name, honey?" Oscar asked her.

"Shelly."

"Here's the thing, Shelly," he said. "We're leaving this afternoon, so there's not going to be any repeat business, but you can earn yourself an easy hundred bucks right now."

She hesitated. "Like how?"

Oscar took his money clip from his pocket and peeled off a hundred-dollar bill. "By telling us the God's truth, honest from the heart."

"Like, what do you mean?" Shelly asked, confused.

"Come here," Oscar said. "Come get the hundred."

She didn't move.

"It's okay," he said.

Shrugging, she clomped toward him in her four-inch heels and tight little gold miniskirt. Oscar handed her the bill.

"Now go on to the door," he told her.

She did as he asked.

"Here's the question," he said. "As far as johns go, how was Rico last night?"

She looked back and forth between them as though she figured she was being set up for something.

"The honest truth," Oscar said. "There's no right or wrong answer, just tell me how he was."

Rico looked at him, wondering what the hell was going on.

"Well," she began cautiously, "he was...all right."

"Be more specific," Oscar said. "Was he a great lover? Did he blow you away?"

She cleared her throat. "He was...well, really into fucking me, I guess."

"Meaning?"

"He was kinda rough."

"Kinda rough, huh?"

"Rougher than most guys, I'd say."

"Last question, Shelly," Oscar said. "Say you're setting your little sister up for her first trick. You get to pick the john. Scale of one to ten, ten being the best. What do you rate Rico, here?"

"My sister?"

"Right."

She pondered the question, then said, "I don't know. Three, maybe four, something like that."

"Thanks, Shelly," Oscar said. "You can go now. Buy yourself a new dress."

The woman left the suite.

Rico glared at his cousin. "What the fuck was that supposed to prove?"

"I wanted you to see yourself through Rhonda's eyes," Oscar said.

"Rhonda? What does *she* have to do with this?"

"I'll give you odds she'd rate you the same way as Shelly."

"Yeah, well, fuck you, Oscar! If you're so goddamn smooth, why'd the Reymond woman jump out of the window? Why wasn't she begging to suck your cock?"

"Excellent point."

"Huh?"

"I mishandled her, I admit. Next time I get hold of her, it's going to be different."

"Don't tell me. You're going to have her on her knees, begging for it."

Oscar drew on his cigar, smiling. "Rico, you're smarter than I thought."

Rico gulped down some coffee and got to his feet. "All right, Casanova, you've had your say. Now we both know that you think like a whore. Great. How about getting your butt out of here and finding that goddamn housewife? Seems to me a perfect job for a guy with your talents."

Oscar got to his feet. Chuckling, he left the suite.

Rico stared after him, feeling the same hatred for Oscar he'd felt toward him as a kid. It was like having to take his clothes off in front of the girls all over again. Fuming, he went to the bathroom to shave and have his shower.

He was in the middle of lathering his face when he slammed the brush down in the sink and stomped into the bedroom, where he picked up the phone. He dialed a number in Long Beach. It took him five or six rings before there was an answer.

"Yeah?" came the sleepy voice on the other end of the line.

"Driscoll? Rico Behring. Look, I know it's the middle of

the night, but I want to know what my fucking wife has been doing?''

"Doing?" the groggy voice replied. "She hasn't been doing anything special."

"Do you have somebody watching the house?"

"Yes. We've got her under surveillance twenty-four hours a day, just like you wanted."

"And she's alone there with the kid?"

"As of the last report I got."

"When was that?" Rico asked.

"Seven o'clock last night."

"Christ, she could have fucked a motorcycle gang since then. Find out what's happened since seven, will you? I gotta know."

"You want me to find out now?"

"Yes, something wrong with that, Wayne? I'm paying you good money, aren't I?"

"Right, Mr. Behring. Let me try to raise Jerry on the radio. Give me a minute."

"Take as long as you want. I just want to know what the bitch has been doing."

After Wayne Driscoll put down the phone, Rico stood there impatiently, looking at the bed. The hooker had been gone for ten minutes, but he could still smell her perfume in the room. What was it about cheap hookers and their cheap perfume that always gave him a hard-on? He almost wished now he'd had her stay.

In a couple of minutes the private investigator came back on the line. "I talked to Jerry," he said.

"And?"

"Your wife has been at home all night."

"Anybody come over?"

"Not a soul, Mr. Behring."

"You sure? Your guy didn't go out for a pizza or anything?"

"Somebody's been there watching the house every minute."

"When she leaves, I want to know every fucking place she goes, Wayne. I don't want thirty seconds unaccounted for."

"I know that," Driscoll said. "That's what you're paying for, that's what we're doing."

"I'll call for a report later."

"Yes, Mr. Behring."

Rico put down the phone. There was a crumpled pillow on the side of the bed nearest him that the blonde had wedged under her hips when he'd fucked her. He picked it up and pressed it to his face. But he didn't picture the blonde, he pictured Rhonda and thought about what Oscar had said. It was true, Rhonda sometimes told him he was too rough, but he'd hardly given it any thought. She came when he fucked her. What more could she want?

In a sudden pique of anger, Rico hurled the pillow across the room, hitting a lamp and knocking it over. "Bitch," he muttered under his breath. Somebody was boffing her, he was sure of it. He'd have sworn it was her personal trainer, especially when Rhonda insisted the guy was gay. So Rico had hired a couple of thugs to take the sonovabitch apart. They beat him to a bloody pulp, but they didn't get a thing out of him, except that he really was a queer, like Rhonda said. Rico ended up having to give the guy ten grand to quiet him down, and he still didn't know who was fucking his wife.

And now he had this bitch, Stephanie Reymond, to worry about. She was making fools of all of them. She was also on the verge of slipping away with their money. Rico was determined that wouldn't happen. Whatever it took, he'd nail her ass and he'd get their money back. She'd find out it didn't pay to fuck with Rico Behring. If the world didn't know that already, it would soon enough.

Isola Lovejoy

It was after nine when Stephanie awoke. By the time she'd showered, done her hair and put on one of the little summer dresses Malva had left her, it was quarter to ten. She wandered into the kitchen where Tess, perspiring despite the mild temperature, was squeezing oranges, having half filled a pitcher with fresh juice.

"Malva's out in the garden, doin' her books," the cook said. "She say you can come on out, have your coffee and breakfast, if you wants. I got the fixins for a nice cheese omelet, if you want."

"That'd be fine, Tess. Where's Captain Kidwell, by the way? Is he up yet?"

"Oh, he been up before me. We have us a cup of coffee with the birds and he gone down to his boat. Say he be busy all day long. 'Spect he's comin' back when he gets hungry enough."

Stephanie thanked Tess and headed for the garden, wondering what Jack was thinking...and if she'd have the courage to look him in the eye after last night. The sleep she'd gotten had refreshed her, but she was no less confused than she'd been the night before. Common sense told her what he really wanted was a cut of the money. He'd said as much. Sure he'd tried to seduce her, but she'd be a fool to think that had anything to do with his feelings. It was all part of his scheme. And yet, as certain as she was of that, she didn't want to believe it.

Stephanie found Malva, sleek as a fashion model in a little purple crepe dress and ivory jewelry, at a table in the garden. Her ebony hair was slicked back like the night before, but she had on more makeup. Light filtered down through a vine-covered lattice arbor that sheltered the patio. The area was enclosed on the back side by a rock garden with ferns and a gurgling fountain. Open before the housekeeper on the table were a commercial checkbook and ledger, and what appeared to be a stack of bills.

"Good morning, Mrs. Reymond," Malva said, looking up. "How did you sleep?"

"It's Stephanie, please. And I slept well, thank you. Your hospitality has been wonderful. I'm very grateful."

Malva indicated for her to sit. "Any friend of Jackie's is a friend of ours."

Stephanie sat across from her. "Do all his friends call him Jackie?"

"I don't know about all. Alicia did. I'm not sure which of us started it."

"Alicia is your cousin, the one Jack was engaged to."

"Yes."

Stephanie wondered if Jack and Alicia were a sensitive issue for Malva. But she was curious about Jack's past and she wasn't sure she'd have other opportunities to hear about it from a third party. "He must have loved her very much," she said tentatively.

"Oh, he did. Told me once when they were together it was the only time in his life he was happy. She made him feel good like his money never did. Stopped drinkin' for her, too. 'Course, she gave him an ultimatum. For two years he didn't drink at all. After she died...well, it wasn't pretty."

"Losing someone you love is the hardest thing in life to bear," Stephanie said.

"Jackie's had his miseries, all right. He lost his baby when he lost Alicia," Malva said. "She was pregnant when she drowned."

"Oh no."

"Nobody but Jackie and me knew she was carryin' his baby. That's when they decided to get married. Not that they wouldn't have, anyway. That girl was so happy. She talked what a lovin' man he was. Strong man with a soft touch. And she was the prettiest little thing you'd ever seen. Could have been a model if she wanted."

Tears welled in Stephanie's eyes at the thought of the pain Jack had been through. "Poor guy."

"I been tellin' him he needs to fall in love again, but he don't want to hear it." Malva closed the check register. "I don't know if I should be sayin' this, but when he's around you, I see a little extra sparkle in his eye."

"Jack likes women."

"No, Stephanie, this could be different. He likes you, I can tell."

Stephanie's first thought was that Jack had enlisted Malva in his conspiracy, that he was going to slip her a little money to help him win the woman confidence. But that was so cynical, she didn't want to believe it any more than she wanted to believe Jack's attraction to her was insincere. And yet, how could she ignore the possibility?

"He has a definite business interest in me, Malva," she said. "My late husband's business has created a...financial opportunity...and Jack wants to help me exploit it. We're kind of in negotiations now. That's probably as good a way to put it as any."

"I see."

"If you were in my shoes, would you trust him?" Stephanie asked.

"That's a little like askin' if you're going to like my favorite chocolate cake as much as I do. I trust Jackie personally, but should you? Lordy, how would I know?"

"Seems to me a man is either trustworthy or he isn't," Stephanie said.

"I think it's a whole lot more complicated than that, honey. Every situation has many questions."

"Relative morality."

"Ma'am?"

"I think I understand you, Malva."

"I won't say a bad word about Jack Kidwell," the woman said. He's always been a friend to me. And I've never known him to hurt a soul."

"He's had trouble with the law in the past."

"That was in a different life. I don't expect you're the same person today you were ten years ago," Malva said.

It was a good point. If Jean Claud Reymond's wife of ten years ago could have seen her on the beach last night with Jack Kidwell, she had no doubt she'd have been aghast. But sexual mores weren't her principal concern. The fact remained—if Jack was thinking twenty percent of thirty million, they were talking six million dollars. That was enough to test anyone's values.

Malva began gathering her papers. "Well, if you'll excuse me, please, I've got a lot to do. Mr. Lovejoy had a little surprise for me this mornin' when he called. Him and his French girlfriend are comin'. They'll be arrivin' tomorrow night."

"He's coming here?"

"Yes, ma'am. He likes to drop in without much notice."

"I guess that means we'd better start looking for a hotel."

"No, no. When I told him Jackie was here with a lady friend, he was thrilled out of his shoes. They've been close for years, you know."

"They cut a wide swath across the Caribbean from what I understand."

"Mr. Lovejoy likes nothin' better than to have a good time. So I hope you're ready." Malva got to her feet and lifted the stack of papers. For some reason there was sadness in her smile.

"I think I'd better talk to Jack," Stephanie said. "I'm sure he'll give an honest opinion whether I should go or stay."

"He already told me he's expectin' you'll stay."

Tess came out the door with a tray. Malva gave Stephanie a conspiratorial smile and left.

Stephanie didn't know what to make of the conversation. Was the hand of Jack Kidwell behind Malva's advice, or was she being paranoid again? There was much she would have to accept on faith, Stephanie realized, if she was going to do business with the man. Should she trust him or not? And just as important, could she trust herself?

After breakfast Stephanie found a book in Nigel's library and went onto the veranda to read. From the big wicker chair where she sat she was able to see the *Lucky Lady*. Occasionally she caught a glimpse of Jack, shirtless and in sunglasses, moving around the deck. But most of the time he was below, probably repairing the damage caused by the storm.

Having thought about it, she decided he was avoiding her, probably to give her space, knowing she'd be embarrassed. She needed time to recover her dignity, time to fret about what to do, time maybe for her desperation to grow and to want to throw her lot in with him.

Only two things were certain—Jack always had the option of selling her to Oscar Barbadillo, but if he wanted the quarter of a million, he needed the disks. They were her ace in the hole. With them, she was worth much more. What she couldn't be sure of was whether Jack was really going for the grand prize, the six million. And, if so, should she be glad?

Tess came out the door then, interrupting Stephanie's brooding. The woman was puffing hard and seemed to be looking for someone. "'Scuse me, missus, but you seen Joseph?"

"No, not this morning."

"Oh, Lord, wouldn' you know. Malva say he got to tell Captain Jack Miss Sonia done call again. He have to call her back, urgent-like."

"Do you want me to tell him?"

"Would you mind, missus? The way I move it'll be suppertime by the time I get down there, and I still got lunch cookin' on the stove."

"I'd be glad to," Stephanie said, getting up.

She headed for the steps and Tess went back inside. Stephanie was halfway down the sloping lawn when Jack reappeared on deck, flipping his dark glasses down from where they were nestled in his sun-bleached hair. She called out to him, but he didn't seem to hear her. So she hurried to catch him before he went belowdecks again. "Jack!" Running, she called to him again. "Jack!"

This time he looked up, shading his eyes as he peered toward the shore. She waved. Spotting her, he waved back.

"Want to come on board?" he called to her.

"Malva said you've had an urgent phone call."

Jack acknowledged her with a flick of his hand. He went to the other side of the boat, where she assumed the launch was located. Seconds later, she heard the outboard engine start. The boat appeared and, within minutes, he'd reached shore, stepping out into the ankle-deep water.

"Do you know who called?" he asked.

"Your friend Sonia."

"Oh, maybe your pals at Inter-America have upped the ante. Could be you're worth half a million now," he said with a sly grin as he dragged the launch onto the beach.

"Great. Is that remark meant to put me at ease?"

"Better than playing coy, isn't it?"

They started up the lawn, and he surprised her by putting his arm around her waist. "So, how are you this morning?"

"I'm okay. How are you?"

"I've been worrying," he said.

"About what?"

"The way you'd react after last night."

"I'm doing my best to salvage my dignity, but frankly, Jack, I'd rather not talk about it."

He pulled her against him and their hips bumped. "That's cool."

Stephanie couldn't believe he was being so open, so carefree. It wasn't the response she'd expected. She managed to separate herself from him, and they walked along, side by side.

"So, Sonia is the go-between with Oscar. Is that how it works?"

"Yes."

"You must feel she's trustworthy."

"I do. Why?"

"I've been thinking. She knows where you are and therefore where I am. What's to keep her from doing business with Inter-America herself?"

"Friendship."

"She must be a very good friend."

"Don't worry about Sonia. She's good people."

They'd arrived at the house. Stephanie stopped at the top of the steps. "Well, good luck," she said.

Jack glanced back. "Let's hope all's well." He went inside.

Stephanie drifted over toward the wicker chair where she'd been sitting, wishing she didn't feel so powerless, so out of control. For all she knew, Jack was selling her at this very moment, and there wasn't a damn thing she could do about it.

The number on Malva's note was not Sonia's telephone number. That gave him pause. Jack calculated the possible dangers and could see nothing immediate. He dialed.

"*Sí,* hello?" came a frail, Spanish-accented voice on the other end of the line. It was a woman's voice, but totally unfamiliar to him.

"Is Sonia Velasco there, please?"

"Who thees is?" the aged-sounding woman asked.

"Jack," he said, warily.

There was fumbling on the other end of the line, then Sonia's voice. "Jack?"

"What's going on, Sonia?"

"Trouble. A friend of Enrique's in the police department called late last night and told me your friends were offering five grand for the name and address of your white lady friend with a European accent. He told me to get out, so I tossed some things in a bag and came to Enrique's mother's place on Fortuna Bay."

"Is that where you are now?"

"Yes, and I'm not feeling real good about it."

"Will you be safe there?"

"I think so, but I can't hide out forever."

"You won't have to, Sonia," he said. "This thing should be over in a few days. I'm really sorry it's come to this. I'll make it up to you. I promise."

"I don't expect anything. I did it to help you."

"I appreciate that, too," he said, "believe me."

"I don't know what you've gotten yourself into," Sonia said, "but that woman is trouble. Enrique's friend said the police are trying to track down everybody who was on her flight to St. Thomas. Unofficially, of course."

"You're kidding."

"No, you can't believe the money that's being waved around, Jack. I wouldn't be surprised if the governor declares a territorial holiday so the citizens can pitch in and help find Mrs. Reymond."

He couldn't hear anything in Sonia's voice that indicated Inter-America's largesse was talking to her. She had money and, though she wasn't rich, she lived comfortably—before her marriage to Enrique Velasco, during and since.

"Maybe you should lay low," he said. "No sense taking unnecessary risks."

"You don't want me to tell them what you've decided?"

Jack thought for a moment. "Can you get word to Barbadillo without compromising yourself?"

"A phone call should be safe enough."

He glanced toward the closed door of Nigel's study, lowering his voice. "Tell them I should be able to put my hands on the disks in two or three days."

"Is that all?"

"No, say I've confirmed that they contain Reymond's complete book of accounts, including the skinny on Inter-America Ventures. And tell him the price is five hundred thousand for the package, half on delivery of the disks, half for the woman."

There was a silence on the line. Then, "Jack, are you sure about this?"

"Trust me, Sonia. I know what I'm doing. But I don't want you taking any risks. Keep your pretty head down, okay?"

He could almost hear the wheels turning.

"Speaking of pretty heads," she said, "what does this woman look like?"

He drew a long breath. "She's attractive."

"Somehow I thought she was."

"Why?"

"Oh, Jack," Sonia said with a sigh, "I just know."

Her tone, more than her words, made him uneasy. "It's business," he said.

"Yeah, sure," she said. "Well, you've got this number if you need anything." Then she hung up.

Stephanie had been thinking about Nigel Lovejoy's arrival and wondered if he might not be her best bet for getting back to the States. True, he was Jack's friend, but Nigel was also a successful businessman, and bright men were usually reasonable. Jean Claud had been…at least when it came to business.

"My, but aren't you a study in rapture?"

She looked over to see Jack leaning against one of the columns. "Hardly," she said. "I was thinking about my husband, to be perfectly frank." That was a bit of an exaggeration, but it was close enough to the truth.

"Maybe reality is beginning to hit you."

"I don't think so. I can regret his death, but not my loss."

Jack walked over, pulling up a straight chair, signaling he wished to talk. He'd washed, but hadn't shaved. The Jack Kidwell she saw was reminiscent of the one she'd seen that first day on the *Lucky Lady*. His proximity, his direct, unapologetic manner, made her feel wobbly. This, she now knew with certainty, was a man who could put practically any woman off her game.

"I'm afraid your enemies have turned things up a notch," he said. He told her what he'd learned from Sonia.

Stephanie had an awful, sinking feeling as she calculated the implications of questioning the other passengers. What were the chances the police would track down Brian and Tiffany? She didn't know how long they planned to stay in the Caribbean, but chances were they hadn't left for home, which meant it was a good bet Barbadillo would eventually find out the alligator case had been stored in the locker.

"If they're talking to people from the plane, the game may be over soon," she said obliquely.

"Did you give the disks to another passenger?"

"To put in safekeeping, yes. But they'll have no problem making her say where."

"Can you contact her?" he asked.

"I don't know where she's staying, Jack. Or even if she's still on St. Thomas."

"We can hope she's left."

"I wouldn't want to bet on it."

They each considered the situation in silence.

Then Jack said, "If you'll tell me her name, maybe I can have Sonia track her down so you can warn her. A dozen calls would probably do it."

It was the closest he'd come to asking outright where the disks were hidden. Did that mean Oscar Barbadillo had asked him to find out if a passenger from the plane was involved and, if so, who? "The poor girl's on her honeymoon," she said. "I don't want to spoil it for her by making her worry."

"The police could spoil it for her if you don't."

"Yes, but all she'd have to do is tell them the truth, and she has no reason not to."

"Meanwhile, you lose the disks and maybe your inheritance," he said.

She looked him in the eye. "I guess that's a risk I'm willing to take."

Jack did not seem pleased, but he didn't argue. "It's your decision," he said. With that he got up, but he didn't walk away. He stared up at the sky as though there were something in the big fluffy clouds he needed to know. After a while he turned to her, his face relaxed, the intensity gone. "I've got work to do, so if you'll please excuse me."

Stephanie immediately felt bad. It was as though she'd accused him falsely. Poor Jack, damned by his past. "Need help?" she asked.

He smiled. "Thanks, but no. I'm used to working alone." With that, he walked away.

Brentwood,

Los Angeles, California

Julius Behring, unshaved and in a foul mood, peered out the window of the big Mercedes SL500 as it pulled to the curb a few doors down from his son's home. Abe Green, a friend from the old days, was next to him in the back seat. A man who worked for Abe named Sammy was driving. The other car with four more of Abe's men were behind them.

Julius and Abe rarely saw one another anymore, not since Julius had severed all connections with local organized crime some twenty years ago. Abe understood and, because their relationship had been more personal than professional, there had been no repercussions. Five years ago Julius had done his friend a favor and now he was calling in the marker. He didn't like needing Abe's help, but he couldn't see any way around it. Julius knew that, left to his own devices, Rico would kill somebody and end up in prison or worse. So, Julius had reluctantly taken matters into his own hands.

"That must be the private investigator," Julius said, gesturing toward the sedan parked across the street. It was dawn and the light was still a bit weak for his aging eyes.

"Whoever it is, he's getting out," Sammy said. He was a big kid, with the bad habit of talking a little too loud. "Want him to come here, Mr. Behring?"

"Yes."

Sammy lowered the window and waved his hand. The door of the sedan slammed closed and Wayne Driscoll, looking disheveled, made his way toward them. He walked to the Mercedes and climbed in front on the passenger side.

"'Morning, Mr. Behring," he said, glancing at the others and looking none too pleased with what he saw.

"These are friends of mine," Julius said, knowing it was best not to be more specific than that. "So, what's the story? Romeo still there?"

Wayne Driscoll, a bland man in his late forties, nodded. "Yeah, Mr. Behring, that's his Carrera in the driveway."

Julius looked, shaking his head. "He couldn't even park up the street?"

"It's been there all night and so's he."

"What could the bitch be thinking?" Julius said, incredulous. "It's like she wants to get caught."

"She must not know Rico's onto her," Driscoll said.

"Well, let's not get into that," Julius said.

The previous evening, when Driscoll had telephoned to say Rhonda's lover was at the house, Julius decided the time had come to act. "Two things," he'd told the P.I., "first is, Rico can't know about it. I don't care what he asks, Rhonda's clean. Second, I've got to hear everything that happens first, like when the guy arrives and when he leaves. If he stays with her tonight, I'm going to pay him and Rhonda a visit first thing in the morning. I'll have a few friends with me. Plan on meeting me at the house at six."

Julius had telephoned Abe, who'd gotten back to him on a clear phone. "I'm going to need that little favor we talked about," Julius had told him.

"Sure thing," Abe had replied. "Just tell me where and when."

So here they were at Rico's, and the guy's car was in the driveway. Julius didn't have any of his son's Latin blood in his veins, but he was outraged on Rico's behalf, just the same.

"Tell me about Romeo, Wayne," Julius said.

"Name's Dan Hachigian," Driscoll replied. "Sells rugs out of a store on San Vicente. Fancy stuff, Chinese, whatever. Guy wears Italian suits, gold Rolex, diamond pinkie ring."

"Real cute," Julius said. "And Rhonda's fucking him?"

"She's been in the rug store four, five times the last two weeks. She was in there yesterday maybe three hours. When she came out she didn't have any rugs. Nothing ever gets delivered to the house. This is the first time he's come to see her, best we can tell. That's why I called you. He hasn't left since we talked and I don't think they're in there playing gin rummy, Mr. Behring."

"Good thing Rico's in the Caribbean. Otherwise there'd be two corpses in there right now. What else do we know about Hachigian?" Julius asked.

"Married. Lives in San Fernando. He's got two sons about eight and ten."

"The schmuck's not a fucking Arab, is he?"

"Armenian."

"That's better, anyway."

There was an extended silence. Julius considered the situation. He hated the thought of violence, but in this instance he could see no other way. Hachigian needed a lesson, but Rhonda needed one even more. If she didn't learn it this way, she'd never learn it.

"Okay, Wayne, thanks," Julius said. "You can take off now."

"What do I say when Rico calls?"

"Same as before. Everything's normal. I'm the one that gets the straight story, and only me."

"Right, Mr. Behring." Driscoll got out of the Mercedes and returned to his own car. Starting the engine, he drove off.

As soon as he was out of sight, Abe spoke in his grumbly voice. "So, what are we going to do to the motherfucker?"

"Mr. Hachigian's going to have to learn that if he fucks another man's wife, he pays. I want him convinced, but not permanently injured. I'm open to suggestions on how best to accomplish that. The important thing is that I don't see him and he doesn't see me. It's Rhonda, my daughter-in-law, I need to speak with."

Abe rubbed his jaw. "How about this. We'll go in the back and, if they're in bed, we'll drag them out. Scare the shit out of them. One of the boys can bring the woman to the front room and let you in the door when you ring the bell. Meanwhile, we'll work the guy over in back, make the shithead understand that if we ever see his face again, he's a dead man."

"My granddaughter will be there, but she's just a toddler. I'd rather she not be disturbed."

"We'll ask the guy to keep his voice down while we squeeze his balls," Abe said, his burly body shaking as he laughed.

"You might wish to suggest he sell his store and move to Jersey or something," Julius said.

"He'll be glad to go by the time we finish with him, Julius."

"I'll need to speak with Rhonda for a while, then I'll leave."

"And we'll take Hachigian out in the desert someplace where he's got a long walk home. Preferably without shoes."

"You're the expert."

"We ready then?" Abe said.

"Yes."

"All right," he said to Sammy, "let's do this quick and be out of here before the newspaper is delivered and the kid wakes up."

Abe and Sammy got out of the Mercedes. Julius heard the doors of the car behind them open and close. He consulted his watch as the men made their way to Rico's house, a Mediterranean job with a tile roof. After they'd entered the side gate and disappeared from sight, Julius sat staring at little Andrea's tricycle, which was at the foot of the steps where Rhonda's goddamn lover could have tripped on it. He shook his head. Christ, why couldn't Rico have found a woman like his mother? Rhonda was a slut. She'd told Rico she was an actress when they met, but all she'd done was sleep with producers and directors, hoping to be an actress. What kind of wife and mother did a woman like that make?

After another three minutes Julius got out of the car. He slowly made his way up the street, his arthritic joints barking until he came to the walk leading to Rico's house. There was a big magnolia tree in the middle of the lawn. It was beautiful but it needed work. Julius made a mental note to have his tree man come over. At the foot of the steps, he picked up the tricycle and carried it to the door. Cocking his head, he listened. Inside he could hear voices. And Rhonda crying. He rang the bell. After a few seconds Sammy opened the door. Still carrying the tricycle, Julius walked past him into the entry hall. He went to the arched doorway leading to the front room.

His daughter-in-law stood by the fireplace, weeping into her hands, her red hair disheveled, her long white legs protruding from a filmy moss-colored peignoir. One glance and Julius could see it was all she had on.

Muffled cries came from the back of the house. Sammy had already gone off in that direction. Julius stared at his son's wife, barely able to disguise his contempt.

"Rhonda!" he called, his voice sharp.

She looked up, her eyes rounding in horror. She crossed her arms over her huge breasts and began shaking her head pleadingly, her eyes ghoulish from the mascara running down her cheeks. She sobbed and moaned, but could manage no words.

"Who's bike is this?" he asked, lifting the plastic tricycle.

Her mouth opened but no words came out.

"Does it belong to Dan's kid?" he shouted.

She stared at him incredulously.

"Rhonda! I asked you a question. Does this belong to Dan's kid?"

She shook her head. "No, it's Andrea's," she squeaked.

"Andrea? Who's Andrea? Is that Dan's kid?"

"No," she said, sobbing. "She's Rico's."

"Oh, she's Rico's. Your husband. That's who you were sleeping with last night, then. Andrea's father, in his bed. Is that right, Rhonda?"

She couldn't speak. She could only sob and shake her head.

Julius dropped the tricycle on the carpet. "Am I in the wrong house?" He went over to the big wing-back chair and dropped into it heavily. He rubbed his chin. "No," he said, "it's the right house. But the wrong guy is in the bed. That's what's the matter with this picture."

A horrible muffled cry came from the back of the house. Rhonda peered toward the doorway and began wringing her hands. Her body trembled.

"How do I explain this to my son?" Julius asked miserably.

"Pop, he'll kill me. You know he'll kill me. Please," she implored. "Please."

"Fine time to be thinking about that, Rhonda. Better you keep your pants on when your husband's gone instead of dick around with some scummy rug salesman. Don't you see this is my name you're screwing with?"

"What can I do to make up for it, Pop?" she begged. "Please, tell me what I can do."

He stared at her, hating the fact that he had a whore for a daughter-in-law. There was nothing as despicable as a woman without morals. If Rico found out, she was dead. Rhonda had that part right.

"Come here," he commanded. "We have to talk."

"Pop," she said, beseeching him. "Let me get dressed. Please."

"Dressed? What for? Doesn't matter what you've got on. You're the same whore clothed or naked. Come here."

She inched her way toward him, covering her pubis with one hand and doing what she could to cover her breasts with the other. Reaching his chair, she dropped to her knees at his feet. Tears continued to flow down her blackened cheeks.

"I'm going to ask you some questions," he said. "Some of the answers I already know, some I don't. But you're going to tell me the truth. Do we understand each other?"

"Yes, but are you going to tell Rico?"

"That was a question, Rhonda. I'm asking. You're answering." He cleared his throat. "How long you been sleeping with Hachigian?"

"For about a month."

"Where?"

"Mostly in his office at his store. Once at the Beverly Hilton. And once…"

"In Rico's bed?"

She dropped her face into her hands. Julius wondered if he wouldn't be doing everybody a favor by telling Abe to take her and Hachigian both out in the desert and put holes in their heads. But Rico wouldn't be able to live with somebody else having to do it for him, and Rico definitely did not need to kill his wife.

"How many other guys have there been?" Julius asked, his stomach turning to acid.

"Two. Once with a beach bum in Jamaica when I went there with my sister. And a guy at the Mercedes dealership. The mechanic."

"You fucked a grease monkey?"

"It was after Rico went to Las Vegas with that whore. Pop, he made me watch a video of him screwing her while he made love with me in our bedroom."

Julius rolled his eyes. "Jesus."

"It was only once. I was so upset with Rico. I…wanted to punish him. It was the first time since my marriage I was with another man. I swear it. It was because of what Rico did."

"I don't want justification. Rico is hotheaded and when he's drunk he does stupid things. You knew who and what he was going in. You're a woman. You're supposed to understand his mistakes."

"What about *my* mistakes, Pop?" she implored.

"That's what we're talking about now, Rhonda, your mistakes."

"What do you want me to do, Pop? I'll do anything you want. Swear to God. I'll cut off my finger. Anything."

"Just answer me this. Do you love Rico?" He held up his hand. "Think before you answer because I want the truth."

She thought for a moment. "I love him, but sometimes I hate him."

"Are you going to tell me you were screwing Hachigian and thinking about Rico?"

She lifted her chin, looking him right in the eye. "A couple of times I did. I wanted to make Rico watch a video of me, just like he made me."

Julius swallowed the bile in his throat. "I guess you're saying these disgusting things because they're true. Okay, fine, Rhonda, but that isn't how things are going to be from now on, so listen real careful. I can't make you into a saint like Rico's mother, but I can be sure you don't mess around behind my son's back. First time you get out of line, Rico hears everything. But he won't have to believe my words because I got a video of you and Hachigian in his office. I went to a lot of trouble to get it. So I'm glad you told the truth about fucking him in his office, because if you didn't, I would have known you were a goddamn liar in addition to a whore and the same thing would have happened to you that's happening to Dan."

Just then a moan of agony came from the back of the house, followed by cries for mercy. Rhonda looked as though she'd be sick.

"What are you going to do to him, Pop? You aren't going to kill him, are you?"

"Do you care?"

"Only because it's my fault," she said, looking him in the eye. "He thinks Rico is always gone because he doesn't love me."

Behring was surprised. It was the first honorable thing he'd ever heard her say. "Assuming he does as he's told, he's not going to be killed. Right now I'm more concerned about you. You're either going to become a new person, or wish you had. You see, Rhonda, from today on you're going to be a *Good Housekeeping* wife and mother, or you're going to die trying."

"I will, Pop. I swear I will."

"I want you to tell Rico that, not me."

"Rico?"

"Yes, we're going to call him and you're going to tell him how much you love him and then you're going to tell him I'm here and that I've come to take you and Andrea to Disneyland. Then you're going to let me talk to him. Do we understand each other?"

"Yes, Pop."

Julius Behring reached into his jacket pocket and took out his cell phone. Then he got out his glasses and the slip of paper with the number of Rico's hotel in St. Thomas. He dialed. "Rico Behring, please," he said to the operator.

"Yeah?" came his son's voice after a moment.

"Rico, it's me."

"Pop, I was about to call you, but I figured it was still too early."

"Yeah, well, we need to talk, but first I've got somebody here who wants to say hello. Hang on." Looking deep into Rhonda's eyes, his finger on the mute button, Julius said, "This is your last chance to become a good wife and mother. Start now, Rhonda, or as God's my witness, I'll kill you myself before Rico has a chance. It's up to you."

Rhonda's eyes were huge blue puddles as he shoved the phone in her direction. She took the phone, looking as though she might die before she could speak.

"Hi ya, bunny," she croaked, her lip trembling. She looked up at Julius, wiping her eyes, smearing the black all over her cheeks. "No, honey, Pop's here at our house. He's come to take Andy and me to Disneyland. Isn't that sweet?...Yeah, but I wish you could come, too. Andy and I really miss you....I love you so much, Rico," she said, staring at Behring. "And I've been thinking about you, wishing you were home....No, everything's fine. Can't a woman miss her husband?...Do you really miss me, Rico? Swear you do?" She gave Julius a beseeching look. "Yeah, bunny, I love you more than ever and I want you to hurry home. Now here's Pop."

Biting her lip, she handed the cell phone back to Julius and sobbed softly. He pressed the mute button. "That's a good start," he told her. "If you can learn to believe what you just said, you're going to be a happy woman. It's all in your hands, Rhonda."

She nodded. "I know, Pop."

He released the mute button and spoke into the phone. "Hang on a second, Rico." He pressed the mute button again. "All right," he said to Rhonda, "now go get dressed. It's going to be a little messy back there. You're going to have to clean up the place later. But don't say a word to anybody. As far as you're concerned, Hachigian's dead. You never met the schmuck. You're never going to think about him."

"Okay, Pop."

"Now go."

She got to her feet and ran from the room. Julius glanced at her ass through the negligee, shaking his head. He figured she had a fifty-fifty shot. She'd keep her nose clean for a year or two, but he knew in his heart that making the marriage last was more up to Rico than it was to her.

"Okay, what's up, son?" he said into the phone.

"Things are moving fast, Pop. The captain may be delivering our friend *and* the goodies in a matter of days. I think he's being straight with us. Sent word that there are copies of Reymond's account books for our investments on the disks, which means our ass is hanging out."

Julius did not like the sound of this. "That makes getting those materials doubly important, Rico."

"Yeah, and the sonovabitch knows it. He's getting greedy. Wants five hundred big ones for the package."

"So, he's a businessman."

"Goddamn pirate's more like it."

"A sharp trader takes what the market will bear, Rico. Tell him I'll pay five hundred once we verify the content of the goods and have the woman in our hands. But tell Captain Hook if he tries to squeeze any more, we might find it cheaper to sink his boat and catch our own fish."

"I'll tell him, Pop."

"Anything else develop?"

"You know the captain's lady friend, the one we been talking to?"

"Yeah."

"Well, we know who she is, but she felt the heat comin' and took a powder. So we're lookin' for her, too."

"Christ, Rico, before this job is done you'll be looking for half the people in the Caribbean. Next it's going to be that bastard Fidel Castro. Better I go ahead and hire the goddamn Marine Corps."

"We'll take what we're owed, plus expenses, out of Reymond's money," Rico said. "I figure that'll come to about thirty million, if we include profit."

"Yeah, well, there's one more problem. Our sources tell us that the money is coming down earlier than they thought, could be as little as a week. So there's a little more pressure to get those items, Rico. It would be nice if you turn something up in the next day or two."

"I'm workin' on it, Pop, believe me."

"And how's Oscar?"

There was a silence on the line, then Rico said, "Oscar's Oscar. Sometimes it seems he's more interested in tail than the work, but he's fine."

"You two getting along okay?"

"How could we not, Pop?"

"Yeah, well, remember what I told you about two heads being better than one."

"Right."

"One other thing. I've hired a man named Alexander Manring to watch things for us in the Cayman Islands. He came highly recommended. He knows people in the banks and the government. Manring has your number and will be contacting you with updates and to coordinate operations," Julius said.

"Pop, the Cayman Islands are a thousand miles away. The woman and Kidwell couldn't have gotten that far."

"I know, but if they know what we know, that's where they'll be headed. And if they slip through your fingers, they could always fly there. I decided the smart thing was to be waiting for them."

"Okay. Anything else, Pop?"

"Yes, a piece of advice. When you come home, why don't you bring your wife a nice present?"

"What for?"

"Because she loves you, son."

Rico was silent, then he said, "All right, Pop. If you say so, I'll bring her something."

"And another thing. You're a grown man, I know, but I'm going to say this anyway. Don't come home with a case of the clap, Rico. It's not good for your marriage."

Monday,
September 30th

Isola Lovejoy

Stephanie had breakfast on the veranda where she could watch Jack at work. She'd gotten up fairly early, but the household was already buzzing. Malva, Tess and Joseph were busy preparing for Nigel's arrival, and Jack, determined to get the *Lucky Lady* shipshape, had, according to Tess, gone out shortly after dawn. Stephanie had poured herself some coffee and, over Tess's objection, had carried a plate of fruit, bread and jam onto the terrace.

The previous evening at dinner she'd asked Jack if it was really all right for her to be there when Nigel arrived, and he'd assured her everything was copacetic. They hadn't talked a great deal more, though Jack had confirmed his intention to phone Jean Claud's investment bankers, Meriwether & Handley, in the morning. Stephanie knew it was a good idea. Due to the time difference, they agreed to make the call after lunch.

Since she'd arrived on the veranda, Jack had been working in plain view, moving around the deck of the boat. Once, when a small plane had flown overhead, he'd stopped to watch it. Was he concerned, or was it an expected visit from Barbadillo and his friends? Stephanie's momentary panic dissolved to guilt as the plane flew off.

After she'd finished her breakfast, she carried the dishes back into the kitchen where she found Malva folding laundry as she talked to Tess. "Anything I can do to help?" Stephanie asked.

"You're a guest, honey," Malva said. "You should be enjoyin' yourself. Why not go for a swim? You'll never have a better chance. Let me find you a suit." She went off without waiting for an answer.

The suit Malva found was a red bikini, but not totally immodest. Ten years ago, Stephanie might even have picked it out for herself. She still had the body for it, but she was also past forty, no longer a kid.

It was a modest, matronly thought, especially for a woman who'd taken off her clothes only two nights ago and gone skinny-dipping. But which woman was she? The one who'd married Jean Claud, or the one mixed up with Jack Kidwell?

Stephanie changed into the suit, lathered herself with sunblock and slipped on the cover-up Malva had provided. Then, with a big floppy hat on her head and a beach towel under her arm, she followed the path she and Jack had taken Saturday night.

The beach was gorgeous, the white sand fine and pure, the water the color of an emerald. She got a lounge chair from the shelter and spread a towel on it. Before sunning herself, though, she decided to go for a swim.

This time she dived into the warm sea as Jack had done. She swam out forty or fifty yards. The waves were higher than they'd been the other night, and it was windier, so she swam parallel to the beach. After twenty minutes, she felt as though she'd had a good workout and decided to go in.

Trudging to shore, Stephanie made her way across the hot sand to the lounge chair where she put on more sunscreen and lay down. The sun was warm, sensuous, and despite herself, she was reminded of those exquisite moments she'd spent with Jack. The image of him and Tanya making love came to mind, as well. That vision had been plaguing her for days, buzzing through her brain like an insistent fly.

She hadn't realized she'd drifted off to sleep until she felt somebody gently shake her. "Hey, sweetheart, you'd better wake up before you're burnt to a crisp."

Stephanie opened her eyes and found Jack hovering over her. She blinked and sat up, a bit disoriented. "I guess I did fall asleep," she mumbled, only then recalling she was in the skimpy red bikini.

"They sent me down to tell you lunch is ready," Jack said, "and make sure you hadn't been eaten by sharks."

Stephanie grabbed the cover-up and slipped it around her. "What time is it, anyway?"

He glanced at his watch. "Nearly noon. How's your skin feel?"

"It's a little tender," she said, patting her shoulders and chest. "I lathered up with sunblock."

"You're lucky."

She wondered what he was thinking. Jack had avoided making suggestive remarks ever since their sexual encounter, though she didn't know if that was out of respect or a desire not to spoil his business opportunity.

She slipped on the rubber thongs Malva had given her and got to her feet. Jack picked up her hat and plopped it on her head. She straightened it and they began walking back toward the house.

"You look every bit the tourist," he said good-humoredly.

"Is that a compliment?"

"Sure. Tourists are good. They're my livelihood."

"With all the money I'm worth on the black market, I must look like a first-class meal ticket to you."

"That remains to be seen."

She decided it was best not to ask him to explain exactly what he meant.

"I talked to Sonia again a little while ago," he volunteered.

"Oh? Good news or bad?"

"They've accepted my offer of half a million."

"What offer?"

"I decided to see if I could squeeze a little more out of them, and they bit."

Stephanie didn't know if he was joking, but she certainly considered her situation no laughing matter. "You agreed to sell me?"

"It's a package deal. You *and* the disks."

Stephanie forced a tight smile. "Nice of you to tell me, Jack. Out of curiosity, did you decide it was kinder if I knew in advance that I'd been sold, or is this just more good old Kidwell honesty?"

"Good old Kidwell honesty."

She wondered if he was testing her, but his grin did give her hope. "That's nice, but not good enough. Really, what's going on?"

"I wanted to see how desperate these boys are. They seem to be both desperate *and* determined. They want your sweet little fanny pretty bad, my dear."

"I am not reassured," she said.

They were in the thickest part of the vegetation on the path back to the house, and Jack pushed a hanging vine aside. "In any partnership, trust is essential," he said. "I'm doing my best to demonstrate where my heart is."

"You must know I have my doubts."

"Sure, you'd be foolish not to."

"So that leaves me where I started," she said. "With no idea what to make of you and even less idea what I should do."

"The trouble is, anything I say sounds self-serving. So, we'll just have to rely on your intuition. I think deep down you know you can trust me—at least I hope so. The real question is if you're willing to trust your own instincts."

Stephanie gave him a sideward glance as they came out into the open. Jack Kidwell, she decided, was a crazy-maker. The harder he tried to put her mind at ease, the more suspicious she became. "We both know I'm stuck with you, Jack. That isn't the foundation for a stellar relationship."

"Maybe I'm a little more optimistic than you are."

He put an arm around her shoulders, giving her a friendly squeeze. It was the same sort of fearless camaraderie he'd shown when she'd gone to get him from the boat for the phone call yesterday. Friendly, jocular, happy-go-lucky Jack. It was as hard not to like the man as it was to trust him. But was his immediate objective sex or business? The safest bet, she concluded, was that it was both.

Jack sat behind the desk in Nigel's study, reviewing his notes. During lunch, Stephanie had told him enough about Jean Claud's finances for him to sound convincing when he spoke to Tom Handley about the Halcyon sale. Stephanie held the cordless phone Malva had gotten for her so she could listen in on the conversation.

"Are you sure you're up to playing lawyer?" she asked.

"Sugar, once a con, always a con."

"That's not very reassuring."

He gave her an amused smile. "Between your propriety and my practicality, we're unbeatable. And, as for playing lawyer, all you need is the mentality of a whore. That's a quality I'm familiar with."

"Make the call and let's get this over with," she said.

Jack dialed information in San Francisco and got the number for Meriwether & Handley. Stephanie wasn't entirely sure what he was going to say, but she knew she'd find out soon enough.

Jack spoke to Tom's secretary first, saying only that he was an attorney in Florida and needed to speak with Mr. Handley. Stephanie pushed the mute button on her phone while they waited for Tom to get on the line.

"This is Tom Handley," came the voice Stephanie had heard so many times over the dinner table.

"Mr. Handley, this is Arnold Milburn, attorney-at-law, Immokalee, Florida," Jack said. "How are you today, sir?"

Jack had affected a southern drawl that was so unexpected Stephanie nearly burst out laughing. He gave her an admonishing look.

"Fine, thank you," Tom said. "What can I do for you, Mr. Milburn?"

"I represent Edith Conroy, who is the aunt of the late Mrs. Stephanie Reymond of Mill Valley, California. I believe you did business with her husband, Jean Claud Reymond, also deceased. Is that correct, sir?"

"Yes..."

"Well, Mr. Handley, it seems that shortly before her death, Mrs. Reymond spoke with my client concernin' her—Mrs. Reymond's—inheritance, a considerable sum that Mr. Reymond had invested on her behalf in a company he'd financed, an outfit called...let me see here...Halcyon Technologies. Does that sound familiar, sir?"

"Yes, Halcyon is being sold to the public and my firm is representing the offering."

"That's my understandin', Mr. Handley," Jack continued. You see, the difficulty is that Mrs. Reymond expressed concern to her aunt that the sale was bein' conducted under...shall we say unusual circumstances, and that her inheritance was therefore in jeopardy. Since subsequent to that conversation Mrs. Reymond has passed away, my client wants to inquire as to the status of her niece's estate, most of which is invested in the company you're representin'. Am I makin' the nature of our inquiry clear, Mr. Handley?"

"You are. But I'm afraid I can't be of much help. I have no information regarding Stephanie's estate. You'd have to speak to her lawyers about that. My understanding is that death certificates haven't been formally issued because of difficulty in identifying the bodies. And the only reason I know that is because I happen to be a personal friend of Mr. Reymond. The situation seems to be very confused at the moment."

"Yes, Mr. Handley, that's my understandin' as well. Let me be direct. Our primary concern is the Halcyon sale, particularly since Mrs. Reymond expressed doubts about the manner in which it's bein' handled."

"I assure you, Mr. Milburn, the sale is being conducted according to S.E.C. regulations and in the most professional and competent manner."

"Oh, I have no doubt about that, sir. Please don't misconstrue my meanin'. The sale itself is not my concern. It's the disposition of the funds followin' the sale. Mrs. Reymond's attorneys have no information on that and suggested I contact you."

"Well, all I can tell you is that the proceeds will be distributed in accordance with Jean Claud Reymond's instructions."

"But he's dead."

"Yes, but the instructions were issued by him in his capacity as president of his firm. Since his corporation continues in existence, despite his death, those instructions will be carried out to the letter."

"Tell me this, Mr. Handley, will you be distributin' the proceeds of sale directly to the investors?" Jack asked, giving Stephanie a wink.

Tom Handley hesitated before answering. "I shouldn't discuss that," he said, "but Jean Claud had us follow the same procedure for years and it's hardly mysterious. The funds are always distributed to a trust account controlled by his firm. Exactly what happens after that I don't know. It's not within our area of responsibility."

"I appreciate that, Mr. Handley," Jack said, his drawl more pronounced. "But the reason I'm speakin' to you is because of our concern that Mrs. Reymond's piece of the pie is goin' to…shall we say…fall through the cracks. You see, we understand the money is goin' to an overseas account."

"Stephanie told her aunt that?"

"Well, yes. Unfortunately, my client, who is quite elderly,

failed to make note of where. I'm assumin' it's Switzerland or perhaps the Cayman Islands, Panama or even Monaco. But as you can imagine, it makes a bit of difference which country and which bank.''

"That information is confidential.''

"Most assuredly it is, sir,'' Jack continued without missing a beat. "And if I were Jean Claud Reymond I would expect my investment bankers to keep that sort of information in the utmost confidence, but I think it's safe to say Mr. Reymond is not in a position at this juncture to register much protest. In fact, who is? As I understand it, Mr. Reymond has no partners. His wife and child are dead. The only parties who could possibly care where that money is are the investors themselves.''

Stephanie found Jack's performance truly impressive. No wonder the man had made a million by the time he was thirty-five. She could envision buying swampland from him and could only hope she hadn't done just that.

"You have a point,'' Handley conceded, "but if you need that sort of information, there are legal avenues you can pursue.''

"Most assuredly, Mr. Handley. And if you are unable to take compassion on us, I will pursue those avenues. I'll subpoena documents, deal with receivers, executors, the S.E.C., the courts. And after spendin' eighteen months and fifty thousand dollars of my client's social security money, I'll know that the proceeds of the sale of Halcyon Technologies are in, say, the Union Bank of Switzerland. Now that's okay, but simple human decency on your part, a few whispered words, perhaps, would save poor widow Conroy a great deal of heartache and grocery money.''

Handley chuckled. "You make a persuasive argument, Mr. Milburn. However, I'm a fiduciary with obligations that extend far beyond those of your client, who is, after all, only one of the parties in interest. But you have an even bigger problem. The sale of Halcyon Technologies has been moved up. That was Jean Claud's last instruction to us. With the sale taking place in four days, you may not have time to intervene with the bank before they do whatever they've been instructed to do with the funds.''

Stephanie had a terrible sinking feeling, but Jack forged ahead with the tenacity of an old-time southern lawyer.

"One thing I've learned practicin' the law these thirty-odd years," Jack said, "is never say never, Mr. Handley. All I need is the opportunity to be of service to this sweet little old lady in any way I possibly can."

There was a long silence, then Tom Handley said, "My advice, Mr. Milburn, is to forget the sale and take a nice vacation. I understand the Caribbean's nice this time of year."

"Never have been to the Cayman Islands," Jack said.

"It's a good choice."

"Travel can be expensive. Know a bank that has exceptional exchange rates?"

"A friend of mine likes Grand Cayman Bank Ltd., but I don't know from personal experience. Never been there. But if you'll excuse me, I have a client waiting. Sorry I can't help you with your legal problem," Handley said, "but I wish you luck."

"Sir, you are a scholar and gentleman."

Jack hung up and Stephanie sat shaking her head.

"You're a genius, Jack. I'm impressed."

"Glad I'm *your* sonovabitch, sugar?"

"Are you?"

He held up his hand. "Scout's honor."

"I bet your investors loved you," she said, "right up until you left with their money."

"Actually, it was my partner who absconded. I stayed and took the heat."

"Why did you, anyway?"

Jack shrugged. "Too softhearted, I guess."

Stephanie sighed. She was starting to believe in him again—which either showed she had great people instincts or she was an even bigger fool than Tom Handley. Of course, there were probably dozens of women out there who, at one time or another, had felt the very same way.

Tess came with a pitcher of lemonade and a couple of glasses. "Y'all must be thirsty," she said, setting the tray she was carrying on the desk.

"You're a mind reader, Tess," Jack said.

"Well, I won't have time to do no more mind readin' this afternoon, Captain Jack. We done got word Mr. Nigel's goin' to be here for supper, so I be mighty busy next few hours. You enjoy your lemonade while you can."

She left the room and Stephanie poured them each a glass, handing Jack his. He held it aloft.

"Here's to a promising beginning," he offered.

"To the finest criminal mind I've ever seen," she replied in toast.

"You may be hoping so, sweetheart."

They drank their lemonade and contemplated each other. Stephanie wasn't sure why exactly, but she found Jack incredibly appealing. Worse, she was letting down her guard, as though the lesson of the other night had been completely forgotten. Maybe she wanted too badly for things to be right between them. Or maybe Jack Kidwell simply had her number.

As she watched him, he picked up a pencil and made a couple of checks on the pad, his expression pensive. He was intelligent, but also very clever. From her perspective, that was where the danger lay.

"So, we know where my money will be and when," Stephanie said, "but I'm not sure what good that does us."

"I'm not, either," he confessed.

"Once I get home, I guess I can commence legal action to get what's coming to me," she said.

"Yes, possibly. But it may not be all that simple. Offshore numbered accounts are not easy to crack, even for the best of lawyers with the best of reasons."

"What are you saying?"

"That if your husband had any experience in these matters at all, he'd set it up so that no one could get access to that money but him and perhaps somebody he trusts."

"Like my sister."

"Yes, like your sister. We know this was a shady transaction involving shady people. For that reason your husband must have intended to keep the money out of sight, not only to hide it from the authorities, but maybe from you and your divorce lawyer. It's hard to say what he was thinking, but I doubt that money will be easy to recover."

"So, what are you suggesting I do?"

"I think the first thing we do is find out what we can from Grand Cayman Bank Ltd."

"Are you saying Arnold Milburn needs to make another call?"

"No, I think this time it should be the widow Reymond. You won't have any trouble playing the role, Stephanie, and I doubt your recent demise made the news in the Cayman Islands. Call them as the grieving widow now trying to sort out her husband's business affairs. Jean Claud told you about his account in the bank and you'd like to find out what you can about securing the funds."

"Do you think they'll tell me?"

"I doubt it, but any information you get out of them would be helpful. It would be nice to know what the procedure is. They probably won't tell you who's authorized to withdraw funds, but there's no harm in asking."

Stephanie was suddenly nervous. She'd never done anything like this before. Posing as Jane had been about the shadiest thing she'd ever done. "I don't know if I'm cut out for this, Jack."

"Hey, it's your money they've got, isn't it?"

"Part of it is."

"What's wrong with going after what's yours?"

"Nothing, but I hate to lie."

Jack shook his head. "Sweetheart, if I were asking you to

hurt anyone innocent, I'd understand. But this is like a game of chess. The bank doesn't care what happens as long as they collect their interest and don't run afoul the regulators. Jean Claud hid the money and you're trying to find it before the competition does."

"You really are amoral, aren't you?"

"Yes, but I don't steal from the weak, the infirm, orphans or widows."

"Including me?"

"Especially you."

Stephanie looked him in the eye, then reached across the desk for the phone. She took a sip of lemonade, then dialed the operator and asked for information in the Cayman Islands. After obtaining the number from directory assistance, she dialed the Grand Cayman Bank Ltd. in George Town. Jack listened in on the portable phone.

A woman with a distinct British accent answered.

"Hello," Stephanie said. "I'm calling on behalf of one of your customers, Jean Claud Reymond in San Francisco. May I speak with the manager, please?"

The woman hesitated. "And you are...?"

"Stephanie Reymond. Mr. Reymond's wife."

There was another hesitation. "One moment, please."

After thirty seconds a man came on the line. "Mrs. Reymond, this is Harris Ivory. I am the manager. How may I help you?" His accent was also British, but with a Caribbean undertone.

"Mr. Ivory," she said, her voice quavering, "I regret to inform you that my husband was recently killed in a tragic accident."

"Oh, my. Mrs. Reymond, my sincere condolences."

"Thank you." She drew a deep breath, surprised at how easily her tragic frame of mind came to her. "The reason for my call is to inform you that as my husband's heir, I will be handling his business affairs from now on."

"I understand."

"My immediate concern is the account Jean Claud has with your bank. He told me about it before his death and I wanted to confirm its status with you."

"Mrs. Reymond, I would be pleased to assist you in any way I can. However, I cannot give information about the account over the telephone. I'm sure you understand."

"Naturally, I wouldn't want you to do anything inappropriate, but if you could give me general information that would aid my attorneys, accountants and me in sorting out Jean Claud's affairs, I'd be most grateful."

"What do you wish to know?"

"How would I go about gaining access to the account?"

"Already we're in a sensitive area. I'm sorry."

Stephanie looked over at Jack woefully and he signaled with his hand for her to keep plugging. She drew a ragged breath, tears in her eyes. "You'll have to forgive me, Mr. Ivory, but as you can imagine, this is an emotional subject."

"I understand, indeed."

"I suppose I should be truthful. I'm especially concerned that Jean Claud invested my personal inheritance in a start-up company that's being sold in an initial public offering in a few days. The money from the sale will be deposited in the trust account Jean Claud established with your bank. I was remiss in not insisting on getting account information from my husband before his death, but these things are unexpected and now I'm…stuck."

"Quite. I understand your dilemma."

"Is there anything you can do to guide me?" she asked, feeling every bit as desperate as she sounded.

The man did not respond immediately, and Stephanie, surprising herself, broke into tears.

"You have my compassion, Mrs. Reymond," Ivory said, sounding genuinely uncomfortable, "but regretfully, it is the bank's policy to keep everything in the strictest confidence."

Stephanie wiped her eyes, feeling silly, despite the authenticity of her emotion. Jack, to his credit, appeared pained rather than amused. An idea suddenly came to her.

"Let me ask you this, Mr. Ivory," she said. "Should I wish to establish additional trust accounts for our clients in the future, what would you recommend?"

"We have a variety of types and classes of accounts," he replied.

"Well, as you may know, confidentiality and close control is important in our business. My interests and objectives are the same as my husband's. We're talking similar sums of money to be deposited and withdrawn in a similar fashion."

Stephanie looked at Jack and saw a huge grin. He gave her an enthusiastic thumbs-up. She didn't know whether to feel elated or ashamed.

"Well," Ivory said uncertainly, "a numbered account might suit your needs."

"How exactly does a numbered account work?"

"Well, the funds to be deposited, from whatever source, would be placed in an account identified only be a special number supplied by the bank. Your name or your company's name would not appear on the account."

"And should I wish to disburse monies to my investors, how would I do that?"

"You would simply authorize the disbursement, which, of course, is a form of withdrawal."

"I would personally?" Stephanie asked.

"If that's the arrangement you make when establishing the account, yes."

"I would write a check like any checking account?"

"We have demand accounts, of course," Ivory said, "but that may not be the most desirable arrangement for transactions of the nature you describe."

Stephanie again looked at Jack. "What would you recommend, Mr. Ivory?" she said, rolling her tongue through her cheek.

Jack gave her the most delightful grin. The sheer mischief

in it excited her, making her wonder if maybe he wasn't right about their chemistry, after all. Who would have thought that one day she'd end up like Bonnie Parker, throwing in her lot with the Caribbean version of Clyde Barrow?

"Some account holders like the security of limiting account access to in-person withdrawals on the bank premises by the principal upon a showing of proper identification and signature verification," Ivory said.

Stephanie again had a sinking feeling. Jack signaled for her to keep going.

"That's awfully restrictive, isn't it?" she said.

"You could authorize another person to have access to the account," Ivory suggested.

"By putting them on the account?"

"Yes. Another way would be by providing them with an access code."

"What sort of code?"

"One example would be a series of numbers known only to you, the person you provide the code, and, of course, the bank."

"You mean, if I give this code to a person of my choice, they could withdraw funds from the account simply by presenting the numbers? They wouldn't need identification or to have their name registered?"

"That's exactly right, Mrs. Reymond."

"Isn't that dangerous? I mean, anybody who found my wallet with the code written down could withdraw all my money. Or do I misunderstand you?"

"There are safeguards. The person would need to know the account number and they would also have to be aware of the parameters of withdrawal."

"What do you mean?"

"You might wish to restrict a nonsignatory's ability to withdraw funds by using the code to certain amounts of money or to certain times. That is, for example, code withdrawals could be made only within so many days following a deposit. Access would be denied if the withdrawal were attempted for greater amounts or outside the specified time frame.''

Stephanie was bewildered. "I can see how this can get awfully complicated," she said, looking at Jack.

He frantically scratched out a note and passed it to her.

She cleared her throat and again spoke to the banker. "Let's assume I've decided to open an account, Mr. Ivory, and that I'll be down there in a few days to make arrangements. Based on your experience, what would you recommend for the type of business I'll be doing?"

Stephanie knew she was pushing. Harris Ivory knew it, too. She could tell by the way he hesitated before answering.

"If the window of opportunity for making code withdrawals was short enough," he said, "I shouldn't think you'd need place any restriction on the amounts."

Jack pointed to his note and Stephanie nodded.

"What's a reasonable period that would be effective, yet safe?" she asked.

Ivory cleared his throat. "I don't know…perhaps five days."

Jack's face lit up and he gave her the thumbs-up once more. She was pleased.

"Five days isn't long," she said.

"No," the banker replied, "especially if you don't have reasonably precise information about deposits. But these are the sorts of things we can discuss when you come in to set up the account."

"Yes, of course. This has given me food for thought and I'm grateful," Stephanie said, feeling elated. "I expect to be making a trip to the Cayman Islands soon. You've been most accommodating, Mr. Ivory. I'll definitely be seeing you."

"I look forward to that, Mrs. Reymond."

Stephanie hung up the phone as Jack came around the desk. She got to her feet and they embraced. It started as a gleeful hug between comrades, but another sort of awareness came into play: he was holding her body, not just her.

"You were sensational, Mrs. Reymond," he said. "You know that?"

"Jack, this is far from over. I can't get to that money because I don't know the code."

"A mere detail."

"What do you mean, a mere detail?"

"It's got to be on the disks," he replied.

"What makes you so sure?"

"I'm not, but it makes sense. Why else would Inter-America be so hot to get their hands on them? It couldn't be just to look at your husband's books. My guess is, Jean Claud destroyed his files or otherwise put them out of reach of Inter-America and so they figured they have to get your copy if they have any hope of getting the code."

"I think that's exactly what Jean Claud did," she said. "And I know Oscar Barbadillo thinks so, too. At least that's what he told me when I was being searched.

Jack nodded. "It may also be that they want to avoid the embarrassment of the information about their operation falling into the wrong hands. In any case, I think they're convinced the code is on the disks, and so am I."

"It could be you're both wrong."

"Possibly," he said. "But I'd rather go with the assumption there's a map leading to this treasure."

"Jean Claud didn't need the code."

"No, but your sister did. And he'd never have set up the arrangement if he didn't intend it to be used."

She pulled her head back so she could look into his eyes. "Jack, you have a devious mind."

He tightened his grip around her waist. Then he gave her that quirky smile of his and kissed her mouth. It was sexy, it was sensuous. And when it was over he didn't apologize.

Charlotte Amalie, St. Thomas

The BMW pulled into the circular driveway in front of the hotel and stopped. Rico Behring waited for one of the step-and-fetch-its to open the door so he could slide out of the back seat. Oscar Barbadillo, who'd been driving, came around the car. Rico was pissed, and he was hot. He headed directly for the door, relishing the thought of the air-conditioning. This tropical-humidity shit was getting to him.

"I hope that's the last schoolteacher from Cleveland the stupid cops have us talking to, Oscar," Rico said, slipping off his coat and slinging it over his shoulder. "That was a god-damn waste of time and I don't like to waste my time."

"From now on I'll talk to them first," Oscar said as they went through the doors.

"The cops in this fucking place don't know what they're doing," Rico lamented. "It's now what…three days they've been looking for the Reymond broad, and almost as long for the captain's friend and they don't got a clue where either one of them is. Not only that, they're supposed to bring me the passenger that's got that bag and what do I get? An old lady with denture breath. Jesus, Oscar, what do we gotta do?"

Oscar shrugged. "Well, the old lady *was* keeping a suitcase for her friend who went to St. Croix."

"Yeah, well, the wrong friend and the wrong suitcase."

They'd come to the bank of elevators and Rico watched the floor panel impatiently. He removed his tie and cuff links, stuffing them in the pocket of his jacket.

"So, how many of the passengers have we tracked down?"

"About half," Oscar replied.

"The other half will be gone if we don't get our asses in gear. Can we get more cops on the payroll?"

"We're already making a lot of waves, Rico. Maybe too many. The governor's starting to ask questions and people are thinking about their jobs."

The elevator car arrived and they stepped inside. Oscar pushed the floor button.

"I think we've got to put the fucking governor on the pay-roll," Rico said.

"Yeah, well, good luck. We're on thin ice as it is. What you'd better hope is that Kidwell comes through for us. I think he's our best shot."

"What's he waiting for? Isn't half a mil enough? What is this guy, a leech?"

"My guess is, he's having trouble putting his hands on the disks."

"Well, if she won't tell him where they are, he ought to beat it out of her."

The doors opened and Rico pushed his way past a middle-aged couple standing in the hall. Oscar followed him toward the suite.

"What's with the broad from Miami?" Rico asked over his shoulder. "Is she here yet?"

"Should be. Her flight was due in an hour ago."

"I hope so. I could use a piece of ass."

They came to the door of his suite and Rico took the room key from his pocket. Unlocking the door, he pushed it open.

Standing at the window opposite was one of the finest sights he'd ever seen. Her back was to him, the waist tiny, ass round and tight, well-shaped legs protruding from a black leather miniskirt that dropped just below the cup of her rear end. She was small, but propped up on four-inch heels, her legs looked long. Her feet were spread apart and her hip cocked, a hand with bright pink, inch-long nails resting on the curve of her haunch. More than anything, her appearance was dominated by the huge mane of hair that dropped to below her shoulders. It was tawny-colored with dark streaks.

She turned at the sound of the door opening. Rico stood looking at her. She wore a leather halter top, exposing a well-tanned midriff. Her boobs were not huge, but they were round and firm and proportionate to her figure. Her face looked small under the hair, except for her leering dark eyes. She had a small nose and mouth, though her pink lips were full, like Rhonda's after she'd gotten the collagen shots.

"Well," Rico said, sauntering into the room, "what have we here—Miss Miami?"

"This is Maria," Oscar said. Then to the woman, "Honey, meet Rico Behring."

She smiled at him, smacking her gum. "So, Mr. Big, huh?"

"Baby," Rico said, feeling an erection coming on, "if you're lucky, you'll find out just how big."

She grinned, chewing her gum loudly. "I can hardly wait."

"Yeah, well, ditch the gum. You're coming to a classy operation here."

Maria took the wad of gum out of her mouth and looked around for a place to put it. Oscar pointed to the ashtray on the table. She walked over and deposited the gum. Rico, who had his shirt half unbuttoned, finished taking it off and tossed it on a chair as he watched Maria return to her place at the window.

"Thanks, Oscar, you done good," he said.

"Anything for my favorite cousin. But if you'll both excuse me, I've got business to tend to."

"Hold on, Oscar," Rico said. "Could I ask a favor?"

"What do you need?"

Rico removed his wallet and took out his company American Express corporate card. "You've got good taste," he said, handing the card to Oscar. "Will you run downtown to one of those fancy jewelry shops and pick up a little something for Rhonda? A ring or a bracelet or something."

"How much do you want to spend?"

"I don't know. Five, ten G's. All I care is that it looks impressive."

"It'd be my pleasure."

There may have been some sarcasm in Oscar's voice, but Rico didn't care. He was liking what he saw too damn much. As his cousin left, Rico went to the most comfortable chair in

the room, which also happened to face the window where
Maria stood preening. The phone rang.

"Shit," Rico said, deciding to ignore it. Instead he contemplated the curves of Maria's body, silhouetted by the late-
afternoon sunlight coming in the window. Her big dangly earrings sparkled through her hair. Rico gazed at the hem of her
miniskirt, half consciously calculating the distance to pay dirt.
The phone persisted, so he got up and answered it.

"Yeah?"

"Mr. Behring?"

Rico didn't recognize the voice. "Yeah?"

"This is Alexander Manring in the Cayman Islands. I have
some information for you."

Rico tore his attention away from the woman, concentrating
instead on the voice on the other end of the line. It was the
man his father had hired to cover the Caymans for them.
"Yeah, Manring, what you got?"

"We've had contact with Mrs. Reymond."

Rico's brain clicked into full consciousness. "No shit?"

"Yes, sir."

"Hang on a second, will you?" He put down the phone
and went to the window where Maria stood. He moved to
within inches of her, close enough that he could smell the
heavy scent of her perfume. She gazed up at him, tilting her
head, smiling as though it was the happiest moment of her
life. He casually reached his hand out, letting his fingertips
touch her bare thigh. Then he brought them up so that they
were just under the edge of her skirt.

"You got panties on under this, babe?" he murmured.

"Yeah," she said, her mouth twisting into a wry grin. "I
happen to be classy, too."

"What say we get down and dirty? You go into the bedroom and take off your panties. Leave everything else on,
though. I like the outfit."

"And?"

"There should be a bottle of champagne in there. Think you're strong enough to open it?"

"You'd be surprised what I'm strong enough to do."

Rico gave the hem of her skirt a firm tug, winked, then tossed his head, signaling for her to leave. He watched her pick up her shoulder bag from a chair, then swing her butt as she made her way to the bedroom, closing the door behind her. He went back to the phone to finish his call.

"So, Manring, are you saying she's there, she's in the Caymans?"

"No, but she called the bank. My informant, Cynthia, rang me up a little while ago with the news."

"So what happened?"

"Mrs. Reymond asked to speak to the manager. Had a five-minute conversation with him and that was it."

"We know where she called from?"

"No, unfortunately."

"Anything else?"

"Cynthia tried to eavesdrop, but couldn't get much except that they were talking accounts. Mrs. Reymond asked a number of questions. At the end she indicated she was coming to the Caymans."

Rico beamed. "Hey, that's beautiful! Good work!"

"Yes, but we didn't get anything specific. She didn't say when she was coming."

"It's got to be soon, doesn't it? The money's going to be there in a few days. Are you watching the airport?"

"Yes, around the clock."

"Well, start watching the bank every minute the doors are open. Hire as many men as you need. Got that?"

"Yes, sir."

Rico hung up the phone, feeling great. If Stephanie Reymond slipped out of the Virgins, then they'd be waiting for her at the other end. One way or the other, they had her cold. Finally had something positive to report to his father.

Rubbing his hands together, he thought of the piece waiting

for him in the next room. He was going to have himself the
fuck of his life.

Isola Lovejoy

Stephanie checked herself in the mirror, knowing she didn't
have long before her host arrived. She'd slicked her hair back
again. The image was sexier, more in keeping with the tropical
setting. She wanted to look her best, and there was nothing
surprising about that—except for the fact that it was Jack's
reaction she cared about.

To her surprise, she'd enjoyed the tricks they'd played on
the banker and Tom Handley that afternoon. She was probably
showing more enthusiasm for the enterprise than was wise,
but she couldn't help herself. She was not only succumbing
to Jack's allure, but to the adventure. Her inheritance was at
stake, true, but the appeal went far deeper than that. Her whole
life had been staid, predictable, proper, controlled. Now her
situation was the antithesis of all that, and she found herself
not just drawn to it, but wanting to embrace it.

Jack had made a convincing case that, if she wanted her
inheritance and the estate she and Jean Claud had built, she
had to join forces with him. Other than giving up, and leaving
the field to Inter-America, she had no real alternative. Even if
she tried to get the money through legal channels, by the time
the bank was compelled to pay her—assuming that was even
possible—the money could be gone.

Trust was the sticking point. She'd been inching toward
throwing in her lot with Jack, though she continued to hedge
her bets. She was in a vulnerable position, and he knew it.
And though he didn't quite have her wrapped around his finger, she could not deny that she'd never before felt the kind
of connection with a man that she felt with Jack.

Of course, there was probably a certain amount of self-
delusion going on. She badly needed a champion. And she

wanted it to be Jack. He made her laugh. He excited her. He even scared her, in a thrilling way. Most of all, he made her feel vital, alive. That was a lot from a man who had bad news written all over him. It also meant she was in danger of being made the fool. That, more than anything, held her back.

There was a knock at her door. "You about ready, sweetheart?" It was Jack. "Nigel called fifteen minutes ago. They should be pulling into the cove any minute."

Stephanie took a last look at herself. "I'm ready. Just a second." She tucked a stray curl behind her ear and went to the door.

"My, my," he said giving her the once-over. She was in a turquoise silk shift, the last thing she could find that both fit and was decent. "My last partner in crime didn't have your figure, or your brains."

"Thank you," she said, stepping into the hall, greeted by the light scent of his cologne. "But need I remind you we haven't made a deal? I'm not your partner yet."

"Hey," he said, taking her chin. "You aren't going to bust my balls over this, are you?"

"I might."

"God," he said, rolling his eyes, "I hate women."

She snickered. "Since when?"

"Well, maybe hate's a little strong," he said. "I lose patience. Let's put it that way."

"You mean you can't stand it when a woman says no and you're programmed to hear yes?"

"For example."

"Jack, you're nothing if not predictable."

He drew her along the hallway, folding her arm over his. "You can say that already?"

"I'm a fast learner."

"That's right—Stanford. Learned everything there is to know, except about life."

She gave him a coy smile. "You never give up, do you?"

"Give up what?"

"Seducing."

"Is that what you think this is?"

"That's exactly what I think it is," she said.

"Well, we're under some time pressure, Stephanie. We've...excuse me...*you've* only got a week to ten days, which means I've only got that much time to win your confidence. Once that five-day window closes, the thirty million is gone."

"I know that, Jack. Better than you. Don't forget, it's my money that'll be lost."

"If you lose, sweetheart, I lose."

"Nice you can be so forthright about it."

"Be honest. Would you believe me if I said I'm doing it out of friendship or for the cause of justice?"

"You've got a point."

As they passed by, they could hear Tess in the kitchen. They went through the entry hall.

"I wanted to say a few things about Nigel before he gets here," Jack said. "He can be very direct, so don't take anything he says too seriously. He's basically a teddy bear and he has an awfully good heart."

"Don't worry," she said, "I'm not made of china. I've survived knowing you, haven't I?"

"So far."

They went onto the veranda where they found Malva waiting in the dusk, an extra glint in her eye. Stephanie looked out and saw a gleaming white motor yacht, all lit up, pulling into the cove. Jack had told her Nigel's boat, *Rubber Soul,* was a fifty-five footer, a real gem. It certainly was beautiful.

Stephanie glanced again at Malva and, seeing her expression, wondered if perhaps she wasn't discovering what kept the woman on the island. This repressed emotion was not an employee's anticipation at the arrival of the boss. There was something more between Malva and her employer than the job, Stephanie was almost certain. The only thing she couldn't be sure of was whether the relationship was reciprocal.

When the yacht glided to a stop in the middle of the cove, not far from the *Lucky Lady,* Joseph, down at the shore, climbed into a launch and putted out to greet the arrivees. The three of them stood on the veranda watching the disembarking process. Half a dozen suitcases were handed down to Joseph by a crewman. Then a man in white yachting togs climbed down the ladder into the launch, followed by a slender woman, also wearing white.

"That is Françoise Gaudier," Jack said under his breath. "Nigel's goddess of the hour."

Stephanie checked, but Malva had moved on down the veranda and hadn't heard. She was glad. "You speak of her with such reverence, Jack," she said. "Do you know her well?"

"Not the way you mean. But I did meet her once a few years ago. Françoise was married to one of Nigel's clients at the time."

"Small world."

"Incestuous one, anyway."

The launch putted over the still water of the cove. It was a calm night, not so much as a breeze.

"Shall we walk down and meet them?" Jack said.

They went down the steps and the sweeping lawn, leaving Malva on the veranda. They were halfway to the water when the launch reached shore. Joseph clambered out and pulled the boat up onto the beach as he had when Stephanie and Jack arrived.

Nigel stood, his chest puffed, a big, affable grin on his ruddy face. His yachting cap was perched jauntily on his head. He was a roundish man, but not heavy. "Kidwell, you old brigand," he chortled as they approached. "Jolly good luck to find you here!"

"Took haven from the storm," Jack returned. "We're in your debt."

Lovejoy stepped out of the boat and turned to help a darkly elegant woman who was about Stephanie's height and similar in build. Stephanie guessed she was around fifty. Françoise wore white pants and a white gauzy cotton blouse that left no mystery as to what was underneath. The diamond on her right hand was enormous.

Jack stepped forward and he and Nigel clasped one another in a manly embrace. "It's been much too long, old bean," the Englishman said, sounding genuinely thrilled. "You know Françoise, of course."

To Stephanie's surprise, Jack kissed the woman's hand, making her laugh giddily.

"Silly boy, Jack," she said, pronouncing it "Jacques." "When did you become such a gentleman, eh?"

"It's a recent conversion," he said, glancing back at Stephanie.

Stephanie wondered if this was more compulsive candor. She moved closer and Jack introduced her. Nigel held the hand she'd extended in both of his.

"A pleasure indeed."

"Welcome home, Mr. Lovejoy," she said.

He chuckled. "Lovely. How delightful." He glanced at Jack. "Smashing young lady, mate. You *are* coming up in the world."

"Good Lord," Jack said. "You two've been here what, a minute? And already all my hours of image-building are shot."

"Rubbish," Nigel said. "If Miss Reymond is half as intelligent as she looks, she bloody well saw through you from the start." He gave her a wink. "Stephanie, let me introduce my dear friend, Françoise Gaudier, light of my life, lamp of my soul."

"Nigel," Françoise said with Gallic disdain, "you and Jacques are both full of *sheet*." As she shook Stephanie's hand, she arched her eyebrow conspiratorially and said, "*Monsieur* and I sleep together, he buys me things and that is all that binds us for this moment. No lights and no lamps."

Nigel laughed with sheer delight. "What wit, what charm, what a woman." Françoise put her arm around his waist.

"So," he said, looking back and forth between Stephanie and Jack, "I trust you two have been comfortable."

"It's been wonderful," Stephanie said. "I've been clothed as well as housed and fed."

"Ah, but of course," Nigel said. "I thought that frock looked familiar. Forgive me for saying so, but I believe the last time I saw it I was taking it off somebody."

"You see, *chérie*," Françoise said. "The man may have boats and islands and offices all over Europe, but he's still a beast."

"Tut, tut, Françoise," Nigel replied, taking her hand and starting for the house. "Having a man to clothe and *un*clothe you is what you ladies live for. It's no good denying it."

"Men are a necessary evil, I admit that much," Françoise replied.

Stephanie and Jack smiled at one another, then followed along behind as the other two led the way, nattering with good humor.

"Nigel's quite a colorful character, isn't he?" Jack said, slowing to allow the others to move off.

"I can see why the two of you are friends."

He gave her a sideward glance. "It was the clothe and unclothe remark. I can see we may be in for a long evening. Blimey."

Stephanie laughed, taking his arm again. "Some things are just unavoidable, Captain Kidwell."

During the course of dinner Stephanie made the decision to trust Nigel and Françoise enough to take them into her confidence. They were only vaguely aware of her situation so, over after dinner drinks in the drawing room, she told them about the last week of her life, withholding only those details she hadn't yet told Jack. They listened. From time to time Françoise would mutter, *"Mon Dieu!"* or Nigel would say, "How extraordinary!" or "Good gracious me!" or "Bloody hell!" Jack added details, particularly in areas where he had special knowledge, but mostly it was Stephanie who recounted her ordeal.

Her story took long enough that Nigel refilled their glasses with Courvoisier, except for Jack who clung stubbornly to soda water. "To what do we attribute this unseemly display of temperance, old bean?" Nigel had asked when Jack first declined a drink.

"I don't want drinking to get in the way of my responsibilities," he replied.

That brought Nigel up short. He squinted at Jack from his vantage point in the big overstuffed chair that was clearly his favorite, his ruddy complexion yet more florid from the brandy. Nigel was balding and unconsciously took a hank of his white hair, pushing it over his pate with his palm. "Good God, man," he said. "You haven't found religion or a woman, have you? They're the only two things I know that'll keep a bloke from a good time."

Françoise pulled her sandal off her foot and hurled it at Nigel. "Scoundrel!"

Nigel, who'd caught the shoe, grinned at her. "Ah, that tempestuous spirit of yours, my love. My, how it turns me on. This may be a night for ropes. Otherwise I may not be able to cope."

"Petit coquin!" She flipped her chin at him in typical French fashion.

Nigel roared, sharing his glee with Stephanie and Jack. He caught his breath. "But we digress," he said. "Françoise and I shall sort this out later. Back to your predicament, Stephanie. I confess I'm completely enamored with the tale."

"Someday I may laugh about it," she said, "but right now I have knots in my stomach."

"If you wouldn't mind an observation," Nigel said, "I quite agree with Jack, those disks must be recovered at all costs. I dare say, thirty million American is worth a bit of risk. There's no chance this alligator case you speak of could be recovered discreetly?"

"It would be tricky," she replied.

"Perhaps if you sent someone. Jack. Myself. Françoise, for God's sake."

"Why should she trust us?" Françoise asked. "Thirty millions of dollars is still thirty millions, whether you have a boat and an island or only an apartment in the fourteenth *arrondissement*."

"True, my love, but even those with gold must learn to trust. Otherwise life is nothing but misery, paranoia and fear. It was one of my earliest lessons in life…that trust in one's fellow human beings is essential."

"Something a man would say," Françoise scoffed.

"What would *you* recommend Stephanie do, then, my darling?"

"If she wants help, she'll ask for it."

"I know I'm in no position to get those disks by myself," Stephanie said, "but I hate to ask anyone to take a risk for my sake, especially knowing there's no guarantee they've got the information I need to get to the money."

"Well, I'd help you for the sheer hell of it," Nigel said. "It would be a lark."

"Stephanie hasn't asked for your help, *chéri*," Françoise reminded him.

They all looked at Stephanie, who knew she'd reached a moment of truth. She'd been putting Jack off out of fear, but she either had to walk away from her inheritance or get help—that much had become clear. Fortunately, even without her inheritance, she'd be able to live comfortably. She still had the house and any assets Jean Claud hadn't squirreled away. And yet it was becoming obvious that money wasn't the only issue. Something tugged at her to go for this. It was the same insistent urge that had been drawing her to Jack.

"I think Nigel's right," she told them. "At some point I have to trust. If you're willing to take a chance for me, I'd be a fool not to accept your help." As she said it, she turned to Jack, who actually looked relieved.

"Splendid!" Nigel said. "We must set about making a plan without delay."

"It would help if we knew just what we're up against," Jack observed.

"Quite right, mate."

Again they all looked at Stephanie.

"Where *is* the bloody case, love?" Nigel asked.

She took a careful breath. "In a locker at the airport at Charlotte Amalie."

There was silence as everyone pondered that. Stephanie glanced at Jack, wishing she knew what he was thinking.

"I shouldn't think fetching a case from an airport locker is an insurmountable challenge," Nigel opined.

"You can be sure the airport is being watched," Jack said. "And a locker is such an obvious place. I'm surprised they didn't think of it."

"They had me under surveillance constantly," Stephanie said, "so I asked a young woman from the plane to stow the case for me. I gave it to her on the plane and she gave me the key to the locker when we were in the ladies' room, so they weren't aware what we did."

"Then Barbadillo and his friends were only half-right when they assumed you'd given the case to another passenger," Jack said. "The problem is, if they track this girl down and she tells them what happened, they'll be able to retrieve the case."

"Without a key?" Françoise said.

"Sure. The maintenance people would have a master key," Jack said. "Unless Barbadillo is unable to find that girl, it's only a matter of time before they have the disks. It could even be happening as we speak."

"It appears time is of the essence," Nigel said. "We've got a bloody ticking bomb on our hands."

"We have several ticking bombs," Jack said.

Nigel threw his head back, draining the Courvoisier from his glass. Then he rubbed his hands together. "I've been

seized by the spirit of adventure, mates. My juices are beginning to flow, as they say."

"God help us," Françoise said.

Nigel wagged his finger at her. "We need a plan, my love,
not prayer."

They engaged in a spirited discussion of how best to retrieve
the alligator case. Nigel suggested that the four of them go en
masse, there being security in numbers. Françoise couldn't see
why they didn't simply hire someone to go—they didn't have
to tell them what was inside. "Half of St. Thomas is on the
alert for Stephanie and the case," Jack said. "I wouldn't hand
the key over to just anyone. It's got to be one of us."

Stephanie pointed out they were looking for him, too, so
they tentatively decided that Nigel and Françoise should make
the trip. Unfortunately, that didn't solve the problem of the
ticking bomb. It would take time to sail to the international
airport at Beef Island. Jack said the solution was to fly directly
from Isola Lovejoy.

"You're suggesting a seaplane," Nigel said.

"Yes."

"Your friend, Bobby Brown?"

"Yes, that's what I was thinking. Bobby's always been willing to skirt the rules if a buck's to be made."

"Precisely the sort of chap we need."

"Not only would a seaplane get you to St. Thomas more
quickly," Jack said, "but on the way out, there would be
many more potential destinations."

"Anywhere there's water," Nigel said.

"Exactly."

"I like it," Nigel said.

"And," Jack went on, "assuming the disks have the information Stephanie needs, we'll want to get to the Cayman Islands posthaste."

"You can fly."

"That would be dangerous," Jack said. "Especially if
they're expecting us. It's a thousand miles, but we'll have the

better part of ten days. The *Lucky Lady* may be our best bet. Stephanie and I could get a head start, leaving here first thing in the morning. Then, after you and Françoise get the disks, we can rendezvous at sea, thereby saving a couple of days.''

"Bloody clever, that," Nigel said admiringly. "Splendid. Splendid."

"Now that you men have planned your war," Françoise said, "we must hear what Stephanie thinks. After all, the decision is hers, *n'est-ce pas?* Everybody but me forgets that." The Frenchwoman turned to her. "What do you think, *chérie?* How do you feel about the way these men have organized your life?"

Stephanie appreciated Françoise's sisterly compassion. Having her there brought a little balance to her thinking. When she was alone with Jack, she lost all objectivity.

"I like your plan, Jack," she said, turning to him, "but it's asking an awful lot of Nigel and Françoise. Maybe I should go to St. Thomas. It's for my benefit so I should take the responsibility.''

Jack insisted it was too dangerous. She'd almost certainly be recognized.

"There's another way, Jacques," Françoise said. She sipped her Courvoisier, all eyes on her. "Stephanie could go as me. We are about the same size and, though my passport would make her older than she is, under sunglasses and a big hat, who would notice?''

Stephanie perked up at the suggestion.

"You were married to a Frenchman, *chérie,*" Françoise said, "surely your French is not so bad."

"It's not as good as it could be, but I'm fairly fluent."

"But you would have no trouble speaking to the officials in English with a French accent."

"No."

"There you are," Françoise said, again sipping her brandy.

"It would still be risky," Jack said. "As a woman traveling

alone, you'd attract attention. And if the customs people made you take off your sunglasses and hat, it'd be all over.''

"You have a point, old bean," Nigel said, smoothing the thin hair lying on his pate. "But she'd attract far less attention traveling with me. Bobby Brown certainly wouldn't think anything of it. As a matter of fact, flying out here, Françoise and I talked about a shopping trip to Charlotte Amalie. We can still make that trip, only Stephanie would go in Françoise's place.''

"You see how quickly he becomes enthusiastic when firm flesh is involved," Françoise quipped. She winked at Stephanie.

With Jack demurring, it was agreed that Nigel taking Stephanie posing as Françoise was the best plan. But they still had the problem of where they would go after they'd retrieved the disks. A rendezvous at sea with the *Lucky Lady* was risky, especially if Bobby Brown couldn't be trusted. They all pondered the dilemma. Stephanie had an idea.

"What if the seaplane rendezvoused with Nigel's yacht, which in turn rendezvoused with the *Lucky Lady?*" she said. "Your friend would never see you or your boat that way, Jack, and nobody would be the wiser.''

"Brilliant!" Nigel exclaimed. "Capital idea!"

Jack regarded her. "Then you're going to St. Thomas?" he asked.

"Do I have to decide right now?"

"No," he replied, obviously concerned. "I don't have to set sail until morning. You'll either board or you won't. Either you'll be flying to St. Thomas with Nigel, or Françoise will.''

"In any case, I should ring Bobby now," Nigel said. "We're assuming he's available to make the trip. I'll tell him I've a lovely lady I want to take shopping in Charlotte Amalie. It's Stephanie's decision who it'll be.''

"Would it be all right with everyone if I slept on it, then?" Stephanie asked.

"But of course," Françoise said. "So long as it is understood that if Nigel buys the black pearl earrings I've been talking about, *I* get them, *chérie,* not you!''

"Deal," Stephanie said.

Nigel got to his feet. "I shall ring Bobby straight away and get matters settled. And you, my lovely," he said, pointing to Françoise, "have had a very long day. Why not have a nice relaxing bath and make yourself comfortable? I shall join you forthwith." He went over to Stephanie and took her hand, leaning over to kiss it. "Fear not, my dear, we shall conquer this little problem. Between Jack's sterling brilliance, my indomitable courage and Françoise's good judgment, not to mention great legs, the odds are in your favor."

"Thank you, Nigel. You've been so incredibly kind, so hospitable." She glanced at Françoise. "Both of you."

Françoise came over. The women embraced.

"You've had some terrible tragedies, *chérie,*" Françoise said, "but you've had good luck, too. Jacques is a wonderful boy, a valiant knight." Then she arched an eyebrow. "But don't trust him too far. Some men are too attractive by a turn."

"Françoise," Jack said, "you were doing great right up to that last remark."

"Oh, posh, Jacques. You know what I say is true. And so does she." She kissed Stephanie on each cheek, then said, *"Bonsoir."*

With that, she and Nigel left the room. Stephanie turned to Jack. He didn't seem too upset.

"And you thought I was a lot to contend with," he said.

She sighed. "I'm beginning to wonder if I'll ever get off of this roller coaster."

He stepped over and took her by the shoulders. Stephanie sagged against him, suddenly feeling exhausted. He held her, stroking her head.

"Do you really think I should let Françoise go with Nigel?" she asked.

"I think you'd be safer on the *Lucky Lady* with me."

Her first thought was that there were all kinds of safe. And though she'd thrown her lot in with Jack, a part of her still felt a niggling doubt about his motives. Somehow it seemed that with Nigel she'd have more control over her destiny. When she was with Jack, she was definitely lost—not altogether in a bad way—but lost nonetheless.

Jack paced back and forth in his room. Through the open window he could hear Françoise's muffled cries of pleasure. No surprise there. His friend was a typical satyr and Françoise the female equivalent. But they were not his concern at the moment. It was Stephanie who was on his mind.

Jack had been thinking all along that he and Stephanie would retrieve the disks, or that she might even send him to get them alone. He hadn't anticipated Nigel would throw himself into the venture, though it wasn't out of character. Actually, sending Nigel and Françoise made a lot of sense. What didn't make sense was Stephanie's going.

At first, he was certain that meant she didn't trust them. But she'd been forthright about the disks being in a locker. That showed trust, considering it gave him the information he needed to sell her down the river. Of course, if she'd lied about the location of the disks, it meant *he* was the one being double-crossed.

Jack didn't want to think she could be that devious. In fact, he knew she couldn't. But she could be that paranoid. After all, she'd been a prisoner of sorts ever since they'd set sail. *His* prisoner. Now she had a chance to do as *she* wished.

As he heard Françoise Gaudier's final cry of pleasure drifting through the night, Jack turned off the light and slipped from his room. He made his way through the dark to Nigel's study. He was about to enter when he heard voices from the veranda. Stealing to the door, he saw Stephanie sitting at the far end with Malva. They were both wearing nightgowns. He moved a little closer to hear better.

"I think you're the only person who's ever noticed," Malva said. "I don't know if that says more about him or about me."

"Men never pick up on those things," Stephanie replied. "Even when you do come right out and say something, half the time it scares them to death. I can't tell you how many times I tried talking to my husband about our marriage, only to have him run from it. He just didn't want to hear how I felt."

"Don't I know."

"I think you owe it to yourself to have a talk with him," Stephanie said. "I really do. You aren't doing yourself any good letting things go on this way."

"I've wanted to for the longest time, believe me. Just never had the chance."

Jack wondered what in the hell they were talking about.

"Do you think he has any inkling?" Stephanie asked.

"I think he knows that to me this is more than just a job. But I'm not sure he's wanted to figure out more than that."

"Sounds like a man."

"He cares about me as a person," Malva said, "but he's careful to keep it at that. I've always felt there could be more, but in my heart I don't believe he wants that."

Were they talking about Nigel? Jack wondered.

"There's a reason he's always got somebody," Malva said mournfully. "Havin' a woman to play with keeps him from worryin' about havin' a life with somebody. I run his house. I'm always here for him. Don't you know that makes me a whole lot like a wife. Honey, I got the worst of both worlds, and I know it, but I just can't let go of the man."

They *were* talking about Nigel! Jack was astonished. He knew Malva was fond of Nigel, of course, but this really took him by surprise. Peeking out, he saw Stephanie had put her arm around Malva's shoulders. Her compassion impressed him.

"Only you know how long you're willing to wait," Stephanie said. "But at some point you've got to ask what's best for you."

"I know," Malva lamented. "I'm lettin' my life pass me

by. I should tell him I'm leavin'. It won't make any difference. He'll be sad because he'll have to replace me, but that'll be it.''

"Sometimes it's best to face the facts."

They sat in silence, Stephanie rubbing Malva's back.

"Ain't this crazy though," Malva said, wiping her eyes. "You comfortin' me. You're the one who's in duck soup, contendin' with Jackie and all."

Jack could hear Stephanie sigh. "Why is it women totally lose their objectivity when it comes to men?" she asked.

"Because we want them to be stronger and better than they are," Malva replied.

"You know," Stephanie said, "I think you're right."

He felt a surge of guilt, and though her distrust cut deeply, he couldn't claim to be wounded. There was too much truth in her words for that.

There was a silence, then Malva said, "You fallin' in love with Jackie?"

Stephanie didn't immediately respond. "I'm charmed by him," she finally said.

"There's a difference, honey."

"Yes, there's a difference."

"Well," Malva said after a moment, "I've kept you up listening to my woes, when you've got a big day tomorrow."

"Yes, I've got an important decision to make. I have to decide if I'm going to take charge of my life or leave it to somebody else. And that's a big issue for me because for years I deferred to a man. I don't want to do that again. It's probably another reason I'm resisting Jack."

He heard them getting up and walking across the veranda. Hurrying back to Nigel's study, he ducked inside, just making it to safety as they entered the house. Malva closed the front door and the women walked toward the rear of the house.

"I don't know how you feel about Jackie or how he feels about you," he heard Malva say, "but there's one thing I noticed in him I ain't seen in a long, long time."

"What's that?"

"He hasn't seemed so alive to me in years. Not since he was with Alicia."

"The question," Stephanie said, her voice dropping to a whisper as they passed by the door to the study, "is whether it's me or the thirty million dollars."

"Thirty million?" Malva said as they left the entry hall.

Jack couldn't hear what Stephanie said next, but he could have guessed. Carefully closing the door, he retreated to the chair behind the desk, where he sat in the dark, pondering the situation. He felt both pangs of conscience and an aching tug at his heart. His plan was still good, he told himself. But he did need insurance.

He picked up the phone and dialed the number at Sonia's former mother-in-law's place. It took a long time before the old woman answered. Jack apologized for the late hour and asked for Sonia. When she came on the line he said, "I know it's a bad time to call, and I'm really sorry, but tomorrow's D day."

"Then it's about over."

"Yes."

"It couldn't come too soon for me." Her Scandinavian accent was stronger, perhaps because she was tired.

"It's been rough, I know," he said, "but I'll make it up to you, I promise. But there's one more thing I need."

"What's that?"

"I need for you to call them one more time, babe," he said. "Just once more."

Tuesday,
October 1st

Isola Lovejoy

" "**M**orning, everyone," Jack said, entering the sitting room. Malva had called him in from his boat where he'd been working since dawn. To Stephanie, he seemed more solemn than the day before, perhaps because he knew what she'd say. He only gave her a fleeting glance as he plopped down on the sofa next to Françoise. He patted the Frenchwoman's knee.

"Sleep well, sweetheart?"

"As well as one can expect sleeping with Don Juan."

"Complaining, my love?" Nigel asked.

"After last night, *chéri*, how could I? The entire household could not have missed my pleasure. You were *magnifique*. There now. It's been said. No need for red faces. *Allons!* I believe we have business to discuss."

Nigel beamed. "Don't you love a woman who can bloody well tell it like it is?" He gave Stephanie a wink. "All right, then," he said, his tone taking the timbre of an executive calling a meeting to order. "The time is upon us, my friends. Bobby Brown should be arriving in two hours' time to take…whoever…to Charlotte Amalie. Stephanie, what's your pleasure, love?"

Stephanie had made her decision, but when she engaged

Jack's steady gaze and felt his magic at work on her, doubt welled. She wanted to be with him, but she wanted it out of weakness, and that was the worst possible reason.

"I've decided," she said, clearing her throat, "to go to St. Thomas, posing as Françoise." She took a breath. "Then, after I've gotten the disks, I'll rendezvous with Jack as we've discussed. If we have what we need, we can sail to the Cayman Islands, assuming you still want to, Jack."

He did not look happy, but she wasn't surprised. "I'll do as you wish," he said.

She glanced at Nigel and Françoise before giving Jack her full attention. "If we're going to be partners, we should have a firm agreement, Jack. Here's my offer. I'll pay you twenty percent of everything I recover from the bank, unless it's through legal processes, in which case I'll pay you five percent. If we're unable to get any money, I'll pay you ten thousand for your time. But I won't take money that rightfully belongs to innocent investors. Once I've examined Jean Claud's books and tracked the money, I'll know how much I can keep. You'll get your cut out of that. Is that acceptable?"

"Yes," he replied without hesitation.

She turned to Nigel. "You're spending a great deal of money on this," she said. "I'd like to pay your out-of-pocket expenses, regardless of the outcome."

"I won't have it," Nigel said. "Not on your life."

"But, Nigel, I—"

"Good God, woman, this is the most fascinating distraction I've happened across since…well, since I rung up Françoise last month and she agreed to have dinner with me. Lest you've mistaken my financial situation, I'm quite solvent. I'm doing this for the sheer hell of it. Adventure. Isn't that right, Françoise?"

"*Mais oui!*" she said. "*We* should thank you, Stephanie. Excitement is so important in life. Last night was especially good for Nigel and me. It's no mystery why."

Stephanie chuckled. "Well, had I known…"

"I dare say your contribution has been quite sufficient, Stephanie," Nigel said with a laugh. "There'll be no more talk of money. Disgusting American habit, that." And he laughed again.

"On that happy note, I'd better make preparations to set sail," Jack said, getting to his feet. "I've got some distance to cover and I don't want to be in the cove when Bobby arrives."

The others rose.

"I've already talked to my men on the *Rubber Soul*," Nigel said. "The captain has his charts ready and is prepared to discuss coordinates and so forth. Françoise will sail with them rather than stay here."

"I will say *au revoir* now, Jacques." She took him by the shoulders, pulled him down and kissed each cheek. "*Bon voyage, eh chéri?*

"Have a good trip, Françoise," he said.

She patted his cheek. "*Ciao.*" She was gone.

Jack turned to Nigel. "With Joseph's help, I've helped myself to some fuel and supplies from your stock. And I've borrowed some batteries and emergency equipment from your crew."

"If there's anything more you require, Jack, don't hesitate to ask."

Jack turned to her. "Stephanie, I do need to talk about the arrangements I've made for you in St. Thomas."

"Why don't I wait for you outside then, mate?" Nigel said. "We can walk together down to the launch."

"Fine."

Stephanie knew Nigel was giving them a chance to be alone. She was glad for the privacy, but also tense, not knowing what Jack was going to say. Once Nigel had gone, Jack moved over to where she stood. The grin on his face was vintage Jack Kidwell, but she saw disappointment in his eyes.

"Nobody will ever accuse you of being overly cautious," he said. "You've got balls, sweetheart."

"I hope you don't take my decision personally," she said.

"I do, but that's okay."

Jack took both her hands and Stephanie stared down at his fingers, feeling the way she had when she'd said goodbye for the last time to her high-school boyfriend. Derek had been headed to Princeton and she to Stanford. They'd been in love the way children are. After he'd kissed her, she'd been certain they'd marry someday. But by Christmas they were no longer corresponding, let alone thinking of marriage. Derek spent the holidays skiing in Vermont while she'd gone to Hawaii with her mother and Jane. She'd met a guy from Cal, Berkeley, on the beach in Maui and he had dispelled any notion of a correlation between physical attraction and a boy's suitability for marriage or any other serious relationship.

Now here she was with Jack Kidwell, in many ways still the naive girl she'd once been. The difference was, she was looking back on a misspent life, not a lost love or two. At eighteen she'd been looking ahead to a lifetime of happiness. What she saw now was a rare, perhaps final, chance at romance slipping through her fingers. She could grab it, sure, but there would almost certainly be a price to pay.

"Are you mad at me, Jack?" she asked.

"Of course not. Why should I be?"

"Your lips are saying one thing, your eyes another," she said.

"Stephanie, if you knew what I was thinking, you'd have slapped me already."

She tilted her head defiantly. "You're trying to make this hard for me, aren't you?"

"Hey, sweetheart," he said, caressing her cheek, "this isn't goodbye forever. It's just for a couple of days." He paused for a heartbeat. "Isn't it?"

"That's what I was thinking. Weren't you?"

"Well, once you get the disks, there's nothing to keep you from heading right for the Caymans."

"I wouldn't do that," she said.

He contemplated her for several moments. "No, I guess you wouldn't."

"What if our situations were reversed, Jack?"

"I won't insult your intelligence by saying I'd do the same. The truth of the matter is, I don't know what I'd do."

She peered into his eyes, feeling a deep stirring. "Thank you for having the integrity to admit it."

"I guess having integrity is something," he said, smiling sadly.

"You know why I decided to go get the disks myself, Jack? Because I feel the need to take charge of my own life. That's suddenly become very important to me."

He considered that before he finally nodded, his eyes a bit moist. "Oddly enough, I think I understand." Then he reached under his shirt and pulled a small handgun from under his belt. "I keep this on the boat, but seeing as I won't be transporting precious cargo until we rendezvous, I want you to have it. It won't hurt to be prepared."

"What about customs?"

"If they're suspicious enough to search your purse, you're already in trouble. If you're determined to do this, then you should have the gun, Stephanie."

He weighed it in his palm. She gazed down at the shiny metal and shivered. Jack put it in her hand and said, "I've talked to Sonia. She'll be waiting for you outside customs."

Stephanie nodded. "I'm looking forward to meeting her."

"Well, time's a wasting," he said. "I've got a long way to go."

A deeper feeling of desperation went through her. Jack must have seen it in her eyes because he took her hand.

"You know, I'm basically a gentleman," he said, "hard as that may be to believe. But I'm going to risk my reputation and kiss you goodbye."

With that, he took her into his arms and kissed her, lightly on the lips at first, then more deeply. She kissed him back, glad he'd read what was in her heart. And after brushing her cheek affectionately with his fingers, he gave her chin a squeeze. "Good luck, sweetheart," he whispered. "I'll be thinking about you." Then he left.

Malva had found a suitcase for her as well as more clothes. Françoise had brought a few things, too. Stephanie picked out what she wanted and Malva helped her pack.

As Stephanie folded the jacket, skirt and blouse she'd worn on the plane from San Francisco, she marveled at how much they seemed like artifacts, relics from a bygone era. It was incredible to think that had only been four days ago. Four morning papers, four breakfasts. At home it wasn't even time for a change of sheets. And yet she felt not only that her life had changed, but that she was a different person—or at least one in transition.

"I've decided to quit my job," Malva told her. "I'm not tellin' Nigel until he gets back, but I wanted you to know. I've been livin' on my dreams too long."

"I know the feeling."

"What was *your* dream?" Malva asked.

"I guess all my dreams were for my daughter. I was just existing. Looking back on it, I'm embarrassed that I was so passive for so long."

"Weren't you gettin' a divorce when your husband was killed?"

"Even that was more Jean Claud's doing than mine. He forced my hand and I didn't even know it."

Malva held up two nightgowns. "Want to pack both or choose one?"

"Neither. I kind of like sleeping in a T-shirt. I've been doing it since the boat."

"A lot of folks in the Caribbean don't wear a thing to bed."

Stephanie wondered if she could do the same, if she could spend her life in the tropical air, living slowly, sensuously, like Malva and, for that matter, Jack. What would she be giving up if she didn't go home? A few friends, her house. She'd always liked San Francisco. Northern California was a wonderful place, but had it outlived its usefulness? With Zanny and Jean Claud both dead, there was no compelling reason to return. But did she belong anywhere else?

Stephanie glanced over at the picture of Zanny, which she'd put on the dresser. Though she'd looked at it a couple of times since her arrival, she hadn't really dwelled on it. Her daughter had not been central to her thoughts to the same degree she had been the past year.

She went over and picked up the photograph. That knot she always got in her chest soon followed. She sank onto the bed, caressing the frame with her thumbs.

"You miss your baby, don't you?" Malva said, sitting next to her.

Stephanie couldn't speak. She gave a little nod.

"I never had a child," Malva said. "Which probably explains why I'm the way I am."

"It's no consolation, I know," Stephanie croaked, "but the one thing worse than not having a child, is having one and losing her." She stared at Zanny's beautiful face. "But you know, Malva, this ordeal has awakened me to one thing I didn't fully appreciate before—it isn't right to live on the memory of my daughter, any more than it was right to live my life through her when she was alive."

"You're a lot stronger than you think, honey. We all are," Malva said, putting her arm around Stephanie's shoulders.

"I don't feel it now. In fact, I feel like crying."

"How long has it been since you've had a good mama-like hug?"

"Far too long."

"Well, you come and get yourself one now."

The two of them embraced and within moments Stephanie was weeping, the pent-up anxiety of days pouring out of her. She hadn't had anyone hold her when she cried since her mother died years before. When she finally stopped, Malva got her a few tissues from the dresser. Stephanie blew her nose and dabbed her eyes.

"I'm sorry."

"Tears are never a reason to be sorry."

"I didn't realize how badly I needed to do that."

"I did," Malva said. "I could see it comin'."

"You've been very kind. A godsend."

"And you've been like a fresh breeze for us, honey," Malva said, sounding a bit wistful. "I can see why Jackie likes you so much."

Stephanie carefully wiped the corners of her eyes. "You really think he does, Malva?"

"Oh, he does, all right. And if I had to guess, I think he might regret that money that's standin' between you as much as you do."

"I'm not sure I believe that."

"Time will tell, now, won't it, honey?" The woman laughed. "Believe me, it's a whole bunch easier to solve other people's problems than your own." Malva gestured for her to get up and get to work. "Come on, now, let's finish packin'. Bobby Brown should be circlin' overhead any minute now. You best be ready."

"You know about Bobby?" Stephanie asked, putting the last of the folded clothes into the case.

Malva gave her a level look. "Stephanie, there ain't nothin' that goes on in this house that I don't know about. Not a thing."

Stephanie and Françoise stood on the veranda waiting for the seaplane. Stephanie wore a big floppy hat and huge sunglasses. In her purse she had Françoise's passport, the locker key and the gun. While they waited, Françoise had been talking about shopping in Charlotte Amalie. Stephanie managed to say enough to keep the conversation going, but she was thinking about Jack and second-guessing herself. A big part of her wished she were on the *Lucky Lady* right now.

"I'm sure I don't have to say this," Françoise said, "but don't worry about Nigel. He might be randy, but he's a gentleman."

"Oh, I know. I'm not worried about him."

"Jacques, then?"

Stephanie nodded. "In my shoes, would you trust him?"

"Trusting *any* man is a gamble. *Tiens.* It always comes down to what's in it for them. But if I had to put myself into some man's hands, Jacques would not be a bad choice."

Everybody seemed to like Jack and had good things to say about him. But they weren't the ones dangling millions of dollars before his nose. Stephanie decided the one absolutely honest thing he'd said was when he told her that he wasn't sure what he'd do if their situations were reversed.

"It could be that I'll never find out how trustworthy he is," Stephanie said. "Nigel and I may fail to get the disks. We might even get arrested."

"But you're brave, *chérie,* that will help you carry the day."

Stephanie could only hope that was true. Yet *brave* was not a word she normally associated with herself. Nor would Françoise, had she known her just a week ago. But if Stephanie truly had grit, surely it had been there all along. What had made the difference? Circumstance?

They gazed out at the cove. The *Lucky Lady* was gone but Nigel's boat remained anchored. Françoise wouldn't set sail until after the seaplane left. Then—with Nigel's assistance—Stephanie realized it would all be in her hands.

"Le voilà!" Françoise said, pointing to a plane emerging from a big fluffy cloud to the west. "Finally."

As the plane descended, Stephanie was able to see the floats hanging below the craft. Chartering a seaplane had been a clever idea. It was fortunate Jack had a friend that owned one. She could only hope not *too* fortunate.

The plane circled a hundred feet above the treetops, its engine loud. Nigel, who was with Joseph at the water's edge, waved at her to join him. All morning, he'd been like a boy waiting for a pony ride.

"*Allez,*" Françoise said. "*Monsieur le général vous fait venir.*"

The woman embraced. Malva and Tess had come to the door to witness the departure. Stephanie gave them each a final hug goodbye. Before they'd left her room, Stephanie had given Malva five hundred dollars to help her get started in her new life, which the housekeeper had refused to take until Stephanie insisted.

Her purse in hand, Stephanie walked down the lawn. Joseph had their bags in the launch, ready and waiting. He and Nigel helped her aboard, then Nigel climbed into the boat. Joseph, with scarcely any strain, lifted the bow and shoved the launch back into the lapping waves. Once they were floating, he lifted his large legs over the gunwales, his pant legs dripping wet at the bottom. After moving to the stern with the agility of a big cat, he started the outboard motor. As they putted out into the cove, Stephanie turned and waved to the three women on the veranda. They all waved back.

Passing Nigel's yacht, they glanced up at the two crewmen who'd been observing the proceedings with equanimity, breaking their stance only to give Nigel a casual salute, which he returned. He was seated in the bow and looked back at Stephanie, grinning from one ear to the other.

"Grand, isn't it?" he said enthusiastically. "Splendid morning!"

Stephanie nodded in response, amused and afraid, aware once more how terribly far she was from Mill Valley.

"Another proof that the dragons in life are every bit as important as the roses!" Nigel said over the loud putting of the outboard. "Every man needs a good battle from time to time."

"And a good nurse, *n'est-ce pas?*" she could almost hear Françoise say.

They slowed as they approached the seaplane, which

bobbed in the gentle waves at the mouth of the cove. The door had been opened and Bobby Brown, a tall, slender man wearing a khaki shirt and pants and aviator glasses, was standing on the float, waiting for them. This, Stephanie reminded herself, was the father of the girl Jack had been making love with on the *Lucky Lady*. There was no particular significance to that, apart from the fact that Jack had entrusted them to Bobby's care, and yet she felt a sense of shame, if only on Jack's behalf.

Joseph slowed the launch. Bobby, obviously a veteran with tourists, had a chamber-of-commerce smile on his lips as he waited for the bow of the boat to nose up to the plane.

"Bobby, old chap!" Nigel said heartily. "Jolly good to see you."

"Hi, Mr. Lovejoy, good to see you, too," he said, taking hold of the gunwale. His voice was a bit higher than his looks would suggest.

After tying the bowline to one of the struts on the plane, he pulled on the side of the boat until the port side of the launch was flush against the float. A broad smile still on his handsome face, Bobby nodded at Stephanie.

"I'd like to present my dear friend and travel companion, Bobby Brown," Nigel said. "This is Françoise Gaudier from Paris, France."

"Enchantée, monsieur," Stephanie said, offering her hand.

"Howdy, ma'am," Bobby said. "Nice morning for flying." He inclined his head in a conspiratorial signal to Nigel as if to say he approved. "Let me help you aboard and we'll get under way."

It only took a few minutes to get their luggage in the hold and for them to clamber aboard. Stephanie took the rear seat. Nigel sat in front with Bobby.

As the pilot prepared for takeoff, Stephanie watched for signs of treachery. So far there'd been nothing. Bobby Brown seemed like a man eager to make a buck, doing his thing with the tourists.

The engine roaring, Bobby turned the plane into the wind and eased the throttle forward. They were soon skipping across the water, the waves thumping at the floats like speed bumps. Then, as they became lighter in the water, the vibration was reduced to a rapid tap, a sort of tattoo that suddenly stopped as they lifted steeply into the sky.

Stephanie glanced back over her shoulder as the Isola Lovejoy dropped away. It had the appearance of a giant lily pad fringed with sparkling sand. Before they banked, she caught a glimpse of the beach where Jack had taken her to swim. A stab of sadness went through her as she recollected that evening. A part of her deeply regretted they hadn't made love.

In front, Nigel and Bobby chatted, but Stephanie couldn't understand what they were saying because of the noise of the engine. She felt oddly calm, though underneath there was residual tension.

After they'd been airborne for fifteen or twenty minutes, she pressed her head against the window and stared down at the sea. They weren't flying at a very high altitude, perhaps only a couple of thousand feet. In the aqua blue water she caught sight of a yacht, its white sail gleaming in the morning sun. She wondered if it was the *Lucky Lady*. It seemed about the right size and, as best she could tell, they had traveled about the distance Jack would have covered in the time he'd been at sea. Before the boat slipped from view, she had a glimpse of a solitary figure in the cockpit. She wanted to think it was Jack, that he was doggedly making his way to their rendezvous point.

If she'd gone with him, they'd be looking up at the seaplane now, knowing Nigel and Françoise were on their way to St. Thomas. But for better or worse, she'd chosen a different course.

Long Beach, California

Ruth Moskowitz, Julius Behring's secretary of eleven years, arrived at the office at seven and was dismayed to see her boss already at his desk. "Mr. Behring, Mr. Behring," she lamented, "why didn't you tell me you were coming early today? I would have been here to make your coffee. You think I don't care about these things?"

"It's not necessary, Ruth. I don't need coffee the minute I arrive."

"Not necessary to you maybe, Mr. Behring, but for me, it's necessary. It doesn't feel right."

"All right, Ruth. So get me coffee now, like a good girl. You're keeping me waiting."

She ran off, leaving Julius amused, shaking his head. Ruth was the one constant at Inter-America Ventures, his "faithful woman" in the office, nearly as devoted to him as his dear Anita had been at home.

"Here's your coffee, Mr. Behring," she said, returning. Ruth never called him Julius, except on those rare occasions when they discussed personal matters. In a business context it was always "Mr. Behring."

"Fine, thank you, Ruth," he said, continuing to look over the financial reports from the folder she kept up-to-date on the credenza behind his desk.

The ritual was still observed though with less ardor now that he was only marginally involved in the day-to-day operations. Inter-America's chief financial officer worried about the little numbers these days—Julius concerned himself only with the bottom line. And now that he was down to visiting the office only two or three times a week, he was perfectly aware he couldn't affect the little things, anyway. Still, it was wise never to admit it. People knew an old dog lost his teeth, but they had to be kept uncertain if and when he might bite. That was true of everyone—including his own son.

"Anything else you need, Mr. Behring.?" Ruth asked.

"I'm expecting a call from Rico," he said. "Be sure it comes right through."

"Yes, of course."

Julius gave a little flip of his fingers and Ruth withdrew, closing the door to his office behind her. He stared after her, her presence staying with him longer than usual. He wasn't sure why he was feeling nostalgic of late, but he was. That trip to Disneyland with Rhonda and the baby over the weekend had affected him. He'd strolled around the teaming park, realizing that he'd never once done that with his own wife and child. It had been an eye-opener. Julius knew that, as a family man, his son was a jerk, but in his own way, he had been just as bad.

The intercom line buzzed and Julius picked up the phone.

"Mr. Behring," Ruth said, "Mr. Green is here to see you."

Julius had asked Abe to report to him about Rhonda's rug salesman, and they'd agreed it would be in person rather than on the phone, though Julius wasn't thrilled at the thought of Abe visiting their offices. But dirty work required the services of dirty people. "Send him in," he told the secretary.

Abe Green opened the door, stepping inside and closing it carefully behind him. "'Morning, Julius."

"Hi, Abe. Thanks for coming. Sit down."

His old friend looked around. "Nice setup you got here, Julius. I assume it's a safe place to talk."

"This is the age of technology, my friend. Daily sweeps of the office for bugs is a way of life."

Abe unbuttoned his coat and dropped into a chair. "Yeah, well, I guess I'm old-fashioned."

"So," Julius said, "you got a report for me on the rug schmuck."

"Yeah."

"Did Mr. Hachigian get our message?"

"He shipped the wife and kids off to Michigan and he's trying to sell the store."

"Sounds like he did get the message."

"I think so, Julius."

"According to Wayne Driscoll, he hasn't tried to get a hold

of Rhonda. She's been staying home with the kid, going to the grocery store, the usual stuff.''

"Looks like maybe your kid's marriage is saved," Abe said, folding his hands over his stomach.

"Thanks to your persuasive powers," Julius said.

"Hey, anything for a friend."

The intercom buzzed again. Julius picked up the phone.

"Mr. Behring," Ruth said, "it's your son on line two."

"Thanks." He put down the receiver a moment. "So, what's your assessment, Abe? We seen the last of Hachigian?"

"I'd say yes, but he's a putz. Sometimes they fool you."

"Stay on him, if you would, until you're sure he's out of town."

"Right. By the way, Julius, how's it going with my one point five mil?"

"Don't have anything definite yet, but I'm expecting a counteroffer on that frozen-fish company I mentioned. It's a nice little business, Abe."

"Clean?"

"Very clean."

"No heads to knock around?" Abe said.

"None. Clean business is good for the heart, my friend. The older I get, the more I appreciate that fact. Now if my son would just grow up."

"I hear ya," Abe said, getting to his feet. "I know you gotta talk to him."

"As soon as I have something on the fish place, I'll call you."

"I'll do the same with the rug guy," Abe said before slipping out of the office, quiet as a thief.

Julius picked up the phone and pushed the button for line two.

"Rico," he said.

"Pops, we did it."

"You got our friend?"

"This afternoon we'll have her. The sea captain's woman called. He's taking our deal. Two o'clock give or take, he'll hand our girl over here at the ferry port at the other end of the island from town. In an hour I'll have her sweet ass."

"What about the half million, Rico?"

"He wants it. We won't get the disks until the money's in his Swiss account."

"He gave you the number?"

"I'll get it at the dock when he hands her over."

"Wait a minute. He's handing her over and *then* we're getting the account number?"

"Sure, Pop. We can't get the disks without payin' so he knows we're going to deliver the bread."

"But if we've got her, won't we be able to get the disks as easily as he can?"

Rico didn't say anything for a moment. "Maybe he's already got the disks, Pop."

"When?"

"Shit, I don't know. None of that was in the message."

"That's my point," Julius said. "If you don't know the answers, you should be asking yourself if any of this makes sense."

"I don't know what you mean."

"Let me say it straight, son. The sea captain is fucking with you. If he's had the disks all along, where did he get them?"

"From her."

"But she didn't have them when she left the island…unless she picked them up on the way to the boat. And that doesn't fit with the way people have been behaving."

"Shit, Pop, maybe he came back himself and got them since."

"That's possible, I suppose, but I still think the sonovabitch is fucking with you."

"What makes you so sure?"

"Some things you feel in your gut, Rico. It's like when you

know your wife's playing around. It just comes to you. Understand?''

Rico was silent. "I was wondering if maybe it wasn't a little too easy."

"That's always a good indicator. Seldom is anything that matters easy. What did Oscar say about Kidwell's offer?"

"He didn't say nothing, Pop."

"Nothing?"

Rico hesitated. "All right, so he said maybe it sounded a little too easy."

"But you didn't listen to him."

"We had an argument, Pop, what can I say?"

"So what's Oscar doing?"

"We got this call from the cops that they got a passenger from the flight who said she took a bag from some other passenger and hid it. Some girl on her honeymoon. Oscar went to check that out."

Julius thought for a moment. "You know, Rico, I don't like it that the captain's got you going to the far end of the island. You probably intend to have your entire army there, don't you?"

"I've got most everybody down here, yeah. I'm here myself."

Julius groaned, trying to decide how to deal with his son's stupidity. "If you want my guess, son, at two o'clock the captain or the broad will be coming into the airport or someplace else that is a long, long way from the ferry port."

"You think?"

"Let's put it this way, I wouldn't assume he's showing up where he says. *When*, however, is a pretty good bet."

"Fuck."

"My sentiments precisely. Look, Rico. Post some of your people at the ferry port, but you might want to scatter the others around, keeping their eyes open. Could be you'll spot Kidwell and the woman someplace else. And if I'm wrong, then I'm wrong."

"Right, Pop, whatever you say. Anything else?"

"That's it for now," Julius said. "Keep me informed, will you?"

"Sure."

Rico sounded a little dispirited, but Julius wasn't going to hit him while he was down. "Talk to you soon."

"Bye, Pop."

Julius hung up. He thought for a minute, then buzzed Ruth on the intercom.

"Yes, Mr. Behring?"

"Ruth, get me on the next flight you can for the Virgin Islands, will you?"

"Yes, sir."

Julius slipped the receiver back into the cradle and sighed. After living a charmed life, he realized that bastard, failure, may have finally slipped up on him and had slapped him in the face.

St. Thomas

They had flown down the Sir Francis Drake Channel, past the northern shore of St. John, and could see the rugged profile of St. Thomas looming ahead. Below them, the St. John ferry was doggedly moving toward Red Hook Dock on the western tip of the island. Stephanie gazed down at it, recalling how she and Jack had made that same passage in the dead of night, unaware of how severe a whack they'd get from the tail of a hurricane. Thinking back on it, she was amazed that they'd made it. And still more amazed that she was returning to St. Thomas of her own free will.

Bobby Brown got on the radio to check the weather. As he did, Nigel turned to her, a grin on his round, sunglasses-masked face. "Well, *madame,* only minutes to duty-free shopping."

"I can hardly wait, *chéri*," Stephanie said, trying to affect the sort of enthusiasm Françoise would have showed.

Nigel reached over the seat and patted Stephanie's knee. If he guessed she was nervous, he was right. They'd land soon. The first challenge was to get safely through customs, then hope none of Oscar Barbadillo's boys would be waiting on the other side of the gate.

Another five minutes and Charlotte Amalie appeared through a break in the puffy cumulus clouds. Bobby began his descent, having gotten clearance to put down at the seaplane facility in the harbor. As they approached Fisherman's Reef Point, Bobby pointed out one of the larger, twin-engine sea-planes taking off from the harbor on its way to St. Croix.

Tracing the rim of the bay, they dropped below a thousand feet, then banked sharply over the town. Bobby aligned the craft with the lane as they passed over a parasailer moving parallel to the shore. Then they dropped sharply toward the water, leveling off just before the floats began clicking the tips of the waves. Once the engine had been cut, they slowed quickly, settling into the water. Bobby taxied to the edge of the course and waited for a launch to pick them up and take them to the customs house. Stephanie had to will her muscles to relax.

"I fancy you'll adore Charlotte Amalie, Françoise," Nigel said.

Stephanie peered out the window through her dark glasses. *"Oui, c'est beau."*

"Your first trip to St. Thomas, ma'am?" Bobby asked.

"No, *monsieur*," she replied in her phony French accent. "The last time I was just passing through and I didn't get to see much."

"This time we'll pick up a few things, won't we, darling?" Nigel said.

"You can't beat the shopping," Bobby said. "That's for sure."

The launch from the seaplane airline arrived and they disembarked under Bobby's supervision. Stephanie took a seat while Nigel stood where he could talk to Bobby, who'd climbed down on the float. The wind tossed Nigel's thin hair and he patted it down with his palm.

"We're agreed on arrangements, are we, then?"

"You've got my beeper number, Mr. Lovejoy," Bobby said. "I'll be standing by the next forty-eight, like I said."

"Capital."

"You figure most likely tomorrow, right?"

"My guess is it'll be tomorrow afternoon."

"I'll be ready."

Nigel nodded and took a seat next to Stephanie. He took her hand, as he would Françoise's, but Stephanie thought nothing of it. If she had to return to St. Thomas, she could imagine no better way than in the company of a flamboyant Englishman. Nigel was better than the best disguise.

The launch, operated by two men, headed for shore and the customs house. The American flag flying over it seemed somehow false. Stephanie had become so distrusting of the world that nothing familiar seemed safe anymore. The only certainty in her life was uncertainty.

When the launch pulled up to the dock, Stephanie was overcome with dread. Her legs felt weak. With help, she climbed onto land as two uniformed officers watched. One of the men from the boat pointed toward them and an officer beckoned them over as a porter with a hand truck took their bags. Nigel grasped her arm and they began walking toward the building. With Jack's gun in it, her purse felt as if it weighed a ton.

"Steady, love," Nigel said from the corner of his mouth.

Stephanie had to remind herself to breathe.

"I'll be stocking up on spirits, you can count on that," Nigel said with full-throated cheer. "Marvelous prices. Even our own scotch whiskey is incredibly cheap."

The officers, both in sunglasses, watched them approach.

"Is this true of champagne, *aussi?*"

"Oh, yes, my love. Better prices than in Paris." He nodded to the officers. "Gentlemen."

They entered. The building was virtually empty except for three customs officers, one of whom was speaking with a woman voicing a complaint rather loudly.

Nigel bellied up to the counter a few steps from the woman. "Afternoon, gentlemen," he said cheerily as he presented their passports.

"Afternoon, sir," a young, lanky fellow said. "Welcome to the U.S. Virgin Islands."

"Thank you indeed."

He glanced at Stephanie. "Ma'am."

"Bonjour, monsieur."

"You're coming from…"

"British Virgins most immediately," Nigel replied. "Popped over for a bit of shopping."

The officer looked at the covers of the passports, then opened them. He gave Stephanie a long, appraising look and she smiled back at him, her heart tripping wildly under the calm demeanor she affected.

"Vous êtes française?" he said.

"Oui, monsieur, c'est juste. J'habite à Paris."

"Gay Paree, huh?"

Stephanie smiled. "Eet ees not always so gay, *monsieur*, but eet ees always Parec."

"No place like home."

"Mais oui, monsieur."

The officer turned his attention to Nigel and asked if they had anything to declare. Nigel said no. "And when we returned to Virgin Gorda we planned to say the same thing to the British customs chaps. I trust you don't have any mates over there."

The man laughed as he stamped their passports. "Man, you can smuggle on that side of the border all you want." He handed back the passports. "Have a nice visit."

It was all Stephanie could do to keep from sighing with

relief. Nigel signaled to the porter to follow and they went out the front door to freedom.

"God," Stephanie said out of the corner of her mouth, "I thought I'd die."

"Françoise would be proud of you."

Ahead was the gate. A single police officer stood outside, chatting with a boy with a small tub of iced soft drinks at his feet. At the curb beyond them was a blue Toyota, the driver an attractive blonde in a tank top, her hair swept up. Judging by her conspicuous sensuality, Stephanie figured it had to be Sonia Velasco.

As they drove, Oscar Barbadillo peered out the window of the patrol car at the sea. The young couple in back were whispering between themselves, the cop humming softly what sounded like a reggae tune, all of them oblivious to the fact that thirty million dollars was hanging in the balance.

Rico had been so sure that Kidwell was going to deliver the woman and the disks, that half a million dollars had done the trick. But when Oscar had heard that this was all to take place at the other end of the island, he knew something was wrong. "Fine," he told his cousin, "go down there and deal with Kidwell, I'll talk to the honeymooners."

Oscar had been disgusted by his cousin's stupidity. Rico had been so sure that Stephanie Reymond was within his grasp that even that hooker, Maria Riveros, in her usual state of undress that morning, hadn't been able to distract him. In a surprising show of maturity, Rico had sent her off to the pool so that he and Oscar could talk business. Their discussion had soon turned into an angry shouting match. Finally they'd settled their differences by agreeing that each would do his own thing.

The main problem now was that Rico had all their resources at the ferry terminal and only one man was left at the airport. The important question was whether the bag and the disks were still in the locker as the honeymooners said, or if Kidwell and the woman had already managed to get to them.

The kid in back leaned forward and tapped Oscar on the shoulder. "Excuse me, but are we going to be able to go after Tiffany shows you where she put the bag?"

"Yeah, that's all we need."

"We aren't going to have to stay in St. Thomas and be witnesses in a trial or anything, are we?"

"No," Oscar said. "It's nothing like that. All we need is that bag."

Tiffany spoke up. "I didn't know there was stolen money in it," she said. "The lady made it sound like you were some kind of criminal or something. If we'd known you were working with the police, we'd have given you the bag right then, honest. I really thought she was in danger."

"In danger of being caught," Oscar said. "But don't worry. Once I've got the bag, you can go back to your hotel and finish your honeymoon."

"We've only got two more days," Brian lamented.

"But you're earning yourself five hundred bucks for a few hours of your time. That's a new dishwasher or whatever, right?"

The cop driving glanced over at him and smiled faintly. Oscar checked his watch.

"How long before we reach the airport?"

"Ten, fifteen minutes, Mr. Barbadillo."

It was nearly two-thirty, which meant that if Kidwell and Stephanie had arrived when they said, they'd either be in Rico's hands or on their way to the airport. The question was who would arrive first.

Stephanie leaned forward between the front seats, sighing with relief at the blast of tepid air whooshing over her from the air-conditioning vent. They were on the highway leading to the airport now, Nigel in front, next to Sonia.

Sonia had taken them to a quiet little bar on the waterfront where they spent a few minutes laying plans. Jack had wanted them to go to the airport immediately, but they needed to be clear on who would do what, and where they'd go afterward.

Sonia had been friendly, but businesslike. Stephanie had watched her with near-pathological fascination. She checked out her skin and her figure, which was voluptuous, if augmented a little by the odd extra pound or two. This was a woman with ripe, earthy beauty, and she was most definitely Jack's lover. Stephanie had absolutely no doubt about that.

Stephanie was fairly confident now that Sonia was as trustworthy as Jack had said. The woman was most definitely taking a chance in helping them, which, in Stephanie's mind, confirmed her devotion and allegiance to Jack. The realization left Stephanie feeling as jealous as she was relieved. Sonia glanced at her in the rearview mirror.

"Jack tells me you're a recent widow."

"Yes." Stephanie stopped to calculate. "Very recent. It hasn't even been a week." God, she thought, how was that possible? She felt as though she was midway through a second lifetime.

"Then you're still numb."

"That hardly begins to describe it."

Sonia glanced at Nigel. "You ever been married?"

"Regularly," he replied, giving her a wink.

"You're an addict, in other words."

"I'm addicted to women, not wives, love, but I confess to occasional bouts of weakness."

He chuckled, pleased with himself. Sonia glanced back at Stephanie with a knowing look.

As Sonia and Nigel chatted, Stephanie opened her purse, dug out the locker key and weighed it in her hand, feeling a curious sort of reverence. To Jack and Inter-America Ventures, it was likely the key to thirty million dollars. But to Stephanie, money wasn't the only issue. There was principle involved. This was *her* inheritance Jean Claud had taken, after all, money that had come to her from her father. Likewise, the portfolio they had accumulated over twenty years of marriage belonged to her. She was simply trying to reclaim what was rightfully hers.

It seemed odd that the three of them were on this joint escapade, each for very different reasons. Sonia was doing this for Jack. Nigel was doing it more for his own pleasure than any other reason. Stephanie couldn't help wondering if they'd have the same enthusiasm for the venture if they knew Oscar Barbadillo the way she did.

Sonia came to the turn for the airport. Stephanie started giving herself a pep talk, still disbelieving that she'd put herself into this position. Perspiration ran off of her, despite the blast of cool air from the front. In some ways, it was like her wedding day—a curious mixture of hope and dread. That probably wasn't a good omen, when she stopped to think about it.

The terminal building came into view. Taxis were leaving and arriving. Jack was probably right—it was best to attempt this amid the hubbub. Sonia pulled up to the curb.

"I'll wait here as long as I can," she said. "If they make me move, I'll pull up to the far end."

"Lovely," Nigel said, the expression, tossed off lightly, sounding particularly absurd.

Stephanie reached for the door handle, but her hand was so wet with perspiration that it slipped and she broke a nail. "Damn," she muttered. Another bad omen.

She and Nigel were on the sidewalk now. A couple of children came running by. One bumped into Nigel and went on without a word. A porter approached. Nigel waved him off. Stephanie wiped her upper lip and adjusted her glasses, suddenly losing confidence in her disguise. The locker key was in her fist. She'd been holding it so tight that her palm hurt.

"You look lovely, my darling," Nigel said. "Never more beautiful."

It was an odd thing to say and completely irrelevant, but

somehow it made her feel better, which may have been his intent. Stephanie girded herself and took his arm.

They started for the entrance when she noticed a police car pull up. Her insides clenched. When the door opened and she saw Oscar Barbadillo emerge, she stopped dead. His sinisterly handsome face, so frightening that day, made her quail.

"Darling?" Nigel said.

Stephanie managed to catch her breath only when she realized Barbadillo hadn't seen her; he wasn't even looking her way. Instead, he opened the rear door of the car. A young woman emerged, followed by a young man. When she realized it was Brian and Tiffany Harvey, the newlyweds from the plane, she gasped.

"Who are they?" Nigel asked quietly.

Stephanie ducked her head and pulled Nigel in the other direction. "My God," she said under her breath. "It's the man who kidnapped me and they have the girl with them who put the case in the locker. They must be coming for it."

Nigel's mouth was agape. "What rotten bloody luck."

Stephanie took a peek. Barbadillo, Brian and Tiffany headed into the building. She was unsure whether to leave or stay to see what would happen next. Since the trio seemed unaware of her presence, it seemed safe enough to watch them from afar. The one good thing was she at least knew they weren't lying in wait for her.

Still holding Nigel's arm, she went with him inside the cavernous building. A tour group flowed around them like sheep passing a rock. A baby cried, drowned out by the incoherent bellow of the public address system. Barbadillo and the Harveys met up with Carlos, the man at the apartment where Oscar had taken her. The entourage headed for the bank of lockers. Stephanie and Nigel drifted along behind.

"Rotten bloody luck," Nigel mumbled again.

Stephanie saw that, barring a miracle, the game was over. But something drew her along. She worried about the Harveys. Presumably the kids weren't in danger, probably having been duped by Barbadillo. Still, given the kind of person Oscar was, she couldn't be certain. And the fact that she was responsible for the pair even being there made her sick.

The group had reached the bank of lockers where a couple of passengers were busy depositing or retrieving luggage. Tiffany went to the lockers and walked back and forth, as though trying to remember which one contained the alligator case. Judging by the way she shook her head, she wasn't sure. Stephanie and Nigel ventured a bit closer, but knew they had to keep a safe distance.

"One thing certain," Nigel whispered, "they won't be opening the locker without assistance."

"Yeah, but what good will that do?" she replied, squeezing the key in her fist.

The group at the lockers conferred for a minute or two, then Carlos, Brian and Tiffany went off, leaving Oscar Barbadillo behind.

"They're dividing their forces," Nigel said. "Probably going to look for somebody with a master key. This jolly well may be the opportunity we need."

"But Oscar's still there," Stephanie said. Then, the gun in her purse coming to mind, she added, "What can we do, shoot him?"

"If we could only divert his attention somehow."

It was apparent that would be necessary as Barbadillo kept an eye on the people opening lockers, standing right behind them until he was satisfied an alligator case wasn't being removed.

"Do you suppose if we set off the bloody fire alarm he'd leave?" Nigel asked.

"I doubt it. Not until the flames overwhelmed him."

"There must be something…"

Stephanie got an idea. "Oscar's a ladies' man," she said. "A woman might turn his eye long enough for us to grab the case."

Nigel looked around them. "But who could we bribe or convince on short notice?"

She stared at Barbadillo. "Maybe he likes Frenchwomen."

"You, Stephanie?"

"I think it's our only chance."

"Don't you think he'd recognize you?"

"Maybe. But the accent might throw him." She pressed the key into Nigel's hand. "When I get his back turned, you get the case. It'll be one of those lockers where Tiffany was looking. The number's on the key."

He examined it.

"Once you've got it, go to the car," she said. "When you're out of sight, I'll follow."

"For God's sake, are you certain you want to do this?"

"Wasn't it James Bond who said, 'You only live once'?"

"I never paid much attention to *him* in those films, to be perfectly candid."

Stephanie gave him a quick kiss on the cheek. "Wish me luck, Nigel."

He could only mutter, "Good God…"

She headed for the lockers, weaving her way through clusters of passengers, exaggerating the swing of her hips. Oscar Barbadillo, wearing a red polo shirt, spotted her when she was about twenty feet away from him, his eyes immediately sliding up and down her frame.

"Pardon, monsieur," she said. "But ees eet possible you have a cigarette?"

Oscar smiled and for a terrifying moment Stephanie wasn't certain whether it was because he recognized her or because he was flattered by her attention to him.

"I've got a cigar, *mademoiselle*. Would that do?"

"Mon Dieu! Do I look like a *cowboy?"*

Barbadillo chuckled, flexing his large biceps. "Sorry, I can't help you with a smoke. But maybe there's something else I could…"

She dismissed him with a wave of her hand, throwing her head. "It's useless. Americans don't smoke anymore. *Merde.*"

"You could always buy a pack," he said, checking out her body.

In the corner of her eye, Stephanie saw Nigel moving around behind the Cuban to the bank of lockers. "I have only French francs," she said, "and the money exchange is…how do you say…temporarily closed."

"I could loan you a buck," Oscar said. "And later maybe you could buy me a cup of coffee. You arriving or leaving?"

"Arriving, *monsieur.*" She gave him a coquettish smile. "How about you?"

"Oh, I'm here for a while. You alone?"

In her peripheral vision Stephanie could see Nigel struggling with the key. She had a terrible feeling the lock had been changed. "Very alone," she said.

Barbadillo, growing wary, started to turn. Stephanie moved forward, putting her hand on his chest.

"But I would love company, *monsieur.* Perhaps I could buy you a drink. Where do you stay?"

Behind Barbadillo, Nigel had gotten the locker open and was pulling the case out when Oscar suddenly spun around, perhaps sensing something was going on. Seeing Nigel, he walked swiftly over as the case dropped into Nigel's hand. Stephanie froze with horror.

"Hey, what are you doing?" the Cuban demanded, taking Nigel's arm. "Who are you?"

"I beg your pardon, sir!" Nigel blustered.

"This case doesn't belong to you."

"It most certainly does! Take your hand off me! I insist!"

Stephanie knew she had to act and act quickly. Opening her purse, she reached in and grabbed the gun, but didn't remove it. Then she poked the Cuban in the back with the purse. "Let go of him, Oscar!" she commanded.

He glanced back over his shoulder and down into the open purse near his kidneys.

"It's loaded and I'd like nothing better than to shoot you!" she hissed, trying to sound as vile as she could.

Oscar Barbadillo looked positively incredulous. "*Caramba!*"

"Let go of him, damn it!" she said through her teeth.

He complied, but somehow managed to smile. "So, it's you, Stephanie. I thought you seemed familiar." Then he shook his head. "You're never going to get out of here in one piece."

"Yeah, well, if we don't, you're dead."

She glanced at Nigel, who was white as a sheet, his lower lip trembling.

"Let's go, Nigel," she said. "You lead the way. Mr. Barbadillo and I will follow."

They started across the terminal building, Stephanie keeping her purse clutched in her arms with the gun pointed toward the Cuban's back. She had no idea what she'd do if Oscar turned and hit her or started to run, but she knew her best hope was if he was as uncertain as she.

"Keep your hands where I can see them," she muttered, recalling the line she'd heard in a hundred movies.

Though she felt weak in the knees, there was also a sense of triumph welling inside her. The tables had been turned.

They stopped outside the building. Sonia's car was no longer where they'd left it, though the police car was still at the curb. The sight of it broke her confidence. Then, remembering Sonia saying she'd be at the end of the loading area, Stephanie peered along the row of taxis and vans, finally spotting Sonia on the sidewalk, waving. Nigel saw her at the same time.

"There she is!" he said, sounding relieved.

"Yes, but we have to walk past the cop."

"I'll divert him with a question," Nigel said. "When I've gotten his attention, you go on."

"Okay," Stephanie said, glancing toward the entrance, afraid Carlos would appear. "But hurry."

Nigel, the alligator case in hand, went off to speak to the cop.

"You actually think this will work, Stephanie?" Barbadillo said under his breath. "We've got this island sealed up, tight as a drum. You might have gotten in, but you'll never get out."

"I'll worry about that."

"It's not too late to deal," he said. "You take your inheritance, we'll take our money and everybody goes home happy."

"Oscar, in case you haven't noticed, you're bargaining from a position of weakness."

"You'll be sorry, *querida*."

Stephanie saw that Nigel was talking to the officer. It was time to go. She gave Oscar a nudge in the back. "Start walking," she commanded. "And no false moves."

They made it past the police car, Barbadillo strolling casually. He almost seemed too cooperative. She knew he was planning something, but what? It also occurred to her she didn't know what she would do with him. He'd probably figured that one out, too.

They reached Sonia, who stared at them quizzically.

"Who's he?"

"The guard dog," Stephanie replied. "We couldn't get the case without taking him prisoner."

"Prisoner? What do you plan to do with him?"

Just then, Nigel came hurrying up, red-faced and perspiring. "Now what?"

Stephanie agonized. "I guess we have to take Oscar with us. Maybe if we put him in the trunk."

"Here?" Sonia said.

"Pull the car up ahead, past those Dumpsters," Stephanie said. "Oscar and I will walk."

Sonia and Nigel got in the car and drove on. Stephanie and Barbadillo began walking.

"You're making a terrible mistake," he said. "These people, that European woman, works for Kidwell. They're going to take advantage of you, *querida,* believe me."

"Unlike you, right, Oscar?"

"You have the disks," he replied, "but I have the island. You're better off with me than with them."

"At least they haven't knocked me around, Oscar. I recall how you treated me."

"That was a mistake."

"You certainly have that right."

"They're going to take everything," he insisted. "I can guarantee you your share."

"Regretfully, I can't guarantee you *your* share, Oscar. I'm going to have to take it all."

Walking around the large industrial Dumpsters, they came to Sonia's Toyota. She and Nigel were standing beside it. The trunk was open. Oscar stopped and, turning to look at her, for the first time appeared a little bewildered.

"Okay," Stephanie said, finally removing the revolver from her purse and pointing it at his midsection. "Get in the trunk."

"Shouldn't we make sure he doesn't have a gun or something?" Nigel asked.

"Good point. Do you have a gun, Oscar? No," she said, catching herself. "Stupid question. Lean up against the side of the car, your hands on the roof."

Barbadillo complied.

"Search him, Nigel," she said.

Nigel felt around Barbadillo's waist even though there were no obvious bulges. Then he tentatively felt the Cuban's legs, down to his trouser cuffs. Nothing. Nigel told Oscar to get in the trunk. Muttering, he complied. Sonia slammed it shut.

"That's that," Sonia said, "but now what?"

"I couldn't shoot him and I couldn't leave him there." Stephanie looked over her shoulder toward the entrance to the terminal. "We'd better get out of here."

They piled in the car and Sonia took off. Stephanie, in back, only now began to realize what she'd done. Her heart was racing and her hands shaking. Nigel, who'd had Jane's case at his feet, handed it over the seat to her.

"Here you go, love. I believe this is what you came for."

She stared at it as she cradled it on her lap, amazed. Then it occurred to her it would be a good idea to check it out. How ironic if somebody had already removed the disks. She opened the zippered top and peered inside. Jane's laptop was there, the money and the disks, as well. Stephanie took a deep breath and sighed. "Lord, I can't believe it."

"We still have a problem," Sonia said. "That man in my trunk. We must dispose of him some way."

"We can't kill him," Stephanie said.

"I'm not advocating that, but we can't take him with us, either."

"Can we dump him in some remote spot?" Stephanie asked.

"It's not a large island. It wouldn't take long for him to walk to safety."

"Perhaps if we tie him up," Nigel volunteered.

"I don't have any rope in the car," Sonia said. "We'd have to buy some. Within minutes the police will be searching for us. We've got to hide quickly."

"I think I have the solution," Stephanie said. "Is there a remote spot on the way, someplace that's off the beaten track?"

Sonia thought for a moment. "Yes."

"Let's go there."

Back on the Harwood Highway, they headed west, instead of east toward town. After five or six miles, Sonia exited the highway, driving on a gravel road into the mountains. They were soon in dense vegetation. Sonia turned into a side track that was scarcely more than two ruts in the road. They passed a deserted shack and up a ravine, finally coming to a clearing, where they stopped.

"My former husband, Enrique, liked to do nude paintings of me in nature," Sonia said. "This is where we came."

She said it in a way that struck Stephanie as poignant. "I'd hate to desecrate it," she said.

Sonia dismissed the comment. "It's for a good cause. Besides, I don't own the place. Just the memories."

They got out and Sonia opened the trunk. Barbadillo squinted at them in the light.

"What now?" he groaned.

Stephanie pointed Jack's gun at him. "Get out."

He climbed out, his expression defiant, disgusted, but not quite so confident as before. "So?"

"Take off your shoes and socks and throw them in the trunk."

The Cuban did as she said.

"Now take off your clothes."

"What?"

"Do as I say," she commanded, pointing the gun insistently, "before I lose my patience."

"I dare say, I can jolly well miss this part," Nigel said, returning to the car.

"Doesn't bother me," Sonia said.

Oscar took off his shirt and pants, throwing them in the trunk. He stood in his shorts, unashamedly, though he was clearly angry.

"What do you think, Sonia?" Stephanie said. "Would it be completely unladylike to humiliate him?"

"With a gun in your hand," she said in her soft Scandinavian accent, "it's impossible to be ladylike."

"I agree. It's too late for virtue. Okay, Oscar, take off your shorts."

His eyes narrowed. "I promise you, you will hate the day you did this. I *will* make you sorry. You will pay, Stephanie. You will pay dearly."

"Take off the shorts and put them in the trunk."

He complied, peeling down his shorts and flinging them in the trunk, clearly too proud to be ashamed. His pride wouldn't let him turn his back. Stephanie and Sonia both stared at him.

"I've seen better," Sonia said after a moment. She slammed the trunk closed, then returned to the car.

Stephanie couldn't say the same. He was considerably larger than Jean Claud, but that was hardly enough in itself to make her want to linger. "Back away, Oscar."

He did as she told him, stepping gingerly on tender feet. Once he was thirty feet away, Stephanie went to the car.

"Pray you never see me again," he called to her, "because you'll hate it. I promise you that."

"Maybe we should both pray we never see each other again," she said and got in the back seat.

Sonia turned the car around as the Cuban watched. Then, as they started down the track, Barbadillo picked up a chunk of wood and hurled it at the car. It thumped on the trunk.

"*Puta!*" he screamed.

Sonia stuck her arm out the window, giving Oscar the Italian salute.

"Good gracious me," Nigel said. "I've just witnessed a side of the female psyche I've never ever seen before."

"Kind of scary, isn't it?" Sonia said with a grin.

The sun had set but the suite was still aglow with color from the western sky. Julius Behring sighed uncomfortably. His lower back was killing him. It had been a difficult trip and his body no longer tolerated long hours of sitting as it once did.

The virtually naked young woman seated across the room had not spoken for ten minutes now, and neither had Julius. But, judging by the way she was bouncing her leg, she was getting impatient again.

After cracking her gum a couple of times, she recrossed her legs and said, "So, tell me, Mr. Behring, why, just because you're Rico's old man, do I have to do what you say? Rico's the one paying me."

"Well, I've got news for you, Miss Riveros. Rico can pay because of me. If he can't buy a cup of coffee, it's because I say he can't. What I'm trying to tell you is that you're really working for me.''

"Hey, don't go getting any ideas, mister. *I* decide who fucks me and who doesn't. This is still a free country."

"I said nothing about sex."

"What *are* you saying, then?"

"I already explained. I want us to wait together for Rico to return, as we found each other."

"No offense, Mr. Behring, but that's kind of kinky. Why should I sit around in a wet swimming suit? If you was a gentleman, you'd let me get dressed."

"I need you as you are so Rico will learn a very important lesson. Now, please, I don't want to discuss this anymore."

"Geez," Maria said, snapping her gum before falling silent, though her leg continued to bounce. Julius was beginning to think he'd done Rhonda no favor by saving her marriage. Not that Rico seeing a hooker was a big deal in the ordinary course of things. It was Rico's timing that was all wrong.

Dusk had fallen and Julius decided the room needed light. He got up to turn on a lamp and had just dropped back down in his chair when the door opened and Rico came flying into the suite, Carlos right behind him.

"If Oscar double-crossed us," Rico was saying, "I'll rip his balls off with my bare…" His voice faded as he saw his father seated under the pictures of the Calypso dancers, the lamplight shining on his pale face. "Jesus…Pop."

"Good evening, Rico."

His son glanced over to the other side of the room where he saw Maria in her bikini, a severe frown on her face. "Oh, Christ," he said.

"Miss Riveros and I have had a nice chat while we waited for you, son. I'm glad you've had an enjoyable time in the Caribbean."

"Pop, it's not what you think."

"Oh?"

Rico flushed. He turned to Carlos, who'd stopped in the doorway. "Wait outside," he told him.

"Come in, Rico," Julius said. "And close the door."

He did as he was told.

"Look, Pop, I don't know what this cunt said, but she's just here, same as a maid or a chauffeur or somethin'. She doesn't mean anything. I've been working my ass off. A guy's got to eat and stuff."

"At thirty-five hundred a day, she's a very expensive meal."

"And nobody better think of screwing me out of my money neither," Maria said. "I blew off a regular to stay and party with Mr. Big Shot, and now I find out he's only junior."

"Shut the fuck up!" Rico roared at her.

"Rico," Julius said, "sit down."

"Pop, listen to me. We got a problem we gotta talk about."

"Rico, right now *you're* my problem. We're going to deal with one thing at a time."

"But listen, Oscar was at the airport with the people who hid the disks for the Reymond broad. And when Carlos went with the couple to get a master key, Oscar disappeared. He'd stayed behind to watch the locker, and when they came back he was gone."

"That makes no sense, Rico."

"The cop outside said Oscar never came out of the terminal, which means he sneaked out another way. The bastard double-crossed us, Pop."

Julius held up his hand, silencing him. Then he turned his attention to the girl. "Can you dress and get out of here in fifteen minutes?"

"If I get paid."

"How much do we owe you?"

"Well, it's more than five thousand now, but I'll settle for that. I didn't have to screw the prick this afternoon."

"You shut the fuck up!" Rico roared again, pointing his finger at her.

''Up yours, Rico. I'm dealing with your old man now. He's at least polite.''

Rico started to get up, but Julius ordered him back in his seat. ''Pay her five thousand, Rico,'' Julius calmly said. ''And make it fast.''

''I've got to go in the bedroom to get my roll.''

''Go.''

Rico left the room. Julius and the girl stared at each other.

''Your son can use his cock,'' Maria said, ''but he don't have clue one when it comes to using his brain.''

''I appreciate your opinion,'' Julius said, seeing she had more insight than Rico could ever hope to have. ''I'm sure I don't have to tell you that ten minutes from now you'll never recall having been here.''

''Piece of cake.''

''I'm serious, Miss Riveros. I have friends in Miami with big ears. I'll know exactly what you say and do. Am I making myself clear?''

She stared at him, her jaw dangling. ''Yes, Mr. Behring.''

Rico returned. He went to where Maria sat, holding a stack of one-hundred-dollar bills over her head. He let them rain down on her. She gathered them up in silence, then scampered off to the bedroom. Rico again took his seat.

Julius looked at him sternly. ''Back to Oscar. Are you saying he took the disks?''

''Yeah, Pop. That's exactly what I'm saying.''

''How could he without a key to the locker?''

Rico said nothing.

After a moment, Julius continued. ''The only possibility I can see is that Kidwell and/or the Reymond woman showed up while Oscar was alone,'' Julius said.

''If so, they talked him into joining up with them.''

Julius didn't want to believe that could happen. He searched for another explanation.

''Oscar might be blood relations,'' Rico went on, ''but we're talking thirty million bucks, Pop. We find the sonovabitch and we find the disks and the woman. I'll bet you anything.''

Julius continued to reflect. "Whatever did happen, this may be an opportunity for us, Rico.''

"How do you mean?''

"If Oscar disappeared, and we knew Kidwell and the woman were coming to the island, there's a good chance Oscar was kidnapped by them.''

"What?''

"At least that's the story we give the police. And that should justify a massive manhunt. Instead of relying on bribes, we get the police officially involved. As far as I'm concerned, my nephew has been kidnapped. I want you to get on the phone and inform the police.''

"Now?''

"Now. Tell them we believe he was kidnapped by Kidwell, Mrs. Reymond and Kidwell's European lady friend. The more of them that are arrested, the better our chances are of getting the information we need.''

Rico went off to make the call and Julius pondered the situation. He had no idea what had actually happened, but there was one thing certain—the disks were at stake and they most certainly contained the key to the money. Why else would Reymond's widow be taking such risks to recover them?

Julius hadn't wanted to admit it to Rico, but he was concerned about Oscar. It seemed unlikely his nephew had thrown in his lot with Kidwell, but Rico was right—they were talking many millions of dollars. And Oscar was clever enough to be dealing on the side with Kidwell without Rico knowing. Still, Oscar would have to find a way to get the money out of the bank, and he had to know Julius could have a battalion of marines waiting for him in the Cayman Islands, if necessary.

So the question was whether Oscar's greed exceeded his intelligence, or whether Kidwell and Stephanie Reymond had outsmarted them all. Time would tell, but there was one thing

Julius was certain of—he should have handled this himself from the beginning. If he had, they wouldn't be in this mess now.

Rico returned. "Okay, the cops are on it, Pop."

"Good. Now, why don't you see if Miss Riveros is ready to leave. And if not, perhaps you can gently hurry her along."

Rico seemed to like that and marched toward the bedroom door.

"Gently!" Julius reiterated.

Moments later Rico reappeared, dragging Maria after him by the arm. She was in a tight little leather skirt and halter top that was only barely fastened. Her purse was in her hand, her hair flying. Rico carried her half-open bag.

"Don't be so rough, asshole!" she screeched.

Rico opened the door, shoved her into the hall, tossed her bag after her, kicking a bra that had fallen on the floor across the threshold. "By the way," he barked, "did I mention I got syphilis?" Then he slammed the door.

Julius closed his eyes, only to see Rico's grin fade when he opened them.

"You got to admit she was a bitch, Pop."

Behring could see his son would never learn. "I was hoping that knowing Rhonda loved you might have changed things," he said sadly, "but apparently it hasn't."

"Look, Pop, this shit doesn't mean anything. Maria was a hooker, for chrissakes. She has a nice ass, that's all. You know I love Rhonda. Christ, I bought her this huge fucking ring. The nicest thing in town. I'm going to take her and Andrea to Hawaii or someplace when I get home. This is nothing, really."

Julius wished his son was man enough to admit what he really was. "That would be nice, Rico," he said. "You do that."

They sat in a weighty silence. Rico fidgeted. Finally he spoke.

"Pop, how come you didn't tell me you were coming down here?"

"Because I wanted to tell you something in person. A decision I've made."

"What decision?"

"That I'm taking over, Rico."

His son looked shocked. "But that's not fair."

Although Julius didn't want to break his son's spirit, he decided Rico needed a dose of humility more than anything. The boy wasn't entirely to blame. Julius had given him too much power, and too much responsibility, too quickly.

"Rico, remember when I told you to stop gambling?" he said. "Remember why?"

"You said the dice was in control and not me."

"That's right. And do you remember why I said it was good you had that problem?"

"Because I could learn from it," Rico said sullenly.

"Right. Well, I want you to know I screwed this up as much as you did. I gave you a job you weren't ready for. So *I* learned an important lesson. Now I'm correcting my mistake."

"Pop, you're wrong. I can do this! You don't understand. It was bad luck."

"Maybe," Julius said. "But you know what? When you're the top man, bad luck is no excuse. It comes down to you win or you lose. And if you lose big enough, you're dead. When Inter-America and everything else I have is yours to lose, you'll understand what I'm saying. But that day hasn't come."

Fortuna Bay, St. Thomas

Stephanie could not sleep. It wasn't just the crickets or the frogs—whichever was making that racket—nor the sticky heat, nor the pungent smell of the pigpen behind the house, nor Nigel's sonorous snoring in the front room. More than anything it was the adrenaline rush. There was something transforming about what had happened with Oscar Barbadillo. She'd discovered a strength she didn't know she had. Most important, perhaps, she'd found a way to survive.

They'd made it to the house of Sonia's former mother-in-law, a shriveled up old woman with shining eyes who made up in spirit what she lacked in strength. Señora Velasco lived in a modest dwelling in junglelike woods a quarter of a mile from Fortuna Bay. She occupied it with her grandson, Angel, Enrique's child by a previous marriage. Shortly after dinner, Sonia sent her stepson, a handsome young man of nineteen, off on his motorbike to find out what their adversaries were up to. Angel was tall and slender, with broad shoulders and a well-shaped head. His handsome face reflected his diverse racial background, a mélange of Spanish, African and Anglo. By the time they'd gone to bed, Angel still hadn't returned and Sonia was clearly worried. That was another reason Stephanie hadn't been able to sleep.

Knowing she was accomplishing nothing tossing in bed, she got up and stole from the tiny room, nominally Angel's, but which had been Sonia's in recent days. The plan had been for Sonia to sleep on a roll-away bed in Señora Velasco's room, and Angel on a cot in the screened-in porch. Stephanie suspected Sonia wouldn't bother going to bed until the young man was safely home.

Creeping past the sleeping Englishman flaked out on the lumpy old sofa, Stephanie, in her T-shirt, went to the front doorway and looked out onto the porch. The first thing she noticed was the aromatic scent of cigar smoke. Because of the density of the surrounding vegetation, not much moonlight made it through the screen and she could not see well, but she did manage to make out a figure seated in a high-back wicker chair at the far end of the enclosed area.

"Sonia?" she whispered. She heard the sound of exhaling, though she couldn't see the smoke.

"Yes?"

Stephanie made her way closer, able to make out Sonia's

features only when she got close. "Still no word from your stepson?"

"No."

"Mind if I join you?"

"No, of course not. Sit down."

Stephanie sat in the nearby straight-back wooden chair, the seat of which was covered with a thin cushion. Sonia, she could see, hadn't yet dressed for bed. She still wore her tank top, though she had changed into a pair of shorts. Her feet were bare and she'd gathered her blond hair into a ponytail at the side of her head, probably to get it off her neck.

"You couldn't sleep?" Sonia asked.

"No," Stephanie replied softly. "Too keyed up, I guess."

"Me, too. And I'm a little worried about Angel."

Stephanie watched her draw on the cigar, making the button of fire glow brighter. This time when Sonia exhaled she could see the cloud rise before disbursing into the darkness.

"I feel badly about all the trouble this has caused," Stephanie said. "And you've done it for somebody you don't even know."

"Well, Jack's a friend," Sonia said. "And his friends are my friends, etcetera, etcetera."

The wistfulness Stephanie heard made her want to downplay her relationship with Jack. "He and I are business associates more than friends."

Sonia turned the cigar in her fingers. "With Jack things are rarely that straightforward, especially when a woman is involved."

"You're…" Stephanie had second thoughts but, after brief reflection, plunged ahead anyway. "Speaking from experience, I guess."

Sonia laughed softly. "As you might imagine." She leaned her head against the back of the chair and contemplated the night. Her chest rose with a deep breath, the cigar resting between her fingers on the arm of the chair.

"Are you and Jack lovers?" she asked.

"No," Sonia said. "Not like you're thinking. Technically, I guess we once were, though."

"What do you mean?"

Sonia rolled her head toward her. "Love wasn't involved. It was sex and friendship. You see, I was married when Jack's and my relationship was most intense. But I wasn't just having an affair, and he wasn't just screwing a married woman. We were taking care of each other, if that makes any sense. Jack knew I was using him to feel good about myself. My husband was a philanderer and Jack made me feel desirable...and appreciated. What I did for him was a little more vague. I guess you could say I made him feel needed."

"I see."

"I don't know if you do," Sonia said. "I don't know if anybody could. I'm not sure I completely understand myself. It started with great sex and beyond that there was affection, compassion, but it ended at that. I loved my husband and Jack knew it. More than that, he was glad I did, because he didn't want all of me. Mostly, he wanted my body, but he also needed someone who understood him and cared about him."

"That sounds an awful lot like love to me, Sonia. Regardless of what he said."

"I know why you say that, but it wasn't love, on either side. You know what the proof was? The way it ended. When Enrique died so did Jack's and my passion for one another. Not our friendship, but our passion."

"Sounds like Jack got scared."

She could see Sonia smile in the darkness. "You know him better than you're willing to admit."

In the course of the ensuing silence, Stephanie anguished over her feelings for Jack, knowing fear played a major role. Sonia probably saw it, too. A man like Jack Kidwell had a recognizable effect on women, touching them in similar and predictable ways.

"I won't deny I find him attractive," Stephanie finally admitted. "That's not the part about Jack that concerns me, though. I'm always off balance because I don't know if I can trust him."

"You *can't*," Sonia said. "Unless and until he realizes he wants to make a commitment."

"I don't mean trust him emotionally. I mean as a business partner. I haven't slept with him, and I have no intention of doing so." She realized she sounded almost too adamant. "What I mean is, that's not where I am. Jack knows it's business. He looks at me, he sees dollar signs and he puts on the charm. That much I'm certain of. I just want to know if I can rely on what he says."

Sonia tapped her cigar into the ashtray on the table next to her. "I'd like to tell you not to worry, Stephanie. In my experience Jack's always been honorable, but I haven't been in your shoes."

Stephanie sighed. Sonia's comments were all too reminiscent of the things Malva had said. She knew why—there was more than principle involved. Thirty million dollars was at stake, enough to make anyone unpredictable.

They sat in a companionable silence. Inside, Nigel snorted so loudly that he coughed, perhaps waking himself. But within moments he was snoring softly again. Stephanie's thoughts turned to what dangers lay ahead.

As soon as they'd arrived at Señora Velasko's house, Nigel tried phoning Bobby Brown, but was unable to reach him, either at his business number or on his beeper. Their first thought was that Bobby had either sold them out or had been arrested—a possibility that had them all worrying. When darkness fell, it became clear they'd have to spend the night. Nigel tried calling Bobby again after dinner and reached his wife. She indicated that he'd gone with some charter passengers on a brief trip, thinking he'd be back in a few hours, but had gotten hung up on St. John and wouldn't be back until morning. Nigel asked if Bobby could pick them up at Fortuna Bay instead of the port. Bobby's wife said that would work, and they set their rendezvous for eleven o'clock. Angel said he would arrange for a boat to meet them at the shore and take them out to the plane. Now all they had to do was survive the night.

Amid the clatter of the insects and frogs, Stephanie heard the put of an engine. Moments later she saw a light flashing through the dense vegetation. It was coming down the road.

"That will be Angel," Sonia said, sitting up.

The sound grew louder and the headlight brighter. It was Angel's motorbike. He stopped just behind Sonia's car, the motor and light dying. He hurried to the porch. Sonia met him at the door.

"You must go!" Angel said, his eyes round in the darkness. "The police are looking for you. They are searching every house! They came to the bar and asked about you, Sonia! No one betrayed us, but who knows for how long?"

Stephanie's stomach dropped.

"They spoke of a kidnapping, and your friends," Angel went on excitedly. "The man who was kidnapped was found and told the police you were headed to this end of the island. There are dozens of them, going house to house. And there are boats patrolling the sea. It will be hard to escape."

Sonia turned to Stephanie.

"We'd better leave," Stephanie said. "I don't want there to be trouble for your mother-in-law and stepson."

"Yes, but where?" Sonia turned back to Angel. "We must meet that plane on the bay in the morning. Where can they hide until then and still be able to get to a boat?"

Angel was silent for a moment, then said, "There is an old restaurant on the beach that is to be torn down soon for the new resort. The windows are boarded up, but we may be able to break in. In the morning I can bring a parasailing boat from work right to the beach."

"That would be good, Angel," Sonia said. "We'll get ready to go. Meanwhile, you can hide the car in the woods. I'll get you the key and a flashlight."

"And I'll wake up Nigel," Stephanie said.

"Yes, hurry and dress."

Stephanie went into the front room where Nigel Lovejoy continued to purr on the sofa. She gently shook his shoulder. "Nigel, old bean," she whispered. "We've got to leave. The police are coming."

"Huh? What's that?" He lifted his head, looking around.

"We're the object of a manhunt, I'm afraid. We're going to a new place to hide."

"Good God," he muttered. "What time is it?"

"Nearly midnight."

He rubbed his face. "And I was having such a lovely dream."

"The price of an adventurous life, Nigel."

He sat up. "Right you are, love."

Stephanie patted his shoulder and hurried off to dress. Five minutes later she assembled with the others in the front room. She had the small bag Malva had given her and Jane's alligator case. Sonia had lit a candle, not wanting bright lights in the house to attract anyone's attention.

"As soon as Angel gets back, he'll take you to the beach," she said.

"What about you?" Stephanie asked. "The police will be looking for you, too. Eventually you'll be arrested."

"I'll be okay. You'd be surprised how many friends I have. My father was in the underground during the war. I learned many tricks from the stories he told."

"I don't know what Jack's promised you, Sonia," Stephanie said, "but I'll see that you get it."

Sonia squeezed her hand. "First you must get safely off the island, then go and claim your money. It's no time to worry about me."

A few minutes later Angel returned. He was perspiring and out of breath. "I parked in the undergrowth behind the Woodruffs' house, the retired Americans from Ohio. It's half a mile up the road. They won't be arriving for another two months."

He gave Sonia the keys. Stephanie opened her purse.

"Here, Angel," she said. "I want you and your grand-mother to have this." Stephanie handed him ten one-hundred-dollar bills from the stash that had been in the airport locker.

Angel's eyes rounded.

"But to enjoy it, you'll have to get us to safety, lad," Nigel said.

"Can you get them to the beach without the police spotting you?" Sonia asked.

"If we're careful."

"Perhaps you should go, then. I'll pack my things and, when you get back, you can help me find a place to hide for the night."

"There is a tree house in the woods where I played as a boy," Angel said. "You will be safe there, Sonia."

"Good. Hurry then."

Stephanie and Sonia hugged goodbye. Nigel also gave Sonia a kiss and a hug.

"When this is all over," he said, "we're having a big party on my island. You're all invited. It will be glorious. I promise."

They said their goodbyes and Angel led the way out of the house. They trooped in single file along the drive. The air, Stephanie noticed, had cooled and the moonlight was brighter outside the screened porch.

When they reached the road, they turned toward the beach. Nigel muttered something about nighttime hikes in Wales as a boy and Stephanie recalled her girlhood experiences at summer camp. She felt the same thrill of adventure, but the stakes in this adult version were so much higher. Jane's case in her hand was a constant reminder of that.

They'd only gone a hundred yards when they heard the sounds of a vehicle behind them. "Quick," Angel said, pointing to the undergrowth. "Into the bushes."

They were no sooner secreted before two vehicles passed by.

"Police cars," Angel said. "I bet they're going to check the beach."

They discussed the situation briefly, deciding to press on. As they marched in silence, Stephanie worried that the escapade might be at its end. With so many police looking for them, could they possibly escape?

Soon Angel took them to a track leading through the trees. Stephanie assumed it was the direction of the beach. The vegetation was not so dense, and enough moonlight came through the foliage that Angel didn't have to use the flashlight. It was a good thing because, as they came to the edge of the beach, they saw a police car parked next to a low building silhouetting the night sky. Officers with flashlights came around the building from opposite sides. Stephanie and the others froze.

Angel signaled for them to back into the protective overhang of the trees, where they could watch in safety. "They're checking everyplace," Angel whispered. "It's a good thing we didn't come sooner."

"Unless they search the same places more than once, we could be safe here," Nigel said. "This may turn out a bloody good stroke of luck."

The police had completed their inspection, and the two officers piled back into their car. They turned around and headed out toward the road. Once they were gone, Stephanie sighed with relief, her heart slowing from its rapid beat. She'd had plenty of excitement, but her instincts told her the ordeal was far from over.

The three of them made their way down to the ramshackle building. Most of the windows faced the sea and were boarded over. There was a padlock on the door, but the hasp had been pried off and was hanging loose. Angel eased the door open and, using his flashlight, peered inside.

The place had been gutted. There were broken chairs and pieces of tables. Part of the bar had been torn out. It did not look hospitable, but it was a place to hide.

"I should get back to the house now," Angel said.

"You've been a godsend, lad," Nigel said, grasping the boy's shoulder.

Stephanie hugged him. "What time should we start watching for you?" she asked.

"I'll try for ten-thirty," he said. "Earlier if I can."

"Good luck," she said. "Be careful."

Angel nodded and dashed off, heading for the woods.

"Fine lad," Nigel said, looking after him.

"We should probably try to get some rest," Stephanie said.

"Right you are, love."

They went inside. They didn't have anything they could use as ground cloths, but Nigel swept a spot on the floor under one of the boarded-up windows. Then they sat, using the bags as cushions. The air outside remained pleasantly warm, but it would cool during the night. Fortunately the structure would afford enough shelter that they would be comfortable. Their biggest concern was the police.

"Sorry now that you came, Nigel?" Stephanie asked him after they were settled.

"Wouldn't have missed this for the world," he replied, not altogether convincingly.

"For your sake I wish you were on your yacht with Françoise instead of this."

"Lovely thought, my stateroom and Françoise, but I'll be with her soon enough. How about you, love? Where should I wish you to be at this moment?" he asked, stretching out.

Curiously, Stephanie's first thought was of Jack and the *Lucky Lady*, not her bed at home, not some elegant hotel or cozy nook from childhood.

"That silence must mean it's none of my bloody business," he said.

"If I could, I'd like to be with Jack on his boat," she confessed.

Nigel chuckled softly. "The way you said that, it almost sounded like a dying woman's last request. You must be more optimistic, love!"

"I'll try," she said.

A silence ensued. Incredibly, Nigel was snoring within minutes, though the sound was dulled by the pounding of the surf.

Stephanie's mind went back to the evening she'd spent on the beach with Jack. Though her very survival was now in doubt, she knew that a transformation had occurred sometime between then and now. Emotionally she'd committed herself to Jack Kidwell. And if she lived to see him again, the first order of business would be to tell him that she cared.

Wednesday,
October 2nd

St. Thomas

Ten-thirty had come and gone and there was no sign of Angel. Stephanie and Nigel had been taking turns peering through the cracks in the boarded-up windows for the past two hours, keeping watch, but no ski boat came into view. At ten-forty Nigel stepped onto the veranda to look up and down the beach, thinking perhaps Angel had landed nearby and was waiting for them. He came back inside, a worried, discouraged expression on his face.

"I don't see him anywhere."

"Perhaps the police arrested him last night," she said.

"If so, he didn't tell them where we are. Regardless, should he fail to show up soon, our goose is cooked. Bobby will be here in fifteen minutes. God only knows how long he'll wait out there before he gives up."

"And there's a chance he'll have heard the police are looking for an Englishman and a woman. If so, we definitely won't be going anywhere," Stephanie said.

"Unless he intends to claim the reward."

She had an awful, sinking feeling. "It's all my fault, Nigel. This was much too risky."

"It's too early to despair, love," Nigel said. "Angel and Bobby may yet come through."

Stephanie was losing hope. What would happen to them, she didn't know, but she was almost certain Oscar Barbadillo would have a hand in it. She'd have been better off going home when she could and facing the music, even if it meant losing everything she had.

No sooner had that thought entered her mind than she gave herself a mental kick in the rear. If any good had come of this ordeal, it was that she had finally taken control of her life. At least she'd go down fighting. Nigel would admire her for it, and so, too, would Jack. Her pride was worth something.

But for the moment all she could do was wait. Nigel kept consulting his watch. Stephanie paced. It was seven minutes before eleven and still no sign of Angel. In a way, she almost hoped Bobby wouldn't show, either. That would be the greatest torture of all, seeing the plane sitting out on the bay, ready to take them to freedom, and having no way to get to it.

Stephanie went to peer out through a crack between the boards. A quarter of a mile out, a police patrol boat was approaching a small sailboat. "Oh no," she said. "There are police boats out in the bay."

Nigel looked, too. "I know, I saw one earlier. I didn't want to say anything. Looks like the bloody bastards are challenging every craft that enters the bay."

Stephanie felt sick. She wondered, if she turned herself in, Nigel might be spared. But when she suggested the idea, he immediately dismissed it. "I must reject the notion categorically," he said. "We sink or swim together."

Suddenly they heard what sounded like an airplane. They both looked out.

"Looks like a seaplane!" Nigel said enthusiastically.

Sure enough, it was a Cessna 205, same as Bobby's. It made a big looping circle of the bay, much as it had Isola Lovejoy, then made a landing from west to east, well out in the bay, at least half a mile offshore.

"Splendid," Nigel said, beginning to pace. "Now all we have to do is find a way to get to it. Maybe I should take a walk up the beach and see if I can find a boat."

"Hold on," Stephanie said. "Isn't that a ski boat with a parasailer coming around the point?"

Nigel returned to the window and peered through the cracks. "Could it possibly be Angel?" he asked.

"Maybe."

"Clever ruse that, if it's him."

They both watched as the boat made its way in their general direction, bouncing over the waves as it sped along, holding the parasailer aloft. Stephanie glanced anxiously at the seaplane, wondering how long Bobby would wait. It was five after eleven. The ski boat was nearing their location and seemed headed straight for them.

"I think it *is* Angel!" Nigel exclaimed. "Get ready to dash out."

Stephanie looked for the police patrol boat, spotting not one, but two. The first seemed to be making its way toward the seaplane. The other was making a circuit of the shoreline, headed in their direction. Could they possibly know? she wondered with despair.

Meanwhile, the ski boat had nearly reached them. It slowed, then stopped right in front of the restaurant, gently depositing the parasailer at the edge of the water.

"That's Angel," Nigel said. "Let's go."

"Wait!" Stephanie cried before he pushed the door open. "There's a patrol boat coming. If they see us run out there, they'll know."

"Bloody hell," Nigel said, their bad luck finally getting to him.

Angel had backed the ski boat right onto the beach and stared up at the building. The parasailer, obviously one of Angel's friends, arranged the sail and harness on the sand. The patrol boat had just about reached them and was angling toward shore.

"The moment of truth," Nigel muttered as he and Stephanie watched, agonizing.

Over the next couple of minutes an unheard dialogue transpired between Angel and the cops. Finally, the patrol boat moved on. Stephanie and Nigel both sighed with relief. Farther out in the bay, the other patrol boat had pulled alongside the seaplane. Stephanie knew that if Bobby told them what he was doing here, the game was lost.

"Is Bobby going to betray us?" Stephanie wondered aloud.

"I told him this was a discreet trip," Nigel said. "Nor has he been paid yet. Perhaps he'll be mindful enough to give them a story."

The patrol boat near shore had moved on and Angel waved at them to come out.

"Let's go down one at a time," Stephanie said. "I'll go first."

She pushed her hat firmly on her head, put on her sunglasses and strolled casually down to the boat, clutching both her purse and Jane's precious alligator case. Angel, in a swimsuit and tattered tank top, greeted her at the water's edge.

"No need to get wet," he said, lifting her into his arms and carrying her to the ski boat.

The parasailer put his harness back on, preparing to take off again as Nigel came down the beach with their bags. Stephanie glanced in the direction the patrol boat had taken, hoping they wouldn't notice, and she was relieved that they hadn't altered their course. The other patrol boat was still alongside the seaplane. It was apparent they'd have to stall, but not on the beach.

They decided to cruise around for a while. If they couldn't make the connection with Bobby, then they'd head back to Charlotte Amalie and look for other transportation.

Angel checked with his friend, who'd moved to the edge of the water and was billowing his chute as much as the breeze would allow. Angel revved the motor and slowly moved seaward until the towline was taut. Then, when the parasailer gave him the sign, Angel took off at high speed, lifting his friend into the air as though the chute was a kite.

They didn't head directly toward the seaplane even though the patrol boat had begun moving off. They made a loop around the bay, then circled back in the direction of the seaplane, giving the appearance of passing by it. But as they neared, Angel cut the power and the parasailer slowly dropped to the sea right next to the aircraft. They circled back as if to pick him up, pulling right up next to the plane in the process.

Bobby looked out, actually appearing surprised to see them. The parasailing guise was clever, Stephanie had to admit. Bobby opened the door, consternation on his face.

"Good to see you, old chap," Nigel chirped. "Françoise and I are ready to head for home."

Bobby helped them aboard but said nothing. Angel bid them goodbye and putted over to pick up his friend. As the ski boat went off, Nigel turned to Bobby.

"Shouldn't we be getting under way, mate?"

"Sorry, Mr. Lovejoy, but we ain't goin' nowhere. The cops were here and wanted to know what I was doing. I said I was here to pick up passengers and they told me I was not to leave until they checked you out." He pointed toward the patrol boat speeding toward them. "So we'll have to wait. Sorry."

"Shit!" Stephanie said.

"Surely there's something that can be done, old bean," Nigel said, trying to sound calm. "I'm in a bloody rush to get home and misunderstandings with the police can take hours to correct. Let's say I double your fee."

"You know I would if I could," Bobby said, almost pleading, "but if I take off without their permission I could lose my license and then my plane. Besides, I got a family to think of."

"Ten thousand, American," Nigel said, his voice demanding now.

"God, I wish I could," Bobby said.

The patrol boat was only a hundred yards away. Stephanie could see it was life or death. She reached in her purse and took out the gun, pressing it against Bobby's neck.

"Will you take off to save your life?" she asked.

Bobby looked back at her, his eyes round. "Jesus. You're joking, right?"

"Let's say I'm not, so you can tell the police you were highjacked. In fact, you're both innocent because I'm taking over the plane. Come on, Bobby, let's get this plane in the air."

Bobby sighed mournfully. "Can't argue with a gun." He flipped the master switch, then primed the engine. The police patrol boat was almost there, lights flashing. Bobby turned the ignition switches on, then pushed the starter switch. The engine fired. Seeing they were trying to take off, the patrol boat swung in front of them. Bobby threw the rudder sharply to one side and eased the throttle forward. The plane slowly pivoted, its wingtip passing over the boat, then Bobby thrust the throttle fully open and the plane roared off toward the open sea. Stephanie had no idea if shots were fired, but when the floats lifted from the water and the plane rose sharply into the sky, she realized that, at least for the moment, they were saved.

The Caribbean Sea

Off St. Croix

When they reached the site where they were supposed to rendezvous with the *Rubber Soul,* some forty miles southwest of St. Croix, they found the sleek craft waiting for them in the crystal waters. They made their descent, stopping within fifty yards of the yacht. Bobby turned off the engine of the seaplane.

"I'll have a bank check in the amount of ten thousand, American, to you within the week," Nigel told Bobby.

"But that's only for your inconvenience," Stephanie added. "Nigel had nothing to do with this highjacking. It was my idea and he's an innocent victim, just like you."

"Where do I tell them I brought you?" the pilot asked.

"Here, I guess," Stephanie said. "We rendezvoused at sea with a cabin cruiser I hired. You weren't able to get any identifying numbers. I took Nigel with me as a hostage."

A small craft piloted by a crewman appeared from behind the yacht and slowly made its way toward them. Stephanie told Nigel to get out and wait on the float. After he'd climbed out, she handed the bags to him. Then she said to Bobby, "How much would a new radio cost?"

"A radio? What for?"

"If you needed one."

"Five, six hundred bucks. Why?"

Stephanie opened her purse and took out a stack of hundred-dollar bills. "Here," she said, handing them to him. "I'm buying you one." Then she aimed the gun at the control panel and fired, shattering the radio.

"Jesus Christ," Bobby screamed, covering his head. "Why'd you do that?"

"You need an excuse not to have radioed for help," she said. "And you're going to have to sit here for three or four hours, long enough for us to have gotten away. Later I'll have the captain of the cruiser put out a distress call on your behalf. You can keep the ignition key in case you have a problem, but put it in your pocket and say I threw it overboard."

The launch from the yacht pulled alongside and Stephanie climbed out onto the float with Nigel. They tossed their luggage aboard, then climbed in themselves.

"Sorry to put you through all this, Bobby," Stephanie called to him, "but trust me, it's for a good cause."

They headed back to the yacht.

"Bloody clever, you are!" Nigel chortled, a huge grin on his face.

"I swear to you, I don't know where it came from, Nigel. I've never done anything like that in my life."

"You picked a good time to become an action hero, love," he said as they bumped along, the bottom of the craft slapping the waves. "Jolly good."

They went around to the far side of the *Rubber Soul* where a boarding ladder had been dropped over the side. Françoise was waiting for them on deck. She and Stephanie embraced, then she kissed Nigel when he clambered aboard.

"Were you successful?" Françoise asked.

"We got the disks," Stephanie said.

"Félicitations, ma petite!" Françoise said. "Congratulations!"

"Thanks to Annie Oakley here, we averted catastrophe," Nigel said. "The woman has been watching too many action films, I promise you that, Françoise. You wouldn't believe the transformation."

"Necessity is the mother of invention," Stephanie said, embarrassed.

Nigel put an arm around each of them. "Perhaps we should put some distance between ourselves and the authorities," he said.

"Do you think we should sail off in a different direction than where we'll be meeting Jack?" Stephanie asked.

"I should think that wise," Nigel said. "Once we're over the horizon, we can circle around in the direction of the rendezvous site. I'll just have a word with the captain. Why don't you ladies go below and make yourselves comfortable. I'll join you momentarily. I dare say we've earned ourselves a drink." He went off.

Stephanie looked down and saw the alligator case lined up with the other bags. She picked it up. "Think I'll hang on to this since we risked our lives for it."

The two women went off, Françoise with her arm around

Stephanie's waist. "You must be relieved," the Frenchwoman said.

"I'm waiting for a little privacy so I can completely fall apart, if you want to know the truth."

"You've been transformed, *chérie,* I can see it in your eyes."

Stephanie sighed as they went down the stairs. "From board of directors of the Stanford Alumni Association to the FBI's most wanted list. I'd say I've transformed all right."

"FBI?"

"Françoise, I'm wanted now for kidnapping and air piracy and, for all I know, attempted murder. If they catch me I could spend the next fifty years in jail."

"Ah, but you're so much more interesting for it, Stephanie. Jack will be thrilled. I'm sure of it." Turning, Françoise slinked toward the bar. "Now, *madame,* may I offer you a drink?"

Stephanie collapsed into a chair. "Whatever you've got, make it a double!"

Charlotte Amalie, St. Thomas

Julius Behring sat in the lounge chair on the balcony, sipping his martini, staring at the sunset. There was a light wrap on the glass slider behind him. He looked back over his shoulder. It was his nephew.

"Oscar, come."

Oscar Barbadillo stepped out onto the balcony. He went to the railing and stood gazing at the sea. "They found the plane and the pilot, Uncle Julius. He was sitting out in the middle of the ocean. Told them he was highjacked by the woman. She wasn't with Kidwell. It was some Englishman. She shot up the plane and left the pilot to the sharks. They got away on a cabin cruiser."

Julius considered that. "She's making fools of us all."

"If I ever get my hands on her, I swear I'll kill her," Oscar said through his teeth.

"You're sounding like Rico," Julius said. "We already have enough of that."

"Twice she's humiliated me, Uncle Julius. A stupid housewife. A man cannot endure that."

Julius understood his nephew's feelings. As if being kidnapped and stripped naked wasn't enough, Oscar had to slink back to the hotel in a pair of shorts stolen from a clothesline. Rico had derided his cousin unmercifully, but Julius was grateful that Oscar hadn't betrayed them. That would have been the most painful cut of all.

He nodded at Oscar, knowing that if fate had been kinder, this would have been his own son. "A man must do what he must do. Our work, the company, has to come first. Rico is depressed and not much use. I need clear heads. You must put aside your anger, Oscar."

"Don't worry. I want her more badly than ever. Yes, we'll get our money, but I will also have her."

"To do what?"

"To regain my dignity."

Julius drank more of his martini. That was one thing about the Latin culture that he did not respect. Pride, *machismo,* got in the way of clear thought. He'd seen it time and time again—men refusing to use their brains when that was the one thing that could save them.

"Your dignity is your business, Oscar, but the company is mine. I must have your promise that you will keep your eye on the ball."

"First things first, Uncle Julius. You can count on me. I have made mistakes, but not because my priorities were screwed up."

"No, the woman is either very clever or very lucky. In either case, we have underestimated her. We will not make the same mistake again."

"For sure."

"The question is what we do now. Can we trace the boat she escaped on?"

"The pilot claims he was unable to identify it."

"Strange."

"Says the English guy was an innocent victim right along with him, but I don't buy it. The Brit and the Swedish broad were both at the airport. They're all in on it together. The Swede wasn't on the plane, which means she's still here in St. Thomas. We find her, maybe we'll know where to find the others."

"Where was the pilot found?"

"Two, three hundred miles south of here."

"South?"

"Yeah, but when they left, they went east, back toward the British Virgins where the English guy's got some island or something. Cops are askin' the Brits to check it out."

Julius stared at his half-empty glass. "Maybe we can learn something from the Englishman and the Swede, but there's no mystery about where Stephanie Reymond is headed. One way or another, she's on her way to the bank. There's only one thing to do now—alert our people in the Caymans she's headed their way."

"What about us, Uncle Julius?"

"We pack up and first thing tomorrow morning we head there ourselves. We'll want boats and planes and good relations with the police. There's a lot of work to be done, and," he added with a groan, "more money to spend. Will you take care of that for me, Oscar?"

"Sure. Anything else we need to discuss?"

"There's one thing that has me perplexed. What happened to the sea captain, Kidwell? He seems to have disappeared."

"Maybe the broad sunk his boat. One less cut to dole out."

"Somehow I doubt it."

The phone at Julius's elbow rang. He picked it up.

"Yes?"

"Mr. Behring, it's Wayne Driscoll. I've got news concerning your daughter-in-law. This a good time to discuss it?"

Julius felt the acid in his stomach splash. He glanced up at Oscar, covering the mouthpiece of the phone. "I think we're through."

His nephew went back inside the suite. Julius returned to his call. "Yeah, what do you got, Wayne?"

"This morning Rhonda left the house with the little girl and some suitcases. They drove up to Van Nuys where she dropped off the kid."

"At her mother's place, I gather."

"Yeah. After that she turns around and drives back to L.A.X."

"And?"

"She gets on a plane for Paris."

"Christ."

"I don't know if Hachigian was on the plane, too, Mr. Behring. We're trying to track him down. Could be she just decided she needed a vacation, but I thought you'd better know."

"Thanks, Wayne. Keep me posted, will you?" Julius hung up the phone.

Rico was an adult and deserved to know what was going on with his wife. But Julius knew his son was a lot more fragile than people realized. He decided to hold off telling him until emotions subsided.

Shaking his head, Julius drained the last of his martini. Life, he realized, was never without complications.

The Caribbean Sea

Jack Kidwell was exhausted. Except for a catnap now and then he hadn't slept in nearly two days. Sitting in the cockpit of the *Lucky Lady,* staring wistfully at the night sky, his brain fuzzy, he coaxed his thoughts along, though they seemed only to come in half-digested chunks. He'd been struggling with the weather—or more accurately, a lack of weather—for a couple of days and he was way behind schedule. He'd actually welcome rough seas, if that's what it took to get some wind in his sails.

The past dozen hours or so, the *Lucky Lady* had drifted as much as she'd sailed. During a particularly extreme calm spell, he'd cranked up the auxiliary and traveled a dozen nautical miles or so under motor power, but he could hardly make a habit of that. Getting to the rendezvous point was critical. Once he had Stephanie safely under his wing, the urgency would be over.

That was assuming Stephanie and Nigel made it, of course. Jack had his doubts that they would. The escapade hadn't felt right from the beginning. Far too risky. But if she did get the disks, it would be a brilliant stroke. The trouble was, he wouldn't know if they had pulled it off until he rendezvoused with the *Rubber Soul*. Meanwhile, the course of his life hinged on whether Stephanie had the guts and the wile to succeed.

Jack had never cared much for situations where things were completely beyond his control—he preferred creating his own problems, finding his own solutions. When he stopped to think about it, the real miracle was that he cared at all. Only days ago all that had stood between him and rock bottom was the nagging of Bill Toussaint. Now he was worrying about the future. That in itself was a dramatic turnaround.

Malva attributed it to Stephanie. But was it Stephanie or the thirty million? He didn't know. If he took a good, hard look at the situation, and asked himself if, without the money, she meant anything to him, what would his heart tell him? Sure, she was a nice person, a lovely person. She was attractive, intelligent, different, even intriguing. Hell, he liked her. He was more than happy to go to bed with her. But she was still just a woman and there were countless appealing women. What set Stephanie apart was her millions and what they could do for him. Why pretend otherwise?

So why did he feel shitty? Guilt? After years of fucking for his own pleasure, why would charming this particular woman bother him? Hell, they hadn't even been to bed. He'd taken nothing from her. Nor had he lied, exactly. Sure, he'd put the best light on things—he'd been coy—but he'd been honest about wanting a piece of the action. Christ, when you came right down to it, she was using him as much as he was using her. So, what was the big deal? Was he getting a conscience in his old age, or was it that he did not really want what he thought he wanted?

That was a scary notion. Allowing himself to get emotionally involved was the very last thing he needed to do. Money, on the other hand, was safe. It was quantifiable and it didn't make demands, it didn't have needs, it didn't get hurt and it didn't die. You couldn't say that about people. People possessed you as much as you possessed them.

Securing the wheel, Jack got up and walked along the deck. The boat was moving so slowly that he could barely hear the hiss of the water on the hull, and the sails were as lifeless as the wings of a dying bird. At the bow Jack stood staring ahead at the darkness. It was as ominous and obscure as the future. He was moving inexorably toward a destiny that might prove as painful and empty as his dream.

The doubt, the self-doubt, was the source of the pain. And pain had never been his friend. The pain of his childhood, the pain of his marriage, the pain of Alicia, the pain of not caring enough to care.

So why was he sticking his finger in the fire now? It would be so much easier to surrender. Hell, the odds weren't even good.

Gripping the spare jib halyard as he stared into the darkness, Jack thought, as he had so often the past couple of days, about that bottle of scotch stowed in his cabin. The desire to retrieve it was as strong now as it had ever been. It would be so easy to have a drink, so understandable. Who did he owe his self-restraint to, anyway? Stephanie Reymond?

No, he owed her nothing. She was as much a problem as an opportunity. She made him question himself, and that was never good. Never. He could choose to have a drink because the choice was his.

Jack felt that terrible tug-of-war beginning inside him. Half his body wanted to go for that bottle *now*. The other half was more afraid of weakness than fear. He either stayed and faced his demons, or he went below. He either drank or he didn't.

He held the halyard so tightly that his arm began to ache. His legs felt wobbly and he thought longingly of the comfort of drink. Would it hurt to hold the bottle in his hand? Didn't a man know the fire best by creeping close?

Jack let go of the halyard and turned to face the stern. The sails were completely slack now, the *Lucky Lady* was scarcely moving in the water. Putting one foot in front of the other, he moved in the direction of the companionway. There was no sound, not even the lapping of waves. He was as alone as a man could be—the devil his only companion.

Reaching the companionway, Jack stared into the dark abyss. Almost without thought he felt his foot descend to the first step. Then he took the next. Moments later he was stumbling through the dark salon, drunk without having taken a drop. Once in his cabin, he didn't bother turning on a light. The bottle was in the back of the locker, buried under a bunch of crap, but he was able to put his hand right on it. Pulling it out by the neck, he stood. Clutching it to his chest, his eyes closed, he gripped the cap with his fingers.

Then he felt the boat gently sway. Glancing over at the open port, he listened. Though he couldn't hear anything, he did feel a gentle rush of sea air waft through the cabin. It entered like a specter, cooling the sheen of perspiration on his forehead, promising to take him to his rendezvous with Stephanie and Nigel.

For a second or two Jack was torn—did he open the bottle of scotch or not? He considered stepping to the port and shoving it out. He even took a step in that direction. But he stopped himself. He wasn't prepared to go that far. No, at this point in his life he needed temptation as much as he needed hope. He needed to know the choice remained in his hands.

Stephanie stood at the railing, staring out at the dark sea. Below, Nigel and Françoise were continuing to party, the music going and the champagne undoubtedly flowing. They'd invited her to join them, but she wasn't in a party mood. She was thinking of Jack and had been all afternoon. They'd reached the rendezvous site as the sun was going down, finding no sign of the *Lucky Lady*. Stephanie's anticipation had turned to worry.

The captain, seeing her concern, told her that sailing alone, Jack had set quite a challenge for himself. It was a considerable distance to cover and the winds had not been favorable. When he'd told her he didn't expect to see Jack until morning, Stephanie had been overwhelmed with frustration and had gone below, where she lay on her berth, brooding. It wasn't just her concern for Jack, though; she'd also been agonizing over what she'd found on the disks.

Within ten minutes of their arrival on the *Rubber Soul*, she had gotten out Jane's computer, slipped the disks in the drive, and started perusing the directories in search of information on the account Jean Claud had set up in the Grand Cayman Bank Ltd. At first, she hadn't found a thing. Then she spotted a small file, only a few thousand bits in size, labeled JT, probably for her sister, Jane Turner. In it was a heading, Grand Cayman Bank, Ltd., and an address. Then, Account Number 011566473. She'd been thrilled until she saw the accompanying code. Typed below the account number was: Access Code: chalk == 4, book == 5, nut == 4, runway == 7, wound == 2, cow == 1.

What did that mean? Surely she couldn't walk into the bank, present the account number, then start spouting out words and numbers. The banker, Harris Ivory, had implied the code consisted of a series of numbers, which meant the access code

Jean Claud had recorded as words and numbers had to be reduced to simple numbers. Her husband had obviously encrypted the code. And to decipher it, she'd need the key.

After showering and having lunch with Nigel and Françoise, Stephanie had again returned to her cabin where she'd spent the next few hours searching every file on Jean Claud's disks, searching for a key to the code. She'd found nothing and began dreading having to tell Jack that everything they'd been through might have been for naught. But then they'd reached the rendezvous spot and the *Lucky Lady* wasn't there. Problems on top of problems.

There was a lull in the music and after a minute Françoise came up on deck. She wore a silk sleeveless aqua-colored blouse and matching pants, looking chic, outrageous, a coquette with mature intentions.

"*Mon dieu*," she said, fanning herself, "I think that man could party his whole life and never grow tired. I had to say to him, 'Enough, Nigel, I'm going up on deck for air.' You know what he says to me, Stephanie? 'I'll find us another bottle of champagne, so don't be long.' Can you believe it?"

"Nigel seems to be good for the French wine industry."

"Nigel is…how do you say it…a party animal?"

"That's a pretty good description."

Françoise turned to look at her in the moonlight, caressing Stephanie's cheek in a sisterly way. "So tell me, *chérie*, why are you sad? Is it the letdown?"

Stephanie peered out at the sea. "A little, I suppose. That, and knowing the challenge I'm facing is awesome."

"You'll have Jacques to help you."

"Assuming he shows up."

"Oh, he will. Jacques would swim here, if necessary."

"Thirty million is a lot to swim for."

Again Françoise caressed Stephanie's cheek. "I see you are holding back in case of disappointment and perhaps that is good, but I think it is better what I do. A long time ago I stopped worrying about men and their motives. I decided the best thing is to worry about my own desires. I try not to hurt anyone, but that is my only rule."

"I think I could learn a lot from you, Françoise."

Nigel came up the stairs just then, a bottle of champagne in his hand. He was ruddy-faced, his shirt unbuttoned, and looked to be in no pain. "Well, my lovelies, conspiring, are we?"

"We are solving the men problem," Françoise said.

"Going to let me in on it, love?" he asked, grinning.

"You're part of the problem, *chéri*, not part of the solution." She gave him a kiss on the cheek. "Now, be a good boy, go downstairs and I'll join you shortly."

"Join?" he said with a drunken grin. "As in conjoin?"

"Allez!"

"Okay, but first a word of advice for Stephanie. Treat Jack just like Françoise treats me and he'll make you a happy woman."

"That's not where Jack and I are," she replied.

"Oh, but you could be, love! Trust me, you need to let go. It would be good for your soul. We've survived a bloody ordeal, for chrissakes."

"Okay," Françoise interjected. "Now you've had your say. Go pour me some champagne."

He handed her the bottle. "Who needs a glass?"

Françoise rolled her eyes. "Why are the English so barbaric?"

"Blame it on the Norman conquest," Nigel said, turning and staggering back down the stairs.

Françoise shook her head, looking after him. "They do it because they can't have a good cry like we can."

"I feel sorry for them," Stephanie said.

"I, too."

For a while they leaned on the railing, side by side as they looked out at the night. The soft balmy air was fabulous. The moon, fuller than the previous night, had come up, illuminating the sea. Stephanie scanned the horizon, but saw no sign of the *Lucky Lady*. Only now was she beginning to realize how eager she was to see Jack. Her adventure in St. Thomas had been a turning point. She was a criminal on the run, true, but she knew it wasn't as bad as it seemed—armed with the full facts, the authorities would probably be understanding. And yet, she had never been in a situation like this, living on the edge. What surprised her most was how it seemed to have transformed her.

"How about you, Stephanie?" Françoise said. "Will you be all right?"

"What do you mean?"

"If you don't get your money."

"Oh, yeah, I'll be fine. Not so rich as before, but I'll survive."

"It's not so bad for women now as it used to be," Françoise said. "It is easier to be alone."

Stephanie heard a little wobble in her voice and turned to look at her. "Would you say you're happy?"

"I'm content to let come what will. And I smile. *Tiens,* life is not so bad, especially not here in paradise."

"I never realized what a staid, uptight person I was until I came to the Caribbean," Stephanie told her.

"This place will do that to you."

"I don't know if I'd ever be able to be free like you and Nigel and Sonia and Jack. I don't know if it's in me."

"A certain amount of daring is necessary to life, *ma chérie.* You've already proved you understand that. But trust is important, too. Trust in yourself, in fate, or whatever."

Stephanie didn't know if Françoise was referring to her attitudes toward Jack, but there was no disputing he was at the heart of her fears.

"I am probably the last one you should listen to," Françoise went on, "but if I were you, I'd give Jacques a try."

"Why?"

"He would be fun. I can tell simply by looking at him. Surely you can as well."

"Yes, he'd be fun."

"*Alors,* that's all you need to know."

"Françoise!" Nigel called from below.

"There, it sounds like it is time for me to have some fun of my own." Then, kissing Stephanie on each cheek, she said. "*Bonsoir, chérie.*"

Stephanie watched her go belowdecks, then she turned her attention to the tranquil sea. Incredibly, it was this same body of water that had nearly claimed hers and Jack's lives. Ferocious one day, meek as a lamb the next. Melancholy, she continued gazing at the far-off moonlit horizon, when she saw what looked like a sail. She looked up toward the flying bridge of the *Rubber Soul* but didn't see the captain. Walking around the boat for a view from a different angle, she saw that he was seated, talking to his crewman. Both men were smoking.

"Captain," she called. "I see a sailboat. Could it be the *Lucky Lady?*"

The man, a Brit with a closely trimmed white beard, got to his feet and stared off in the direction she was pointing. He picked up his binoculars and peered at the craft.

"Aye, ma'am," he said. "She may well be the *Lucky Lady*. She's the right size and she's rigged the same. We'll know soon enough."

Stephanie returned to her vantage point and watched the craft slowly make its way toward them in the light breeze. The closer it got, the more excited she became. Soon she was certain it was Jack. The captain confirmed it when the sailboat was within a couple hundred yards.

"That's the *Lucky Lady,* all right, ma'am."

Jack began luffing his sails to slow the boat. She finally drifted to a halt thirty or forty yards off the port bow of the motor yacht.

"Ahoy," Jack called. "That you, Stephanie?"

She waved at him. "Yes, it's me!"

"Nice to see you alive and well. How was your trip?"

"More exciting than I expected, but fairly successful."

"Are we going to the Caymans?"

"I guess we can give it a try."

He gave her the high sign. "Give me a minute and I'll be over."

As she watched, Jack backed the jib and eased the main while bringing the bow closer to the wind. He lowered his rubberized launch into the water. Then he came putting over to the yacht through the gently lapping waves. When he was alongside the *Rubber Soul,* he tossed the crewman a line, then clambered up the boarding ladder.

Stephanie waited for him and he surprised her by taking her into his arms as the crewman withdrew.

"I know business partners aren't supposed to show this kind of emotion, sweetheart, but I sure am glad to see you." He gave her a warm, affectionate kiss.

She hadn't expected him to be so direct, but was secretly pleased. "Tell the truth, Jack, you're happy because you were sure I'd duck out and leave you hanging, right?"

"No, I figured you were too honorable for that. But I wasn't sure you'd make it in one piece. That's why I'm so relieved to see your shining face." He stepped back, taking a look at her. "Damn, if you don't look lovely."

"Thank you."

"No trouble from the bad guys?"

"Oh, there was trouble, but we survived."

"With your virginity intact?"

"Morally speaking, yes, but legally I'm a fallen woman, Jack."

"Legally?"

"In all probability I'm now wanted for kidnapping and air piracy, plus an assortment of lesser charges."

He laughed, cuffing her chin playfully. "I knew you had it in you, sweetheart."

"The sad part is, it may all be for nothing. I've had a look at the disks. The code's there, all right, but I don't see how we're going to be able to decipher it."

"You mean the code's in code?"

"Yes."

He rubbed his grizzled chin. "Well, I'm sure there's a way to figure it out. We're not dealing with the CIA and the KGB." He took her in his arms again, holding her as they rocked back and forth, luxuriating in the feel of each other.

It felt so natural, so good, she resisted questioning it, resisted the impulse to doubt and pull back. Pressing her head against his chest, she tried to sort out her feelings and, more important, his. "Jack?"

"Ma'am?"

"Hypothetical question. The code's unbreakable and we fail. Or the computer falls overboard tomorrow and everything's lost. Then what?"

He thought for a moment. "Are you probing my intentions or my values?"

"Both."

"In your hypothetical question, Stephanie, is all that money in the alligator case lost, too?"

"No, I still have a few thousand to my name."

"Well," Jack said, "I guess what I'd do is clean you out as best I could, *then* take off for greener pastures."

Stephanie pulled her head back and gave him a whack on the shoulder. "I wish you wouldn't do that."

He laughed. "Sweetheart, how can it matter what I say to an unanswerable question?"

"You might be surprised," she said.

"Okay, have it your way. I'm your man, Stephanie, through thick and thin. Scout's honor, till death do us part."

"You're making it worse."

"Then stop asking dumb questions."

She stared into his eyes. "Okay, from now on it's blind trust." She turned to the *Lucky Lady* bobbing peacefully, hove to in the moonlit water. "So, when do we leave?"

"I don't expect Nigel and Françoise are dying for our company at the moment. In fact, I expect the old goat has already lured her to bed.''

"I think you can safely say that," she agreed.

"Then I say we ride what wind we've got and head for the Caymans.''

"Right now?"

"There's no time like the present," Jack said.

"I guess I'd better get my things then."

"You'd better unless you want to wear whatever frilly little numbers I'm able to dig up."

"Resupplied, have you?" Stephanie said.

Jack slapped her behind. "Come on, lady fair. We've got a week to make snide remarks. No point wasting our time doing it now. Our destiny awaits."

Stephanie took a few steps in the direction of the companionway, then stopped, turning to face him. "I've become dangerous since you last saw me, Jack. I even terrified Oscar Barbadillo. It's only fair I warn you of that."

He laughed. "Dangerous women turn me on, sweetheart. Only fair to warn *you!*"

That was enough. Turning, she hurried down the steps, headed for her cabin, her cheeks burning.

Thursday,
October 3rd

The Caribbean Sea

The sun coming in the port awoke her. Checking her watch, Stephanie saw that it was after nine. Poor Jack. If conditions permitted, the plan had been for her to take the wheel at first light so he could get some sleep. She jumped out of bed, slipped on shorts and a tank top. Then she grabbed her toothbrush and comb and went to the head.

Back in her cabin she put on sunblock, her hat and dark glasses, then went up on the deck. She found Jack in the cockpit. He was sprawled out on the seat, a towel covering his face.

"Jack," she said, shaking him.

He sat up with a start, squinting in the bright sun. "Oh."

"Sorry, I overslept," she said.

"Christ, I must have dozed off." He stood and surveyed the sea ahead, then checked the compass heading. "That's really bad. If I'm going to screw up, though, this is the place to do it—out in the middle of nowhere." He looked up at the nearly slack sails. "There's so little wind, we're not doing much more than drifting. It's been like this off and on since I left Isola Lovejoy."

"Have you slept since then?"

"Not really."

"Jack, that's terrible."

"Falling asleep at the wheel is terrible."

"Show me what to do, then go down and get some real sleep," she insisted.

Jack tacked, explaining the steps as he went through them. She'd watched him enough on their voyage to the island that she already had a fairly clear understanding of the procedure. Afterward he gave her a brief primer on sailing in general, what to look out for and what to avoid. He explained how to gauge sail trim by easing the sheet until the leading edge began to shake, or luff, then cranking it back in until it stopped. "When in doubt, ease it out," he told her, then asked if she had any questions.

"If I keep headed this way long enough, will I eventually run into China?"

Jack pinched her cheek. "Yeah, Christopher. Piece of cake."

"Okay, now go get some rest," she said. "I insist."

"Can I bring you some breakfast first?"

"No, I can wait. You worry about yourself."

Jack gave her a contemplative look of uncertain meaning, as though there was something he was trying to decide. "You've got to take care of yourself, too, you know."

The kindness of his tone struck her. It was as though she really mattered to him. "Maybe a piece of bread or something then."

Patting her knee, he went off. She watched him go. Jack was in his faded cotton shorts, a tattered, sleeveless shirt and topsiders without socks. His shaggy hair seemed more sun-bleached than before, his muscular arms and legs more tanned. He was as appealing as ever, and not so frightening as before. She was getting comfortable with him. That had to mean something, but she was almost afraid to consider what.

Stephanie locked the wheel the way he showed her and lay back, glancing around at the sun-drenched sea and nearly cloudless sky. This was the most relaxed she'd felt since her ordeal had begun. There had been moments of peace on Nigel's island, but there had also been uncertainty. There was still uncertainty, of course, but now, like Françoise, she felt more accepting of what was to come—whatever it turned out to be.

The mainsail and jib began fluttering and Stephanie knew she needed either to make a slight course adjustment or trim the sails. Checking the compass, she decided to tack. She was in midprocedure when Jack appeared, carrying a tray. He stood aside as she completed the maneuver.

"Hey, not bad for a plebe," he said, dropping on the seat beside her. "You into this sailing stuff, Mrs. Reymond?"

"I'm enjoying it." She checked out the tray. Jack had made coffee. There was also a small can of orange juice, bread, jam and a couple of thin slices of cheese. "That looks great, but you shouldn't have gone to the trouble."

"I found that good service makes for repeat customers. You know—keep 'em coming back for more." He grinned.

"Jack, you're bad."

"Bad and dangerous go together, sweetheart."

"So do fatigue and mistakes," she said, sipping her coffee. Jack winked at her.

Stephanie tore off a piece of cheese and ate it with a corner of bread. Then she drank more coffee. It was strong. She liked the bite.

Next to her, Jack stretched out his long body, his legs open and relaxed, his head back. He was obviously wrung-out, maybe too tired to go to bed. Or maybe he just wanted to talk a while first.

"Sonia told me all about your relationship," she said, figuring she might as well come at him out of the blue.

He opened one eye and regarded her. "Did she tell you that now we're only friends?"

"I think she loves you, Jack, if you want my honest opinion. And if you were honest, you'd admit that you love her."

"Oh, really?"

"Well, that's my opinion."

"Maybe I'm not that honest, Stephanie," he said, closing his eye.

"I'm serious."

"So am I."

"You admit that you do love her."

"Of course. But not the way you're thinking."

She picked up a piece of bread and began slathering jam on it with excessive zeal.

"Why do you ask, anyway?" he said. "Concern for my sake or hers?"

"Both, I guess."

"Well, don't worry your pretty little head. Sonia and I understand each other just fine." Jack picked up the can of orange juice, pulled open the tab for her and put it back on the tray. "Don't forget to drink this," he said. "You need vitamin C to protect against scurvy."

She gave him a little nudge with her elbow, then picked up the can and dutifully took a sip. Whether it was true or not, she had the feeling Jack cared about her. It was a nice feeling, an increasingly warm feeling.

Jack yawned. She liked his company, but she knew he needed rest.

"Go take your nap," she ordered. "I've got everything under control here."

"Aye, captain," he replied, giving her a little salute. Again he patted her knee. "Damn happy to have you aboard again, sweetheart. Didn't realize how much I missed you until you were gone." Then he got to his feet, looking down at her meaningfully for a moment or two before retreating along the deck.

As he disappeared from sight, she played his last comment over in her mind. He could have said it for effect. And it was possible—even probable—that he had ulterior motives. Yet he sounded entirely sincere, so she chose to believe he was.

The warm glow she felt came somewhat as a surprise. Her heart was beating a bit rapidly. Early on she'd elected to ignore Jack's seductive games. Now she wasn't sure she wanted to. She could never be like some of his other women, wiggling her tits, exchanging a few suggestive remarks, then leading him off to bed. But neither was it out of the question for her to be with someone for whom she felt warmth and concern, not to mention a very strong attraction.

It was odd how feeble the human spirit could be when it came to love, she decided. Or, maybe it wasn't odd at all. Maybe it was simply normal, and she was only now discovering what it meant to be normal. Normal and alive.

Four hours passed and presumably Jack was still sound asleep. Half an hour earlier she'd locked the wheel and gone below to use the head. Peeking into his cabin, she saw him flaked out in his berth in his undershorts, dead to the world. She'd decided to let him sleep as long as he wished. The poor man had earned it.

She had been content, though the sun was hot and her skin felt tender despite the sunblock. Fortunately a shadow from the sail fell across her when she was on the more southerly tack.

With time to herself, she'd been able to think. The one thing that kept eating at her was Jean Claud's secret code. In light of everything else, she hadn't dwelled much on her resentment. By getting killed, Jean Claud and Jane had insulated themselves from her wrath, but when she stopped to think about it, she realized what a snake her husband had been. The bastard had put all her money, plus the money from their joint portfolio, into an offshore account, and then he'd given *her sister* access to it! It was a flagrant case of adding insult to injury.

When she'd looked at the disks in her cabin on the *Rubber Soul*, she'd been concentrating on the Cayman bank account and hadn't closely examined the source of the funds that had been invested in Halcyon. There was a lot of research to do. When Jack came up on deck, she'd go down and spend time on the computer.

It occurred to her then that she was really doing little more than keeping watch for traffic and tacking every once in a while. There still wasn't much wind and they couldn't be covering more than two or three miles in an hour. So why not work on the computer now?

She secured the wheel and went below to retrieve Jane's computer and the disks. On her way back up, she tripped on the top step and the computer nearly went flying over the lifeline and into the water. The horrible vision passed through her mind of thirty million dollars sinking to the bottom of the sea. She was so shaken she stood there for a moment, her hand to her chest, trying to recover. It brought home just how fragile the whole enterprise was.

Settling down in the cockpit, Stephanie scanned the horizon. Seeing nothing in sight, she turned on the computer and took another look at Jean Claud's files. First, she examined the Halcyon portfolio. It was then she noticed that Jean Claud's initial capital investment was only nine million dollars—five million of it her inheritance, two million their joint portfolio, a million and a half of his family's money and half a million was attributed to somebody named Dave Martin. She wondered who he was, then remembered the man Jean Claud had talked to on the phone that day was named Dave.

Stephanie contemplated the implications. Based on what she saw, there was no Inter-America Ventures money invested in Halcyon, no funds from other outside investors except for this Dave. Essentially Jean Claud had taken eight and a half million dollars from various family portfolios, plus the half million from his friend, and parlayed it into thirty million dollars, based on the estimated appreciated value of the stock. With Jean Claud dead, seven-ninths, or roughly eighty percent, of the thirty million was rightfully hers, the rest belonging to her husband's French relatives and Dave Martin.

"Have you broken the code, Sherlock?" She looked up to see Jack, sleepy-eyed, making his way toward her.

Stephanie perked up at the sight of him. "No, I was just looking to see how my husband manipulated my money." She smiled warmly, her annoyance with Jean Claud already slipping from her mind. "How do you feel? When I looked in on you earlier, you were zonked."

Jack dropped down on the seat. "Better, but I'm not quite ready for a marathon."

"You have a big sleep deficit to overcome."

He surprised her by taking her hand. "So, how's it feel to be captain?" He leaned over and checked the compass. "Course looks good."

"No problem, except that it's been slow going."

Jack perused the sky. "Yeah, the wind gods aren't looking on us very favorably at the moment. Many days like this and it'll take us a month to get to the Caymans."

"Where are we, anyway? Do you have a map?"

Jack pulled a small scale chart from the locker. He pointed to a spot about a hundred nautical miles south of Puerto Rico, between sixty-six and sixty-seven degrees west longitude. "I'd say we're right about here." Then he dragged his finger across the chart toward Mexico, stopping at a couple of specks below the eastern end of Cuba. "And we have a week or so to get all the way over here. A thousand miles or thereabouts."

"Can we make it?"

"If the wind picks up. This sort of calm is very unusual."

"We're being tested, Jack," she said, aware of his knee bumping lightly against hers.

"Ain't that the truth?" he said, rolling up the chart. He glanced at the computer resting on her lap. "So, how about the code? Been working on it? Or is that privileged information?"

It was a pivotal question, her answer depending on the degree of her trust, and they both knew it. "I don't see why it should be privileged. We're partners, after all." Looking into his eyes, she saw a smile in them. "And God knows I can certainly use the help. Let me call up the file."

Stephanie pulled up the document then pointed to the series of word-and-number pairs. "I think each of these represent a digit in the code. The banker implied there'd be a numerical access code. There are six word-number combinations. A six-digit code seems logical."

"The words are connected to the numbers by an equal sign," Jack observed.

"That's the part that baffles me. Why an equal sign?"

"The words must represent a number of some sort themselves."

"Undoubtedly. That part I think I understand," she said. "Jean Claud made this code for my sister, and Jane, like our mother, was into numerology. In fact, Mom was so fanatical she'd change her phone number or the license plate on her car to get the right numerological indications. She was obsessed and it rubbed off on Jane."

"But not you?"

"I was into numbers, all right, but in my case it was the sort you find on a profit-and-loss statement." She laughed. "Good old Stephanie, the oddball in the family."

"Numerology is sort of like astrology, isn't it?"

"Yes, sort of. I think it started with the belief that the numbers in a person's birth date determine the influences in their life. But it was extended to words, as well, by giving each letter in the alphabet a numerical value. A equals one, B equals two, C equals three and so forth."

"All the way to twenty-six?"

"Not really. In numerology there are only nine pure numbers, one through nine. Every multiple-digit number is reduced to its base by adding the digits. For example, the number ten is equal to one because one plus zero equals one. And eleven is equal to two because one plus one is equal to two. Similarly, twelve equals three because one plus two equals three."

"So two hundred and forty-three equals...nine," he said,

doing a quick calculation, ''because two plus four plus three equals nine.''

''Exactly,'' Stephanie said. ''It sounds complicated, but it's really pretty simple. Keep adding digits until you get to a base number. My mother could look at a person's name, do a quick calculation and tell you whether they were sociable, technically inclined or destined to be rich and successful, all because each base number has intrinsic qualities. For example, the number one is pioneering, six represents sociability, eight money and success and so forth.''

''That must have come in handy at family seances,'' Jack quipped.

Stephanie gave him a look. ''The point is, each of these words in the code would have a numerical value in terms of numerology. 'Chalk,' for example, is three plus eight, plus one, plus three, plus two, which…let me see…adds up to…seventeen, if I'm not mistaken, which reduces to eight because one plus seven equals eight. Understand?''

''If you say so, sweetheart.''

''My point is that the first digit of the code, chalk == 4 in numerological terms is eight == 4, but I have no idea what that means. Why the equal sign?''

''Maybe this code has nothing to do with numerology,'' Jack suggested. ''Maybe it's just the number of letters in the word.''

''But that still doesn't explain what the equal sign means.''

He considered that, rubbing his chin. ''True…''

''At first I thought the number after the equal sign indicates the position of the digit in the code. In other words, chalk == 4 means that the numerological value of chalk, or the number eight, is the fourth digit in the code.''

''That makes sense,'' Jack said, his interest rising.

''Yeah, but look,'' she said, pointing, ''the numbers he lists here after the words are, in numerical order, one, two, four, four, five and seven. That would mean two fourth digits and a seventh digit, but no third and no sixth, so that eliminates that possibility.''

Jack studied the screen. Stephanie slipped the computer onto his lap and stood to take another look at the sea. Off to the north she spotted a small steamer, but it was several miles away and on a different course. She sat down again.

"What if the equal sign represents something else?" he said. "For example, what if equal really means plus."

She watched as he put his hand on her knee, caressing it unconsciously. "Sure, Jack, that's possible, but it could also be a minus sign or a multiplication sign. There's no way to know."

Now he rubbed his chin again. "You're saying we're screwed?"

"Maybe. But I'd like to think there's a nice, clear, logical explanation. My sister wasn't dumb, but she was a plodding thinker. My intuition tells me this code is straightforward and mechanical, not deceptive. The equal sign really means equal in some way. There's obviously a key, but I can't figure it out. The only thing I feel fairly certain of is that numerology figures into it. Even Jean Claud was into our family's obsession with numerology, though usually with tongue in cheek."

Jack leaned back, folding his arms over his chest. "I'd like to be encouraging, Stephanie, but I have a hunch this is something that's going to come to you intuitively, if it comes at all."

She regarded him. "Discouraging, isn't it?"

"Oh, I don't know," he said, putting his arm around her shoulders and bringing his hip right up against hers. "Maybe the numerological gods are on our side."

Stephanie leaned toward him and he kissed her temple.

"Hey," he said. "I just realized. You worked right through lunch, didn't you? Are you hungry?"

"Not really."

"Can I get you a drink or anything?"

"No, but I've been thinking I'd like to wash up and maybe rest a little. I'm not used to this much sun."

"How thoughtless of me," Jack said. "You go on below. Take a nap, if you like. Maybe we can have an early dinner."

"That sounds good."

Stephanie lifted Jane's computer off his lap, turned it off and closed the cover. "Maybe I'll work on this again first thing in the morning, when I'm fresh."

"Sounds like a good plan."

She got up, holding the computer carefully this time, and headed for the companionway. As she got to the top of the steps she glanced back and saw Jack looking at her legs. She smiled. He smiled. The more things changed, she decided, the more they were the same.

Stephanie came back up on deck at about sunset and found Jack staring absently at the sails. The air was strangely warm and still. He glanced at her, shaking his head.

"What's happened?" she asked.

He pointed up at the sails, sagging like old skin. "We're in a dead calm. If we move at all, it'll be because of a current."

"You mean we're stuck?"

"Until the wind comes up."

"How long will that be?"

"It could be a few hours, or a day. Now that I've got a working radio, I've learned there's a huge high pressure area covering most of the gulf. Until it starts moving off, we'll sit here bobbing like a rubber ducky." He stood.

"Where are you going?"

"I thought I'd go below and fix you a special meal. We might as well have a pleasant evening instead of one of us being stuck on watch. And, since we're not going anywhere, anyway, I figured I'd get a good night's sleep. Once the wind comes up, we can sail around the clock."

"You're the captain."

Jack reached out and caressed her cheek. "I always liked hearing that, especially from a beautiful woman."

"Why? Because it sounds like 'lord and master'?"

He chuckled. "You see right through me, don't you?"

"God, I hope not."

Jack looked her over. She'd put on a little sleeveless cotton dress and slicked her hair back. "My, but don't you look gorgeous."

"Amazing what a shower will do for you," she said.

"I thought I'd shave and have one myself." Reaching out, he took her hand and gently pulled her to him. "Meanwhile, you don't mind if I smell you, do you?" he said, gathering her in his arms.

They stood on the deck, holding each other in the dead calm air. The sea was so still the boat hardly moved. She was aware of his masculine scent, his strong arms and the feel of the stubble on his chin against her temple.

Jack lightly stroked her neck, making her shiver. She pulled her head back so she could see him. The sun had dropped below the horizon and the light had that peculiar, luminescent quality that comes only at dusk.

He seemed aware of the question in her eyes. "What?"

"How long has it been since you've had a drink, Jack?"

He reflected. "How long have I known you?"

"A week."

"Then it's been a week."

"But that's coincidental."

"No, since you came aboard I've been gainfully employed," he said. "But that's not the whole story."

She wasn't sure she wanted clarification. Jack rubbed her cheek with his thumb.

"Aren't you going to ask me to explain?" he asked.

She gave a half shrug.

"A lot of it's because of the way I feel about you…. No, not a lot," he said, correcting himself. "It *is* because of the way I feel about you."

Stephanie lowered her eyes, but he lifted her chin, making her look at him.

"That's the sincerest compliment I can give," he said, a quaver of emotion in his voice.

"Has it been hard?" she asked. "Not drinking, I mean."

"It's been a bitch."

"You must feel good about it, though."

"When I'm not thinking about having a drink."

Taking her face in his hands, he leaned down and kissed her mouth. It was a tender, affectionate kiss that said a lot about his feelings. For the first time he was suggesting that she was important to him.

"Hey," she said, breaking the mood, "you know what? I haven't paid you yet."

"Paid me?"

"The seven thousand I owe."

"It's six, but don't worry about it. No rush."

"No, it's important that we're businesslike, Jack. I want to do this right."

He kissed her forehead, then the corner of her eye. "Why is that important?"

She forced a couple of quick breaths as he held her by the waist. The message in his eyes was unequivocal. Things, she sensed, were shifting to another gear.

"Maybe it's the accountant in me," she said, "always wanting to keep things tidy."

"Tidy, huh? Don't tell me your house was tidy, everything in its place."

She nodded. "Yeah, pretty much."

He frowned deeply. "Do you suppose that means we're incompatible?"

"Possibly," she said with a shrug.

"Do slobs upset you?"

"Jean Claud was fastidious and I was always organized, so our house was…"

"As antiseptic as an operating room?"

"Yeah."

Jack grinned. "I guess I'm like a breath of fresh air." When she didn't respond, he let his hands drop from her waist. "Why don't we go below then? I can start dinner and get cleaned up."

They went down to the salon. Saying it would be wise to save the batteries, Jack lit a couple of kerosene lamps, one of which he gave to her. The other he took with him to the galley. Stephanie retrieved her purse from her cabin and brought it out to the table in the salon.

"We have the good fortune of being able to eat some of Tess's fine cuisine," Jack called from the galley. "She made a few dishes for me to bring along."

"Great."

Stephanie had forgotten about Jack's gun and, finding it in her purse, she put it on the table. Then she spotted Françoise's passport.

"Oh, damn."

"What's the matter?"

"I left without giving Françoise's passport back to her."

"She can get another. Anyway, it might come in handy. God knows what you'll have to do and where you'll be going before it's safe to be Stephanie Reymond again."

He had a point. She turned her attention to the money. Having spent most of her cash, she had to pay him with traveler's checks. She'd signed six thousand dollars' worth by the time he joined her at the table with a bottle of mineral water and two glasses.

"I could probably dig up a bottle of wine if you'd prefer it," he said.

"No, this is fine. Why make it difficult for you unnecessarily?"

"Admittedly I've been avoiding temptation." He opened the bottle and poured some in each glass. "Ice is a luxury we'll have to do without."

"I'll survive," she said.

Sitting across from her, Jack touched his glass to hers. "To us and our common enterprise," he said. "May all your codes be easily broken."

"It would improve our prospects, wouldn't it?"

They each sipped their water. The way Jack looked at her made her feel strangely aware of herself. His rakishness, if that's what it was, went beyond simple mental undressing. It was connection, a deep connection. She could think of no other way to describe it.

Stephanie pushed the traveler's checks over to him and put the gun down beside them. "I guess I owe you a bullet," she said. "I used one to knock out the radio in Bobby's plane."

"Don't worry about it. It's all part of the service."

"Jean Claud was opposed to having a gun in the house. He said the potential for harm was greater than the potential for good. And he was probably right. Had I not had your gun with me in St. Thomas, I wouldn't be wanted for kidnapping and air piracy."

"But you probably wouldn't be here with the disks, either."

"Sort of bad news, good news, isn't it?"

Jack gave her one of his particularly endearing smiles. "I'm glad things worked out this way, but whether we have the disks or not, I can't think of anyone I'd rather be with."

She wondered at that, but didn't comment. They contemplated each other for a long time.

Finally Jack said, "I think I'll go get cleaned up now." He picked up the traveler's checks and the gun, which he stuffed in the waistband of his shorts. "I've got some rice steaming and seafood stew simmering on the stove. If you wouldn't mind, check them occasionally."

"Sure," she said.

Jack started for the head, then stopped. "Oh, by the way, do you play cribbage?"

"Not for years."

"But you know how?"

"Yes, Jean Claud and I played a lot when I was pregnant.

But as soon as Suzanne was born we stopped. I can't tell you why. Maybe with the baby we were too busy.''

He had a funny look on his face.

"What, Jack?''

"Oh, nothing.''

"Tell me.''

He sighed. "Alicia and I used to play cribbage. Especially toward the end.''

"When she was pregnant?''

Jack's expression was questioning.

"Malva told me,'' she explained.

He nodded. "I guess she would have known.''

There was an awkward silence.

"Maybe cribbage isn't such a good idea,'' she said.

"Would it bother you?''

She shook her head.

"Let's let fate decide,'' he said. "If the board hasn't been pinched, it'll be in that locker over there against the bulkhead. If you can find it, we'll play. If not, we'll leave our cribbage memories to rest. Fair enough?''

"Fine.''

Jack went off to shave and shower, and Stephanie got up to search the locker. In an odd way, it seemed significant whether she found the board, though she couldn't begin to say why. Nor did she know whether she wanted to find it. Like Jack said, fate would decide.

Seven Mile Beach, Grand Cayman,

The Cayman Islands

The barkeep put another rum and Coke in front of him. Rico Behring picked up the glass, examining it as if he wasn't sure he wanted to drink it. "How many's this?''

"That's your fourth, sir.''

Rico regarded the man. He was of medium height, a little on the heavy side. His dark skin glistened in the heat and a huge mustache dominated his face. They'd spoken very little despite the fact that Rico was the only one at the bar. A couple of gangly old guys who looked like fishermen were sitting in the back corner, talking and laughing over their beer, but the beach café was otherwise empty.

Out on the patio, under the thatch cabana, the barmaid was cleaning the metal tables. Her hair was cut short like a man's and she wore large hoop earrings that hung nearly to her shoulders. She was on the small side, but she had the roundest, juiciest ass he'd ever seen. The way her little T-shirt dress stretched over it was enough to give a guy a hard-on.

When she drifted from sight, Rico turned his attention back to the bartender. "What's your name again, sport?"

"George, sir."

"George. Why is every fucking thing in this fucking place named George?"

"I don't know, sir, perhaps it's our colonial past."

Rico found the guy's even temperament sort of surprising. Every nigger he'd ever known had some kind of attitude, but this one he liked. George picked up an empty glass and polished it with his bar rag. Seeing not a flicker of hatred in the bastard's eyes, Rico took his roll from his pocket and peeled off a twenty.

"Here, *amigo,*" he said, handing him the bill. "That's for you. It's got nothin' to do with the drinks. Put it in your pocket."

George smoothly tucked the twenty away. "Thank you, sir. You're very kind."

Rico smirked because it sounded strange. Nobody he could think of ever called him kind. Not even his mother. Generous, funny, happy-go-lucky, life of the party, but never kind. "To tell you the truth, George, I'm in a shitty mood."

"Sorry to hear that, sir."

"Problems with my wife. I'm down here on business and

the bitch is back home, jerking me around. I've tried calling her three times in the last twelve hours and nobody's home, not even the kid with a fucking baby-sitter.''

"I can see how that would be vexing, sir.''

"Fucking A,'' Rico said, knocking back more rum and Coke. "If she's screwing around behind my back, I'll cut her goddamn heart out.''

"You obviously love her.''

"Christ, I married her, didn't I? How much more can you love a broad than that? And she wasn't exactly Miss Virgin Queen when we met, neither.''

"I understand, sir.''

Rico looked at him appraisingly. "You know, George, I think you do.'' Draining the last of his drink, he put the glass down on the bar. "Give me another, sport.''

"Yes, sir.''

Outside, the barmaid was sweeping the patio now. With every stroke of the broom her ass rocked. Rico could imagine thrusting his cock in her with each hitch. God, how he'd love to have those legs wrapped around him, squeezing the bejesus out of him. George placed a fresh rum and Coke in front of him.

Rico's eyes were still on the girl. "Tell me, my friend. Can that piece out there be had?''

"I don't think so, sir. She has a man.''

"Does her man have money?''

George hesitated. "I believe not.''

"Then I've got something her man doesn't have. How much do you think it would take to get her in bed, moneywise?''

"I really wouldn't know, sir. But if that's your interest, there are places in town…''

"No,'' Rico said, shaking his head. "I like that one. She's got a great ass.''

George resumed his polishing.

"Do you think she'd have dinner and share some fun and games with me for five hundred pounds?''

"Honestly, I have no idea, sir, but I tend to doubt it."

"Tell you what, George, I'll give you a thousand pounds to negotiate with her on my behalf. Go make a deal for me. You can keep the difference."

"Sir, I really don't think…"

"Here," Rico said, pulling another twenty from his roll. "Don't be shy. Go ask her. What can it hurt?"

The bartender headed off. As he went out the door, Carlos, Oscar's sidekick, came in the front entrance. He seemed surprised as he hurried over to the bar.

"*Jesucristo,* we've been looking for you everywhere, Señor Behring," he said anxiously. "It's your father. He's had a heart attack. They took him to the hospital."

Rico felt his heart clench. "Pops?" he said through an alcoholic haze. "Pops had a heart attack?"

"They think so," Carlos said. "They were at dinner and he fell right over. Oscar was with him. Everyone's been searching for you, *señor.* We been combing the beaches, looking in every bar and restaurant between the hotel and the town."

"This isn't a joke?"

"No, I swear it, *señor.* Please come. I got a car out front."

Rico numbly got to his feet. He felt so light-headed, he had to hold on to the bar.

"You all right?"

"Yeah," he said, dazed. "Just give me a minute."

As Rico stood there, his heart racing, the bartender returned. Rico stared at him mutely, only half recalling what they'd discussed. George leaned across the bar and lowered his voice to a confidential tone.

"Corine said to tell you, sir, that she's not a prostitute."

Rico considered that. "So what does that mean, that she wants more money?"

George appeared uncomfortable. "She said she'd be willing to come by your hotel and have a drink with you, sir, and get acquainted. But it would have to be tomorrow afternoon. Two o'clock.''

Rico was beginning to get the drift of the conversation. "So, how much bread we talkin', George?"

The barkeep lowered his voice still further. "Twenty-five hundred, sir."

"Dollars?"

"Pounds."

Rico knocked back a big gulp of rum and Coke. "Jesus, virtue is expensive on this fucking island."

"Corine is not a professional, sir."

"Amateurs are more expensive, huh?"

George shrugged.

"Señor?" Carlos said. "You coming?"

"Yeah, go get in the car, Carlos. I'll be right there."

The man went off.

"Tell you what, George," Rico said. "I'll have somebody come by tomorrow and pick her up. But I'm not paying over two grand. That's more than top dollar for *any* piece of ass."

George frowned.

Rico smiled. "The five was going to you, wasn't it, sport?"

The barman lowered his eyes.

"I'll pay her two thou," Rico said, taking his roll from his pocket and peeling off three twenties. "Here's sixty bucks. If you can get more out of her, more power to you." Glancing up, he saw the woman at the door leading to the patio, half hiding behind the door frame. He could see trepidation in her eyes. He smiled. "Hi there, doll," he called to her. "You're lookin' beautiful."

She shrank from sight. Rico chuckled, liking the thought of an amateur. Then he turned to face the entrance, his hand still resting on the bar. He refocused his thoughts on what he was doing. Carlos's shocker entered his brain again. Jesus, he thought, what if Pop died? Well, he knew what it meant, of course. This whole thing would land right in his lap. And

Oscar would have to kiss his ass right along with everybody else. Christ.

Rico patted the bar with his hand. "Thanks, George."

"Yes, sir."

He headed for the entrance, walking as straight and true as he could. Even so, he wove a little. Shit. He wasn't sure he was ready for this. But not a fucking soul would find out he had doubts. Not even his father.

The Caribbean Sea

Stephanie cleared their dinner dishes while Jack went topside to check out conditions. They'd played two games of cribbage before they'd eaten. She'd won the first, pegging out with Jack sitting twelve points back and holding a sixteen-point hand. She'd been thrilled since Jean Claud had usually beaten her. Perhaps it was an omen, though of what she couldn't say. The second game had fallen into a more familiar pattern. Jack trounced her, coming within a few points of skunking her. They'd agreed to play the rubber game of the match after dinner.

Jack came back down the steps. "That's the calmest sea I've ever seen in my life. And it's a gorgeous evening. Venus looks big enough to sit on top a Christmas tree and the moon's so bright you could read a newspaper by it. What do you say we play our rubber game up there?"

Jack grabbed the board and cards and she followed him up the stairs. He was right about the evening, it was glorious, the air incredible. While he set up some chairs and a small folding table on the deck, she gazed at the sea. Far to the north a freighter and a cruise ship slipped along the horizon, the latter aglow with lights. The sky was a carpet of stars.

They were in their own little floating world, just the two of them, joined in a common enterprise. But at times, that almost seemed to her like an excuse. Though she wouldn't have admitted it at the outset, part of what she was doing was simply being with him. This was becoming clearer to her all the time, though it remained unspoken on both their parts.

"This is truly magnificent," she said in awe.

"It's the kind of night you want to last forever," he said meaningfully.

Stephanie sat quietly as Jack set up the board and shuffled the cards. She thought about how attractive he was, how his presence alone could arouse her. The fact that he knew it, too, made the feeling all the more intense. She wondered if he was determined to make love with her tonight, and if he tried, how she'd react.

"All right," Jack said. "Rubber game." He contemplated her. "You know, more should be riding on the outcome than just bragging rights."

"What do you mean?"

"We need a bet of some kind."

"Like what?"

Jack stroked his chin as he considered her question. She noticed his eyes glide down her and it wasn't hard to guess what he was thinking.

"Nothing immoral," she warned. "Losing a bet is the worst possible reason I can think of for having sex."

"I don't recall saying anything about sex."

"It's what you were thinking."

"No, Stephanie, it was what *you* were thinking."

She blushed, hoping he couldn't tell. "There's more than one way to suggest something, you know."

He leaned back in his chair, folding his hands over his stomach. "You're still afraid of me, aren't you?"

"I'm not afraid of you. We haven't always wanted the same thing, that's all."

He reached over and took her hand, surprising her. "Look, Stephanie," he said, "I know this isn't the life you're used to and I'm not the sort of man you've associated with in the past. But I want to be really clear about this. As long as we're together, I'll never make you do anything against your will. Whatever happens between us, it'll be what you want, what feels good. So don't worry."

His words touched her, even if they were calculated for effect. They showed he understood what was on her mind. "I appreciate that," she said. "I really do."

"But we still need a meaningful bet."

"Why is that so important?"

"The more you live on the edge, the more alive you feel. That's why people gamble, Stephanie."

"I don't need to gamble to be happy."

"Then why did you come with me?" he asked.

"Why did *you* come with *me?*"

"Because I *am* a gambler."

She watched him riffle the cards. He was daring her to play his game. "Okay," she said. "What do you want to bet?"

"Tell you what. Let's play for an extra five percent of the booty. Our deal now is I get twenty percent of whatever you get out of the bank, right?"

"Unless it's through legal action, yes."

"All right. We play this game to see whether it's going to be fifteen percent or twenty-five percent."

She blinked. "That could be a difference of three million dollars."

"That ought to get your palms to sweating," he said with a grin.

"No," she said, shaking her head. "I won't do it. That's crazy."

"You offered me twenty percent out of the chute, Stephanie, so what's five percent one way or the other?"

"A million and a half, that's what."

"You're afraid."

"I am not," she said indignantly. "Besides, the way things stand with the code, we may not be getting a nickel out of the bank, either one of us."

"Then you shouldn't have any trouble making the bet."

Even in the soft light of the moon his features betrayed a certain arrogance and self-satisfaction.

Stephanie felt herself rising to the bait. "All right, Captain Kidwell," she said with forced confidence. "I'll bet you the five percent."

"Excellent," he said, rubbing his hands together. "I love a woman with courage."

They cut the cards. Jack got the first deal and crib. Her palms *were* sweaty, and at some level the excitement, the expectation, did appeal to her. It was just a game of cards, but she'd never been more nervous playing in her life.

The game progressed, the lead swinging back and forth. The ebb and flow from exhilaration to despair was incredible. But at the one-third mark she took a commanding lead, bettering him by nearly twenty points. She felt the thrill of blood sport. It was a strange high.

"Having second thoughts, Captain?"

"Don't get smug, my dear. The game's not over."

No sooner had he said it than his luck changed. He had a couple of good hands in a row, one a sixteen-pointer, and passed her at the final turn. Stephanie felt as though the wind had been knocked right out of her. She sat watching him shuffle the cards, her nails dug into her palms, a sheen of perspiration on her lip as she considered what was at stake.

They were tied, fifteen points from the finish, and it was his deal. That meant he would get the crib, but she got first count. If she mustered fifteen points between play and count she'd win, regardless of how many points he ended up having.

"Hmm," Jack said, studying the board. "Fifteen points, a million and a half dollars riding on the hand. That figures out to a hundred thousand dollars a point. What do you think of your odds?"

"Not good," she said despairingly. "Less than fifty-fifty."

He nodded. "Yeah, I'd agree. Of course, I may not go out, either."

"But next hand you count first, which means your chances

are probably better. You're definitely in control of the game,'' she said, trying not think of the stakes as real money. When she looked up at him, she actually saw pity on his face. ''What?''

''Let's make it interesting,'' he said. ''I'll let you buy an extra card.''

''What do you mean?''

''I'll deal you an extra card and you can discard one and keep the best four out of five in your hand.''

She considered that. It could make a big difference, increasing her chances considerably. ''What'll it cost me?''

''Hmm,'' he said thoughtfully. ''What do you have that I might want?''

His quirky smile told her he was having more suggestive thoughts. But instead of sharing them with her, he dealt six cards to her and six to himself, then stopped. ''Okay,'' he said. ''Here's what I propose. You get a free card if you come with me for a moonlight swim.''

''Here? In the middle of the ocean?'' she said.

''The water's warm and it couldn't be calmer.''

She contemplated him, wondering what the catch was. ''No sex?''

''Nothing you don't want to do. We just go skinny-dipping.''

Stephanie looked at the board. ''Do I get to see the turn card before I have to discard the extra?''

Jack chuckled. ''Ah, practical as well as virtuous, I see.''

''Yes or no?'' she demanded, flushing.

''Sure,'' he said. ''You can see the turn card.''

''All right,'' she said. ''It's a deal. Give me my card.''

Jack, thoroughly amused, gave her the extra card. It was a five. The turn card was a king. She also had a queen, a ten and another five in her hand. That was fourteen points. If she managed to get two points in play, she'd win!

She discarded a six from her hand and put another six and nine in the crib for Jack. They began the play. Her queen brought the count to thirty, but Jack had an ace and got the two points.

"Damn," she muttered, losing a chance at a point.

Next round he was high card, winning another point. Stephanie got a point for playing last card in the final round, but with the fourteen points in her hand, that gave her a total of fifteen, which put her in the stink hole, one point shy of victory. Now the question was if Jack had thirteen points in his hand and crib, or if they'd have to play another hand.

Stephanie counted her hand for him and placed her peg in the stink hole.

"Oh, poor Stephanie," he said. "So close and yet so far."

"Come on, Jack," she said, her heart pounding, her face damp with perspiration. "Let's see your hand. What do you have?"

"Only five points," he said grimly.

He showed her his cards. She smiled, feeling a spark of hope.

"Now the question is if I have eight points in my crib," he said, surprisingly cool.

He began turning over the cards one at a time, starting with the six and the nine she'd given him. That was two points. He knew what he'd put in the crib, which meant he also knew whether he'd just won or lost a million and a half dollars. There was no sign on his face, nothing in his eyes indicating the result.

"Jack?"

He turned over a seven. Her heart stopped. If the next card was an eight, she'd lost. His hand rested on the card.

"Damn it," she said. "Turn it over."

Jack picked up the card and turned it over. The eight of hearts! That gave him eight points in his crib. He'd just won another five percent of the Halcyon money, her money. Stephanie was stunned.

She swallowed hard, feeling as though she'd just been

kicked in the stomach. She glanced up at him. Jack actually looked embarrassed.

"Tough luck," he said.

She only half comprehended what had happened. In one sense it was cataclysmic, in another it was all pretend, anyway. "I guess I should hope that cost me a million dollars," she finally said. "Because if it's worthless to you, it's worthless to me."

"Whatever the outcome, it was good for a little excitement," he said, sounding a touch too upbeat.

"I guess I'm a double loser," she said. "I owe you another five percent of the deal and now I've got to take off my clothes."

"Forget it," he replied. "I think you've taken a big enough hit already."

"No, I bought that card. If I'd picked up just one more point in play, you'd be singing the blues."

"A woman of honor," he said.

"I pay my debts. Do you want me to undress now?"

"No, I already feel like Simon Legree."

"Good," she said, managing to smile. "You *should* suffer a little."

Jack shook his head, like maybe he'd heard it before. But she was going to get it over with. Standing, she turned her back to him and removed her T-shirt. Next she took off her shorts, sliding them down her legs before kicking them aside. Finally she slipped off her panties, knowing Jack was not ten feet away, his eyes poring over her. If anything, her heart was pounding harder than when they were playing cards.

She did not look back at him. Instead, she moved to the gate in the lifeline where the boarding ladder was normally deployed. Gazing down at the dark water, she told herself not to consider what dangers might be lurking there. Rather, she considered how beautiful the sea was in the moonlight. Then, rising to her toes, she dived into the water.

The initial sensation was coolness. But she surfaced and

after a moment the water began to feel tepid. Over the gentle swells she saw another ship far to the south. Behind her there was a splash. Stephanie turned to see Jack surface three feet from her. He pushed his hair back off his face.

"You like the deep water?" he asked.

"How deep is it, you suppose?"

"I don't know, around two miles, I imagine. Ten, twelve thousand feet."

"My God," she said.

Jack smiled. "Quite a sensation to be in it though, isn't it?"

"Feels wonderful, I admit."

They treaded water, facing each other. His wet face glistened in the moonlight. She moved closer, drawn to him, until their faces were only a foot or so apart.

"Funny how stimulating water is," he said. "I wonder why."

"Millions of years ago we were probably doing it in the water," she said.

"The more things change, the more they're the same."

Stephanie wondered if he'd just propositioned her. His eyes said yes, but that came as no surprise. The question was what *she* wanted. The moment had come either to retreat from the possibility or to advance. She knew it, Jack knew it.

Stephanie reached out and put her palm against his chest. He touched her waist. The water suddenly became an impediment. She wanted both his hands on her, she wanted to be in his arms.

Breaking away, she swam back to the boat where she grasped the boarding ladder. Jack continued to tread water, only turning around to face her after a minute. Seeing she had not climbed back onto the boat, he slowly swam toward her, through the reflection of the moon on the surface of the water.

Her back to the boat, Stephanie reached behind her head and held on to a rung of the ladder. The waves lapped at the top of her chest.

"What did you think when I told you I'd watched you and Tanya make love?" she asked.

"I figured you were trying to be provocative."

"Maybe I was. I've thought about it a lot, wondering what it would be like to be her."

"Are you trying to tell me something?"

"I don't know," she said, her voice tremulous.

Jack inched closer. When they were about to touch, he reached behind her and grasped the lower rung of the ladder. His body bumped up against hers, his thigh, his hip, his chest coming into contact with her. She drew a nervous breath.

"I'd like to think you just propositioned me," he said in a low voice.

She didn't have the strength to respond. Jack encircled her waist with his free arm and kissed her deeply, his tongue passing her lips. She wrapped her legs around his hips, drawing him close enough that she could feel his erection against her. The kiss ended and he pressed his face into the crook of her neck.

Through half-closed eyes, Stephanie saw the low, sleek lines of an oil tanker slide across the black horizon. But the image faded when Jack slid his hand between her legs.

She gasped when he began caressing her.

"You like it when I touch you, don't you?"

"Oh, yes."

"Like it when I put my finger here?"

"God, yes."

She writhed against his hand. He fingered her for several minutes, bringing her to the precipice of orgasm three or four times, but always backing off just before she came.

"Let's get back in the boat," she said. "You go first."

Stephanie moved aside so he could go up the ladder. He waited on deck, helping her up, then embracing her. The air felt cool on her wet skin as they kissed, his salty lips pressed against hers.

"Will you make love to me the way you did Tanya?" she asked, trembling.

"No, we'll do it in a way that's just for you."

She held him, suddenly frightened. "Jack, I haven't had sex in years," she blurted. "Not even with Jean Claud."

He took her face in his hands. "I know how to be gentle, sweetheart, don't worry."

Taking her hand, he led her toward the companionway. They went down the narrow passage and through the dark salon to her cabin where he embraced her and lowered her onto the berth in one motion. His wet skin was cool but still warmer than hers.

Enough moonlight came through the ports that she could see his face hovering over hers. She tried to understand from his eyes the full meaning of what was happening, but it wasn't there. This was about pleasure—and if she was lucky, about tenderness and affection. But in a way it was also about finally getting her due, getting from Jack what she'd never gotten from Jean Claud.

Propped on his elbow, Jack pushed the wet strands of hair off her cheek. He seemed in no hurry. And though her heart still slammed against her ribs, she felt herself begin to relax.

"What do you like best, babe?" he asked, running his fingertip over the top of her chest.

"I haven't done a lot. My husband didn't have much of a taste for sex, and I guess not much skill, either."

"That means we have to experiment. But we each have responsibilities, Steph. Mine is to be intuitive and creative. Yours is to tell me what feels good."

Stephanie swallowed hard. His words alone aroused her. Sex with Jean Claud had been a bit like a bumper-car ride at a carnival. There was contact, but it was brief and harsh and exciting only in a negative sense.

"Can you do that?" he asked.

"Yes, I'll try."

Jack cupped her breast and lowered his mouth to her nipple,

taking it between his lips. He sucked it, lightly running his tongue over the tip.

"Do you like that?"

"Yes."

"How does it feel?"

"You're making it throb."

"Good," he said, kissing and teasing it some more.

He moved to the other breast, repeating the ritual, moving his mouth back and forth from one breast to the other, occasionally nibbling the nipples lightly.

"God," she murmured. "I can even feel it in my stomach."

Jack slid his face down to her abdomen, dragging his moist lips across her skin. "Here?"

"Yes, everywhere."

He moved his head still lower and parted her legs. His breath was hot. She purred.

"Does this feel good?"

"Yes," she croaked. "It feels very good."

His face sank deeper and he moved her legs still farther apart. His tongue lapped her again and she lifted her pelvis.

"How about this?"

Air passed through her throat, but words were hard to form. She'd never before done this, save in her fantasies—fantasies involving dark men with dark intentions.

Jack looked up at her. "Stephanie?"

"Oh, don't stop, please," she begged, taking his head and pressing his face against her.

Again his tongue caressed her with perfect pressure. When she felt her orgasm coming, she grasped his head and squeezed it hard between her legs.

The sensation was so intense that she had to ask him to stop. The pleasure was becoming pain. But she'd never felt so purged, so out of control.

"You liked that, didn't you?" he said, rimming her navel with his tongue. "Did I satisfy you?"

The answer was yes, of course, because she couldn't imagine an orgasm more intense. But maybe that wasn't what he was asking. Did she want him to fuck her? That's what he wanted to know.

"Yes," she told him, "but I want you in me now."

She could feel his erection and tentatively grasped his penis. It arched slightly. She traced the upward curve with her palm, unsure how to pleasure him. But what she was doing seemed to be working. Stephanie pictured that girl straddling him. She wanted to do the same.

Rising to her knees, she got astride him. Jack gazed up at her as she guided his sex into her opening.

"God, you're big," she gasped as he slid into her.

"You feel good," he said, touching her breast.

She sucked a deep breath of air into her lungs. They both smelled of sex and the sea. She began rocking. It only took a moment before she was as turned on as she'd been earlier.

"Oh, oh," she murmured, realizing it wouldn't take much for her to come again.

Jack took hold of her haunches. She gyrated in concert with his direction, lifting herself so that she could slide back down his shaft. Wanting more contact, she leaned forward. Jack increased the pace by lifting and dropping her more rapidly onto his cock.

"Do you like this?" he asked.

"Oh, yes," she said, panting. "This is the best of all." And it was.

"Your body was made for this, Steph," he whispered. "Made for me to be in it."

Her blood surged and she felt something powerful gathering. As the sensation heightened, her head rolled back on her shoulders and she began to moan. She could come then, if she let herself. "Are you going to come?" she asked, wanting to let go when he did.

"You want me to fuck you now, sweetheart? You ready?"

"Oh, yes," she said, her body trembling.

That was all it took to set him off. He arched high and

Stephanie could feel him gush. She came with a violent shiver, her insides pulsing. Pulling her down on his chest, he held her tightly. A minute passed. She was aware of her breathing and the waves that continued to surge through her, their intensity only gradually diminishing.

Jack kissed her soaked forehead. "You and I just got laid, babe."

"I feel like I died."

"Oh, you're very much alive."

She sucked in his scent. It was male, spiced with the sea, and it seemed as if it should be a part of her, and she of it. She flopped down beside him and Jack took her hand.

"God, it's not always like that, is it?" she muttered.

He took her hand. "No. Sometimes it's quieter. But you've had a little catching up to do."

She rolled her head his way. "You mean I have to wait another five years for that to happen again?"

"I hope not."

She kissed his shoulder. "I hope not, too."

She gazed at him, knowing that dangerous feelings were coming. This next turn was what she had to guard against because she knew perfectly well what and who Jack really was. She could love what he'd done to her, but she couldn't love him.

George Town, The Cayman Islands

Oscar Barbadillo sat at his uncle's bedside in the darkened room. Behind the bed was a whole bank of blinking lights. Julius, an oxygen tube in his nose, opened his eyes and squinted at him.

"Good, you're still here. Where's Rico?"

"He's on his way, Uncle Julius."

"So you found him."

"Yes."

"Where was he? In a brothel?" Julius waved Oscar off with his hand. "Never mind, I don't want to know."

"Rico didn't like it when you relieved him of command. He's been upset, drinking more than usual."

"I know," Julius lamented. "But he's got other problems. Some he doesn't even know about. I'm afraid he can't handle the burdens. This heart of mine couldn't have given out at a worse time, Oscar. I'm dying and I know it. You're going to have to help Rico. He will need you."

"I'll do whatever you want, Uncle Julius."

"Sometimes I wish you were my son, Oscar. But Rico is my heir. Inter-America will be his. I cannot deny him his inheritance. But in my will, you receive ten percent of the company. This to ensure you will stand behind Rico. I want your promise."

"Of course. I will help in any way he lets me."

"I must tell him what I want. That's why he must come. I want him to hear it from my lips."

Oscar watched and listened with compassion, but he knew that Julius Behring's words would mean nothing once he was dead. Only power mattered—and whoever controlled Inter-America Ventures would call the shots. Soon he would be dealing with his cousin.

Julius again closed his eyes, resting while they waited. After a few minutes Oscar heard Rico's voice in the hall.

"I don't care about your goddamn rules," he was saying. "I'm going to see my father *now!*" Rico, looking as though he was in the middle of a drunk, appeared at the door. He stared into the room, disbelief on his face. "Jesus, Pop," he muttered.

Julius had opened his eyes again. "Good, you're here." He motioned for his son to enter.

Rico moved slowly toward the bed. "What's with this hospital shit, Pop? How you going to earn your pay flat on your back?"

"We must talk."

"Sure, Pop." Rico pulled up a chair, ignoring Oscar. He plopped down and leaned toward his father.

"Your time has come, son," Julius wheezed. "Even if I don't die now, I'm through. The company is effectively yours."

"Pop, don't say that."

"It's true. So, we've got to prepare. You've got to starting thinking like a boss, Rico, not somebody who's been sitting in the driver's seat because his old man said he could."

"Pop—"

"No, listen to me, son. You've got the company to worry about now and you've got your family. Your wife and child need your attention. There've been problems with Rhonda you don't even know about. Before we went to dinner I got a call from our lawyers. Rhonda's divorcing you, Rico. She sent papers."

Rico's mouth dropped. "You're shitting me."

"No, son, it happened. You need to go home and take care of it."

Rico sat brooding for several moments. "What about our money?"

"That's the other thing. I'm putting Oscar in charge. You'll have your hands full in California dealing with Rhonda and settling in as CEO. I know you're fired up about the money, but this is something Oscar can deal with. Let him handle Stephanie Reymond."

Oscar watched Rico turn and glare at him. Julius's words were nothing but a futile attempt to control things from the grave. Rico would not listen, he was sure.

"Well, I guess he's had plenty of experience with her," Rico said snidely.

Oscar could have throttled the sonovabitch right then and there, but there was no point in coming to blows until absolutely necessary.

"I want you two to promise me you'll work together," Julius mumbled.

Oscar and Rico exchanged looks again.

"Do you promise?" Julius insisted.

"Yes, Uncle Julius," Oscar said.

"Sure, Pop," Rico added.

"Okay, that's going to be it, then," Julius said. "I can't do more than that." His head seemed to sink deeper into the pillow, his voice becoming a whisper. "It's in your hands, boys."

Julius's eyes closed. He seemed exhausted. Oscar realized the old man had rallied for this speech, he'd passed the torch, and now he was giving up.

The nurse entered. "Please, gentlemen, let him rest."

Oscar and Rico got up and shuffled from the room. They went down the hall.

"Jesus Christ," Rico muttered. "Here one minute and gone the next."

Oscar couldn't resist. "We talking about your father or your wife?"

Rico gave him a dirty look. "I was referring to Pop, but I'm not quite through with Rhonda yet. The bitch hasn't heard the last of me."

They stopped at the nurse's station and faced each other.

Oscar took a cigar from his pocket and fingered it. "So, are you going back to L.A.?"

"I haven't decided."

"Well, am I in charge here? Because if I start giving orders, I want to know they're going to be obeyed."

"Cousin," Rico said, putting his hand on Oscar's shoulder, "Pop said you were the man and Pop ain't dead yet, is he?" Grinning, he walked away.

Friday,
October 4th

The Caribbean Sea

The first hush of a breeze came shortly before dawn. Jack had waited out the lull and the *Lucky Lady* was actually moving when the sun first peeked over the edge of the azure sea. He figured that with some help from the weather they would make it to the Cayman Islands by Friday, the eleventh, which was when the window for withdrawing funds would probably close.

The sale was taking place about now, back in San Francisco, but Stephanie had said it took a couple of days for the funds to be transferred out of the investment banking firm's account and into the designated trust account. They figured the clock would begin ticking at the Grand Cayman Bank Ltd. sometime on Monday or Tuesday. They couldn't be sure whether the deadline would come a week from now or on the Monday after that, but they'd agreed to leave nothing to chance. If necessary, Jack had told her they could put into Jamaica and fly to the Caymans from there, though he wanted to avoid the airport if at all possible. But one way or another, October 11 was drop-dead day for their enterprise.

Jack peered up at the gently rippling sail. There was nothing as exhilarating to a sailor as being at sea with a dawn breeze rising. Of course, there were a few other things in life he found pleasant. Being on intimate terms with a lovely lady was the first thing that came to mind.

Last night with Stephanie would clearly be one of his more memorable evenings. Except for the fact that it had ended on a tentative note with her saying she preferred to sleep alone, it had been near-perfect.

But if Stephanie was unclear how she felt about him, the reverse was no less true. Sex normally didn't alter his feelings about a woman, because he kept emotion out of the mix. But he hadn't been able to help himself with Alicia. It was starting to look like the same thing was happening with Stephanie Reymond.

It was difficult to say why. He had every reason to keep emotionally detached. But realizing that did not tell him what to do, how he should feel, what was safest, what was smartest. In that sense she was a little like his battle with the bottle— ever-present, impossible to dismiss.

The early-morning sun was beginning to warm the back of his neck when Stephanie appeared wearing a Hard Rock Café, Paris T-shirt and white shorts. Her hair was wet and slicked back, emphasizing her cheekbones and giving her normally proper appearance a certain elegance.

"'Morning," she said a touch self-consciously.

"'Morning, sweetheart. How'd you sleep?"

"Well," she said, blushing, "they say good sex will do that for you. Now I understand why."

She'd mentioned it right off. A good sign. She was dealing with what had happened. She turned her face to the breeze and he studied the line of her jaw.

"The train's moving again, I see," she observed.

"Yes, God doesn't let the world stand still, even when you'd like to stay right where you are."

"I thought you wanted to go to the Caymans, Jack," she teased.

"I mean that more in the emotional sense, of course. Last

night was special. I could have stayed there a while, a good long while.''

She didn't look at him, nor did she answer for a moment. "True," she finally said, "but there's no need to dwell on it. We can appreciate what we had and move on, can't we? I certainly would prefer that.''

She was both skittish and defensive, he could see. Her tact—don't make too much out of something that was routine to him. Protect yourself by being blasé.

"Would it offend you if I chose to linger a while?" he asked.

She thought for a moment. "Are you wanting to make a speech, Jack? Because if you feel the need to reassure me, don't. I'm capable of keeping things in perspective.''

She was having a harder time than he thought. He reached over and took her hand. "I hope we aren't going to let a little thing like sex come between us.''

Despite herself, she laughed. "Jack, you're crazy.''

"Hey, sweetheart, I calls 'em like I sees 'em.''

She looked down at his hand. "Maybe the easiest thing would be for us to revert to a business relationship.''

"You mean, we should consider last night an anomaly?''

"It was an itch we both had to scratch. I was curious and you...well, I guess it was just something you had to do.''

She needed reassurance but he wasn't sure how direct he ought to be. "I think we should talk about this," he said.

"No, I'd actually prefer we didn't. At least not now...if you don't mind.''

"You're saying you want to table it.''

She took a deep breath. "Yes." Her expression was tentative. "I don't mean to be difficult, Jack. I'd just rather talk about something else.''

"Such as?''

"Business. Our plan. Maybe we should talk about our plan.''

"Okay.''

"So, what do you think?" she said.

"Well, I'm in good shape, so I'll stay at the helm most of the day. If you could spell me this evening, I'll grab a few winks and take the night watch. This is shaping up to be an around-the-clock undertaking. You'll have plenty to do working on the code, and we can share cooking and housekeeping duties. How does that sound?"

"Sounds good to me."

Stephanie had a lilt in her voice and Jack could see she was happy to have gotten things off to a constructive start. And, to his relief, she seemed reasonably content with the way they'd glossed over what had happened the previous night. He wasn't entirely satisfied, but the important thing was that she was.

"Have you had breakfast?" she asked.

"Not yet."

"How about if I make us some?"

"Perfect."

Stephanie went off and Jack checked out her legs. He felt a sadness, a deep longing, which had nothing to do with desire. Last night, he'd possessed more than her body—in a fundamental way, he'd possessed her. He'd felt it and he knew she had as well. Evidently that had scared her. It was probably what she was running from.

She was back in fifteen minutes with a tray, made up much as the one he'd fixed the day before. "Variety is not one of the strong points of this sort of existence, is it?" she said.

"Nope, we're sort of stuck with the same food and the same company."

"Which do you suppose is going to get old first?" she asked, her pretty mouth bending wryly.

"I'm afraid to answer that honestly. You might take it as flirting."

She gave his arm a playful slap and they ate in companionable silence. After a while she asked a few questions about navigation and sea traffic, but conversation was intermittent.

Jack had trouble looking at her without feeling longing. He would have liked it so very much if she'd put her head on his shoulder.

"Jack," she said after they'd finished eating, "can I get your professional opinion about something?"

"Sure. Which profession are you referring to? Sailor? Investor? Criminal? Or observer of the social scene?"

"You didn't mention gigolo, so I guess the latter."

"Gigolo?" he said, taken by surprise.

"By that I mean a guy who knows his way around the bedsheets."

"Hoist with my own petard, I see."

"No, it's an innocent question, but a serious one. I need some help with my insecurities."

"Shoot," he said.

"As you know, I had a...well, let's say unfulfilling sex life with my husband."

He nodded.

"Somehow, Jean Claud found happiness with my sister. I can't say they had a sterling sexual relationship because I simply don't know. But there's no doubt they wanted each other sexually."

"You're wondering what was wrong with you."

Stephanie lowered her eyes.

"I wouldn't take it personally," he said. "Nobody could say there's a damn thing wrong with you, certainly not me."

"But I did nothing to deserve his rejection," she persisted. "I was a good wife and I tried to be a loving one. I didn't put pressure on him or make unreasonable demands."

"It may have been nothing more than the fact he was married to you," Jack said. "Some guys can't mix sex and marriage. I'm not saying it's common, but there's that Madonna-whore thing. A guy like that can take a mistress and screw her all day long, but can't get it up for the mother of his children to save his soul, not in the middle years of a marriage, anyway."

"You don't think it could have been me, Jack?"

"Not unless you intimidated him. Sometimes a woman can be too much for a guy. It's a psychological thing."

"That ever happen to you?"

He reflected. "I've been turned off by a woman's attitude, but I don't recall not being able to get it up because of it. Of course, I've only had one wife."

"How was it with her?"

Jack sighed. It had been ages since he'd even thought of Ellen, much less their sex life. He really had to dig into his memory. "The sex was good, especially at first. The whole relationship went south pretty damn quick, though."

"Did you love her?"

His smile was wistful. "Back then I was incapable of love, Stephanie. I couldn't tell it from lust. Which should have been a clue, considering it meant I was in love with every other woman on the street."

She blinked.

"I've led a pretty licentious life, I grant you. But I've mellowed in recent years. I'm not as obsessed with sex as you might think. To the contrary, I sort of half gave it up for booze."

"Hardly an improvement," she said.

"No. But I'm in the midst of a campaign to clean up my act," he replied. "After last night I may have to go back to my old ways."

She gave him a sardonic look. "It was just sex, Jack. It couldn't have been that special."

"Oh, but it was."

Stephanie shifted uncomfortably. "I think we're due for a change of subject."

The fishing boat they'd seen earlier was fairly near and Jack checked it out with the binoculars. He saw nothing suspicious. A man on the deck of the boat waved, Jack waved back. They watched it pass them.

"Okay," he said as he put down the glasses, "you asked me a question. Now I've got one for you."

"All right."

"After your mother ran her numbers on me, what would she say?"

She laughed.

"No, it's a serious question."

Stephanie shook her head, amused. "I don't need to give you a numerological reading to tell you you're dangerous, Jack."

"Do me, anyway."

She glanced around. "I'll need a piece of paper and a pencil."

He got up. "You take over here and I'll go get some."

He was gone only a minute, handing her a small pad and pencil before taking his place at the wheel. Stephanie wrote out his name and then jotted a number over each of the letters. Then she did the calculation.

"Hmm," she said, looking at the pad.

"Good or bad?"

"Well, odd actually. The name Jack Kidwell is a seven-four-eleven."

"What does that mean?"

"The numerical value of Jack is seven. The value of Kidwell is four. Seven and four combine to make eleven."

"Which is two, right?"

"Technically yes, but eleven is a special number in and of itself."

"That's what's odd?" he said.

"No, what's odd is that I'm a seven-four-eleven myself."

"You mean we're twins?" he said, tongue in cheek. "Separated at birth?"

"Hey, I don't believe in this stuff," Stephanie said. "I'm just answering your question."

"So, tell me, what are we seven-four-elevens like?"

"Seven is a lonely number. It represents people with singular qualities who are set apart and go their own way."

"That could be us, Steph."

"Four, both our last names, represents technical qualities, people who are engineering, math and science oriented."

"You were an accounting major," he said, "and I was a developer and a navigator. I guess that works. What does the eleven mean? That we're lonely nerds?"

She laughed. "My mother loved people with eleven names. They're successful, high achievers. Alexander the Great was an eleven."

"Sugar, I think you just lost me. Alexander the Great and I are not peas in a pod. Now, you and me, that could be another story."

"Make fun all you want, Jack, I don't take it personally. And my mother's not here to take offense."

He made a slight course adjustment. "What would your mother say about our prospects? Are two elevens like two Pisces, comfortable swimming in the same sea?"

"I never got into it that much," she said, looking away. "It was my mother's and Jane's thing."

"Steph-an-ie," he admonished.

"All right," she said, relenting. "My mother would have been thrilled with you. There, does that make you happy?"

"I knew there was something to this numerology business."

"Yes," she said, "what it is, is the key to that code."

Jack drew a deep breath. "I've learned one thing from this discussion," he said.

"What's that?"

"With two lonely little nerds going after that thirty million, Inter-America Ventures and all its henchmen don't have a chance!"

Stephanie shook her head. "If you'll excuse me, Captain, I'm going to work on the computer." She got up. "Let me know if you need anything."

He reached out and took her hand, drawing her fingers to

his mouth and kissing them. "The sailing life is a lonely one," he said. "If you want to do something for me, come topside every once in a while so we can share a little human warmth."

"Warmth? In a tropical sea?"

"Euphemism," he said.

She gave him a look, then strode off, swinging her derriere a trifle more than before. Jack blew a silent kiss after her. This was a woman he could become very, very fond of. It had taken him a week to figure that out. But it just could be that she ended up meaning more to him than a lousy thirty million bucks. My, but wouldn't his old partner, Larry, have found that a hoot?

George Town, The Cayman Islands

Rico was on the phone, waiting for the office in L.A. to connect him with Milly Wilson, Rhonda's mother in Van Nuys. Through the slider he saw Carlos with the barmaid, Corine. They were across the hotel garden and headed his way. Rico was pleasantly surprised. And relieved. He'd only half figured she wouldn't come, which would have been the shits because he needed to get laid.

He watched them make their way through the palms, the banana plants and flowering shrubs. As they passed the pool, Rico got a good look at her. She had on a short dark skirt, high-heel sandals, a little gold tank top and the same gold hoop earrings as the day before. The legs and the face were okay, but the ass, which he couldn't see from this angle but remembered vividly, was primo. He'd been thinking about it all day.

Milly came on the line. "Rico?"

"Hi ya, Milly, how's it goin'?"

"Okay," she said tentatively.

"Yeah, well, it's not so good with me. As you know, Rhonda's pissed at me. And if that isn't enough, my father's had a heart attack. A big one."

"Oh dear, I'm sorry to hear that, Rico."

"Yeah, we're down here in the Cayman Islands on business and bam, just like that, it hit him. We're hoping he makes it, but as far as work is concerned, this is it. He's out. Retirement or death, one way or another, he's gone."

"I'm so sorry."

"Yeah, Milly, I am, too."

Carlos and the girl had almost gotten to the suite. Rico studied her moves.

"So anyway, I've got something I want you to do for me, all right?"

"Well, if I can help...I suppose..."

"Great, Milly. That's great. But wait a second. I've got another call. Some banker. Can you hold on a second? Thanks."

Carlos and the girl were at the slider. Rico waved them in. Corine entered hesitantly, like some kid going into the spook house. For a second she didn't see him across the room, her eyes not yet adjusting to the relative darkness after the bright sun.

"Hi, there, sugar," he called to her, his hand clamped over the mouthpiece of the phone. "It's Corine, right?"

She nodded like a deaf mute.

"That's great. And you're looking sharp, real sharp. Nice shoes. But listen, I'm on the phone doing some business with this banker, see, and I'm going to be a couple of minutes. Why don't you go into the bedroom over there...show her, Carlos. Yeah. And I'll join you as soon as I finish this call. Make yourself comfortable in there, sugar, and Carlos will bring you a drink. Rum, vodka, beer. Whatever you want. Carlos, take care of the lady, will you?"

The two of them went off, Corine into the bedroom, Carlos to the bar. When the bedroom door was closed, Rico returned to his call.

"Yeah, Milly, sorry about that. High finance. You know how it is."

"Rico, I don't know what I can do," she said. "Rhonda told me she's not supposed to talk to you, only her lawyer, so maybe I shouldn't, either."

"Milly, Milly. You and me don't have problems. We're cool, aren't we? I get you a new car every couple years, don't I? You're not saying you and I've got to talk through lawyers, are you?"

"I don't want to get anybody into trouble."

"Hey, there's no trouble. There's just two old friends talking. No harm in that. I'm not calling for secrets. I want you to give a message to Rhonda. That's no big deal."

"All right, Rico, what do you want me to tell her?"

"Well, first, tell her I'm sorry, whatever it is I did, I'm sorry. She's in France, right?"

"Yes."

"Okay, I'm sure you can reach her because you gotta know in case Andy gets sick or something, right?"

"Right."

"So, first tell her I'm really, truly sorry. Then tell her I don't care if she's got a guy. That don't mean a thing. I'll forget and forgive if she kicks his ass out. That's number two. Three, Milly, because of Pop and all, I'm runnin' things now. Inter-America, the whole thing, is mine. So Rhonda's the wife of the big man. No more second banana. That means we gotta live a little better, right? Tell her that, Milly. Hang on a second, okay?"

He waited while Carlos carried a tall drink into the bedroom. When he came out, closing the door, Rico signaled for him to leave the suite. Rico returned to his call.

"Milly?"

"Yes," came the feeble reply.

"Right. Now number four is a little harder for me to say, but if Rhonda don't like one, two and three, then there's number four. That's the baby, Milly. I know Andrea means a lot to Rhonda and she means a lot to me. So tell her Andrea's stayin' with me, no matter what. Tell her her lawyer might say that her fucking the plumber don't mean shit, but, well, it does because I say it does. I can buy the Supreme Court, if I have to, though it would be much cheaper to buy her lawyer. I think Rhonda understands that, Milly, but if she hears it from her mama, then she know it's serious. Tell her, Milly.''

He paused to take a breath and he heard sobbing.

''Milly? What's with you? I gave you three good things to say, too.''

''Rico,'' the woman said as she sobbed, ''don't fight over the baby, please don't. It will only hurt her. Andrea doesn't need her parents fighting over her.''

''Milly, you're right. But the one you should be saying this to is Rhonda. *She's* the one that's been fucking around while I'm out busting my butt, trying to earn an honest living. Tell her this, Milly, tell her I'm coming home in a few days to live in my house, just like before. My kid's going to be there. It'd be nice if my wife is, too. Now, you call Rhonda in Paris and tell her that her husband's going to be home soon and he's going to have this big old fat ring in his pocket, and who knows, maybe a bracelet or somethin' else. I'd like to see her there with a smile on her face. But if she's stupid, if she fucks with me, she can tell her sorry ass goodbye. Got that, Milly?''

All he could hear was sobbing.

''Well, I've got work to do,'' he said. ''If Rhonda needs to talk to me, tell her to call the office. They'll put her through to me. You understand, Milly?''

''Yes,'' came the feeble reply.

''Good. Meanwhile, be thinking what new car you might be wantin'. Christmas is coming, Milly.'' He hung up the phone. ''Fucking broads,'' he said under his breath.

Rico went to the bar and made himself a rum and Coke, then went to the bedroom. Opening the door, he found Corine sitting on the corner of the bed, the drink Carlos had made in her hand. It looked untouched.

''So, how's it going, doll?'' he said, closing the door.

"I don't know if I should do this, man," she murmured. "I don't even know your name."

He slowly walked over to her. "It's Rico, sugar. Rico. It's a good, honest name. My mother gave it to me. And I can tell you, no mother of mine would raise a son you wouldn't be proud to call a friend," he said, putting his hand on her shoulder. She smelled like lilacs or something.

She gazed up at him from under her brow. "I've never done nothing like this before, man. Never."

"You want to know something?" he said, massaging her shoulder. "I haven't either. But you're such a good-looking woman, I couldn't resist asking you over."

"Still..."

"Believe me," he said, "if I had the time, I'd have taken you to dinner a couple of times and sent you flowers and all that because I can see you're the kind of girl who'd like that romantic stuff. But then I said to myself, gee, with two thousand dollars in her pocket, Corine could go out and have all the dinners and buy all the flowers she wants, maybe buy her mama a little present or something."

"My mother's the reason I came. She's been sick and couldn't work. We've lots of bills."

"Hey, that makes me think all the more of you, sugar. I like the idea of helping out a loving daughter." He gave her chin a pinch. "So, drink your drink, doll. I'm a busy man. It'd be nice if you got more comfortable, maybe take off your top so I can see those tits."

Corine stared down at the floor, biting her lip. Rico started getting annoyed. What the fuck did she want? For him to get on his knees?

"Something wrong? You don't like me?"

"How can I not like you, man? I don't even know you!"

Rico took her jaw in his hand and turned her face up to him. He smiled. "Look at me, sugar. I ain't a bad-looking guy. Good sense of humor. I got a little bread. What's not to like?"

He could see that she was agonizing, fidgeting nervously.

"It's the easiest two grand you'll ever make," he said softly.

"Okay, I'll do it," she said, her voice trembling. "But two things. You got to give me the money first, and you've got to wear a condom."

Rico smiled. "Now you're sounding like a businesswoman. I like girls who learn fast."

"And man, I'm telling you now, I won't do nothing kinky."

"Babe, I just want a piece of ass."

Corine took a long drink, obviously fortifying herself. Rico went and got his money, returning with a stack of hundred-dollar bills, which he counted out. "Okay, babe, I've done my part. Now take off your clothes. Everything but that little skirt and the sandals."

"Everything else?"

"Yeah, the panties, the works."

The girl tucked the bills into her purse and went over to a chair, where she began stripping. Rico watched her, enjoying this more than usual because she was nervous and embarrassed. He undressed, dropping his shorts as she took off her panties. She seemed surprised to find him already erect, saluting the flag.

Rico went over to her, his cock leading the way. She was short and her big, round eyes gave her a childlike air, despite the womanly body. She gave a little flinch when he took her nipple between his fingers. After he rubbed it for a few seconds, it started getting hard.

"You get wet easy?" he asked.

She shrugged, lowering her eyes. She was trembling.

"So, reach under your skirt and play with yourself."

She blinked.

"Go on," he said as he continued toying with her nipples. "Play with yourself."

The girl complied, closing her eyes. Rico listened to her breathing, liking it that she was getting excited.

"So, you got a boyfriend?" he asked.

She nodded.

"What's his name?"

"George."

"George? The bartender?"

"No, man, my George is a turtle farmer."

"Turtle farmer? Christ, next I'm going hear all the turtles in this fucking place are called George, too. So, what's your turtle guy like? He got a big cock?"

She nodded, averting her eyes.

Rico took her free hand and guided it to his cock. "See how you like this one."

Corine squeezed her eyes closed again and bit her lip. But he noticed she was working the hand between her legs real good. And she was tugging pretty good on his cock.

"I think I'm ready, sugar," he said. "How about you?"

She nodded without opening her eyes.

"Okay," he said. "See that chair over there by the window? Go bend over it and point your ass at me."

She opened her eyes and gave him an uncertain look.

"Go on, I'm not going to do nothing but fuck you from behind."

Corine looked as if she'd decided that might be all right. Before going to the chair, she grabbed a pillow from the bed. Putting it on the arm of the chair, she bent over it. The little skirt hiked right up, exposing the goods. And what a beautiful sight it was. Rico could have given himself a couple of yanks and it would have been over.

"The condom, man," Corine said. "Don't forget the condom."

"Yeah, right." Rico went over and fiddled with the drawer on the bedside table as if he was getting something, but he didn't. He faked like he was putting on a rubber. Then he approached her, his cock like a divining rod. "You've got one hell of an ass, baby."

"You're not going to hurt me, are you?" she whined, child-like.

"Sugar, I'm going to have you begging for more."

Rico lifted the girl's skirt and ran his chalky white fingers over her ebony ass. His cock strained toward her, eager. But he wanted to take a minute to admire the goods before ramming her.

"So, George ever do you this way, Corine?"

She shook her head. "Not so much."

"Turtle farmers got no imagination. Well, this'll give you something to think about when ol' George is doing you."

Taking her haunches in his hands he moved up against her, his rod so stiff it didn't need any help finding the mark. Corine shuddered when he touched her opening. Rico leaned hard against her, his cock sliding right to the hilt. She gasped and he almost came then. Taking several moments to get control, he began thrusting. At first it was long and slow, then when he felt his balls gather, he really started ramming her. He watched her gold hoop earrings swing and shudder as he pounded her, her scent rising in his nostrils. She gave a little cry every time he hit bottom.

After a while she cried out more loudly. Whether in pain or pleasure he couldn't tell, and he didn't really care. "Jesus," he said, feeling it coming.

Just after he exploded in her, he looked up and saw a face glaring at him from the shrubs outside the window. It was a big buck nigger whose round eyes turned to rage as he realized what was happening. The head disappeared as quickly as it had appeared and Rico shuddered with a final thrust, collapsing on Corine's beautiful round ass.

The girl was definitely crying. "Can I get up now, man?" she managed to say. "Are you through?"

Just then there was a terrible noise in the other room, the sound of shattering glass.

"What the hell?" Rico exclaimed.

Seconds later the bedroom door flew open and the buck

who'd been outside loomed in the doorway. He wore a tattered muscle shirt that barely stretched over his huge shoulders and chest, long pants and work boots. His fists were clenched and there was rage in his eyes.

Corine, with Rico still in her, looked back over her shoulder to see what the commotion was. When she saw the guy, her face went round with horror. "George!" she screamed.

Rico, rubbery from the sex and only half juiced with adrenaline, withdrew from the girl's ass and had just managed to turn around when the guy was on him. George's big fist caught him square in the middle of the face, knocking him to the floor. For a second Rico lay flat on his back, his eyes a blur. He saw George grab the girl and whack her on the side of the head so hard she went flying into the chair.

"Fucking whore!" he raged. "Fucking bloody whore!"

The man advanced again on Rico. He'd grabbed him by the arm and was pulling him to his feet when Carlos and two other men came rushing in. Blows were exchanged. The girl screamed hysterically. George, after getting in a couple of licks, was finally knocked to the floor and subdued.

Rico, with blood streaming from his nose, staggered to his feet. Corine, still frenzied, tried to get to George, but Rico grabbed her arm and flung her back into the chair.

"I'll kill you, man!" George shouted, even with Carlos shoving his face into the carpet.

"How did this sonovabitch get in here?" Rico screamed at the men. "Look at my fucking face!" Enraged, he went over and stomped on George's head with his heel, once, twice, silencing him.

Corine wailed. Rico told her to shut up. He glared at the men.

"Take this fucking bastard out to some swamp and whack him."

"Oh, no," the girl pleaded. "It's my fault. You can have your money back, man. Let George go. I'll take him home. Keep the money, man. Keep it."

Rico grabbed her by the face and gave her a shove backward. "I told you to shut up!"

Just then Oscar came in. He wore a polo shirt and freshly pressed khakis. "What's going on?"

"Our security stinks around here!" Rico shouted, wiping his bloody nose with the back of his hand. "I can't even get laid without some asshole popping me."

Carlos and one of the other guys had pulled George to his feet. Corine was sobbing in the chair, her thighs streaked with Rico's juices. Carlos told Oscar what happened.

"Take that sonovabitch out of here before I shoot his ass right here!" Rico said, pulling up his trousers. He didn't bother with his shorts.

Corine slid to the floor and began crawling around, gathering her clothes. George, who'd taken a couple of pretty good shots, mumbled half coherently. Oscar, looking around as though he were standing in the middle of a freeway accident, told the men to escort George and the girl out the back way and to drive them home.

"Hey, Oscar," Rico protested. "I already told them what to do with this jerk-off."

"You got bigger problems, Rico. We gotta talk."

He motioned for the others to leave. The men dragged George out the door. Corine, still putting on her clothes, trudged after them. Rico, seeing her purse, picked it up.

"Hey, bitch!"

She turned and he threw the purse at her.

"Might as well take this."

She picked it up and ran out of the room. Oscar went over and closed the door.

"Listen, Oscar," Rico said, the rest of his face as red as his bloody nose, "you ever contradict me in front of anyone again, I'll have *your* ass. That's the only warning you'll ever get!"

"Rico," Oscar said, looking at him with undisguised contempt, "Julius had another attack. I just came from the hospital."

Rico was taken aback, sobered by the news. "So, is he all right?"

"No, Rico, he's dead."

Rico sank onto the corner of the bed. "Shit."

Oscar stood silently, waiting. Rico glanced up at him.

"Dead?"

Oscar nodded.

"Fuck."

"So, Inter-America is yours, cousin. Nobody to second-guess you. You going to L.A. or are you staying?"

Rico rubbed his face, careful when he touched his nose. What a way to find out he was suddenly king. He looked at Oscar, realizing he hadn't answered his cousin's question. "I guess we'll do what Pop said, but I'm not leaving for a couple of days."

"What do you want me to do?" Oscar asked, not trying especially hard to mask his contempt.

"Organize things here, like Pop said. But I want to know everything that happens. Same as Pop, I don't want surprises."

"Then I might as well tell you the latest. Alexander Manring had lunch with the girl in the bank today. Cynthia. The sale of that stock went through yesterday in San Francisco. The bank got a wire transfer of thirty-one point five million into Reymond's account this morning."

"Thirty-one point five!"

"Yes, there's a little extra. We got five days, starting Monday, to come up with that code or we lose the money for good."

"Fucking A," Rico said, staring at his bloody hands. He'd heard every word Oscar had said, but he had to remind himself the part about his father being dead. It just didn't seem possible.

"Another thing," Oscar went on. "The men we sent looking for the Englishman found his island, all right, but he's off somewhere in his boat. But he keeps in touch with his house-keeper. She was convinced to share what she knew. Turns out Stephanie and Kidwell are in his boat, headed this way. Manring talked to some sailors about makin' a trip like that. Depending on weather, Kidwell and the woman ought to be showing up here along about the middle of the week.''

"I suppose you're planning a welcome party," Rico said.

"A very special welcome party."

"You've got a thing about that broad, don't you, Oscar?"

"Let's just say I owe her."

Rico smiled, though his nose hurt when he did. "I guess you know what you want, cousin, but take it from me, you're better off with a professional."

"Thanks, but I'm actually looking forward to Stephanie's arrival. I plan to entertain her in a manner to which she *isn't* accustomed."

"Well, I'm anxious to see her, too, but for different reasons." He dabbed his nose with his handkerchief. "So, what's your plan?"

"From what I'm told, we should be able to spot them coming fifty miles away. And this time there'll be no place for them to hide."

"I guess there are advantages to being in the middle of the fucking ocean."

Oscar looked down at Rico's bare feet and the blood all over the front of him. "So, you want a doctor?"

"No, the nose stopped bleeding. I'm okay. The mother-fucker punched me while my cock was still in the broad's ass."

Oscar actually smiled. Rico could see that the picture he painted was a pretty amusing one. If it'd happened to anybody else, he'd be laughing his head off.

"The hospital suggested we should be thinking about what we want to do with Julius's body," Oscar said. "I said we'd let them know."

"He wanted to be cremated. No funeral, no bullshit." Rico

shook his head with disbelief at the situation. "You know what Pop told me once, Oscar? It was when I was a kid and I'd got this girl pregnant. He had to give her parents a big check and afterward he came to my room and he said, 'Rico, when I die, I know exactly what you'll be doing. You'll be off someplace fucking a whore.'" Rico shook his head. "Scary, huh?"

Oscar nodded. "Yeah, Rico, it is."

Saturday,
October 5th

The Caribbean Sea

A woman of many talents," Jack said to Stephanie.

"Don't start giving compliments until you've seen the result," she replied.

He was sitting cross-legged on the deck in front of her and Stephanie was cutting his hair. Earlier he'd confessed to feeling grubby and she'd agreed he could use a haircut, offering to give him one. She was not completely without experience, having regularly cut Zanny's hair as a child. Hair salons had set off the girl's asthma. Stephanie had become rather adept at haircutting, so much so that the child's haircuts had gotten compliments from other mothers.

Before she'd started on Jack, there'd been some negotiation. "I'm willing to go shorter," he'd said, "but don't make me look like a banker."

They'd agreed that a Robert Redford look was about right and Jack had gotten her a pair of scissors and a comb. She'd been at it a while, not wanting to be too aggressive for fear of butchering him.

It was getting toward noon. Jack had taken the night watch and, after Stephanie had spelled him, he'd gotten about four hours' sleep. There'd been a fair breeze during the night, Jack had told her, and a nice stiff one most of the morning. She'd been a little nervous tacking, but her confidence was growing and Jack admitted to being impressed with the way she'd handled the boat.

That was the bright side of the trip. On the negative side, Jean Claud's damn code was getting her down. She'd spent virtually all yesterday afternoon trying to come up with a key. Several ideas had come to mind, but the possibilities were myriad.

"You ever cut your husband's hair?" Jack asked as she made him lower his chin so she could see the back.

"Heavens, no, are you kidding?"

"Didn't he trust you?"

"Jean Claud would have been humiliated, plus he wouldn't have liked the intimacy."

"Is this intimate?"

She surprised herself by having brought up intimacy, and was embarrassed when Jack pressed the point. "Mutual grooming tends to be, Jack."

"It's nice that it doesn't bother you," he said, caressing her bare foot.

She did not recoil. She liked it when he touched her, though he hadn't done it a lot since they'd made love. There'd been a couple of spontaneous hugs and he'd brushed her cheek with his fingers or rubbed her back. Mostly he'd left her hungering for more. Jack, she was coming to realize, understood the female mind.

"What do you think, Stephanie? Are we compatible?"

"Compatible for what?"

"A relationship."

"You mean as business partners? Crewmates? Friends? What?"

"How about lovers?"

His question caught her unprepared, though it wasn't out of character. "What are you doing, propositioning me?"

"No, I've just come to realize how strong my feelings are. I feel real comfortable with you. I think it's an adult thing."

She stopped trimming and rested her hands on her knees. "Adult? You mean I seem different than the girls you usually take for lovers?"

"Yeah, I think that's exactly what I mean."

"Thanks a lot. Is it my wrinkles that turn you on?"

"Hey, I'm trying to say something nice here. I've never felt this kind of rapport with a woman before. Sure, I'm attracted to you physically, but your mind and character and personality turn me on even more. I'm drawn to you in a way I'm not used to. That's what I'm trying to say."

His tone was too serious, too earnest by a turn for her to dismiss it. But still, she didn't know what to make of it. She'd spent so much time damping down her feelings the past week that facing them forthrightly wasn't easy.

"I think it's propinquity," she told him. "We're in the same boat in more ways than one."

"I'm not willing to dismiss it so easily."

"I'm not dismissing it, I'm trying to explain it."

"Do you feel it, too?" he asked.

She started trimming his hair again. "You really believe in putting people on the spot, don't you?"

"Well, to be honest, I've felt a mutual attraction right from the beginning. But I also knew that in one sense or another we were using each other. I did consider you a business opportunity—you were right about that. Now I'm wondering if there might not be more."

"Like what?" she said warily.

Jack caressed her foot some more. "I know you're discouraged about the code," he said. "I'm pretty disappointed myself. So the last couple of days I've been trying to look past next Friday, asking myself what if we come up empty? What happens to you, what happens to me?"

Stephanie froze. This was the very thing she'd been wondering herself. "I don't know what I'll do in the short run.

Eventually I'll go home and try to salvage what I can of my life.''

"Do you have a life you want to go back to?" he asked.

His questions were getting more and more pointed. They began to scare her. "You're trying to get at something, Jack. Maybe you should just say it."

He turned to face her, his gaze intent. "This is not easy for me to say," he began, "but I don't want next Friday to be the end for us, whichever way this deal turns out. I'd like for us to have a chance to get better acquainted…under more normal circumstances."

"I don't know what to say. What is it you really want? A playmate? A lover?"

"All right," he said, "fair question. Say the Cayman deal goes bust, we come up empty. The way I figure, we'll be sitting a hell of a lot closer to the Yucatán in Mexico than the Virgins. I know some people over there on the peninsula. We could rent a place on the beach and spend a month being as happy as fate and circumstances allow. Depending on the way the wind's blowing, we can decide where to go from there."

Stephanie stared into his eyes for a long time, feeling torn. Touched, moved, but especially torn.

"I know I'm not being practical," Jack said. "And I know that drives women batty, but damn it, I can't think of anything I'd rather do than shack up with you."

She weighed her response. "Your offer is a lot more tempting than you might think."

Jack sighed. "That's progress, I guess."

"Look, I'm going to make some admissions that no woman makes lightly. Even to herself." She took his hands. "You've changed my life, Jack. For starters, you literally saved it. If you fell overboard right now and were lost at sea, our lovemaking would live in my heart forever. I'd probably think of it before dropping off to sleep every night for the next fifty years."

"It's nice to be appreciated," he said.

"But nice as the experience was, it's nothing compared to the part of myself that you've given me," she said earnestly. "Since meeting you, I've gotten in touch with a side of me I didn't even know existed. I was closed up. And I don't just mean sexually. I didn't know how to live, to get in touch with my passions, to shuck off my doubts, my fears. I know I've still got a ways to go, but I have lived this past week. I've looked both myself and the world in the face and I've taken chances. Emotional chances, physical chances, you name it."

"I'll say this, Stephanie, I like what I see."

"Thanks. But the real bonus is discovering that I haven't been a whole person. The one role I deeply cared about was being Zanny's mother. My daughter was my life. And I used the fact that she was young and sickly as an excuse not to live, not to realize my potential."

Jack caressed her face and big tears welled in her eyes. "You are a very special lady, Stephanie," he said, his own eyes glistening.

They hugged. She loved the feel of his arms. Especially then. After a minute they settled side by side on the seat and she rested her head on his shoulder. She'd never in her life felt so close to a man, so much in tune with his spirit.

"So, is Mexico a viable option?" he asked.

"You were serious about that?"

"Absolutely."

"Jack, don't you see, I'd just be trading one kind of dependence for another. I won't do that again."

"I'm not asking to be boss," he said. "Partners is enough."

"That's not the issue, either. I need to feel the wind in my hair. And be free."

"And you don't see me in the picture."

"That's not true. I just can't commit to anything yet."

"I'm rushing you," he said.

She pressed his hand to her cheek. "I think we need to take one step at a time."

Jack took her chin and, smiling, he kissed her.

She allowed herself the luxury of inhaling his salty, sun-drenched scent. Putting both her arms around him, she gave him a hug. Despite what she'd said, she liked what she was feeling now. They seemed like a team, a couple. Maybe even soul mates. "Jack," she said, "do you suppose we could let the ship sail herself for an hour or two so we could take a nap together?"

He laughed with delight. "I love a woman who knows what she wants."

They kissed. Stephanie put her hand on his thigh, then drew it up until it rested on the bulge at his loins. "What I want right now," she whispered, "is for you to make mad, passionate love with me. All day long."

"My darling," he said, "I'm sure that can be arranged."

Wednesday,
October 9th

The Caribbean Sea

They'd been lovers for a week. The last four days in particular had been incredible. Stephanie had learned more about her body in that short time than she had in the previous forty years. Jack managed to surprise her every time they became intimate. And great sex, she discovered, existed in a world all its own. Other realities faded into the background; there was only her body and his.

With just the two of them on the boat, they would come upon each other in likely or unlikely circumstances. A touch would follow, then arousal and intimacy. He might enter her from behind as she soaped her hair in the shower, or she'd awaken him by kissing his shoulder and taking his sex in her hand.

With the supply of water running low they had been forced to go for hours at a time perfumed with the scent of their lovemaking, his fragrance as much a part of her as her own. At times she would play the aggressor, then the subdued maiden, allowing him to dominate her. Sometimes they laughed, sometimes the sex was as violent and elemental as the limits of pleasure would allow. Often they made love with care and tenderness. For the first time in her life, Stephanie lived in the realm of her body. They connected more profoundly and powerfully than she thought possible.

But there were many separate hours, as well, hours to contemplate both immediate pleasures and distant dreams. She thought about Mexico and she thought about home. She envisioned Jack as her dream lover and as a life partner. She visualized herself dancing with him at a black-tie alumni banquet, and then would picture him alone in the *Lucky Lady,* reading for the hundredth time the letter in which she said goodbye.

Jack, by his very existence, was everything good and everything painful. Jack was the embodiment of her own contradictions.

And she thought about the Cayman Islands, her siren's call. Yes, it was a ticking bomb, yes, it was fraught with danger. But it was as irresistible as the allure of Jack himself. It was the challenge she had to conquer, the last hurdle before she faced the future.

Jean Claud's code remained a thorn in her side, that frustrating windowpane between her and the dish of candy. She worked on it each day. She fought it, struggled with it, used an entire tablet of paper playing with every conceivable possibility her imagination could conjure up. Jack tried as well, but chalk == 4, book == 5, nut == 4, runway == 7, wound == 2 and cow == 1 confounded them both, haunting her to the point of dementia. Sometimes she awoke in the night, sweating, moaning, worrying if she'd ever find the key to unlocking it.

That morning they'd lost the easterly wind that had been carrying them across the Caribbean. At breakfast, while they drifted under a nearly slack sail, Jack told her that, although they had just two days left to make it to George Town, only an extended calm would put them in jeopardy of arriving late. They were forty miles off the southwestern tip of Jamaica with about a hundred and fifty miles to go.

"It's hard to know whether I wished it was longer or

shorter," Stephanie said. "Part of me is convinced I'll crack the code if I have enough time. Another part of me knows it's hopeless."

"As long as we've got breath, we've got life."

Stephanie sighed, wondering if he wasn't kidding himself. Maybe letting go of the dream of fabulous riches was just too hard. "I may be too much of a realist for this kind of work."

She eyed the stale crust of bread on her plate. It was the last of their "fresh" food. She flicked the bread into the water, thinking how much that would have annoyed Jean Claud, who abhorred waste. Of any kind. Jack, on the other hand, was so easygoing, she never feared being herself around him.

"If it's getting to you, we can slip right on past the Caymans and go on over to the Yucatán," Jack said. "No extra charge."

"And buy a grass shack with the money I've got left?"

"I used to be in real estate, don't forget. Bet I could get us a fabulous deal."

Stephanie smiled. "That's one thing about my sister. She might have been after my husband, but she never tried to get me involved in any hot real estate deals. On the other hand, why should she? Jean Claud gave her the key to all my money."

The words were no sooner out of her mouth when a startling realization hit her. She had her sister's computer which, on the hard drive, contained all the documents from Jane's real estate business, as well as her household accounts. Except for a cursory look early on, Stephanie had not made a thorough examination of her sister's files. It suddenly struck her that she might find something helpful on Jane's hard drive.

"I just thought of something I can check on the computer," she said. "If you're finished with your coffee, I'll take this stuff and go below. Do you mind standing watch a while longer?"

"Far be it from me to get in the way of inspiration."

Stephanie gave him a kiss on the cheek, took the tray and

hurried below. After rinsing the dishes, she got out Jane's computer. On Monday the batteries had begun fading so she'd been working exclusively on paper. To save time now, she went right to the directory. Nothing immediately jumped out at her. Then a folder entitled Family caught her eye. She checked the contents and found files with titles like Birthdays, Gifts, Holidays, and so forth. Stephanie looked inside them all, and as best she could tell, Jane had transcribed years' worth of notes and entries from old calendars, diaries and the like. There was information about things such as gifts Jane had received from their mother on various occasions and presents Jane had given Zanny over the years.

In the gift file there was an entry entitled Jean Claud, followed by something that nearly stopped Stephanie's heart: *craie* == 4, *livre* == 5, *noix* == 4, *piste* == 7, *blessure* == 2 and *vache* == 1. These French words were equivalent to the English words in Jean Claud's code. The corresponding numbers following each word in the two languages were identical. Stephanie's heart beat wildly.

Her first thought was that it was strange that Jean Claud, whose native language was French, should have used the English words in his copy, and Jane's version was in French, a language she didn't speak. Logic would dictate that Jane would have had the English and Jean Claud the French version of the code.

Stephanie did a quick numerological check of the French words and found that they bore no obvious connection to the numbers following them, either. It seemed as random as the English. She racked her brain. What could Jean Claud have been up to? This was his doing, she had no doubt about it. Then it occurred to her that the true code was based on the French word, not the English. Jean Claud had simply used the English to make the code more obscure—not a bad ploy considering how long she'd worked with the wrong set of letters. It was logical since Jean Claud was bilingual and knew the French equivalent to the English. When he saw ''chalk'' he'd know the actual code word was *"craie."* Jane, on the other hand, had in her version of the code the actual word that was to be used.

Stephanie became really excited, though she still didn't know what the connection was between the words and the numbers. But she'd had a breakthrough. The irony was that for days she'd struggled with the right words, but in the wrong language. Realizing she was using valuable battery power, she started to turn off the computer.

In her excitement, Stephanie inadvertently hit a function key and the program's spell check came on, highlighting the word *craie*. In the drop-down screen there were a list of alternative words for what the computer had taken to be a misspelled English word. The words on the list were "Craig," "Craik," "crake," "crane," "crape," "crate," "crave" and "craze." As she stared at the screen, it suddenly hit her. The *spell check* was the key!

Stephanie clasped her hands to her chest, dizzy with awe. "My God," she muttered. "That's it!"

The *craie* == 4 entry must mean the true code word was the *fourth* alternative spelling indicated in the drop-down screen of the spell check for the French word *craie*. In this case it would be the word *crane*. That, Stephanie was certain, was the actual word Jean Claud intended to be in the code, not chalk or *craie!* Its numerological value was the first digit in the access code for the bank. She did a quick calculation. "Crane" was a five word, which meant the first digit in the access code was five. If she was right, she'd just broken the code!

When the computer screen began to flicker, Stephanie broke into a cold sweat. She needed the spell check to decode the last five digits of the access code. What if the damn thing died on her?

She quickly repeated the process she'd just gone through for the five remaining French words. Using this method, she determined that the digits in the access code were 547658. Her hands trembling as she stared at the number, Stephanie told herself that those six little numbers might well be worth thirty million dollars.

Hardly able to contain herself, she ran up to tell Jack. "You'll never believe it," she said, dropping down beside him, "but I think I cracked the code."

He was incredulous as she excitedly told him how the spell check contained the key to unlocking the code. Jack put his arm around her shoulders.

"Steph, you're a genius."

"It was dumb luck. Purely accidental."

"And those French words were in a file on the hard drive all along."

"Yes, the family-gift file, if you can believe it. Maybe Jean Claud did intend to give Jane my inheritance, after all."

"Why are you so sure the spell check is the key, and that the numbers paired with the words indicate the true code word?"

"I can't be positive," she said, "but when you think about it, it makes a lot of sense. Jane had to be able to use the code, which meant whatever Jean Claud set up would have to be simple, yet tricky enough that it wasn't obvious. Since the bank access code is a series of numbers, and Jean Claud's code involved letters, the way to transcribe from one to the other had to be through numerology, given my sister's predilection for it. All along, the stumbling block has been the numbers after each word. Sure, they might be numbers you're suppose to add or subtract from the value of the letters, or whatever, but with this, Jane wouldn't have had to memorize a thing."

Jack rubbed his chin. "I grant you, it makes sense. But are you willing to walk into the bank with those numbers?"

"Seems to me it's worth the risk. How about you?"

He took her hand. "Sweetheart, haven't I been your man all along?"

Stephanie gave him a hug. "God, I think we may have done

it. You may be on the verge of becoming a very rich man, Captain Kidwell!''

"Have you written down the code?"

"I've got it memorized. If Oscar Barbadillo is waiting for us in the Caymans, I figure the thing to do is hand over the disks and let them try to figure out the code."

"Babe, you've got a mean streak in you, know that?"

"One way or another, I intend to get my money back."

He caressed her cheek. "If I was a drinking man, I'd suggest we open a bottle of champagne," he said, sounding almost sad. "Of course, nothing says *you* can't have some."

She took his face in her hands and looked him in the eyes. "A bottle of mineral water would be just fine. Don't forget, we're partners, Jack. All the way."

The wind picked up that afternoon. Stephanie was at the helm for several hours while Jack slept. When he finally came up on deck, sleepy-eyed but in good spirits, she asked if he'd dreamed about being a millionaire.

"No," he said, giving her a kiss. "I dreamed about you."

"Now why would that be?" she said, feigning skepticism. "Could it be because I've got the access code?"

Jack grabbed her by the shoulders and pulled her down over his knee and gave her behind a couple of good whacks.

"Hey," she protested as he let her up. "That hurt! Why'd you do that?"

He wagged his finger at her. "Don't get cheeky with me, young lady. That code may or may not work, you don't know for sure."

"Oh, it's the right code, all right. I've been thinking about it for hours. I know Jean Claud and I know Jane. This is exactly the sort of thing he'd have set up for her. I'm sure of it."

"Needless to say, I hope you're right."

She heard something in his voice. "What, Jack? What's wrong?"

He shrugged. "Nothing."

"No, there's something."

"Well, you having figured out the code does pose a problem," he said.

"What's that?"

"Now I can hardly say what's on my mind because you'll misunderstand my motives. I waited too long."

"What do you mean? What's on your mind?"

He took her face in his hands. "I think I'm in love with you, Stephanie."

"You mean that?"

"Yeah. But, to be sure you believe me, I almost have to hope we fail to get the money. Otherwise..."

"I won't believe you? Jack, if you really loved me, it ought to be obvious. I should be able to feel it. Something as important as that has a power of its own."

"You sound pretty certain about that," he said.

"I have reason to know."

"Which is..."

"Maybe I'm falling in love with you, too," she said.

"Are you?"

"Yes."

He scrutinized her, their expressions equally severe. "Isn't this something," he said, "for two people just having professed their love, we're looking pretty dour."

"It's a complicated situation."

He kissed her lightly on the lips. They peered into each other's eyes.

"It's impossible to ignore the money, though, isn't it?" she said.

"I'm afraid so." Then, shaking his head, he laughed. "I see now why money is considered the root of all evil. The judge in my trial tried to make the point, but I didn't see it at the time. He said, 'Mr. Kidwell, for some people money's a curse. I think you may be one.'"

"I hope you aren't suggesting we're cursed."

He pinched her cheek. "Being challenged is more like it."

"God, here we are worrying how our money's going to affect us and we haven't even gotten it yet. If I'm going to worry about anything," she said, "it should be what happens to me when I try to go back to the States. People will have questions, and it's still not clear how much trouble I'm in."

"Are you going to head right for San Francisco?"

"I may go to Washington first to see my friend Leslie," she said. "Her husband, Warren, will be very helpful in sorting out my problems."

He nodded. "Obviously, I wish you well."

"Jack, I've been thinking it would be nice if you came to Washington with me."

His eyebrows rose. "Really?"

"Yes."

"In what capacity?"

"My friend. And lover."

"Win, lose or draw?"

"Yes," she said. "Win, lose or draw."

Laughing, he kissed her lips. She kissed him back deeply. They held each other for a long time. She didn't know how long, but they both came back from their thoughts at the same time, drawn by the sound of a plane. Looking up, they spotted it, the late-afternoon sun shining on its wings as it approached from the northwest, the direction of the Cayman Islands. As they watched, it made a looping circle high overhead, then turned and headed back the way it had come.

Jack said nothing. He didn't have to.

Thursday,
October 10th

The Caribbean Sea

Stephanie had gone to bed early, but she hadn't slept. Sometime after midnight she heard the door to her cabin rattle and slowly open. Once, a few days earlier, Jack had lashed the wheel and paid her a visit during the night. Since they hadn't made love that evening, she wondered if he didn't have the same thing in mind now. In a way, it would surprise her. They'd both been tense and edgy and preoccupied. Seeing that plane had been a wake-up call.

Jack had said he thought they should stand off Grand Cayman and not put in until after dark the next day, preferably in some marina remote from George Town, assuming one could be found. He had no detailed charts of the area, which meant they would have to approach the island cautiously because of the coral, keeping one eye over the side and the other on the depth sounder. Stephanie knew that now, just as in the beginning, she was very much in Jack's hands.

She didn't say anything as he crept into the cabin, though she was surprised when he went to her locker. Using a flashlight, he began rummaging through her things. She almost asked what he was doing, but something—a vague premonition, perhaps—kept her silent. After a minute he closed the locker and crept back out the door, silently shutting it.

Stephanie wondered what that was all about. What was he looking for? Then it occurred to her it might be the gun. But on her return to the *Lucky Lady* she'd given it back, and Jack had made a point of putting it in a drawer in the galley, where either of them could get it quickly in the event of an emergency. Had he forgotten? She assumed that was it and tried to go to sleep.

As she lay listening to the hiss of the water against the hull through the open port, she relaxed as best she could. It had been an incredible day. She'd broken the code. She and Jack had professed their love. Wealth and happiness both were within grasp. But one obstacle remained—Inter-America Ventures.

Stephanie knew she faced a formidable challenge. Inter-America had resources. She had the code. That made her a target, true, but it also gave her leverage. And she did have Jack, too. She wasn't in this alone.

Glancing over, she noticed that the door to the locker was still open. A thought suddenly hit her. The computer! It hadn't occurred to her until now—she had no idea why—but that's where she kept Jane's computer.

Jumping out of bed, she went to the locker and peered inside. It was too dark to see anything so she felt around. The computer wasn't on the shelf where she kept it. My God! she realized with horror. Jack had taken it!

Stephanie broke out in a cold sweat as she calculated the implications. She'd told him how she'd broken the code, but she hadn't told him what the actual numbers were that she'd deciphered. Surely that wasn't what he was after.

Creeping to the door, she carefully opened it, only to spot Jack seated at the table in the dark salon. He had a flashlight trained on the screen of her computer.

Stephanie's heart nearly stopped. She sagged against the bulkhead. "Dear God," she muttered under her breath. Jack had been playing her, waiting to see if she managed to break the code. It was probably what he'd had in mind from the very beginning. No, of course he wasn't going to sell her out to Inter-America for a lousy half-million dollars. He wanted all thirty million for himself!

She breathed heavily, her heart racing. The implications went much deeper than a simple double-cross. Once Jack had the access code, he wouldn't need her. He could slit her throat and throw her overboard and keep all the money for himself!

The question was, what did she do? Confront him? Pretend she hadn't discovered his treachery? If he did work out the numbers, she'd be in real danger. And she had to assume that he'd be able to decipher the code. After all, she'd explained the theory; any fourth-or fifth-grader could figure it out once they had the key words. If she was going to confront him, it was best to catch him off guard. Now was the time.

Drawing a breath, she opened her cabin door. Jack swung his head toward her. The light from the flashlight shone up from under his chin, giving his face a ghoulish appearance. The surprise in his eyes was plain to see.

"Jack, what are you doing?"

Caught flat-footed, he couldn't come up with a lie. He lowered his head and sighed. "I was checking out the code."

"Why?" she asked, edging into the salon.

"Well, because..."

"Because why, Jack?" She didn't move directly toward him, but rather on a tangent. Her intent was to get to the gun in that drawer in the galley.

"I thought it would be best if we both knew the access code," he said lamely.

She could tell by his voice he knew he was unconvincing. "Why's that, Jack? Why do *you* need to know the code?"

She was nearly opposite him now. The face she'd loved only hours, only minutes ago, now seemed heinous, threatening. She sidled toward the galley, keeping her eyes on him. Jack got up abruptly, his chair noisily scraping on the sol.

Stephanie panicked. She dashed madly toward the galley, tripping over something in the dark and falling to her knees. She scrambled to her feet, getting to the galley first. She jerked the drawer open and found the gun just as he was on her, trying to wrench the weapon from her hands.

"Stephanie, for chrissakes! What are you doing?"

"No," she shrieked, backing away from him. "The question is what are *you* doing!"

They faced each other, the flashlight on the table providing what little light there was.

"I'm not going to hurt you, if that's what you think," he said, almost sounding angry.

Stephanie didn't believe him. In a sudden fit of courage, she lunged, knocking him against the bulkhead. That gave her the opportunity to scramble past him. She ran as fast as she could through the salon to the companionway, then up the steps. Reaching the deck still in the flush of panic, she realized there was no place to go. Could there be another vessel nearby? She peered out, seeing nothing but the dark sea on the port side. She hurried to the bow and searched the starboard side of the *Lucky Lady,* only to discover nothing but a couple of dim lights miles in the distance.

Stephanie spun on her heel, spotting Jack. He moved slowly toward her, the gun dangling from his hand.

"Stephanie," he said, "will you please listen to me?"

She backed as far from him as she could, but she was trapped. In her T-shirt, she trembled, not sure if it was because of the cool wind or her fear.

"Listen," he said, "I'm not going to hurt you."

"I don't believe you."

"I want to explain why I was looking at the computer."

"You don't have to. It's obvious. You want all the money for yourself. What were you going to do? Throw me overboard?"

"*No!*" he said sharply. "I have no intention of hurting you! If I did, I'd do it now."

"Maybe you haven't finished deciphering the code. Maybe you think you may still need me."

He put his hands on his hips. "Damn it," he said. "Why are you so paranoid?"

She was incredulous. Her mouth sagged open. "*You* sneaked into *my* cabin and took the computer with a code worth thirty million dollars and now you ask why *I'm* paranoid? You're delusional!"

"No, just stupid. I should have come right out and asked you to share the code. But I was afraid you'd mistrust my intentions."

"What were your intentions, pray tell?" she said, unable to mask her sarcasm.

"I was nervous, afraid if things got tense, you might forget it. I worried about them grabbing us. I thought if we both knew the access code, the chances of one of us making it to the bank were better than if only you knew it."

"How noble of you."

He grimaced. "My mistake was not discussing it with you. I wanted you to trust me and figured that if you did, you'd tell me the code. And I was afraid if I asked you to tell me outright, I'd undermine what trust you had. So I thought about it for a couple of hours and decided I'd get it surreptitiously so we'd never have to face the issue. I wanted the code for insurance. If I never needed it, if things worked out and you were able to withdraw the money okay, it never would have mattered and you'd never have known."

"I don't believe you."

"It was stupid, I admit. Maybe some of my deviousness is still with me."

"*That* I believe."

"Look," he said, "can't we just put this behind us as an unfortunate example of my poor judgment and you too readily jumping to conclusions?"

"I'll never trust you again as long as I live!"

He groaned miserably. "Why do you have to interpret this

in the worst possible way? Why can't you look at the bigger picture, the way things have been, the way we feel about each other?''

"The way we feel about each other is bullshit!'' she snapped. "You are a liar. I knew that the day I met you and I know it now.'' She shook her head. "I've known all along I shouldn't trust you, but I stuck my head in the sand. You don't care about me. You never have. It was always the money.''

"You're wrong!'' he shouted. "Dead wrong!''

"Oh, so this whole thing is about love and devotion, is it?''

"I told you I loved you, Stephanie, and I do. Yes, I've been thinking about the money. At first, that was all I cared about. I mean, I liked you but I saw this as my big chance to score and I was going for it.''

"But now you love me and that's all changed," she said, her voice dripping with sarcasm. She shook her head. "Nice story, Jack, but I don't buy it. Not after tonight.''

He stared at her for a long time. The wind blew her hair across her face. She pushed it aside, meeting his gaze. Finally Jack extended the hand with the gun toward her, handle first.

"Here," he said. "If you're going to have to protect yourself, you might as well be prepared.''

She stared at the proffered gun. "Why are you doing this?''

"If you're really worried I might steal your money, you might want to shoot me now and get me out of the way.''

"I wouldn't even consider such a thing and you know it.''

"Well, at least now I can't shoot you.''

She took the gun. He gave her a wan smile and headed back toward the cockpit.

"Jack," she called after him.

He turned. "Yeah?''

"Did you decipher the access code?''

"Yes," he said, after a brief hesitation. "I did.''

Jack sat in the cockpit, slumped in his seat, ruing his stupidity. He wasn't afraid of losing his cut of the money so much as he was of having alienated Stephanie beyond the point of forgiveness. If he got her to George Town, she'd probably pay up, then kiss his sweet ass goodbye. This was not a woman who could be won back. Not with sweet talk. Not by any means he could conceive.

"Damn it to hell!" he growled, giving the steering pedestal a kick with his heel, hurting himself. "Shit."

He probed his mind for a workable strategy, but he could think of no good options. His best bet if he loved her was to hope they couldn't withdraw the money. Then, when he asked her to join him in Mexico, it could only be for one reason— because he cared about her, and her alone. How ironic!

The sad part was he had lived enough years that he knew they weren't going to be living on love alone. Stephanie wasn't going to come out of this destitute. She'd still be better off than he, which meant any overture he made would be suspect. He'd put himself in a no-win situation.

Needless to say, he was depressed, angry with himself, disappointed. He'd had a good thing going and he'd blown it. Hell.

That same old craving for a drink began lighting his soul. He'd done a pretty good job of fighting it up to now. Though he'd come close a couple of times, he hadn't fallen off the wagon. But at the moment, he dearly wanted to do just that.

Staring at the dark, empty sea, with the *Lucky Lady* gliding smoothly toward the Caymans, Jack pictured himself going below and digging out that bottle of scotch. Was this what he'd been waiting for, the reason he hadn't chucked the goddamn bottle overboard?

For another fifteen minutes Jack battled his demons, fighting himself as much as them. Finally he went below, digging through his locker until he found the bottle. He stormed from his cabin, only to run into Stephanie, who was coming out of the head.

"Oh!" they said simultaneously, both stepping back.

Stephanie looked at him a moment before she noticed the bottle. He couldn't see her expression in the darkness well enough to divine her thoughts, but when she went to her cabin without uttering a word, he had little doubt it was disgust. Jack couldn't get up on deck fast enough.

Once he was topside, he leaned against the cabin trunk and slowly unscrewed the cap. His hand shook as he lifted the bottle to his mouth. He stopped before tilting his head back and asked himself if he was ready to die. "Yes," one voice cried. But another, quieter one, told him, "No, not yet."

Jack knew he was trapped between weakness and strength. This was a test he'd unconsciously been seeking. In the end, pride won out. He tossed the bottle overboard and turned to watch it bob in the wake of the *Lucky Lady*. He might have lost Stephanie, but he hadn't lost himself. At least not yet, anyway.

Stephanie came up on deck at dawn to relieve him. His bottle was nowhere to be seen and he gave no indication that he had been drinking. Jack regarded her soberly, his expression seeming to say he had as much reason to be disappointed in her as she had in him.

"We're sixty, seventy miles south by southeast of Grand Cayman," he said. "If you hold this heading for a couple of hours, it'll put us about fifty miles due south of George Town. Since we have all day, I'm thinking of circling around and approaching from the north under the theory they may not be looking that way. We need to find some advantage."

Stephanie said nothing in response.

"I'm going to try and get a couple of hours' sleep. Wake me then, if you would, and I'll set a new course."

"All right."

She could tell he wanted to say more, but couldn't find the words. There was no point in apologizing, they were beyond that. But there was need for some sort of understanding. She stopped him from leaving.

"I'm not going to try to make light of what happened last night," she said. "I was...well, you know how I feel. There's no point in going into it. But I need to know where things stand, what we're going to do once we get there."

"What do you want to happen?" he asked.

"I'd like to go to the bank and try to get the money. If I succeed, I'll settle up with you. A deal is a deal. But then I want to say goodbye. For good."

"I expected that," he said. "And I can't say I blame you."

"I'm glad we agree."

"That may be the least of our problems, though. We still have to figure out how to get past that pack of wolves waiting for us."

"Do you have a suggestion?" she asked.

Jack sat back down. "I've given it some thought. It seems to me we increase our odds if we split up."

A well of suspicion rose in her. "Really?"

"Your chances of getting to the bank safely would be better if I acted as a decoy. Say we stand in close to the coast and you go ashore in the dinghy. You can get to a road, have a taxi take you to some small, out-of-the-way hotel and hold up there until morning. Meanwhile, I'll take the boat into Hog Sty Bay. If they grab me, I'll say I dumped you overboard and have been frantically trying to break the code so I could grab the money for myself. I'll show them the disks, like you suggested, and let them have a go at breaking the code."

Stephanie searched for ulterior motives, for duplicity, for a trick. Nothing jumped out at her. What he proposed gave him no advantage she could see, unless he'd decided to try to join forces with Inter-America. But Jack had no reason to believe they'd honor any deal he might work out with them. And besides, once she was ashore, he would be unable to betray her more than he already had.

"That sounds reasonable," she told him. "I'll agree to that. But how will we settle up?"

"We'd better plan to rendezvous afterward," he said. "I

don't know anything about George Town, but there's got to be a café near the bank. Ask where the nearest one is and I'll meet you there, after you've made the withdrawal.''

He sounded surprisingly confident she'd succeed. It could be wishful thinking on his part, but then, too, there was nothing to be gained by being pessimistic. ''Okay,'' she replied. ''We'll meet at the nearest café.''

''Well,'' Jack said, getting up, ''I'd better get a little rest.''

''Yes, do that.''

''You don't look like you got much yourself.''

She shook her head. ''No, I didn't sleep.''

''Sorry, Stephanie.''

She shrugged. ''It'll be all over tomorrow, one way or the other. Then I can sleep for a week.''

He nodded, his expression anxious.

''What happened to that bottle of liquor you had last night?'' she asked.

''I chucked it overboard. Figured it'd be easier if I took my problems one at a time. I'll worry about getting drunk tomorrow.''

She did not like hearing that.

''But you never know,'' he added. ''I might stay sober without you.''

She nodded and Jack went below.

Stephanie sighed. She felt a little better having gotten things out in the open, but even if she ended up pulling this off, she'd still feel as if she'd lost. Jack had been trying to redeem himself, but last night he'd blown it. He'd really blown it.

The sun, a golden sliver, appeared on the horizon to stern. The wind was stiff, and over the next hour, with the sun climbing rapidly in the eastern sky, the *Lucky Lady* made good time. The rising seas crashed against the hull and the rigging whistled in the wind. The calm that had prevailed most of the trip had come to an end.

Stephanie was so lost in thought, agonizing over Jack, that she didn't notice how close two other craft were until they were nearly upon her. Finally the roar of their engines drew her attention, and she looked back to see a large motor yacht and a speedboat converging on the *Lucky Lady* from the port and starboard quarter.

The two boats were about a hundred yards away and closing fast. Stephanie knew instantly who it was.

Securing the wheel, she dashed to the companionway and ran down the steps. "Jack!" she cried as she hurried across the salon. "Jack, some boats are chasing us!"

Sticking her head in the door of his cabin, she saw him lift his head and blink at her. "Boats?"

"Yes, a big one and a little one. I'm sure they're after us."

He ran to a port and tried to look back. Spinning, he dashed to the companionway and up the steps. Stephanie followed. By the time she reached deck, Jack was staring at their pursuers, his hands on his hips. The cabin cruiser was less than thirty yards back and the speedboat was fifteen yards off the starboard side.

"Heave to!" came a voice over a bullhorn from the larger craft. "Heave to and prepare to be boarded."

"Well," Jack said to her, "what's your pleasure, m'lady? Surrender or go out in a blaze of gunfire and glory?"

Her heart chugged. "I don't know if I'm prepared to die for that money, Jack."

"There's no guarantee they'll be merciful."

She swallowed hard. "But it's our best shot."

"Shall I run up the white flag then?"

She instinctively took hold of his arm, though minutes ago she'd half condemned him as a traitor. "Yes," she said. "I don't want anybody hurt if I can possibly help it."

"Even me?" He was amazingly calm.

"Yes, Jack," she said. "Even you."

Their captors, Jack noticed, were a mixed bag. Most of them appeared to be local thugs, probably hired by Inter-America. The man who gave the orders was Latino, perhaps South

American. His name was Carlos and he was no businessman, unless the commerce of drugs or guns could be considered a business.

Stephanie, like Jack, leaned against the cabin house as a man guarded them with a submachine gun. Half a dozen others were belowdecks, searching. Carlos paced, occasionally passing them and muttering.

The *Lucky Lady* was tied up alongside the cabin cruiser. Jack had only had a glimpse of the captain, who he judged to be a mercenary like the others. When a nice-looking Latino guy in a black polo shirt appeared on the deck of the motor yacht, Jack heard Stephanie moan.

"What's the matter?"

"That's Oscar Barbadillo," she said under her breath.

She immediately began trembling and Jack put his arm around her. Considering him the lesser of two evils, evidently, she sagged against him. Jack gave her a good firm squeeze as Barbadillo made his way along the deck.

"Whatever you do, don't give them the access code," Jack whispered, "because if you do, you won't have any leverage. Tell them the story I was going to give them, that we have the code words, but can't decipher them. Offer a little resistance, but not too much."

"Jack, I know that man is going to hurt me," she said, her voice trembling.

"They have no way of knowing you broke the code. Hang on as long as you can."

Oscar Barbadillo was opposite them now. He smiled cruelly. "*Dios mio,* if it isn't Mrs. Reymond," he said, leaning on the railing. "It seems we do meet again, *querida.*"

Stephanie shrank even closer to Jack and he could tell she was terrified.

"Who's that you're with there, Stephanie?" Barbadillo asked. "Your bodyguard?"

She didn't answer.

"Or might that be the famous Captain Kidwell?" Oscar

chuckled. "Are you ready to do business with us now, Captain?"

Jack glared at him.

"Unfortunately the price has dropped to five cents," Barbadillo said, "but that's more than you'll ever be worth, so you might consider it."

"If I had anything to offer you, I would, Barbadillo," Jack said.

"Are you saying the lady hasn't shared the code, Captain? Because if not, I'm sure she can be persuaded to share it with me."

There was some commotion farther along the deck of the sailboat. Carlos, who'd been talking to one of the men, came walking toward them. He had the computer.

"Look, Oscar," he said. "I found a computer and we have some disks also."

"Good," Barbadillo said. "Bring it all on board. And bring the woman. Stephanie and I have a little catching up to do." He smiled broadly. "It was nice meeting you, Captain Kidwell. And I thank you. Your greed saved us half a million."

Carlos gave the computer to one of the men, then stepped over, taking Stephanie by the arm. Jack reached out, touching the man's shoulder.

"You'd better not hurt her, *amigo,* because I promise you, if you do, you're a dead man."

Carlos's lips peeled into a smile. Then, out of nowhere, he swung, hitting Jack on the side of the face, knocking him back against the cabin house. "Fuck you, *amigo,*" he snarled, then led Stephanie away.

"I'll buy you a cup of coffee in George Town, Steph!" Jack shouted after her.

Barbadillo, who'd watched everything from his vantage point at the railing of the yacht, laughed, shaking his head. "You won't be buying anybody anything ever again, Captain," he said. "Unless you're a hell of a swimmer."

"There's no reason to hurt her," Jack said to him.

"Do I look like a man who would hurt a woman? Captain, you misunderstand me. My way is to make myself irresistible. That's how I deal with women. Anyway, Stephanie likes me. She may not yet know how much, but she will learn." He grinned. *"Adiós, Capitán."*

Jack watched him move down the deck to where Stephanie was being helped aboard. Barbadillo went up to her and kissed her on the cheek as if she was an old friend. Jack could tell she was terrified. Clenching his fists, he wanted to vault up onto the deck of the cabin cruiser and tear Barbadillo to pieces. The man guarding him must have been aware of his feelings because he fingered the trigger on his weapon, eyeing him closely.

"It's time to say goodbye, *amigo,*" Carlos said, moving back along the deck of the *Lucky Lady*.

Walking up to Jack, he punched him in the stomach without warning. Then while he was doubled over, Carlos took the submachine gun from the guard, then brought the handle of the automatic sharply down on Jack's shoulder, dropping him to the deck. He lay stunned while Carlos kicked him in the stomach and back, then in the ribs. The last blow resulted in a loud crack and a sharp pain. Carlos reached down as Jack writhed in agony and grabbed a handful of hair, jerking up his head.

"What's the code, my friend? Tell me the code and I won't kill you."

"I don't know," Jack said, wincing with pain. "We couldn't break it. Stephanie has the code words, but they're words, not the numbers. She doesn't know what they mean."

The man stared at him as though he was evaluating Jack's truthfulness. At last he said, "We'll let you die, anyway." Then he slammed Jack's head down, got up and walked away. The guard followed along behind.

Jack lay there in pain, certain he had a cracked rib. He heard the men departing from the *Lucky Lady,* clambering aboard the cruiser. Surely they weren't going to leave him there. The must intend to shoot him from the deck of the yacht. He was sorry now he hadn't resisted. If he'd only shot one or two of them, it would have been something. The one thing he regretted was dying without knowing whether Stephanie would be all right.

Jack could hear them casting off the lines, then the revving of the cruiser's engine as it pulled away. He was incredulous.

It was then he heard a crackling sound and smelled smoke. Rising to his knees, he peered down the deck and saw smoke belching from the companionway. Soon the flames were licking up and the sails began to catch fire. This was how they planned to kill him, he realized—by burning his boat out from under him.

Jack forced the emotion from his brain and tried to think clearly. If he was going to save himself, he'd have to act fast. The dinghy was clear at the other end of the boat and it was deflated. He calculated his chances of getting by the fire. Given the time it would take to get the thing inflated, he'd never make it. And it was also possible they'd punched a hole in it or had already tossed it overboard.

No, he saw what fate was in store for him. He had a fifty-mile swim to land, which would have been a piece of cake if it wasn't for the ribs. Sitting down painfully on the deck, he watched the motor yacht heading off to the north. The thought of Stephanie taken prisoner by those bastards made his heart ache. He didn't want to think what they might do to her.

Wincing with pain again, Jack was aware he had one chance of surviving—if someone saw the smoke and came to investigate. Why the stupid bastards had set the *Lucky Lady* on fire, he didn't know. If they wanted to scuttle her, all they had to do was disconnect the thrull and open the valves and she'd have sunk quietly into the depths. And nobody would have known the boat was going under—except maybe a shark or two.

The fire was raging and the heat had become intense. Jack sidled over to the railing. He'd give it a few more minutes before quietly dropping over the side. He didn't relish the thought of trying to swim with these ribs, and he knew the longer he waited before getting in the water, the better off he'd be. Damn, he thought. What a lousy day this had turned out to be.

Stephanie peered out the port, pressing her cheek to the glass as she watched the *Lucky Lady* slowly disappear from sight. The sails were ablaze and a column of dark smoke rose into the azure sky. Jack, they told her, had elected to stay behind. She wondered if they'd killed him, or left him for the sharks.

When she could no longer see the boat, she turned from the port, wiping her eyes. She'd known from the beginning that this might happen, but she had no idea they would be so savage. She'd seen Carlos beating Jack. They'd hurt him, but when they told her he said she knew the access code, she knew they were lying. If Jack was going to break, he'd have told them the code himself.

So far they hadn't hurt her, but Barbadillo had looked at her as though he had every intention of settling the score. When she'd told him that Jean Claud had devised a code and that it was on the disks, he was pleased. But he became skeptical when she said that it was a word cipher, and the access code was a six-digit number she hadn't been able to figure out. He'd given the computer to one of his men. They'd have a look and then talk some more. "Meanwhile, Stephanie," he'd said, "I want you to make yourself comfortable in your cabin."

Up to now nobody had gotten rough with her. She figured they wanted to keep her healthy so she could help recover the money—though she knew she'd be a fool to count on that. The biggest surprise was the condition of the cabin. It was well-appointed and clean, but stripped bare. There wasn't even any bedding on the berth, nothing in the lockers. Apart from the furniture, all there was in the cabin was her suitcase, a pillow and a few short links of rope. God, she hoped they didn't plan on torturing her.

Stephanie paced, worrying about Jack, about herself, about a future that looked bleak at best. The irony was that even if she gave them the deciphered code, she couldn't be sure they wouldn't kill her.

Once more she went to the port and peered out. There was no longer any sign of the *Lucky Lady,* not even smoke on the horizon. Poor Jack.

Hearing the lock turn and the door open behind her, she spun around. It was Oscar Barbadillo. She tensed.

"I hope you find the accommodations adequate," he said. "I know it's kind of Spartan, but that's intentional." He went to the one armchair and sat, crossing his legs. Then he took a cigar from his pocket and lit it. "More comfortable than the trunk of a car, don't you think?"

"What do you want, Oscar?"

"To talk."

"About what?"

"Us, Stephanie."

"I don't see we have anything to discuss."

"That's because you're fully dressed. We seem to communicate best when at least one of us is naked. I believe it's your turn, *querida.* Take off your clothes."

"What's that going to accomplish?"

Barbadillo drew on his cigar. "It's going to make me feel better and, at this point, that's important. So take off your clothes or I'll invite a couple of my men to come in and assist you."

"You're sick."

"What were you when you had me undress on St. Thomas?"

"I was trying to keep you from going to the police. The alternative was to shoot you."

"Ah, I see. A humanitarian gesture." He took another drag on the cigar. "This, too, is a humanitarian gesture. You can contend with me while you're naked, or with half a dozen of my men. I leave the choice to you. Me or the hungry horde.''

Stephanie's heart raged. Oscar was a monster, but a suave one. She could defy him, or she could try to please him. With luck, he might stop at humiliating her. She decided to make one more attempt to reason with him.

"Isn't the money the important thing, Oscar? You realize, I assume, that you only have until tomorrow to get it from the bank. Then it's gone forever. Shouldn't you be working on breaking the code?''

"I have a computer expert in the salon, doing just that. But I have a hunch I'm going to get the code faster by talking to you. So, as you undress, think about what you wish to tell me. Now get started before I lose my patience.''

Stephanie saw it was hopeless. So she quickly undressed, keeping her back to him. Shivers went up and down her spine and her hands trembled. Once she was naked, she snatched the pillow and sat with it in front of her on the bed. Oscar slowly drew on his cigar.

"Now lie on the bed, *querida*,'' he said.

"What are you going to do?''

"Interrogate you.''

She moved onto the middle of the berth, clutching the pillow to her body.

"Put the pillow under you head,'' he commanded.

She didn't argue. Oscar slowly got to his feet. Her skin crawled as he made his way to the berth, sitting casually beside her. He drew on his cigar, exhaling toward the ceiling. He nonchalantly looked over her body.

"So, was Kidwell a good lover?'' he asked.

"Yes.''

"Really?''

"Yes, Jack's a wonderful lover and a decent man.''

"Your wonderful lover was negotiating to sell you to us, you know,'' Barbadillo said, drawing the tip of his index finger up her side.

She tensed. "I know that. He told me."

Oscar drew light circles on her breasts with his finger, making her dig her nails into the mattress. "And you believed he made love with you because he loved you, *querida?*"

"Yes," she said, her jaw trembling.

"You are a very trusting woman," he said, lightly pinching her nipples.

It took all her willpower to lie still. "You have the disks," she lamented. "What more do you want?"

"I want for us to know each other very well, Stephanie. Only then can there be trust."

He ran the flat of his hand down over her stomach. Unable to help herself, she grabbed his hand. "Please don't," she said, half sobbing.

Barbadillo frowned insincerely. "What are you afraid of, Stephanie? I won't hurt you. You'll like what I do to you. And afterward you'll tell me who was better, Kidwell or me."

"No, Oscar, please."

"Tell you what I'm going to do," he said. "I'll tie you to the bed. Then you won't need to resist. That way, when you enjoy it, your conscience will be clear. You'll have no choice but to accept the pleasure." He grinned. "Isn't that considerate of me? I'm making is so easy for you to have a good time."

"I don't want to have sex with you," she cried.

"Oh, but you do, *querida*. The only unknown is how much."

Rico Behring stood next to the pilot of the speedboat and held on to the windshield for balance as they skimmed along at high speed, the warm sea air stinging his eyes. There were a couple of sailboats in sight and a fishing trawler, but no cabin cruiser.

"Where the fuck are they?" he said over the roar of the wind.

"Should be dead ahead, sir," the pilot replied. "This is the course the captain of the yacht gave in his radio transmission."

Rico was pissed. Oscar was supposed to keep him informed and it was only by chance Rico had learned that Kidwell's boat had been sighted. More than once the last two days his cousin had gotten cheeky with him. "I thought you were going back to L.A.," Oscar had said when they'd had dinner a couple of nights ago.

"What difference does it make to you?"

Oscar had shrugged. "Somebody's got to run the company."

Rico hadn't thought anything of it until he realized what Oscar had to gain. Thirty million was up for grabs. Anybody with the code could walk into the bank and claim it. His goddamn cousin was planning on double-crossing him. When Kidwell's boat was sighted and Oscar went off to pick them up without saying a word, Rico knew he was right.

He glanced back at the three heavily armed men in the back of the boat, nodding. Oscar might have him outnumbered with his little band of pirates, but Rico definitely had his cousin outgunned. He'd called in some real professionals, men who could handle the rough stuff.

"There she is, Mr. Behring!" the pilot said, pointing.

"Great," Rico said, patting the man on the shoulder. He signaled the others to get ready. "The captain knows to stop and let us board?"

"Yes, sir. He knows who's paying the bills."

"Everybody does, except my fucking cousin."

Stephanie cried softly as Oscar ran his hands over her. Her wrists and ankles were tied to the corners of the berth, her eyes closed, her head turned as far from him as she could. He'd tried to make her watch as he'd undressed, but she refused to look at him. She didn't want to feel or sense anything.

When Oscar put his hand between her legs for the first time, she let out a mournful sob. He continued purring into her ear,

undaunted, his tobacco breath washing over her as he tanta-
lized her with his fingers.

"Don't fight it, *querida*," he whispered. "Let go and it will
be so much more pleasant."

Suddenly the boats engine stopped. Stephanie opened her
eyes. Oscar sat upright.

"What the fuck?" he said. He walked naked to the port.
Seeing nothing, he went to the other side. "*Cristo!*" he exclaimed.

"What's happening?"

Barbadillo ignored her.

Moments later they heard shouts up on the deck and what
sounded like gunfire, in short staccato bursts. Oscar rushed
back and picked up his clothes. He was in the middle of trying
to put on his pants when the door burst open and a large man
in dark glasses carrying a submachine gun charged into the
cabin, ready to fire. He ordered Oscar to put up his hands.

As Stephanie stared, mouth agape, a younger man entered
the cabin, glancing first at Oscar, then at her. "Well," he said,
"I see we're having a little fun. What's the deal, Oscar? Figure
you'd fuck the code out of her?"

"Rico, for chrissakes, what's with all the theatrics?"

"Theatrics, cousin?" Rico said, walking up to him. "Is that
anything like double cross?"

"What are you talking about?"

Rico got right in his face. "What the fuck you doing grabbing the broad without telling me, huh? Decide you didn't
need to share the dough with the company, Oscar?"

"Rico, you're nuts!"

"Nuts? No, I'm stupid to trust you. You were going to run
out on me. My old man not dead a week and you're going to
steal our money and run."

"You're not only stupid," Oscar said, "you're insane." He
gave Rico a shove.

Rico's eyes rounded with rage and he reached behind his
back and pulled a pistol from his belt. Then, without a word

he shot his cousin in the chest, the force of the bullet knocking Oscar back against the bulkhead. Stephanie gasped. Oscar's eyes were round with disbelief. He gave a little groan as he slumped to the floor.

"Stupid sonovabitch," Rico muttered. Then he turned to the man who'd broken into the cabin. "Have somebody dump the bastard overboard, will you? All he's good for now is fish food."

The man stuck his head out the door and called in a couple of hands. They entered, casting curious looks at Stephanie before carrying Oscar from the cabin. Rico ordered the gunman out and told him to close the door. Then for the first time, he turned his full attention to her. Stephanie was at a loss for words.

Rico sat on the bed, looking at her face. "You must be Mrs. Reymond," he said in a bizarrely calm voice.

She swallowed hard. "Yes," she croaked.

"I'm Rico Behring, head man of Inter-America Ventures." He reached into his pocket and produced a jackknife, which he opened, waving the blade before her. "You'll have to forgive my cousin, Mrs. Reymond," he said. "Oscar is a stupid, pathological sonovabitch." Then, using the knife, he cut the ropes, freeing her.

Stephanie snatched the pillow from under her head, covering herself with it. "Thank you," she gasped.

Rico got to his feet and gazed down at her. "Get dressed, then come into the main salon. You and I are going to have a drink, then we'll talk." With that, he left the cabin.

Trembling, Stephanie quickly put on her clothes, aware of the pool of blood on the floor where Oscar Barbadillo had fallen. Fighting back her rising gorge, she left the cabin, finding Rico Behring alone at the table in the main salon. He had her purse, with the contents dumped out, and Jane's computer. The framed photo of Suzanne was in his hand.

"Who's the kid?"

"My daughter," Stephanie said.

"How old is she?"

"She'd be twenty-one on her next birthday. That's an old photo."

Rico blinked. "No shit? You're old enough to be the mother of a twenty-one year old?"

"Yes."

"My compliments." He gestured to her. "Come over here and sit by me," he said. "I want you to explain to me how the code works."

She went to the table and warily slipped into a chair. "Mr. Behring," she said, her voice shaking, "Oscar left Jack Kidwell on a burning sailboat out at sea. Can we please go back and pick him up?"

Rico looked surprised. "Oscar did that?"

"Yes."

"Jesus, how long ago?"

"I don't know, half an hour, maybe forty-five minutes."

"Sugar, that long ago, there's no way he's alive. You best forget him." He somehow managed to look sorry. "Don't worry, though. You've got a new partner now. Me, doll." He reached over and pinched her cheek. "You and me are going to get along real well. And we're going to get rich. That's a promise."

Friday,
October 11th

Grand Cayman Island

Stephanie had terrible nightmares about people being shot and drowned and tied up and thrown into burning buildings. But she awoke in the clean hotel bed, the sheets fresh-smelling, the balmy air wafting in the window, fragrant with blossoms. She was alive, unharmed, and had been promised one million dollars by Rico Behring for her cooperation. But she was also scored by a deep wound—Jack, she'd come to accept, was dead.

Though it had taken hours to sink into her brain, Jack's death had hit her harder than any of the many tragedies that had befallen her over the past few weeks. The other deaths had been staggering, but knowing Jack was dead had completely eviscerated her. Sure, he'd disappointed her that last night. His betrayal had been painful, even devastating, but she knew a part of him had loved her and that in the end he'd tried to do the right thing. Now he was gone.

Stephanie had tried to make sense of what had happened. There was no logic to it, no grand meaning that she could see. By luck, pluck and chance she was alive. That was all she understood.

The bedroom door swung open and Rico Behring entered. No knock, no excuse-me.

"Good, you're awake," he said, approaching the bed. "This is our big day, doll. We can't sleep through it, now, can we?"

Stephanie pulled the sheet up to her chin, incensed that he would walk in on her that way, but he'd proven so unpredictable, she wasn't surprised. The man, she decided, was pathological. Yet he'd treated her with courtesy, in a crude sort of way. The closest he'd come to direct intimidation was on the boat when he'd explained what he expected. "Tomorrow morning we're going to the bank together," he'd said. "One of my associates will be with us. You will present the code and if it doesn't produce the money, my associate will put a bullet in your head, no questions asked. You get one chance to come up with the right answer, and one chance only. Do we understand each other?"

Rico Behring was so inherently evil that she had instantly capitulated. She'd admitted she'd broken the code, explaining how she'd accidentally discovered it with the spell check. "But it's only my best guess," she'd said. "I think it's the right code, but I can't be absolutely sure."

Rico had grinned, given her cheek a pinch and said, "Doll, you'd better hope it's right, because if not, you're dead. If we have to do you right there in the bank, we will. Succeed and you'll be a million bucks richer. Fail and it won't matter."

But then he'd given her lunch on the yacht and later he'd taken her arm as they were disembarking at the marina, personally escorting her to their waiting limo for the short drive up the coast to the hotel. "Please don't get any ideas about trying to run for help," he'd said. "There'll be more people guarding you than the president of the United States. Just remember, we're partners and partners gotta treat each other right."

Later they'd shared a room-service dinner, including wine and soft background music. Rico hadn't made a pass at her, though he'd given her a couple of oblique, but suggestive, compliments. "Not to be personal or nothing, but how old are you?" he'd asked.

"Forty-two," she'd said.

"Jesus, you'd never believe it. And I'm pretty particular about my women."

He hadn't touched her, saying good-night politely when she said she wanted to go to bed. Stephanie had found that there was a man posted in the garden outside the suite and probably another in the hall. They'd disconnected the phone in the bedroom. Rico's trust obviously had its limits. Besides, she'd been so numb that laying plans were beyond her. The money no longer mattered. She just wanted to get through this alive. She didn't even care whether Rico Behring gave her a million dollars or not. Jack was dead, everything else paled beside that tragic fact.

But Rico wouldn't let her give up. He stood over her now, a psychotic zealot unwilling to give value to human life. She was his key to the bank vault and he would use her as such to accomplish his purposes.

"So, what's the matter, sugar?" he said after she'd stared at him mutely for several long moments. "Can't get up your enthusiasm for a million bucks?"

"No, I told you I'd do it and I will."

"Great. Come and have some breakfast. The room-service waiter just delivered it."

"I don't care for anything."

"I ordered it and it's here," he said, losing his patience, "so come and eat it while it's hot."

"Can I get dressed?"

Rico grabbed the sheet and flung it back. Stephanie jerked her T-shirt down, covering herself.

"You're fine," he said. "Put on a robe and come eat."

As soon as he'd left the bedroom, Stephanie got up and, grabbing the hotel robe, put it on. Casting a wary eye toward the door to the sitting room, she made a quick trip to the bathroom, pausing at the mirror long enough to run a brush through her hair. Fearing she'd antagonize him, she hurried to the sitting room, cinching the tie of the robe still tighter. Breakfast was laid out on the table. Rico surprised her by holding her chair for her. Stephanie sat warily, fearful of what his bizarre behavior might lead to.

Once she was seated, he let his hands rest on her shoulders. "Think what this means, doll," he said. "You and me are having one hell of a payday. Even after I give you your million, I'm still making a ten-million-dollar profit! Ten fucking million! It's cost me a few hundred thousand, but that's still chicken feed."

"I'm glad you're pleased."

Rico started massaging her shoulders. "Funny when you think about it. When this business started, you were married and I was junior nobody. Now there's only two of us left standing—you and me."

The way he chuckled convinced her he was crazy. She wasn't the most coherent she'd ever been herself, but she could feel the man's insanity. And his touch, while less indecent than Oscar Barbadillo's, was somehow more menacing and dangerous. She was in the hands of a maniac.

Rico began massaging the back of her neck. She could feel the strength in his hands. As he slipped his fingers around her neck, exerting only the lightest pressure on her throat, she quailed.

"You know, you've got nice skin," he said, running his fingers under the collar of her robe. "I've never made it with anybody over thirty-five before. I'm wondering if after we finish at the bank maybe we should come back here and have us a little party. I've got some ludes and there's enough fucking champagne to float a battleship."

Stephanie was torn between ordering him to take his hands off her and playing along. If she didn't stop him sometime, when would it end?

Just then there was a shout outside the door to the suite. A woman's voice, then a man's. The door flew open and a voluptuous redhead in tight parrot green Capri pants, a one-shoulder tunic top in a garish yellow and gold platform slides came barging in.

"Jesus fucking Christ," Rico said, removing his hands from under Stephanie's robe.

The woman fought off the man trying to grab her and stumbled toward them as Stephanie tightened the robe at her throat. Rico stepped around the table.

"Let go!" the woman screamed as the man tackled her. "He's *my* goddamn husband!"

"Mr. Behring?" the man said, his arms wrapped around the woman as she tried to stomp his feet.

"Let her go," Rico commanded.

The man did.

"It's all right," Rico told him. "Go back out in the hall." After the man was gone, Rico stared at the woman, his hands on his hips. "Rhonda, what a pleasant surprise. Where's your fucking lawyer?"

"So," she said, glancing at Stephanie, "you don't like me having a guy, but it's just fine if you play doctor with some slut. Or is this your secretary?" She glared. "Know what? You're a hypocrite, Rico. The biggest goddamn hypocrite in the world."

"As a matter of fact, Rhonda, this happens to be my business partner. Not that I owe you any explanations."

"What business? Prostitution? You pimping now, too, dear?"

He doubled up his fist and made a threatening gesture. "Button it, bitch! I won't put up with any shit from you. I'll do any fucking thing I want."

"Oh, you can screw every whore in the Caribbean for all I care."

"So what the hell are you barging in here for? Why aren't you home with the kid?"

Stephanie was in shock. Her initial impulse was to leap to

her feet and tell the woman she was under the wrong impression—not for Rico's sake, but for her own. But she was too stunned, and things were moving too quickly, for her to react.

Rhonda gave Rico a painful smile, pursing her lips and clearly fighting mightily to keep from crying. "I came because you're going to hear how you've ruined my life."

"Jesus, Rhonda, give it a rest. This ain't the time."

"You need to hear what you've done to me, Rico," she insisted. "I want you to know."

"Fine, say what you gotta say, then get your ass out of my sight."

She glared, pausing for a moment as if summoning her courage. "I was a person when I met you, Rico, not a perfect one, maybe not even a very good one, but I had a life, I had a little self-respect," she said tearfully, her eyes bubbling over. "Then I married you and I didn't feel good about myself anymore. You make me feel like shit, like a cheap whore, if you want to know the truth."

"That's what you are, Rhonda, I got news for you."

"Yeah, well, not everybody thinks so. There are people who like me. Even love me. Men who love me—and I'm not talking about my body. You know what, Rico? You and your damn father even took that away. You drove away the only man I ever really cared for. And you've scared my mother and got her telling me not to leave you because it's not worth losing my baby. You're blackmailing me just so you'll have somebody at home to beat up. A punching bag. You're a cruel-hearted sonovabitch, Rico, the most evil man I've ever known."

He laughed. "You come all the way down here to tell me that? You're an even dumber cunt than I thought."

"Well, that's not quite all," she replied. "I brought my lawyer along to make an official response to your threats."

"What?"

"You won't give me a divorce without taking Andrea away from me, right?"

"You got it."

"Well, my lawyer said a divorce may not be necessary. He said there's a better way. Want to know what it is?" she asked, reaching into her bag.

"What the fuck are you talking about? You on drugs again, Rhonda? That what's going on? You fry your brain again?"

Rhonda pulled a shiny nickel-plated automatic from her purse and leveled it on her husband. "Meet my new lawyer, Rico."

Stephanie gasped.

"Jesus Christ," Rico moaned. "Put that fucking thing away."

"No, Rico. *I'm* calling the shots now. It's payback time. You can either stand there and take it like a man or act like the disgusting little bully you really are."

"You know how this marriage is going to end, bitch?" Rico said, stabbing his finger at her. "I'm going to fucking kill you."

"Sorry, Rico, but I thought of it first."

Without another word, she opened fire. Three shots rang out in quick succession, all crashing into Rico's chest. Stephanie saw the look of utter incredulity on his face as he dropped to the floor. Rhonda calmly stepped forward and administered the coup de grâce just as the door to the suite flew open. One of Rico's henchmen came rushing in, his own weapon in hand. Rhonda fired once, dropping him on the spot. Then she turned to Stephanie, who sat frozen in her chair, cringing.

Smiling, Rhonda put the automatic back in her purse. "Have a nice day, honey," she said, then strolled casually toward the door, stepping over the groaning man.

Rico was covered with blood and didn't appear to be breathing. The man in the garden pounded on the sliding glass door. Stephanie managed to pull herself together and get up from the table. As she went into the bedroom, she heard the crash of glass, probably a patio chair coming through the slider. Her head pounding, she went to her suitcase and hastily put on a dress and shoes. More people arrived and she heard shouts and oaths in the next room.

Spotting her purse on the chest, Stephanie grabbed it and went to the door. Two men were bending over Rico, pressing on his chest and cursing. Another guy tended the wounded man. Stephanie slipped past them and headed for the slider. She made it out into the garden and began walking briskly toward the pool. She expected to hear a shout from behind her, maybe feel a bullet in her back, but nothing happened. In moments she was on the beach. Taking off her shoes, she started running in the sand.

She didn't know how far she'd gone, perhaps half a mile, before she came to what looked like a beachfront bar or restaurant. It didn't seem to be open, but there was a young woman sweeping the patio. She turned, her large gold hoop earrings swinging as Stephanie came running up.

"I need a taxi," Stephanie said breathlessly.

The woman, who had a bad contusion on her cheek said, "I can ring one for you. Come inside."

Stephanie stood at the bar while the girl phoned for a taxi. Afterward, she looked at Stephanie and said, "Man, you look kinda hot. Want somethin' cool to drink?"

"That would be nice."

The girl got her a Coke and put it on the bar. Stephanie opened her purse.

"No, it's compliments of the house, ma'am."

Stephanie took a five from her wallet and gave it to her anyway.

It seemed forever before the taxi arrived. The driver, an elderly man with a grizzly white beard told her they were doing repairs on the only road into town and it would take a while to get to the bank. The warning was not without merit. Arriving at the construction area, they waited a long time before they were permitted to creep through a muddy stretch of temporary bypass.

Stephanie clutched her purse, replaying the scene in Rico's suite over and over in her mind. Her hope was that Rico's men would be so confused by the shooting that they would have forgotten about her. Her best hope was that she could reach the bank and get out of there before any of them showed up.

She thought, too, about going to the police. She'd witnessed Rico's and Oscar's murders, and at some point would have to report to the authorities what had happened to Jack. But there was no urgency on either score, and it was probably in her interest to get back to the States as quickly as she could. Yet, she couldn't get the image of that burning boat from her mind. Just thinking about it made her heart ache.

Knowing Jack, he would have wanted her to grab the money and run. He'd have understood her need to right the scales and get her due. And even if greed had gotten the best of him that last night, she was convinced that there was as much good in him as bad.

Stephanie ran the code numbers through her mind. There was no guarantee that she'd worked out the right one, but she dare not dwell on the possibility of failure, not after all she'd been through. Not after Jack...

They eventually reached town, a village compared to Charlotte Amalie. Bank after bank lined the waterfront road. Stephanie had the driver stop up the street from the building where the Grand Cayman Bank Ltd. was located. She paid him in dollars, doubling the fare. When she got out of the taxi it was ten thirty-five.

She walked slowly along the sidewalk, alert for faces she'd seen in St. Thomas or on the boat. A smiling woman with a baby buggy and a toddler passed by. People were shopping or going about their business. Two boys worked on the engine of a motorbike. It was a slow, sleepy day for the rest of the world. Not a likely time to be picking up thirty million dollars.

Stephanie reached the entrance to the bank. "Grand Cayman Bank Ltd." was written in gold-relief letters on the face of the building, and it was etched in the glass of the door. She went inside, immediately looking around, fearful of who she might see. But she didn't recognize anyone.

The atmosphere was surprisingly tranquil. It was not a large room, the style colonial with ceiling fans, potted palms and clerks in short-sleeve shirts or sleeveless dresses. Stephanie approached the heavy wooden counter, staffed by a slight young woman. She asked for Harris Ivory.

A very proper-looking man in a three-piece suit came to the counter. He wore small, wire-rimmed glasses and though he appeared to be still in his thirties, he was half-bald, his dark dome shining.

"I'm Stephanie Reymond," she said, introducing herself. "We spoke several days ago on the phone."

"Ah, yes indeed, Mrs. Reymond," Ivory said, beaming. "Delighted you've come."

"I'd like to make a withdrawal from my husband's numbered account," she announced without ceremony.

Harris Ivory frowned slightly, pressing his lips together. "Please come to my office," he said.

Then, stepping over to the gate in the wooden railing, he opened it, inviting her to pass through. Stephanie followed him. His office was not ostentatious, but very tidy and suffused with banker dignity. He went behind his desk and invited her to sit in the guest chair. His demeanor was sober as he took a form from his drawer and slid it across the desk in front of her. Taking a pen from the holder, he handed it to her.

"If you would be so kind as to enter the account number where indicated, please."

Stephanie complied, handing back the form. Ivory took the sheet and turned to the computer terminal on the corner of his desk, his expression glum.

"To access this account, I shall need the six-digit access code," he said. "Please be good enough to enter it there, in that device on the corner of the desk."

Stephanie, her palms wet, her blood racing, carefully entered five, four, seven, six, five, eight, then pushed the enter key. She looked at Ivory, who stared at his computer screen for a long while. Her nails dug deep into her palms.

"Mrs. Reymond," the banker said, "you have successfully accessed the account, but I regret to inform you there are no funds available for withdrawal."

She was incredulous. *"What?"*

"The account is empty, Mrs. Reymond."

"But how can that be?" she said, getting to her feet. "There's supposed to be thirty million dollars in that account." Ignoring protocol, she went around the desk and stood next to the man, peering at the screen.

"Please, Mrs. Reymond," he said uncomfortably.

"No, I want to know what happened to my money. Didn't Meriwether & Handley wire you the thirty million?"

He looked up at her over his glasses. "Please return to your chair and I'll explain."

Stephanie, sick with dismay, returned to her seat. Ivory got up and closed the door to his office, then returned to his chair.

"The deposit was made. Thirty-one point five million dollars was the precise amount. I'm afraid the entire sum has been withdrawn. The account balance at the moment is nil. I'm very sorry."

"Wait. The money was withdrawn? When?"

Ivory cleared his throat. "This morning. Right after we opened our doors. I handled the transaction myself. That's why when I saw the account number I had misgivings. It was possible additional funds had been wired to the account without my knowledge, so I didn't say anything, but I'm afraid that's not the case. I'm terribly sorry," he repeated.

Stephanie sat stunned. It made no sense. Who could have known? Then, it hit her. *Jack!* He was the only other person who knew the access code. At least, he was the only one so far as she knew. "Mr. Ivory, I have to know who withdrew the money. Was it Jack Kidwell?"

"Mrs. Reymond, I'm afraid I'm not at liberty to—"

"I don't care what you're at liberty to do. I *have* to know! Jack's my...partner!"

"All the same—"

"He's American, in his early forties, about six-two or three, blond hair, quite good-looking. Does that fit the description?"

Ivory, his frown deepening, slowly but emphatically nodded.

Stephanie fell back in her chair, covering her mouth with her hands. "Dear God."

Somehow, he'd survived. Somehow, he'd escaped his burning boat and made it to shore. She was filled with a sudden euphoria. Jack was *alive!*

"Oh, thank God," she said, her eyes instantly brimming. "Was he all right? Did he seem okay?"

"Yes...though he seemed to be in some sort of discomfort. He held himself rather stiffly, I must say."

"Poor Jack," she said. "My God, I thought I'd lost him." Stephanie took a deep breath. Looking at a perplexed Harris Ivory, she smiled. "It's incredible, but I almost feel better than if you'd handed me a check for thirty million dollars."

The man was at a loss.

"Tell me, Mr. Ivory," she said. "Is there a café nearby, or a tearoom or something?"

"Yes, indeed. There's a coffee bar directly across the road. They serve tea, as well, and light snacks."

"It's the nearest?"

"There's another a few hundred yards farther down the road, but this one's quite pleasant. Aunt Hazel's it's called. You'll see it."

Stephanie got up, feeling lighthearted. She was so relieved to hear Jack was alive that everything else almost seemed unimportant. That said something, considering how angry she'd been. The thought, innocent on its face, gave her pause, followed by a stab of doubt. Jack would surely be at the café. That was what they'd agreed. Suddenly, she wasn't so sure.

"I've got to go," she said. "If Jack should happen to come

back for any reason, would you tell him I'll be across the street in the coffee bar?''

"Certainly.''

Ivory came around his desk and they shook hands.

"Oh,'' he said, "I nearly forgot. A piece of mail came for you a few days ago. Let me find it for you.''

They went out into the bank proper and Ivory retrieved a letter-size envelope from a case and brought it to her. Stephanie glanced at the return address. It was from Françoise and it had been mailed from Guadeloupe. Stephanie stuck it in her purse, thanked the bank manager again and left.

Stepping into the bright tropical sun, she looked across the street and saw Aunt Hazel's a few doors up. Fear rose within her. Jack had her money, but would he be in the café, as they'd agreed? The joy she'd felt only minutes earlier turned to doubt.

She crossed the street, knowing she was about to discover the truth about Jack Kidwell. Her questions, her doubts, the uncertainty were about to be resolved. With each step she took, her skepticism deepened. Maybe she was trying to prepare herself. Or maybe, deep inside, she already knew.

Reaching the open door, she peered inside. The place was tiny, only half a dozen tables squeezed in the small space. Two women sat at one table, the woman she'd seen earlier with the baby buggy was at the counter. In the corner a man was reading a newspaper that masked his face. Unable to bear the suspense, she marched over. He lowered his paper. It wasn't Jack. It was a very British-looking chap with ruddy cheeks and a large mustache.

"Good day,'' he said, as amused by the way she stared at him as he was taken aback.

"Sorry,'' she said, turning away. She went to an empty table by the window and sat down to gather herself.

Well, that answered that. Her brief attempt at being stoic quickly fizzled and her eyes filled with tears. What did she expect? The man had been handed thirty-one point five million dollars. Did she really think he'd bring it to her in some insane fit of honesty?

Stephanie checked her watch. It was just after eleven. Jack had been a multimillionaire for an hour. But when she thought about it, she realized that wasn't such a long time. Was there any chance he might still show up? Could he have gone to buy some clothes or something? Maybe plane tickets? No, Jack had left with the money. That was obvious.

When the counter girl had finished serving the last customer, Stephanie went up to talk to her.

"Excuse me, miss," she said, "but I was supposed to meet someone here this morning and I'm wondering if I might have missed him. He's an American, early forties, over six feet, blond, blue eyes. Has anyone fitting the description been in, perhaps left a message for Stephanie?"

The girl shook her head. "No, ma'am, not that I did see. The only white gentlemen that's been here this morning is that one sitting over there and two gentlemen from Barclay's who get their coffee every morning."

Stephanie was disappointed, but not surprised. She ordered a cup of coffee and a pastry. When she went to pay, she noticed the envelope in her purse. Returning to the table, she read the letter while she had her coffee.

Françoise recounted how she and Nigel had spent several blissful days on St. Kitts where he'd surprised her with a proposal of marriage and a gorgeous ring. She wrote:

> The wedding will be in Paris in May, *chérie,* and we expect you and Jack to be there.

The mention of Jack brought instant pain, but Stephanie read on.

> Nigel and I have a bet as to whether you will come together or separately, but I won't tell you the size of the bet or who bet which way. Please don't disappoint me.

"Sorry, Françoise," Stephanie murmured, "but I will have to disappoint you." She knew what Françoise had bet and was sad to say that Nigel knew Jack better than either of them. The letter went on:

> We also have a bet whether you two will leave the Cayman Islands fabulously wealthy. This one I *will* tell you. I say yes, Nigel says no.

Strange as it may seem, kids, Stephanie thought, you're both wrong and both right. Stephanie continued reading:

> On another subject, you may be happy to learn that you are not the criminal you feared you'd become. Nigel made inquiries from St. Kitts. No charges or arrest warrants were issued for any of us. To the contrary, there was a big fuss in St. Thomas over police involvement in the affair. It seems the bad guys took off without settling with people they owed money to and the authorities are so busy pointing fingers at each other that your little escapade has been forgotten. *Félicitations!*
>
> Sonia, you will be happy to hear, is back in her house and her family is well. Bobby Brown has his ten thousand and won't be making waves. We were very surprised to hear from Malva that she is leaving Isola Lovejoy for good. Nigel pleaded with her on the phone for half an hour, but it was no good. She wants to return to the States to start her own business. Nigel is very sad, but in the end he sent her twenty-five thousand dollars as a bonus for her years of service.
>
> Finally, if my passport did not wash overboard in a storm, perhaps you could send it to me in Paris. Address below. I hope this letter finds the two of you in good health. Indeed, we should be so lucky it finds you at all!

Stephanie was heartened somewhat by Françoise's letter. The

Frenchwoman, too, had been taken in by Jack, which relieved some of Stephanie's embarrassment, if not her pain. And it was good to know she wasn't be a fugitive from justice. Sorting out the mess in California would be challenge enough.

Stephanie checked her watch. Two hours had passed. She knew Jack wouldn't show up, but a part of her had been determined to give him every chance just so there'd never be any doubt.

Around one-thirty she went to the travel agency a few doors down to inquire about flights. She would go to Washington, as Leslie would be returning any day, if she wasn't home already. There were no direct flights, but she was booked on a connecting flight through Atlanta, leaving that evening.

Stephanie returned to Aunt Hazel's. The girl told her there'd still been no sign of Jack. Stephanie went out and had lunch at a fish place a block up the street, not far from the monument to George V. She bought herself a magazine afterward and returned to the coffee bar. The girl didn't wait for her to ask, she solemnly shook her head.

Stephanie had to kill time before her flight and couldn't think of a better place. It was unlikely the police would be searching for her in connection with Rico's murder. His men wouldn't want them to know she'd even been there, much less have her interrogated. But there was no point in advertising herself and this was as unobtrusive a spot as any.

Finally the time came to leave for the airport. Stephanie debated with herself for a while before tossing aside what dignity she had left by writing her address in Mill Valley on a slip of paper and giving it to the girl. "If he shows up, give him this. I'll be there in a week or so. I'm headed for Washington now." Then, feeling as though a part of her had died, Stephanie went out, found a taxi and rode to the airport in tears.

In what may be her final indulgence for a while, Stephanie bought herself a first-class ticket. Cayman Airways was most accommodating about helping her sort out formalities with customs, about her lack of a passport. She did have her driver's license and was told to expect some questioning in Atlanta, but she was on her way home.

As she suspected, there was no sign of the police. Stephanie had a hunch whoever was left at Inter-America wouldn't have wanted to bring Rhonda in on the murder, either, because it would only expose them to scrutiny, and at this point they had nothing to gain and everything to lose. In all probability, Rhonda was as free as she—crude justice maybe, but justice nevertheless.

The first-class compartment of the plane was scantily occupied. Stephanie was glad. She hoped to stretch out and sleep a little. The adrenaline that had been carrying her had finally run out.

She gazed out the window of the plane, getting her last look at the Caribbean. The ground crew was in the process of closing the doors to the baggage compartment in the belly of the plane. She could hear them slamming doors. The fuel truck had pulled away and the fasten seat-belt sign was on. Stephanie closed her eyes and prayed she'd fall asleep soon. She wanted to awaken in a different world.

Over the general hubbub, she heard the commotion of a late-arriving passenger which she tried to ignore like everything else. She felt someone drop down next to her and was annoyed. Why sit next to her when there were plenty of seats available? Opening her eyes to see who it was, her heart all but stopped.

"Hi, sweetheart," Jack said. "Headed for Washington?"

She couldn't speak.

"You're not too happy with me, are you?" he said. "Hell, I don't blame you. I'd be pissed if somebody grabbed my thirty-one point five mil, too."

He put his hand on hers and grinned as though that was going to rectify things.

"Jack, I can't believe this."

"I can't, either."

She stared at him. He was cleaned up and wearing a new white, short-sleeve shirt and dark slacks and shoes. And he smelled good. She was beyond caring about that sort of thing, though. She shook her head. That was all she could do.

"Maybe I ought to explain," he said. "I'll give it to you straight and you can draw your own conclusions."

She waited.

"I was rescued by some fishermen who saw the smoke and came to investigate. The *Lucky Lady* had burned to the waterline by the time they arrived and I was down to my last gasp. A couple of broken ribs and no lung capacity, it's a miracle I lasted in that water as long as I did.

"Anyway, they brought me to George Town and gave me a meal and a place to sleep. This morning I talked my way into some new clothes in a shop in town. I was at the bank when the doors opened, sure I'd be seeing either Barbadillo or you or both."

"And what would you have done if you had?" she asked.

"Negotiated, I guess."

"But nobody was there, so you went in, nervously gave them the code and thought you'd died and gone to heaven when the money started pouring out."

"Basically."

"That's all obvious, Jack. What I'm dying to hear is what happened next."

He stroked his chin. "This is the bad part."

"I bet it is."

"Well, I had the money, all right, but if I wanted to live to enjoy it, I figured I'd better take a powder. I got my butt out to the airport. The first flight I could get on was headed for Houston, but I figured anywhere but here. So I boarded the flight and, as they were sealing the hatch, I changed my mind and got off the plane."

"Why?"

"I asked myself the same thing. For shorthand purposes, let's just say my conscience got the best of me."

"Really. It's good to hear you've got one," she intoned.

He sighed. "Better late than never, Steph."

"So, why are you here? To apologize for stealing my money?"

"No, guilt isn't the only thing that got me off that plane. I started thinking about the way I felt about you, and I realized the money wouldn't mean much without you by my side. Oh, I'd figured all along I could track you down sooner or later, but as I sat on that plane I asked myself why I was leaving you at all. What I really wanted was to be taking you to Mexico. Or Paris or London or Tahiti, if you'd prefer."

"You want to treat me to a trip."

"Yeah."

"On my money. That's quite a payback, Jack. Real generous."

He caressed her fingers. "Let me get to the bottom line. I think we belong together, sweetheart. Long-term. Permanent as you like."

Stephanie longed with all her heart to believe him, but she knew there was a catch. "What about my money?"

"The transfer receipt is right here in my pocket," he said, tapping his breast.

Her eyebrows rose.

Jack reached into his pocket and drew out the receipt, which he handed to her. She read it.

"Jack, this is in favor of a Florida bank account in your name. All thirty-one and a half million."

"Yeah, I know. Basically, it's my money now."

"Yours?"

"Right."

She shook her head, not understanding. "Surely you don't think you're going to end up with my money *and* me!"

"Well, yeah. I guess that's what it boils down to."

"Jack, you're nuts."

"Thirty mil is a lot of bread," he said. "Say I give it back to you and we get married. I'd be beholden to you the rest of my life. You'd always wonder if I was staying with you because of the dough. But if *I* keep it, then the only uncertainty will be whether you're with me because of my charm, my wit and my ability to turn you on, or because I'm a rich sonovabitch. *That's* a scenario I can live with!"

She was aghast. "You've got nerve, Jack Kidwell. I'm amazed you can sit here and say that with a straight face."

"Come on, Steph, be honest. If the money's in your name, you'll never be sure what's keeping me around. On the other hand, if I stick with you even though you're poor as a church mouse, then you'll know it has to be true love."

"Jack, that is the most self-serving argument I've ever heard. Do you actually think I'd marry you after you stole my inheritance?"

He took her hand and drew it to his lips. "Well, not today, maybe. Or tomorrow, either. But after a month in Tahiti...well, I think you might. In fact, it wouldn't surprise me at all."

Detective Jackie Kaminsky is back—in a case that has her questioning her own choices.

Missing person? Murder victim? Or murderer?

One night John Stevenson went out to get baby formula—and didn't come back. On the surface it appears to be a routine case. But for Spokane detective Jackie Kaminsky, the facts just don't add up. Has the "perfect husband and father" simply abandoned his family? Is he somehow connected to the hit-and-run death of his boss's young daughter? Or, as Jackie is beginning to suspect, is John's disappearance the perfect decoy for something more sinister?

"Detective Jackie Kaminsky leads a cast of finely drawn characters…" —*Publishers Weekly*